EMPIRE REMEMBERED

Rebuilding Kysia Book 1

by

Jason R Sank

Copyright © 2021 by Jason R. Sank
Published by Jason R. Sank
Editing done by White Knuckle Copy
Cover art done by Ajayi Olajide
Cover Design by Robert Atchison
Interior formatting by Blessing Daodu
www.sankstories.com

ISBN: 978-1-7379309-0-7 (paperback)
ISBN: 978-1-7379309-1-4 (ebook)

Printed in the U.S.A.

This book is dedicated to my most beloved, Nicole D.B. Sank.

Without you in my life, my dreams would fade away and a better life would just be an illusion.

ACKNOWLEDGMENTS

This book would not have been possible if not for the advice and support from several people. I want to thank my wife for letting me pursue this crazy dream of mine, for having my back and supporting me and never letting me give up. To my parents Dennis and Karen Sank for your love and support and especially my mother who has been there since the initial outline, first draft, and the multitude of phone calls when I needed to talk something out. Robert Atichenson for editing, cover design, and advice. Few things have brought me as much joy as reigniting our friendship after years and finishing this novel with you. This novel would not be as mature of a work if it wasn't for you, old friend. To my test readers for all your valuable feedback Justin Trimpe, Mark Baker, Rob Dalluge, and Adam Wallace. To one of the most amazing bosses that I have ever had the pleasure to work for, Cindy Plaisted, thank you for advice, being flexible with my schedule, and an amazing laptop. It was a real pleasure to work with such a talented digital artist such as Ajayi Olajide for bringing my idea for the cover to life. To my buddies Jake Vetter and Dylan Mcdade for all the hours of listening to me talk about my book and wacky advice given.

Self-publishing is a unique journey and Dale Robert's Youtube series Self-Publishing With Dale provided a lot of valuable insight that made this journey much easier. Additionally, I would like to thank the staff at Book Award Pro, especially Nour and Jay, for all your help with submitting my novel to various book festivals and writer competitions. It was a great load off my mind to have you all handle this so I could be focused on other things. I would like to thank Blessing Daodu for doing an amazing and fast job on the formatting of this book, you are a life saver. Finally, I would like to thank Aram Vartian and his amazing Podcast Godsfall for rekindling my love for storytelling which started a chain of events that led me to write this novel.

PROLOGUE

It was amazing, Rehn pondered, how the death of so many innocent people were nothing more than numbers to him. A person's humanity gets taken from them as they become an item in a report, in this case four hundred fifty-seven instances of lost humanity. That was merely from Certzold's forces and didn't include the body count from Danelik's forces, which remained relatively intact. The conflict had lasted less than a week.

Rhen had just started paying attention to Certzold when the young man decided to launch an attack against his neighbor. Certzold's charisma had allowed him to gather just over five hundred to his army. Their size was offset by their inexperience- both the leadership and experience fighting as a unit. The first battle had been a rout and the rest became statistics in the report a few days later. When would these people ever learn, Rehn pondered. He stretched at his desk and looked at the stack of papers next to this one, only a few more left.

Each report detailed the activities of a psylord whose bastard lineage descended from the Kysian Empire. The empire once spanned the entire continent. Order had been kept by the Wardens, who could read the minds of the subjects and ferret out the guilty as well as the disloyal. They enforced Imperial edict wherever they went, and it was said that they could communicate mentally with the Emperor, regardless of the distance. They were Imperial messengers, judge, jury, and executioner - all in one. If that wasn't enough, they were an elite fighting force for the Imperial army, expanding the Emperor's domain. As soldiers, they could link their minds together and fight with peerless cohesiveness, always knowing where their brothers in arms were and what they were doing.

It was from these Wardens that people with psychic abilities could trace their heritage. Those with multiple talents, or unusual strength, claimed to be descendants, not of the Wardens, but of the royal family, who had greater psychic gifts. No one could verify any of this, but, in a world where might makes right, no one cared. Most were concerned about getting along with their own lives and not attracting the attention of the psylords.

The vast empire was now a cluster of city-states ruled by petty dictators called psylords who possessed strong psychic powers. When the final Emperor went mad, his insanity spread through the wardens and royal family like wildfire. Virtually overnight, the empire broke. There was no one to keep the wardens in check as they savaged the once great Empire and sired their progeny throughout the lands. Over the next several decades, humanity struggled to get back to its feet. Eventually, people reformed society and, naturally, they chose the bones of the old locations as their new cities.

Not all of the offspring would inherit their parents' powers, but those who did would have their gifts manifest as their bodies matured. It caught the world off guard. Once again, the fears of the past emerged as the next generation displayed their psychic inheritance. The madness that had infected the wardens and the royal family was not passed on to their forced-upon progeny.

As the new generation came into their powers, there were few who could restrain their actions and even fewer willing to risk themselves to act as a moral compass. It didn't take long before these progenies realized that most people could not resist them. Fear became the way, as those with psychic abilities soon began to exert their power over others. It was the dawn of the first psylords. Over the next several decades, more and more people were born with psychic powers, as the first generation spread their seed.

From the lowest street urchin to the mightiest warrior, all had a chance to develop psychic powers when they came of age. Some powers, such as telepathy and enhanced senses, or even clairvoyance, were fairly common. Even if you possessed a rare ability, like controlling someone else's mind, it might not be strong enough to do much. Then there were those who were immune, or perhaps resistant, to powers.

Rehn, like the rest of the Cashek Society, lived in quiet, protected isolation from the rest of the world. The Cashek Society had been formed by Emperor Palreon as a way to preserve the knowledge and way of life of the Empire. Many members of the Cashek Society, Rehn included, wondered if Palreon had glimpsed the disaster that was to befall them. While the rest of the world was ravaged by wardens, the Cashek Society was unaffected as they chronicled it all, sequestered away in their secret location. It was all a glorious mess; one that he would never have to see first hand.

CHAPTER 1

TIANNA

While tonight's job wouldn't erase her past, it would allow her to be a part of events that would soon change the world. Slowly, Tianna approached the large squat building that was the tavern. Most of the inns and taverns were over by the entrance to the city, in an area called the merchant's courtyard. This one was located in a rough part of town, and filled with laborers and mercenaries - people who worked long hours, as opposed to the merchants and wealthy who flocked to the inns that horseshoed the merchant's courtyard.

Erlin's spies had told her that her target would be here. A few minutes and it would all be over, at least the part she hated. Tianna didn't mind killing. Over the years, she had killed many people, first as a raider then as a matter of survival. What she did not look forward to, was being the center of attention. If she had her way, the kill would be done quickly and quietly, but that would not serve Lord Merik's purpose. This had to be done publicly, with lots of witnesses.

Theoretically, she didn't even have to kill Bearus to fulfill Merik's purpose. Given his reputation, and the fact that he would be backed by his crew, it would make showing any kind of mercy an opportunity for them to escalate things, and that could slow things, which she could not afford that night. By now, the others were ready, and they were merely waiting on her. Tianna paused to make sure that her face was concealed by the hood of her cloak before she stepped into the tavern. It would not do to have someone recognize the ritual scar on her face and decide to try to claim the bounty on her that it signified.

Bearus the Indomitable sat in the middle of a large table near the center of the tavern with his friends. They were a loud and boisterous group, harassing the serving girls, boasting of their day's accomplishments, and taunting any who dared to look towards their table. This kind of behavior would have ended in a violent brawl and possible death had it been done by anyone else. Even amongst the room of hardened thugs and laborers, none dared to draw the ire of Bearus and his crew.

He was a hulking giant of a man, over six and a half feet of solid muscle. Rumors said that he could shatter the sturdiest shield, and break the arm holding it, on the first strike with his flail. Few could stand against him for more than a moment in combat. However, that was not why he was called "The Indomitable."

With the body of a giant and a mind that couldn't be psychically controlled, Bearus had quickly become Djinar's top enforcer. It had not been long before he became Lord Djinar's top enforcer. Few dared expose themselves to his quick anger and reckless behavior. It was best to hunker down and hope to escape the behemoth's notice. So, as he and his crew shouted and carried on, the patron's of the tavern did their best not to do anything that might draw Bearus' attention.

The tavern was fairly crowded, but Tianna was able to find a seat facing Bearus. She stared at him, and it did not take long for him to notice her gaze. He said nothing but snorted as he took another drink. It would not be the first time someone had come here to challenge him. The man with a rakish mustache sitting next to him turned to say something but stopped when he saw that something held his boss's attention.

Turning his head, he followed Bearus' gaze and locked eyes with her. A smile spread across his lips and lit his eyes with a glow. "Well, well, well, what do we have here?" His comment was loud enough for the rest of Bearus' companions to hear, and they stopped their carousing.

"My dear, don't be shy. Why don't you come and sit on the boss's lap? That's what you want isn't it? For your sake, I hope it is, because the boss doesn't like it when some piss ant interrupts his fun."

It was not long before the others joined in on the taunts and catcalls. The tavern grew quiet. Those seated near her tried their best to fade into their seats, in fear that if they got up to get away they would be noticed and become part of the fun and games. Bearus did not taunt; he never did. He looked her dead in the eyes and returned her stare. As he continued to drink, his glare never waived, but neither did hers. She could tell that her lack of fear in him was something new, something unheard of for him. Tianna slid the hood off and turned her face slightly so that he could clearly see the scar that covered half of her face, knowing the bounty associated with it would spur him into action.

Bearus slid his chair back. As he made his way over to the silent woman, Jarlon leaned back in his chair and smiled smugly as he said, "You're in for it now beautiful. You done made the Boss mad. Even if, all of a sudden, you chose to speak, there is nothing you can say to change his mind. No one does anything with his mind. That's why he's called Indomitable. Personally, I don't know what you think you will accomplish by staring at him so hard, other than your death."

Bearus loomed over her. The only sound to be heard was the scraping of a few chairs being adjusted by those who sought a better view. With his right hand, he drew the knife at his side and raised it high in the air before plunging it down.

It took a moment before people realized what had happened. When they did, you could hear the gasps from even the most battle-hardened mercenary. Bearus had plunged the blade into his other wrist and then drew it up his arm to the elbow. He stood there, blood pouring from his sliced arm. The color had quickly drained from his face and he collapsed to his knees.

Jarlon leaped up from where he was seated, whether to fight or run nobody could say, as his body became rigid. He reached down to the table, picked up a carving knife, and slit his own throat. His companions barely had enough time to register what had happened when the next man did the same. One by one, each member of Bearus' crew slit his own throat.

"No, that's not possible," was all Bearus could say. He struggled to pull the knife out of his arm, but the shock and blood loss made such a task impossible. For a moment or two, he wavered before finally falling over onto the tavern floor.

In the silence of the tavern, mugs of ale could be heard hitting tables as nervous customers cautiously put them down as all who witnessed the event tried to comprehend the impossible. The quiet lady stood up, carefully stepping over Bearus' corpse, and looked around the tavern.

"Lord Djinar is finished. Those who still support him by the cock's crows will be deemed an enemy and all their assets forfeited. Lord Merik is now the ruler of Crestburn."

With that, she left the tavern and disappeared into the evening street. It took several minutes for the shock of what happened to fade and people began to talk. One by one, the tavern's patrons began to leave. Some headed off into the night to warn friends about what happened so that they could flee by morning, while others went home to wait out the violence that was sure to follow the next few days. The tavern keeper locked the doors and left the bodies of Bearus and his companions where they lay, too afraid of possible repercussions of touching them.

CHAPTER 2

BOTUN

The last report had just been finished and he was finishing up his evening meal, which was still a bit warm. There were days it seemed running Crestburn took all of his time. Now, to be technical, he merely administered the city as Djinar's seneschal. While Djinar was the city's lord, most of his time was spent in debauchery. Everything from wine, sweets, dancing girls, and slave boys. There were few psylords as wealthy as him.

Djinar's wealth was due to his control or Twilight Haze, a smokable herb with sense altering properties. The herb was potent enough on its own but, when combined with Rathgar venom, it's effects were dramatically enhanced. It was this additional step, discovered by Djinar, that allowed him to dominate the market. The man's paranoia made sure nobody learned how he created Twilight Haze, as well made it all but impossible for him to be betrayed. As he rose in power, he made sure to eliminate anyone who could be a threat to him and, before long, Crestburn was his.

The door to his study bursts open and a red-faced servant rushed towards him. Botun slid back the chair and reached for the dagger concealed on the inside of the right arm of the chair, ready to thrust it into the chest of his assailant. The servant all but slammed into his desk and tried to speak, but was too out of breath to make his words clear. Upon realizing that this was not an assassination attempt, Botun eased back into his chair and glared at the servant.

"You know I have rules about conduct. This better be important." Botun said.

"It," the servant gasped. "It is sir." The servant paused and tried to collect his breath before blurting out "Bearus is dead!"

"What do you mean dead? How?"

"He was killed at the tavern, him and all his men."

This could not be true. Bearus was a beast of man and would crush most in a fight. The fact that there had yet to be someone strong enough to stun or control his body with their mind made the idea of facing him all the more daunting. Killing him was almost unthinkable, but to kill him and his crew, surely this servant was mistaken.

"There was this lady," the servant began. "She had some scar on her face and she dominated his mind and all of his crew. Made Bearus watch as she made his crew kill themselves before finishing off Bearus. She told everyone there that Djinar was through and that a Merik was now our lord."

"I can't imagine such a thing happening without Jenal learning about it beforehand, unless."

His musing was cut short as another servant burst into the room. "Sir, I have news you must hear immediately."

Botun raised his hand to silence the new servant.

"If it is about Bearus and his crew I have just been informed. I need you to fetch me Jenal Goldentounge. His spies should have warned us about any attack that was planned unless it was his doing. I don't think he had the ambition to rule Crestburn but he has been acting rather unusual as of late."

"Right away sir." the second servant said as he hurried out the door.

"I need you," Botun continued as he addressed the first servant "to order the guards around the manor to double and the gates to the city sealed."

He waited till the servant had left before getting up and leaving the room. At this time of evening Djinar would most likely be with a couple of his dancing girls in the main lounge or the deck. Quickly as he could, and yet still look dignified, for it would not do to have the seneschal seen running like a common servant, he made his way to where Djinar was spending his evening. His sharp glare and rapid approach had the guard opening the door before he got to it. Inside the room, Djinar was reclining on a couch as two scantily clad girls were dancing for his enjoyment.

"My Lord Djinar, I have a report of the utmost urgency."

With a weary sigh, Djinar adjusted his heavy bulk on the couch to a more dignified position, one fitting to receive his seneschal and not a pair of scantily clad dancing girls. With a snap of his fingers, a servant rushed over with a tray of diced fruits as the two girls headed over to the side of the room to submissively wait, kneeling with their elbows in and palms up. Casually he selected a peach and dipped it into the sweet creme before devouring it. He reached for another when he noticed the intense look on Botun's face, instead of his infallible calm face.

"Well, Botun, what is it that you have to tell me? It must be of grave importance for you to rush in as you did. You know how I like to take my time and enjoy things?

"Bearus was murdered!"

Djinar scoffed and took a moment to select a fruit before turning back towards his seneschal.

"You have to be joking. No one could kill that brute of a man. Even if someone could best him in single combat, his crew would not allow such an opportunity to happen."

"Word is spreading like wildfire. Multiple sources are saying the same things for it not to be true. Some scarred woman dominated him and forced him to fatally stab himself. The reports say that not a single one of his crew was able to leave the table before she did the same to them."

Stunned silence filled the room.

Trying to find the words, Djinar managed to stammer, "Was there a message?"

"Yes. She said that you are finished and that someone named Merik is now the lord. I have ordered extra guards to the mansion, city gates closed, and I request that we move you to someplace more secure."

"Are you sure that is necessary?"

"My liege, if ever there was a person who was able to dominate Bearus, then they will probably make short work of the guards, or at least enough of them to get through to you. Might I suggest that you link up with one of the girls and then we take you to another room? You can still enjoy your evening while I see to this insurrection, if it pleases you?"

With frustration, he told Botun "Fine, fine. I shall do as you suggest. Go see what you can do to make sure I have a city to rule by morning, however if I find out this was nothing and that you overreacted and ruined my evening's entertainment then you will suffer greatly my friend."

"I assure you, my lord, that it is as dire as I believe."

"I have a place where I can keep myself hidden and safe."

A moment of effort and Djinar was able to pull his bulk up from the couch. A snap of the fingers and both dancing girls were darting before him. It was all that Botun could do not to scream at the man as he was probably linking up his senses to one of his dancing girls. Even in the midst of a probable coup, Djinar cared more about his pleasure than his safety. It was also this quality that made it possible for Botun to extend his influence a lot further than he would be able to otherwise.

"You two will sit on the couch and then you," as Djinar awkwardly pointed to the second dancer. "will close your eyes and count out loud to five hundred. At that point, you may open your eyes and begin pleasing one another." With that Djinar grabbed a tray of fruit and headed off with a quick pause to tell him to "see to this mess."

CHAPTER 3

SUVAL

He watched his victim, Jenal Goldentongue, as he went stumbling and staggering down the street. The man was beyond exhausted, and yet somehow found the strength to move. Jenal leaned against a building in order to steady himself and quickly dozed off. A moment later, he awoke with a startled jerk from the terrors of his dreams. It was well, for he needed to get word to Botun and Djinar that an attack was happening.

For the last few weeks, Jenal had not been able to find rest and comfort in his sleep. Each night he spent tossing and turning, often waking up in a panicked state. Never once did he see Suval sitting in his rooms, smiling at him as the dreams became more disturbing. Shortly before sunrise, Suval would slip from Jenal's house and walk about the city. He had a room at an inn, but he rarely used it. Thanks to his special ability, he rested when he was in someone else's dream.

He was the first. The first who Merik recruited, the first in the city, the first. He was special, but not in the way his uncle told him he was special. Suval could not help but shiver at the the thought of his uncle. The man was dead and could no longer hurt him.

When Merik said that he was special, he meant it, for Suval possessed an ability that no one else had. He was the first to have a new ability. Well, second actually. With him, Merik would be able to change the world.

That was why Merik had him come to Crestburn before the others. It was his job to make Jenal so exhausted that he would miss any signs that several mercenaries were in town and in the employ of a new psylord. The task was easy, but it took time. People could function fine with little sleep over a few days. It took much longer for true exhaustion to set in.

Suval enjoyed watching Jenal try alcohol, as well as herbal teas, to improve his sleep. No matter what the man did, it would not hamper Suval's ability. Each day began to drag on longer than the one before, and his nights were filled with restless chaotic sleep. At the end of the second week, Jenal was starting to look less tired and that was when Suval realised the man was secretly taking naps during the day. That would not do. For the next two weeks, he rarely left the man's side for more than a couple of hours. Thankfully, Suval had another ability that happened to complement his dream stirring quite well. He could make it so that people did not notice he was there. This allowed him to get close to his playthings.

Suval was with Jenal when a messenger appeared with the news about Bearus. If he was being honest, Suval had completely forgotten that tonight was the night of the coup. It was very easy for him to lose track of the days when regularly messing with someone's dreams. He had not quite figured out why that was, because his mind was very much conscious and awake as he sojourned in his plaything's sleep. As far as he knew, they could not detect him in a dream, but he made sure to be careful nonetheless. Soon that will all change. Merik made him a promise that he could have a place where he could be free to test the bounds of his special powers. All he had to do was deliver Jenal.

"You look weary. Let me help you, friend," he said with a soft voice as he lent Jenal his arm.

"Thank you, but I can," was all Jenal got out before Suval put his finger on Jenal's lips and shushed him.

"You need not thank me, friend. I am here to serve. Let us continue on our way. After all, you have important places to be, and important things to tell, do you not?"

Jenal Goldentongue was too exhausted to put up a fight and nodded in weary agreement. He leaned on Suval as they made their way towards the mansion. The streets were empty and fear was palpable even to his diminished sense. They arrived a short time later to the destination and were ushered in quietly through a side door, through a corridor, and down a flight of stairs. This was not where he wanted to go. In his mental haze, he must have turned towards the cells that Djinar had in his basement.

Jenal turned to Suval and was about to inform him of this mistake when he froze in fear. There was a glimmer of recognition in his eyes as he was looking at Suval. Perhaps he did recognize him. In the future, he would have to be more careful with his playthings, but that would not matter for Jenal. With a gentle push, Jenal fell to the floor as Suval locked the door to his cell.

CHAPTER 4

BOTUN

It was a warm summer morning and the temperatures promised only to get higher. Botun wore a hooded cloak, hoping it would keep him from being recognized, despite the fact that the temperatures made the thing uncomfortable. Summer had just started and, already, it seemed to be hotter than it had been in years. At this rate, the temperature would be unbearable with a cloak, and having one would draw unwanted attention. Wiping the sweat from his brow, he opened the door to look down the street.

While Djinar had been the ruler of the city, it was Botun who ran things. The laws that were signed off by Djinar were drafted by Botun, and little was done by the former lord that hadn't been guided by his seneschal. It was a credit to his planning and resourcefulness that he had not met his fate the night of the coup. Although this was a relief, there was a part of him that felt a bit insulted that he hadn't been removed in the first moments, like Bearus and Jenal had.

Whether by their neglect or by happy accident, it didn't matter; he was alive. With a pause at the doorway, Botun took a moment to double check to make sure the street was safe before stepping out. Although the common citizen never saw him, there were still plenty who might recognize him, and thus warrant concealing his identity. He was a bit surprised that there weren't wanted posters with his likeness on them already. It gave him hope that there was still a chance he might survive this mess.

The first thing he had done, after the attack, was to find a secure place to hold up. The next couple of days, he carefully began to reach out to others that he suspected were still loyal to Djinar. Although Merik was an usurper, he had to give the man credit. The takeover was a wonderful success. It had been both fast and precise, leaving the city unscathed, which was wise, for the average person cared more about getting through each day than who ruled them. To the masses, one dictator was the same as another.

In the days following the attack, there was a roundup of those who didn't declare their loyalty to Merik. Between reports from Hargod and Zarha, Botun had a good idea of who had been escorted to the mansion and not heard from again. It didn't take long for the rest to get the hint and disappear on their own. Now, came the task of tracking them down and

11

convincing them to meet with him. His years as seneschal allowed him to learn a lot about those who served Djinar, even the things they thought were secret, such as where they were likely to hold up.

Last night's rendezvous had been successful. Of the six people who he found, all but one said that they were willing to meet and discuss future possibilities later today. The one that had refused to see him outright also tried to kill him after he left.

Carefully, he weaved himself into the crowd of a busier street. If half of the people that he met with over the week showed up to today's meeting, then there would be about a dozen people in attendance. A fair number to be sure, but it was nowhere near the number of people that had already ended up on the wrong side of the takeover. It would be enough to get things started. There was so much to be done, and the requirement of secrecy would make every task take much longer than it normally would.

Regardless of the outcome of today's meeting, there would still be plenty of work to do. A secure location for regular meetings would need to be found, as well as passage out of town for those who wish to leave. Then, there was the task of finding Djinar. Knowing Djinar, he was more than likely holding up someplace secure and high on Twilight Haze. The former lord was a bit paranoid and probably had several safe houses that even Botun did not know about. Once Djinar was found, then they could plan to take back the city.

The idea of abandoning Crestburn, and Djinar, to their fate was still dancing in his mind. It would make an easier life, and he had little doubt about his ability to integrate himself with another lord somewhere else. While Crestburn had its issues, it was a place where he could impose order out of chaos. Djinar's addictions made him an ideal partner for Botun to work with. As long as Botun made Djinar look good and kept awash in vice, Botun had the virtual run of the city. While Djinar was a lazy addict, he possessed far more charisma and was much better at subtle manipulation than Botun was. Getting people to do what he wanted was something that came easy for Djinar, and was one of the strongest reasons Botun needed him to figurehead the reclamation of the city. There will be little to no chance that he would be able to come to the same arrangement with this Lord Merik or some other lord.

From one street to another, he took a roundabout path to the Merchant's Courtyard. The horseshoe-shaped market place was located near the main gates of the city and was where the majority of the city's merchants set up shop. The innermost section was composed of little more than trade blankets, while the next sections were filled with temporary stalls that are little more than wooden frames for canvas or cloth to be draped over. The layer after that is composed of semi-permanent structures that will have partial walls that can last a few years. Permanent shops compose the outer layer, with a row of inns and cafes framing the Merchant's Courtyard, except on the side that was closest to the gates.

It was a wonderful setup. To those visiting the city, it appeared that different classes were shopping at the same location in harmony, while, in fact, each class stayed within their own area. Although there are no formal laws against the poor coming to the outer ring, the accidents that would befall them were more than enough to deter such things from happening. The wealthy shop at leisure in the outer layer, and then lounge at a cafe without being around the poor. The poor, of course, would only ever enter through the opening of the Merchant's Courtyard by the gate.

Botun found a nice stall near the mouth of the courtyard that provided a view of the city's gates. Feigning interest in the earthen vases, he watched the guards check people as they came in and out of the gate. Anyone going through the gate was subject to a pat down and having their wagons examined. After that, they were questioned for a few minutes by the guards before letting them go. This part was the same as it was when Djinar ruled.

What changed was that there was now one of Merik's new guards standing near and supervising the guard performing the questioning. Botun had little doubt the new guard was a telepath. While telepathy didn't give a person the means to detect lies, a skilled telepath could notice mental cues common with deception. When someone was not skilled at lying, there would often be a mental stutter, or pause, as their mind formed the lie. Additionally, there is often a nervousness or apprehension associated with the deceiving thought. Those who are skilled liars are often too quick to respond and their lies void of emotional association. Although not impossible, it is difficult to lie to a telepath skilled in ferreting out deception. It was an educated guess but he believed that the new guard was making sure the first wasn't letting friends through as well as double check their work.

This drastically increased the difficulty for people trying to flee using the main gates. Hopefully, that cocky kid he planned to hire would perform as well as his reputation suggested. Botun moved from the first stall to one now selling daggers and lingered a bit longer before he decided it was time to head to the meeting. He would be there early, but that was fine, as it provided him a chance to take a short rest and catch up on some much-needed sleep. He wiped the sweat from his brow as he left the Merchant's Courtyard and began the long slow walk to the abandoned house where the meeting would take place.

As long as Botun could remember, Crestburn had a seedy underside. Vice was always popular with the poor and the rich. When Djinar rose to power, he made sure there were several places addicts could go to get high. Dark, dingy, abandoned buildings where the town guards were told not to go, not that they needed to be encouraged, because, with the addicts off the streets, their patrols became easier.

By the time Botun arrived at the house, he had broken into a decent sweat and would be happy to get rid of the cloak. He gave a quick glance to the lookout, a man who appeared to any onlooker as a vagrant on the edge of passing out against a wall. The lookout responded with a cough, letting him know it was safe to enter. The house was a large three-story building that had seen better days. Upon entering, he was hit with the smell of unwashed bodies, vomit, and god knows what else. Half a dozen addicts sprawled out in the front room amongst broken furniture and against the walls. The floor was covered in a layer of grime and garbage, with paths where people came and went. One door was blocked by a broken cabinet and a pile of assorted refuse. The other led to another room where a man sat at a table looking like he was about to light up.

"Order in chaos," Botun said to the man.

Password given, the man got up and went over and unlocked the door that led down a hall to a flight of stairs. The first two rooms were nothing but show. The rest of the house, while abandoned, was nowhere near in such a pitiful state. Rooms on the first and second floor were either boarded up or locked. The third floor was where the meeting would take place. It was far enough from prying eyes and provided an opportunity to escape by the roof should their enterprise be discovered.

"How did it go?" Zahra greeted him as he reached the third floor.

"As I figured it would. It seems like a waste to check what I already know, but, if I didn't, then someone would complain, and then there would be delays as they insist on having the information verified. Delays that we can not afford."

Zahra nodded understandably. She was of average height but had wide shoulders and hips. Her dark, curly hair caught almost as many men's attention as her ample bosom, which she made sure to display. Zahra was one of the youngest madams in Crestburn. In addition to trading flesh, she also traded secrets and was rumored to be one of Jenal Goldentounge's favorites, whether for sex or information was anyone's guess. Botun figured it was both, not that it mattered.

"Who all is here?" he asked.

"Nine have shown up so far, not counting guards," she said.

As predicted, a few had brought a couple of guards, but nothing that couldn't be handled by the brute squad stationed in another room at the other end of the hall. There was at least an hour left before the meeting and his train of thought was derailed by a yawn.

"When did you last sleep, Botun?"

"I got a few hours last night."

"Figured as much. You're running around doing everything yourself, not trusting others to lend a hand."

He shook his head. "That's where you are wrong. I have trusted a few people. Besides, I have much more going on than organizing today's meeting."

"Regardless, you need rest. You are liable to get yourself caught or killed when your sleep deprived ass stumbles into the wrong person. There is a cot with a blanket, water, and some food in the next room. Eat and sleep. I will come to get you when the time comes."

Botun turned from Zahra and headed to the door that she pointed to. The water was warm, but quenched his thirst. The plate of food took the edge of his hunger, for he had not eaten since late last night. After he finished the plate, he stretched out on the cot and closed his eyes.

Knock, knock.

Botun jerked awake. He had no more than put his head on the pillow before he passed out. "Just a minute," he said as he sat up. The pitcher of water and plate had both been refilled, and next to it was a washcloth. Zahra really knew how to take care of people. He ate quickly, and drank another glass before he used the rest to rinse the sweat off his body. Like him, Zahra was smart enough to know how much weight people put on other's appearances. The calmer and cleaner he looked, as if he had been untouched by the current hardships, the more willing others would be to listen to him. He sat at the edge of the cot for several minutes, forcing them to wait on him. He donned the cloak, drew up the hood, and headed to where the others were biding their time.

"Please, excuse my tardiness," he said as he entered the room. There were a lot more people present than he figured, almost twenty in fact. This was a good start, but unless he could get them to follow him, the number of people wouldn't account for much. He took his time crossing the room, slowly taking off the cloak as if wearing it in this heat was inconsequential to him.

"Thank you all for coming. I know that time is precious and leaving your respective safehouses puts you at risk of being discovered. It is safe to say that we were all caught off guard by Merik's coup," Botun said as he surveyed the room, seeing almost everyone nodding their heads in agreement, except for Lucky Liam, paying him no attention as he was focused entirely on Zahra. She, on the other hand, was dividing her focus between listening to Botun, performing the task that he had assigned her, and making sure that Liam had something to distract his gaze.

"Early today I checked out the city's gates. It seems that our new ruler is making a visible show of strength. As expected the guards are checking each person who enters or leaves the city. In addition to this is an extra guard, one that I have never seen before and can only presume that is part of the new lord's retinue. Judging by how much attention they paid to the guard who was questioning people, I can safely assume that they are a telepath and here to catch anyone who is loyal to Djinar trying to flee the city."

A murmur of discontent swept the room. He gave them a few minutes to let this news sink in and allow them to talk amongst themselves. With an extra telepath at the city gates, it would be very difficult for them to escape on their own. If they wanted out then they would have to trust him, hoping that he would not have assembled them all here unless he already had another way out. Of course, they could stay here on their own but that would be a serious risk. The best hope that they had was Liam, that cocky little shit that was ogling Zahra.

In poor neighborhoods, there was never any shortage of errand boys and package runners. Those who were patient and kept their head down eventually graduated to better paying and more rewarding work. Plenty of street crews were in need of a good lookout, or muscle to provide a solid thrashing. Joining a crew was only logical for street kids, for on their own they usually didn't last more than a few years before disappearing.

Liam was an enigma. Most boys leave behind running packages and other minor roles once their bodies start maturing and the extra coordination and strength provides them opportunities previously denied to them. To Botun's best judgment, that should have been several years ago for Liam, and yet he was still running packages and delivering messages. Over the last couple of years, Liam built a reputation as one of the best runners in the city. His slender frame and agility made him a natural at running across rooftops and through dark alleys.

To look at him, you wouldn't expect much. Liam was a little shorter than average and slender, with short cropped black hair. It was hard to pin an age on him, but Botun figured the young man was probably seventeen or eighteen, old enough to have left package running years ago. He had quick reflexes and was fast on his feet, attributes that helped him get out of trouble more than once. His face was pretty, almost feminine, and Liam was quick to use his delicate features when flirting with the ladies. Liam seemed to be at ease no matter where he was, as if being ready for trouble was too much of an effort for him to bother with.

What made him stand out, was the fact that he never got caught. Eventually, a package runner would get caught by another crew or the guards, and take a serious beating (by them or his own crew for getting caught). Liam had never been caught by anyone. There were even a few attempts to set him up for an ambush, but they always failed. With each failed attempt to capture him, Liam's reputation as being lucky grew and the lad was more than willing to advertise this.

Botun began again as the room quieted. "The last few days have been stressful for us all. The attack came out of nowhere and it was over before we knew what hit us. Bearus' body was still warm when Merik claimed the city and put a price on all of our heads. I am not going to fool myself into thinking that you all are here because of your loyalty to Djinar. I know many of you were still trying to figure out which side to bet on by the time everything was done and over with."

"I am not going to fault you for that. Our loyalties don't matter right now, because we all have a price on our heads for not being loyal to the Merik, or at least not being loyal fast enough. Any future we have in this town is over unless we can find Djinar. I have people looking for him and, hopefully, we can find him before Merik does."

"How do you know he ain't been found by Merik?" one of the thugs in the room asked.

Botun smiled and replied "Educated guess. If Merik has him, then he would have publicly executed him by now. Also, there are still patrols rounding up anyone who might be loyal to Djinar. It's reasonable to believe that they are still looking for him. If we can find him first, then we have a chance to get our lives back."

At that, there were several muttered agreements and nodding of heads. All eyes were on him, except for Liam's, whose were glued to Zahra's ample bosom. She smiled at him and responded with a devilish wink as he placed a hand on her thigh and gave it a squeeze. Botun glared at Liam and said "While you are here, you are working for me, Liam. Flirt and seduce whomever you choose, but do so on your own time!"

"Wat's de matter? Mad she likes me more tan yous? Don't worry it none, bossman, tis babe can't handle me."

"Oh really," Zahra says with a chuckle. "Boys like you think their men until a woman shows them otherwise."

"Yous can show me watsever yous like."

With that retort, Liam quickly got up, out of striking range, and came over to Botun, holding his hands palms up, as if to show him he had nothing to hide "Don't worry about me, boss man. I can behave when I have tos, besides da only thing you need to do with me today is ta just show me off ta those gathered here. Let them know you bought my services. So just me being here is what you paid fa today. Now, as far as the other part of the deal, well, when it's time fer that, you can be sure Lucky Liam will be all yours, if my fee is paid."

"Thank you," Botun replied, doing his best to keep as much of the sarcasm out of his tone as he could. Liam went back to the couch and laid his head on Zahra's shoulders.

"I am sure all of you have figured out by now that Liam."

"Uh, tat's Lucky Liam bossman" the boy interjected as he shifted his position to throw a leg over the couch and place his head on Zahra's lap.

"That Lucky Liam will be our guide out of town. He has a route that will get us safely out of the city. Once you are out of the city, you are free to go your own way; however, there are other options available to those who are interested. If you decide to take the risk, then let Zahra know as well as give her the payment. Don't take too long to mull this over, for we will be leaving in a few days.

"I am lucky, not perfect, least not tat I know of. On my way over here I heard tat Lord Merik will be addressing de city after next week. I suggests tat we wait until ten. There is a chance he will back off with the guards once he has addressed the city."

"There is also a chance he may maintain things the way things are," Botun countered.

"True, but it doesn't feel like tat. Trust mes I have a natural instinct fah these kinds of things. If we go in a few days, it doesn't feel right. Next week after de speech tat feels right, tat feels lucky. After all," he turns and looks Zahra in the eyes "Don't yous want ta get lucky."

Botun surveyed the room with his eyes and saw several people nodding their head in agreement with Liam.

"We can wait a week, but no more. I am paying because you're one of the best. Hide all you want behind false claims of luck, but you're not fooling anyone. You have information and resources at your disposal that allow you to succeed as you have. That's why I am agreeing to wait as you recommend, not because 'I want to get lucky'".

At that, Botun turned and made his way over to a group sitting near the window and began talking to them. Over the course of the next couple of hours, he talked with everyone in attendance, answering their questions and reassuring them. People began to slowly filter out in small groups. Finally, it was just him and Zahra.

"Well?" he asked.

"Nothing," she replied. "I couldn't read a single thought in his head. Not that I am sure I want to know what that cocky little perv is thinking. It will take a stronger telepath than myself to read his mind."

"So he does have royal blood then," Botun said using the slang term for someone whose psychic powers were much stronger than the average person, powers strong enough that they could have been inherited from a member of the Imperial family instead of the wardens, from who most of the world got their abilities.

CHAPTER 5

The falcon soared in the sky as it glided along thermal currents. It was a beautiful warm sunny day with few clouds in the sky. Days like this were ideal for flying over the land and snacking on an occasional mousy morsel. While there was some time for pleasure, there were more important things to do today. A few more minutes and it would be time for the boy to take complete control.

Redclaw had grown used to the arrangement. There were several birds in the aviary, but the boy came back to him more than any of the other birds. He said it was because the other birds didn't cooperate with him as Redclaw did. Not that cooperation mattered with the boy's power. Perhaps it was too weird for the others to allow a human into their mind. It might be weird, but Redclaw was more than willing to put up with it if it allowed him some freedom.

It had taken the boy a while to learn how to fly like a proper falcon, and even now there were times the boy was clumsy with his body. Thankfully, he was smart enough to back off and allow Redclaw to take back control of his body when the need arose. Part of him wished for freedom of the open skies, like wild birds. That was something that would never happen, but, then again, the dangers of being hunted, starvation, and storms would also be things that would never happen to him either. It was what it was. At least with the boy, he was able to fly more and, for that, he was grateful.

The boy wanted him back in the city because it was time to pay for the freedom he got this afternoon. Redclaw realized long ago it was futile to do other than as the boy wished, for he could take control of his body in a heartbeat. As he came over the city, he could see that the inhabitants were gathering in a large mass not far from one of the city gates. The bird of prey began a slow lazy spiraling descent. A mouse was skittering down an alley. He wanted the mouse, but now he was no longer in control of his own body.

The boy landed his body on a rooftop and began to look around, and the boy's mind told him something was different. Normally this area was where humans traded things with one and another. Now, however, there was a nice size stage that had been placed in the middle of the area. The area around the stage was packed with people: way more than when they came to trade with each other. Several people on the stage had matching clothes. They must be hunters (guards - the boy's word echoed through their link). There were more of those hunters (guards) spread out amongst the crowd.

Several trumpets sounded off in the distance and announced the coming of a new group. These people were all on horseback, and one wore a cloak in the same green and black color of the guards. That must be the new leader of the city. He was not much to look at, even for a human. His hair was dark and very short, and his face was smooth. There was darkness in his eyes that made him think of a predator. Yes, definitely a predator, but not like a bear or wolf. No, the man was more like a viper, ready to strike and poison.

The group made their way through the crowd, which quickly parted for them. They dismounted the horses and made their way on to the stage. There were six guards with the leader, one of which was a female with a large scar on her face. One guard took a position at each corner of the stage, while the scarred female and the last guard stood behind the leader. Slowly, the crowd quieted down and, when the silence became the rule and not the exception, the leader began to speak.

CHAPTER 6

ASHA

Asha made her way through the crowd, looking for a familiar face that she might be able to use. She knew the merchant's courtyard like the back of her hand and yet today it seemed totally alien to her. Normally, the inner area would be crowded with the lower class, her people, while the rich stayed at taverns and specialty shops at the outer edge. Today was different because it was the wealthy merchants who packed the area in the middle, where the stage had been erected overnight. The poor were pushed to the outer edge of the merchant courtyard, but none dared to actually cross the invisible boundary into the wealthy shops. They were trapped between the wealthy merchants up near the stage and their property in the outermost ring of the merchant's courtyard.

Slowly, she made her way through the crowd. Occasionally she bumped into someone. Those accidental bumps allowed her to swipe bracelets, rings, and other valuable items. By the time she neared the stage, Asha wore enough jewelry to make herself appear wealthy enough to belong in this crowd. Although jewelry would help, it wouldn't be enough. The rich kept to themselves and didn't take kindly to new faces. Of course, if she was on the arm of someone, well, that was a different story altogether.

There! Just a few yards from her was Albrit Deshane. He was a middle aged man of muscular build with a shaved head and a thick beard. Asha had accompanied him before, and he was fond of her. Albrit made his money as a bladesmith who specialized in decorative daggers. His work was stunningly beautiful and functional. In fact, she was carrying the piece he had gifted her last summer. It was a slender, wavy blade that looked like it would shatter if it hit anything remotely solid. In the pomelle was a small emerald that, when depressed, would allow a fine powder to fall out of a carefully concealed groove. The powder was a special blend that she had meticulously ground until it was as fine as dust. When tossed in the face of someone, it would cause pain and temporary blindness.

"My what a big blade you have," she whispered into his ear as she slipped in from behind.

Albrit laughed and turned around and hugged her "Shali, it is good to see you my dear" using the false name he knew her by. "My god girl, you look more beautiful than ever. We must get together again sometime. I see you still have my gift," he said as he slid his hand down her hip where the dagger hung. "I hope you have not had cause to use it."

"Only once or twice and, like it's maker, I was more than pleased with its performance," she said with a coy smile.

Men were so easy to manipulate. All you had to do was make them feel like you were in awe of them and they were more than happy to give you enough attention that you could lead them where you wanted. She did have an advantage with Albrit, since she knew his secret. With her mind, Asha reached out and gave his emotional sense of fondness a bit of a nudge, just to be on the safe side. It wasn't much, but every little bit helped.

"Well thank you, my dear. I am not often complimented in such a way. I would love to have you join me."

"I would love to," she said with a curtsey and palms up gesture, reminiscent of a dancing girl. "As you said, it has been too long and it would be nice to catch up and see what you have been doing." With that, she slipped an arm around his waist and they proceeded to make their way through the crowd. It timed out wonderfully, for, no sooner had they got within a few feet of the stage, horns could be heard off in the distance.

Albrit leaned in and whispered in her ear. "So, what have you heard about this new lord of ours?" he asked.

"Nothing much," she replied.

"Yes, he does seem to keep to himself. I heard that he was badly wounded and has only recently recovered enough to conduct the affairs of the state."

"Oh really?"

"Yes, but, then again, I also heard that Djinar got away and that he has been hunting for him. Or, at least, until now, which is why there is today's speech. Djinar has been found and now will be publicly executed, or so they say."

"Well, that would help explain the stage that was erected last night."

"That's quite a surprise. I wonder how long he intends on keeping it here?"

Now that she was close enough to examine it, she was surprised to see that the stage was very solidly built. A fair amount of effort would be needed to take it down, which meant it was here to stay. The more she examined the stage, the more she came to believe that it was going to be a permanent fixture. That would change the dynamic of the merchant's courtyard, perhaps Crestburn's oldest tradition.

"Longer than we imagine, I think," she replied.

Albrit was about to respond when they heard trumpets much closer. A murmur began to ripple through the crowd, as if an echo to the trumpet blast. Another call came from the trumpets, this time even closer still. The crowd was now silent and heads turned towards where the horns could be heard. It was a rare moment in Crestburn when the merchant's courtyard was void of sound. Even at night, laughter could be heard from the inns, desperate women soliciting their services, and games of chance being played on cheap blankets near the center of the Merchant's Courtyard.

Once again, the trumpets sounded, but this time punctuated by the sound of horses. Necks strained in anticipation at the first look of their new lord. The crowd parted as a party of seven rode towards the stage. Six riders were dressed in the same black and green of the new guard uniform.

The seventh rider must be the new Lord of Crestburn. He was a young man, just a few years older than herself. His clothes were well tailored and he was clean shaven. He didn't look at ease on horseback, and there was a softness to him that wasn't often associated with psylords. Whatever he had been before he took over the city, he definitely had not been a warrior.

The crowd began to murmur as the guards hitched their horses to a spot on the back of the stage. Four of them mounted the rear steps and stood in each corner. The other two stayed mounted by their lord. He waited until the first were in position before dismounting his steed. The two remaining guards did the same in almost perfect unison. Slowly, he mounted the steps and took his place in the middle of the front of the stage.

Asha was good at gauging people. She had years of training in learning how to size people up and figure out what they wanted or needed in Djinar's harem. Girls started their training at a young age. The first years were all about etiquette and how to wait on and serve people. Once their bodies began to develop the bumps and swells that pleased men, they went on to other training. For Asha, that never happened, as her body barely changed when she came into womanhood. When it became obvious that she would never flower like her harem sisters, she was cast out. On the streets, alone, she learned fast how to manipulate and take what she needed to stay alive. She refined the skills that she had been taught, the most important of them being how to anticipate what someone wanted.

Merik wanted power. The other thing he craved was control. His slow steady movements drew eyes to him. His position on the stage made him the center of attention. The way he looked out over the crowd, as if he was looking for a flaw in a horse he was about to buy instead of looking at loyal subjects. There were many small things that she picked up on that led her to believe that this man was trouble.

A loud voice both in her ears and in her mind announced and introduced Lord Merik as the rightful ruler of the city. The crowd grew silent, and the Merchant's Courtyard was void of sound again. Traditionally, heralds made their announcements vocally, for not everyone was a telepath, and to do both was redundant. While most telepaths could send out an unfocused message that could be picked up by any telepathic mind nearby, few could project over such a large distance as the entire Merchant's Courtyard. This was done as a show of power, letting all present feel the strength of the telepath he had at his disposal.

As the herald made his way through this introduction, Asha did what no other psychic could do. Asha could see when a person used a psychic ability. The bit of research that her limited means allowed could not find evidence of anyone else having this ability. It frightened her to think that she might actually have an undiscovered ability. Such a thing would draw attention to her and she would become a pawn of the psylords. So, she planned to keep the ability secret until she found someone else like her, not that she had any hopes of that.

When she used this ability, she saw a faint cloud of psychic energy around a person's head. Each ability has its own cloud and, the more vibrant the cloud, the stronger that person's abilities were. Some people had multiple abilities and, when they used them at the same time, it created a vortex of many-hued clouds around their head. At first, it was tough to tell what powers a person possessed, but, with practice, she had begun to decipher these complex psychic clouds. Clouds only formed around a person's head when they used an ability. Some people were immune to certain powers, such as the late Bearus the Indomitable, and they would have permanent clouds that were fog like.

The herald on the stage was the strongest telepath she had ever seen. His cloud was a rich teal and a faint teal cloud that matched his could be seen around everyone's head that she could see, showing her that he did indeed reach every mind with that telepathic broadcast. The man's telepathic power was staggering. Asha knew a few telepaths who could communicate across the Merchant's Courtyard, but that was only with a focused telepathic thought, which had much greater range.

A quick glance at the female guard with a massive scar on her face didn't show any clouds, which only meant that she wasn't using an ability right then. There was something odd about her, though. It looked almost as if she had clouds, but when she tried to focus on the thing it was gone. Perhaps she was just seeing things. Lord Merik, on the other hand, had two fog-like clouds, denoting psychic immunities against being stunned and having his body physically controlled by another. As she studied him, she began to see a crimson cloud form, denoting emotional manipulation.

Didn't the rumors say it was a scarred woman who slew Bearus? She glanced at the female guard and, again, she thought she could see something more but, whatever it was (if it was real) existed just on the threshold of her perception.

CHAPTER 7

MERIK

Merik stood calmly on the stage, surveying his subjects. There was quite a crowd here today. Of course, after what he had just pulled off, few would dare not attend. It was not often that a psylord was able to take over a city from another with so little bloodshed and collateral damage. The nature of his success spoke more to the people than mere words could, as evident by the sheer numbers that attended his speech. Now that he had their attention, it was time for another show of force by having Erlin demonstrate his strength in telepathy. Power was what made people civilized. When one exerted their power over others, the weaker ones did as they were told. In their submission, they would be better able to work with each other without bickering and arguing or wasting time with indecision. They fell into line and did as they were told. Laws and rules were irrelevant because they changed over time and with new situations. The only thing that mattered to people was power.

"Thank you all for coming out today," he began as he sowed a feeling of hope in the crowd. "I know that most of you out there are scared and worried. It's only natural, and I don't blame you for your fears. History has shown us time and time again that when psylords fight for dominance, it can be a messy and bloody affair. Rare is a victory won without the cost of innocent lives. Without homes being destroyed, families torn apart, and hearts broken.

"That is not what I did. I only targeted Djinar and his people, leaving you unharmed. You all have suffered enough under Djinar's rule and others like him. Like you, I am a humble man with a simple background, a book merchant, if you believe. I got tired of seeing people suffering time and time again at the hands of petty and cruel dictators. This insufferable behavior has been going on since the empire broke. This madness must stop.

"Once, we had a great empire. It lasted for over a thousand years. Peace and prosperity, instead of wars and desolation, were had by the people. The empire of long ago seems like a dream long lost. I tell you, my friends, that this dream is not lost. It is very much alive."

"I know you doubt me, may even think that I am mad or foolish. It's ok. Many before have made false promises about rebuilding the empire.

Countless have claimed to be either the emperor reborn or descended from his family. How many of you out there in the crowd is of royal blood". Merik paused and let a bit of fear make its way into their minds. At the mention of the slang often used to identify people with strong psychic talents a worried twitter rippled through the crowd. In the past psylords, worried about challengers, made it a crime for others to be of royal blood. They made up rules and regulations about what abilities and strengths constituted as officially being of royal blood. It did not take much of an imagination for those in attendance to wonder if Merik would do the same.

"I am not of royal blood," Merik said as he planted calmness in their minds. "I am a common person like many of you. Sure I have a few abilities, but in this day in age who doesn't? My strength comes not with my psychic talents but with what I know. For years I have studied volumes of long-forgotten books from private collections of former psylords. From the laws of the Empire to how the wardens functioned, I have studied it. I have learned by examples set in royal decrees. I have learned more about the old empire than probably any other person and, if there is someone out there who knows more than me, I invite them to join us. To pool our knowledge and increase the realization of the empire being rebuilt.

"As knowledgeable as I am, I can not do it alone. I need you. I need your support. In order to rebuild the empire, we need to become a society of the empire. We must live under the old laws. We must rebuild the wardens of old. We must believe it in our hearts and treat one another as citizens of the great empire. This will take time. Laws won't change overnight. We must have peace and prosperity in the city before we can think about rebuilding the Wardens.

"I come to you not as a tyrant forcing you to obey, but as a man with a dream to make our lives better. We need to end this needless cycle of repetitive violence and destruction. Therefore, I am asking for volunteers to join the city guard. I know it doesn't sound like much, especially coming from a man who wants to rebuild the empire. This is merely the first step. In the days of the empire, the Wardens were both the town guard and judge and military. To do this, they had an education beyond that of the average citizen.

"So, that is where we start - with you, with volunteers. Those who wish to join the guard will come to the training grounds and speak with guards there. They will take care of you. In order to raise you up to be more than just town guards, you will need to be trained and educated. Classes will be set up to educate you on the ways of the old empire, law, and military strategy. You will have extra training in combat so that you will be more than skilled enough to handle any situation. When the time is right, and your education is complete, you will have the opportunity to transition from guard to judge. Who better to lay judgment than someone who has worked alongside the people and knows the laws and the value of peace better than those who uphold it."

"There will be plenty of time for us to accomplish all of this. I know it won't happen overnight, but we can start today. We can start with a few simple laws, things from the time of the old empire, when times were better. It will now be a punishable offense to lie to any member of the city guard or city officials when they are doing their jobs. They also have the right to have a telepath brought in to examine someone believed to be lying. To support this, it will also be punishable to refuse a telepath on official business access to your mind. If you happen to be resistant to telepathy, then you must be forthcoming with that information immediately and arrangements can be made for a stronger telepath," at which Merik turned and smiled at the Erlin "to be found.

"In the meantime, the guards will have an increased presence in the city. There will be extra patrols to assure that there is no longer a lingering threat from Djinar or an attack from an opportunist hoping that I overextended myself. This is so that you all can go about your daily lives as you have always done before. The gates of the city will still be under strict observation. For those of you with nothing to hide, you have nothing to fear and just bear with this minor inconvenience as we take extra steps for your safety.

"A week from today, we shall have a massive celebration, celebrating this wonderful city. I will open up to you Djinar's private reserves of food and drink. There shall be music and plays and merriment to be had by all. You have been through so much and you need time to relax and have fun. Reward yourselves for not giving up and for making the most of your lives. Together, we can make this dream of the old empire being reborn into a reality."

Merik turned and walked off the stage, his guards flowing around him like clockwork. He kept his face calm and serene, waving to the people as he made his way through the crowd on horseback. Before, there was nervousness and apprehension, but now there was hope. He could see it in their eyes, in the smiles that he got. There was even a group of boys, almost old enough to be men, huddled in a group nearby. He waved to them. They waved back, elbowing the few in their group who didn't notice, getting them to wave back as well.

"Erlin," he said, addressing his herald. "Please send a telepathic invite to those boys over there to take a private tour of the guard's quarters."

While he didn't possess the ability to see the telepathic message, no one did, he could see the reactions of those young boys. Each boy all but jumped out of his skin in shock. Once the message was delivered, they all straightened their backs and went from waving to giving their best attempt at a salute. Wonderful. He could guarantee that each one would take up the offer of the tour and most, if not all, would become guards. People were so easy to control and manipulate. All you had to do was promise them something better than they had. So long as it looked like you tried to do as promised, the masses would go along with it and, when you failed to deliver, they would be too set in the new ways to do anything about it. Complacency and hope were a ruler's best friends.

CHAPTER 8

JARIEK

Jariek finished cleaning up the last of the bird cages. It was smelly, dirty work but he didn't mind. He enjoyed working with animals, and most people said he was a natural with them. Of course, they didn't know what he knew, that his talents worked on animals just as well as they did on people. Actually, his talents worked better on animals, it seemed, that is after they got over the initial shock of something touching their mind. Jariek preferred working with animals. Their thoughts were so much more focused and their needs simpler. People were so chaotic in their thoughts, and their desires made them so unpredictable, especially here in the real world and not in the confines of the Cashek Society.

He knew he should be grateful, since most orphans tended not to survive long on their own. Second caravan members had picked him up and taken him to the Cashek Society, or so he was told, for he was too young to remember. The society placed him with a family who raised him as one of their own. Jariek received an education that would be comparable to only the wealthy in the real world. He had friends, family, and safety. Life was good, then the powers came.

Psychic powers were no big deal for the most part Jariek thought. While psychic powers were almost commonplace in the outside world, they were more prevalent within the Cashek Society. The society even provided training, which greatly enhanced one's finesse and control with their psychic abilities, and recorded members' psychic strengths.

It wasn't really hard for Jariek to keep the fact that his abilities worked on animals a secret when the society put little to no effort in looking for something they didn't believe existed. Sure, they asked you about any abilities you possessed. They even had a telepath present to see if you were being honest. The great irony was that the Cashek Society trained those who would be living in the outside world to be able to lie well enough that a telepath wouldn't notice a lie. This, combined with the fact that the questions were mundanely routine and he had been able to prepare for them.

So, Jariek lied when they asked him if he thought he had a new or unusual ability not previously recorded. Between the training that they had provided him and the fact that they were questioning him more out of routine than belief that they might find something, his deception went unnoticed. He even had a backup plan should they have found out. Jariek would have told them that he didn't realize he was influencing the animals and must have done it out of reflex. It wasn't a good plan, but might be enough to prevent serious trouble for his initial deceit, or so he hoped.

Needless to say, the fact that he could use his abilities on animals made it much easier for him to work with them. He was always cautious, so that others did not find out. It gave him an edge over the other kids when it came to animal handling. Jariek was almost too good and came close to drawing attention at one point. This was remedied by having a few accidents with the animals. His special ability was nice, but it didn't grant him animal handling skills. Those he had to work on and develop on his own.

By the time he was old enough to apply to become an informant for the society, he was good enough to be an apprentice at any stable. Horses were fine, but it was birds of prey that he loved to work with. During his training to become an informant, he had been able to work with the society's hawks. When his training was complete, they forged credentials for him and provided him an apprenticeship with Master Gerwald, a falconer in the city of Crestburn. There, he was to work for Master Gerwald and report the happenings of the city back to the society.

While the others went to the speech given by their new lord, Jariek had volunteered to stay behind and watch the shop. Pretty much everyone was at the speech, and that freed Jariek from dealing with any customers. After the others left, he let out RedClaw, his favorite falcon, to work with, and he linked with his mind. Redclaw soared in the skies until it was about time for the speech to start. With the falcon's sharp eyes and keen hearing, Jariek watched the proceedings from the bird's vantage point.

In exchange for watching the shop during yesterday's speech, he was able to take a few hours off this morning after chores were completed. He smiled as he finished with the last bird cage, knowing that he would be done until the afternoon. Jariek had not realized how much work there was in being an apprentice falconer, compared to working with birds in the society. He both worked and lived at the shop, so anytime away was a wonderful thing. Jariek made his way down to his room, cleaned up, and then went to find Master Gerwald. His master was in a back storage room, yelling at one of the young journeymen who screwed up the seeds used to feed the birds that weren't predators.

"Uh, excuse me Master Gerwald." he said.

"What do you want, Jariek?" replied Master Gerwald.

"Well, sir, I have finished with the last of my morning chore list and was wondering if it was ok to head out for a bit? Like we talked about yesterday."

"Already?"

"Yes, sir. I got up a bit earlier today and had a head start. You did say I could be gone when I was done."

"Yes, I did. Didn't expect you to rise early though. Hhhmmm. You know Jariek, if you showed this kind of motivation every day, and not just on the days you are offered time off, you would make it to journeyman much faster."

"Yes, sir."

"Fine, go have some fun. Tell Lara to give you this week's pay so that you can have something to spend." This was met with a scowl from the journeyman who would have to wait another whole day to get paid like everyone else.

"Thank you, sir."

With that, he headed off to collect his pay and then on to the Merchant's Courtyard. The money was a nice surprise that he hadn't been counting on. Master Gerwald came off gruff and angry, but he wasn't that bad, provided you didn't screw up with one of his birds. Jariek was one of three orphans that worked for him. It seemed that Master Gerwald had a bit of a soft spot for boys without a home and often favored them with extra chores that resulted in extra privileges, such as going out and early paydays. The others who worked for Gerwald did not like the preferential treatment and often found ways to retaliate. The morning was cloudy and the temperature a bit cooler than it had been in the last several days. It was a wonderful morning to have off and, thanks to his foresight to start his chores early, Jariek would have an extra couple of hours to do as he wished. The city didn't seem all that different than when Djinar ran things. People still walked the streets, shops were open for business, and guards still patrolled. He browsed a few shops along his way to the Merchant's Courtyard, where the vast majority of shops would be located.

Jariek paused at a food vendor and purchased a spiced meat pie. The smells that came from the small stove made his stomach grumble. Although Master Gerwald fed his apprentices and journeymen well, it was not always enough to keep up with his teenage metabolism. Vendors like this one, where they cooked the food right there on the spot, were his favorite. While the food with the society was filling, it was also bland. Jariek often spoiled himself with such delicacies on his time off.

He had to suppress a childlike smile when he was handed his pie. Jariek quickly wrapped the spiced pie in a piece of clean cloth that he had brought along just for that purpose. It would keep his pie nice and warm until he could find a place to eat that was a bit closer to the Merchant's Courtyard. With a more hurried pace, after all the cloth would only keep the pie warm for a little while, he made his way down the winding streets. Before long, he found an alley near several of the large taverns that were frequented by caravans.

Jariek looked around and found something to sit on so that he could enjoy his snack. The pie was still steaming as he unwrapped it, the smell of the spices making his mouth water. He inhaled deeply, drawing out the moment and taking his first bite. *"Ouch, that's hot"* he broadcasted telepathically in an unfocused manner. Jariek ate the pie, which wasn't as hot as he made it seem, as he waited for the telepathic replies.

When a telepath sent out an unfocused thought, as he had just done, it was received by nearby minds. With weak telepaths, such as Jariek, their unfocused thoughts could only be picked up by other telepaths, while stronger telepaths' thoughts could be picked up by any mind. Now, of course, a focused thought could be picked up only by the mind it was sent to, regardless of the receptor's telepathic ability or the sender's strength. Unless done for a specific reason, such as a herald, it was considered rude to send out unfocused thoughts.

Of course, such things do happen. Those who are just learning to control their telepathic ability occasionally send unfocused thoughts by accident, and even unknowingly, until they get the hang of the ability. Sometimes, such thoughts happen as a reaction to surprise or pain. Then, there are the jerks who do it just because, or are so drunk that they can't control their minds. Often, when an unfocused thought gets sent out to those who weren't expecting it, the responses were less than kind. So, Jariek sat at the mouth of an alley while several harsh telepathic replies were made, as well as one surprising compassionate one from what sounded like a sweet old lady.

He was halfway through his pie when the response that he was looking for came in. The Cashek Society had a very ingenious way for their informants to communicate with the Second Caravan. A generic unfocused thought gets sent out by the informant, such as himself. If a second caravan member receives the thought, they have a specific response that they give, letting the informant know that they are there. Since their minds had been joined by the initial unfocused telepathic thought, the second caravan member can respond with a focused thought and, from that point on, they can have a nice, private conversation without ever having to meet.

The system was far from perfect, but it worked well enough. Sure, there were times he didn't get a response, but members of the second caravan always stayed at the same tavern or inn. He, like all local informants, was provided with a location to give a message from and await a response. Caravan members tried to keep regular schedules, which increased the chance of making contact. This system allowed them to keep tabs on the major events in a timely manner. If something became serious, they could even send an operative to investigate the situation or even one of the wardens to resolve the matter. The thought of the wardens made him shiver.

It only took Jariek a few moments to give his report. Most of the time was spent convincing the second caravan member that, yes, Merik did say "to become a society of the empire" and that he had not misheard it. The phrase was one of several that they watched out for, as it might indicate that a psylord came into possession of an important imperial document that would be key to having the empire rebuilt. Once convinced, the Second Caravan member told him that an operative would be arriving in a week and to assist whoever the Cashek Society sent.

When the report was finished, the pie too, Jariek felt light-hearted. This was what he had been trained for. Over the years, a few had said similar words but, in the end, it had always been just a coincidence. This time might be different and things could get really interesting. He began to imagine what it would be like to have the empire rebuilt. How wondrous would that be? And, he would be a part of that. Granted, he would be a mere footnote in the historical records, but that was better than nothing. Plus, this Merik guy seemed a lot more caring than most psylords. Merik would probably make a good first emperor for the newly rebuilt empire.

CHAPTER 9

ASHA

Asha moved through the streets. She was dressed in a more subdued manner than when she attended Merik's speech. Her skirt and blouse were dull earth tones, nothing that would attract attention. Her hair, although short, was wrapped up in a dhuku that was tied off to one side. She blended in with the poor and working class, the people who were most often unnoticed. As long as she stayed out of the wealthy districts, she would pass unnoticed by those around her.

This was good, for right now she wanted to observe people and see what impact the regime change had on the city. It had been several days since the grand speech in Merchant's Courtyard. By now, people will have started making up their minds about their new leader, not that it mattered really. It was both fruitless and kind of funny. Merik would continue to rule the city regardless of what anyone thought, and the people would continue to have an opinion regardless of the lack of impact it would have on him. She guessed it was just human nature to have an opinion about matters that you could not affect.

Even if the people's opinion didn't affect Merik, it would affect Crestburn, or at least the way its inhabitants interacted with one another. That was the reason she was out and about today. She observed people and looked for changes in their behavior, as well as listened to the conversations discussing Merik and his proposal. While she had a bad feeling about things, her opinion was the minority, if not the exception. His claim to rebuild the empire was dismissed politely. After all, he was their new ruler and his temperament had yet to be fully accessed. The two most popular topics were his humble background and his promise to provide extra education. The stipulation that you had to join the guards in order to get the education seemed such a small price to pay.

Of course, what they didn't realize was that during his speech, Merik had been influencing their emotions. While he did not have the strength to influence a lot of people at once, he did affect a fair number of wealthy and influential people of Crestburn, since they were the ones who were closest to the stage.

Merik did surprise everyone by not having the stage taken down. People speculated that their new lord would make another speech during the celebration that was just a few days away and, shortly after that, the stage would then come down. She had seen the stage up close. It was sturdily built and probably not going away anytime soon, if ever. This meant that he intended it to be used, and she was worried that the use would be a much darker purpose than giving a rousing speech.

Her musings were paused by a rumbling in her stomach. Asha looked around for a food vendor with something decent that she could swipe. It was not as if she needed to steal. Money was not a problem. Stealing was how she kept herself alive when she had been cast out. Back then, she could not bring herself to lay with men for money and stealing food and clothes had been necessary for survival. As the days turned to weeks, she learned other ways to scratch out an existence for herself. Now, she was at a place where things were, well, if not comfortable, they were definitely livable. So, when she stole, it served to remind her of her early desperate days on the street and kept her skills sharp.

Asha found a fruit vendor on a corner that would fit her purpose nicely. She made her way over and started checking out the fruit. The merchant was busy trying to answer why his fruits were bruised to a berating customer. Asha selected a few nice pieces, which she slipped into a hidden pocket in her skirt, and started walking away when someone yelled for her to stop. A quick glance over her shoulder revealed one of the new town guards heading straight towards her.

"Stop thief" the guard yelled, loud enough for heads to turn in their direction.

Asha took off in a sprint, weaving through a group of people who were still unaware of what was going on. By the time the guard made it up to the group, they gladly stepped out of his way. Realizing that the guard was not about to give up so easily, she cursed under her breath. Asha rounded a corner and reached into a concealed slit in her skirt, using her cutpurse ring to slice a special stitch that she had painstakingly sewed into it.

With the stitch cut, an extra panel of fabric was freed at the waist, causing the skirt to slide off of her hips. While the one hand was taking care of the skirt, the other was unwrapping her dhuku. As the skirt hit the ground, she threw herself into a tumble and landed in a semi-prone position facing the way she had just come from. Asha stuffed her head wrap into a pocket of the pants that she had worn under the skirt and quickly snatched her skirt and tucked it behind her body.

All of this took only a moment, and it was well that she had spent hours practicing quick changes as the perusing guard rounded the corner. He paid her no head and charged down the street in vain pursuit. Asha watched as he made his way down the street, only to slow down and start looking around once he realized that he had lost the thief. Carefully, she rose up and made her way to the other side of the street, her eyes never leaving the guard.

Slowly, the guard turned in a circle scanning his surroundings. After he completed his scan, Asha took a second to see if he was using psychic abilities and noticed a faint cloud around his head and groaned inwardly as she saw the teal color. Odds were that he had been telepathically linked to another guard nearby and had called for reinforcements. Asha headed away from him and watched out for other guards. Before she had gone a block, there were two more heading toward the first. One with a telepathic teal, the other with a different kind of psychic cloud around his head.

Just great.These new guards were using telepathy to work together. They probably linked up at the beginning of their patrol, that way if they got separated they could covertly call for assistance. This would make getting away much more difficult for thieves. Merik, apparently, wasn't kidding when he talked about improving the guards. Asha studied the cloud around the second guard's head. Fear crawled up inside her as she realized he had enhanced his senses. He could see, hear, and smell better than the average person, a good deal better judging by the strength of his cloud. If he was strong enough, this would make things rather difficult for her.

Asha had more abilities at her disposal than just being able to see when someone was using psychic powers. She looked at the guards and focused on them. As the guards walked down the street they were carefully looking at everyone they came across. Sweat beaded on her brow, but there was no way to back out now. She walked along as if nothing was the matter, but internally she was a nervous wreck. While she was skilled in using her abilities, she had very little opportunity to use them against someone else's powers.

What she had done to the guards was make it so that they failed to recognize her. As long as she didn't do anything to draw attention to herself, their gaze should slide off of her. It would be almost as if she was not there. The problem lay with the guard who was enhancing his senses. Would his enhanced sight allow him to recognize her before his mind told him that there was nothing to look at?

She had heard of others with this talent, who had pushed the limits of this ability too far. They grew careless and began to act as if the ability made them invisible. Inevitably, they would do something stupid that drew attention to themselves, such as walking towards the guards with enhanced senses, and get noticed. One way or another, Asha was about to find out. The guards were now close enough she could hear their footsteps. She dared a quick glance up, only to meet the eyes of the guard who could possibly notice her.

CHAPTER 10

BOTUN

"I am sorry Botun, but I can't join you, " Artus said nervously.

"Oh," Botun replied with a raised eyebrow.

Artus looked over his shoulder, making sure no one was near enough to overhear their conversation. It was kind of amusing, since the closest two people were his own poorly disguised guards. One was pretending to be passed out drunk a few tables over and the other was taking too long to look at baskets at a nearby vendor. An eavesdropper would have to get past both of these men before standing a chance of hearing anything incriminating.

"It's not that I don't want to. I have commitments that I need to make sure are handled before I am free to leave."

"Is there anything I can do to help resolve these commitments for you?" Botun asked.

"No, no," Artus replied hurriedly "It's nothing to concern yourself with, and won't affect you. I swear."

Botun eyed him for a good minute before slowly nodding his head in consent to continue. The pause would serve as a reminder to Artus who was in charge, as was evident by the gulp he gave and the slower, more measured pace with which he spoke as he continued.

"They are private matters. Personal business as well as someone I want to make sure is safe. I am sure you don't need to be told her name. You know that I couldn't leave without her. As it stands, I have not had an opportunity to get word to her. As it is, I am not sure she would even understand. Even if I could bring her, she would probably put the group at risk."

Botun sighed inwardly as he listened to Artus give a half-hearted excuse as to why he would not be joining his group leaving the city. It did surprise Botun that Artus was using his mother's dementia as the excuse not to go. While the old woman was losing her mind, she was nowhere near as bad as Artus made her seem. It was all Botun could do to keep a straight face when Artus said that he couldn't leave without her. Artus would sell her out to Merik if it meant a chance of living. She was just a shield for him and nothing more. He played his part, as he had done so many times before as seneschal, nodding his head in understanding and sympathy, assuring Artus that it was ok and that there would be no hard feelings about the decision. Privately, he cursed him for being a fool and a coward.

Once the reassurance had been given and there was little left to discuss, they went their separate ways. Botun knew what was going to be said before the meeting started. Whenever someone wanted to meet in a semi-private place, other than the house that he had secured, it was because they were telling him that they would not be joining the group. They needed someplace that they felt safer should his ire befall them. Botun gained nothing by retaliating against people, and such an act would more than likely scare off those who had not committed yet.

This was the third person to decide to strike out on their own. He had another meeting in a couple of hours, also in a neutral place, and that would probably make four. Although it maddened him, he didn't completely blame them, either. What he had proposed was dangerous, almost as dangerous as staying in the city. At least no one had betrayed him yet. Although he was no longer seneschal, they knew how resourceful and determined he was. It also helped that a reminder of what happens when someone betrayed him was still fresh in their memories from early this past spring. Botun felt confident that the exodus from the city would be safe.

He sat in quiet contemplation, allowing Artus to slink away. Botun watched as two guards carefully slipped in behind to cover his retreat. He shook his head and wished that Artus had put as much effort into leaving with the group as he did in protecting his own skin from a friend.

"Well, that didn't take long," came the thought from Zahra. She was stationed a few blocks down and, when Botun passed her, she linked up with him telepathically as well as clairaudiently. While Botun held his meeting with Artus, she could hear everything that Botun did. She could have talked with him telepathically, but she was wise enough to wait until after the meeting so as not to distract him.

"No, it didn't. It went pretty much as I expected it to. Well, hiding behind his mother was a bit of a surprise. I didn't expect him to have the gall to try that."

Zahra responded with the telepathic equivalent of a laugh.

"Still, it means another one that won't be joining us."

"At this rate, will we have enough?" she asked.

"We should. I have enough to pay Liam's fee. Unfortunately, that leaves me with very little funds left to look for Djinar."

"I have some money stashed away that you can use if you need to."

"That would be helpful. I suppose I will owe you a favor for it."

"Several, but let's not be picky about the details. After all, there is no guarantee either of us will survive"

"We will. Speaking of Djinar, anything new from your girls," Botun asked, referring to Zahra's brothel girls that serve as her sources of information.

"Sadly, no. By now I should have heard at least a rumor as to his whereabouts. Either he has managed to vanish completely, which would not be completely out of character

for that paranoid bastard, or he was eliminated and his body removed so quickly that no one realized it happened."

"Djinar did have more than his fair share of secret rooms and hidden passages. Most of the secret passages and hidden rooms I know about, but there are spots that he kept hidden from me. I do have access to a resource inside the mansion that can try to find those locations for me, but I would rather wait a bit before potentially exposing this asset."

"Just be careful, Botun. There are still people disappearing, and I don't think it's just from people going into hiding."

CHAPTER 11

JARIEK

It was hard for Jariek to focus on his chores. Ever since Lord Merik's speech, he had been excited and did his best to suppress it. At first, it had been easy, but the reality of the situation hadn't fully hit him. It wasn't until he had delivered his report with the Second Caravan member that things became real. They were going to send an operative to investigate!

During training, he had been told that there was a chance that he could go his entire life without there being anything significant enough for the Cashek Society to send an operative to investigate matters more fully. Realistically, he would probably have two or three times in his life where things would warrant more attention. He hadn't expected one of those few times to be so soon.

He had been in the city for little more than a year now. In that time, he had gotten to learn a fair amount about Crestburn and its local politics. Sure, he had been briefed before being sent there, but reports could only convey so much. There was much more that could only be learned by experiencing it first hand. Of course, his duties as an apprentice to Master Gerwald took up most of his time. What little bit of free time he earned had been spent exploring the city. Thankfully, the patrons who came to the aerie typically had a large sense of self importance and were talkative. Much of what he reported back to the society was learned at work. All he had to do was stand still, off to the side, and keep his mouth shut. He would hear all kinds of gossip as they made small talk with Master Gerwald or one of his journeymen.

Each month, he gave a report that kept the society up to date with the happenings of Crestburn. Practically everything he reported would be filed away as unimportant news. Occasionally, there might be a tidbit that would be important enough to reach the council's notice. He knew that his primary role was to be the eyes and ears of the society. It was not a bad life, especially when compared to the fate of other orphans.

He couldn't remember life before the society. Jariek knew that he was an orphan who had been picked up by second caravan members and brought into the society. He had been placed with a family and raised as one of their own, and by "one of their own" he meant the society. A family was nice, but the Cashek Society was first in all things. His education was far better than anything he could have hoped to have received had he been adopted by someone in the outside world. He had classes on everything from geography to politics. Training in survival skills, animal handling, and some weapons training. Most importantly, his mind was honed to observe and remember.

Long hours had been spent molding him into something that they could use, all for the greater good. It didn't bother him. With the education they provided him also came an opportunity. On his own, he would never have the possibility of being an apprentice to a trade, let alone something as prestigious as a falconer. In addition, he had a family, kind of. His adoptive parents cared for him very much.

He had made his intentions known to his teachers that he wanted to work in the outside world and, shortly after that, was tested with several other students, many of them older. By the time the testing was done and the initial training complete, several months had passed. Then one day he was hanging out in the park when he noticed her. Sure, he had seen Marla before, but something was different about her now. How he failed to notice her before was beyond him, but there she was. As fate would have it, they would even share a class together and quickly became close. Had he not become an informant, there would have been a good chance that they would eventually be married, or so he had hoped. Her long brown hair and dark green eyes. She was almost enough to make him stay, not that he would have been given a choice in the matter. That fate was an illusion and, eventually, he had to leave.

Sure he was limited in many ways. He was not free to change careers, other than a chance at becoming an operative or move to a different town, but those were minor things. The apprenticeship that he had been given would set him up nicely as a falconer one day. Operatives tended to get placed with jobs that would eventually leave them well off. This did two things. First, it made it less likely for them to abandon their trade and runoff. Secondly, the jobs tended to be in professions that left them exposed to lots of people, making their jobs to observe that much easier. Making a report each month and not being free to move to another town were small prices to pay for what was given.

When the Cashek Society had been first formed, before the collapse of the Kysian Empire, Emperor Palreon commissioned a manuscript that contained hidden lessons within. A clever enough person could extrapolate the lessons from the text. The readers would believe that they were privy to special information that would put them on the fast track to rebuilding the empire. It provided insight into not just how the emperors' thought but how they viewed the empire. The reader was even encouraged to practice these hidden lessons regularly and was told that, in order to understand the minds of the emperors, they should think and speak in the manner which the emperors did. This would make it easier for them to stand out amongst the others and show the common people that they were the best hope for the future. This, combined with several phrases that were repeated so as to be at the forefront of their mind and to increase the chance of their being used often when speaking to others, resulted in a person who would make for a better candidate for the society to work with, as well as a way to recognize them.

Jariek knew that the overthrow of Djinar would be important news for the council. It was the kind of event that took priority. What was not expected was the choice of words that Merik used in his speech. It could be a mere coincidence that he said, "a society of the empire," but Jariek didn't think so. There had been times in the past that other psylords have said the same with no clue of the importance of those particular words, and, by now, there had been enough people to use the phrase over the years that it was beginning to lose its uniqueness, nor was it the only phrase in the text suffering from repeated use. The thing that separates this from those other times, in Jariek's opinion, was Merik's mentioning of the old laws and how he knew how to rebuild the empire. It was enough to make Jariek believe that Merik had discovered one of the manuscripts. Not that his belief in this was of any importance. The use of the phrase alone was enough for the council to send an operative to investigate the matter further.

An operative!

It was exciting. These were members of the Cashek Society who had almost complete freedom. They got sent out to investigate matters that the council deemed important. Occasionally, they intervened in situations, but those times were rare and far between. As a part of his training to become the eyes and ears of the society, he spent time studying under an operative. While observing and reporting was his main function, he was also required to assist any operatives sent to his location. This assistance typically would be to familiarize the operative with the area and situation at hand, run errands, and provide them with supplies as needed. It would be a lot of extra work, in addition to both his job as an informant and his apprenticeship.

"Ouch" Jariek cried out as a pigeon pecked his hands. He pulled his hand back and examined it. The skin had not been broken, but it still didn't stop the strike from stinging. He had been so lost in his own thoughts about the implications of the speech that he didn't pay attention to the cages he cleaned. Jariek shook his head, annoyed more at himself than with the stupid bird that got him. Across the room, Reg, one of the journeymen, laughed at him as he cautiously finished up the cage.

There were five apprentices and three journeymen working for Master Gerwald. The apprentices were in charge of cleaning the aerie, as well as cleaning the cages and feeding the common birds. They also began their training on working with the birds, staying with pigeons and the occasional exotic house bird. When they had progressed to journeyman, they were able to officially start working with birds of prey. The journeymen often made special arrangements with the apprentices that would get them time with the hunting birds in exchange for helping with their chores. Jariek worked out a deal with one of the journeymen which, in addition to some time learning how to work with the falcons, gave him access to Redclaw.

Most of the others got along well enough with him. Master Gerwald's shop was known for having some of the best-hunting birds in the region. Although he specialized in birds of prey, he had quite the collection of more common birds. Everything from ravens to pigeons and the occasional parrot. The shop did a lot of business, and there were people from all walks of life from Crestburn and the surrounding towns who came in and did business with Master Gerwald. It was a wonderful place to gain information.

CHAPTER 12

TIANNA

Sweat dripped off her brow and her breath was growing short. She had been at it for almost an hour with barely a pause. Her sword thrust forward and slightly up before returning to a guard position. The move was fast, barely a blink. She did it again, only this time she rolled her wrist as she finished and immediately transitioned into a swipe that would have struck a leg. This move was also completed with speed and precision that few could match.

Her arms had grown sluggish from use, not that anyone watching could possibly tell. Both the falcata and armor she wore during practice were weighted. A few more minutes and she would allow herself to end her drill session for the night. It wouldn't do her much good to practice her forms if her muscles were too fatigued to do each form correctly. Practicing bad form lead to fighting with bad form, and that lead to death. More than once, she had seen someone cut down because of sloppy swordplay, and she was determined not to let that happen. If she were to die by the blade, then let it be a skilled opponent that took her out.

She floated from one stance to another. Each one took next to no thought for her to assume. Still, she paid attention to the position of her body and her blade. Critiquing every aspect of each move. Seeking out perfection. Once that was achieved she pushed farther. She was determined to be the best. Each day, she practiced her sword forms for an hour. This was in addition to the drilling she did alongside the rest of the city guards.

At first, her practice sessions were a novelty to the city guard of Crestburn. A few even tried to egg her on and get her to spar with them, wanting to test her skill. They wanted to see if she could really fight. Their offers were met with silence as she ignored everything for that one hour. Thankfully, no one had been dumb or brazen enough to have tried to force a match by striking at her.

At last, she closed her eyes and steadied her breath. A rough cough let her know that it was time to resume her duties as captain of the guards. She looked over and saw Sergeant Hurlt waiting patiently.

"Well, Sergeant, don't just stand there. You can give me the report while you help me out of my practice armor."

Sergeant Hurlt nodded and quickly moved to start undoing the buckles at her shoulders. Hurlt was a former mercenary, much like herself. In fact, all of the new guards that Merik used were mercenaries. Even though he was only a sergeant, the other officers tended to defer to him if he made a suggestion. One did not live to be as old of a mercenary as Hurlt without learning a few things, or acquiring a few scars. Tianna didn't mind the veteran and made use of his wisdom by having him as her personal aide.

"Well Captain," Hurlt began. "It seems that Lord's Merik's speech has had the effect that he desired. Today, we have had a dozen young men and women who came and inquired about how to become guards. A few of the youths were so bold as to claim that Merik sent them a personal invitation via his herald. There were about four or five that were here yesterday after the speech as well."

"Good"

Hurlt gave a half grunt half snort as he helped her out of the armor. "Here, I thought it was my job as the grouchy old veteran to give one-word responses."

"Oh, it is your job, just so long as the word is a profanity."

Hurlt responded with another snort as he shook his head. The captain was one of the few people who could almost make her chuckle. She summoned a guard and ordered him to drop off her practice gear to her room and have a servant draw her a bath. Things were still touchy between the old and new guards who didn't trust one another. Most of the original city guards were barely worth being called guards at all. They were lazy and corruption ran thick within their ranks. Thankfully, Erlin and his lackeys were able to weed out the corrupt ones. The trouble makers she sent to the task of clearing out a nearby warehouse full of Twilight Haze, in addition to their regular duties. The city was full of the drug and things would get interesting when the addicts ran out of their supply.

"How is the progress on clearing out the warehouse?"

"Should be finished tomorrow, Captain."

"Have the crew divided up. I want one half to finish cleaning while the rest begin making bunks and bringing in equipment. See to it that there is a master carpenter to oversee the work. Also, I want several rooms made suitable for officers quarters. All new recruits will be stationed there by the start of next week."

Hurlt nodded and then began to go over the next item at hand. She left the training ground and swung by the mess to have a plate sent up to her room. Hurlt following her every step of the way, updating her with the evening's reports. When she reached her room, Hurlt had finished with his reports and waited to see if there was anything else that she needed before leaving. She waved him off and damn near fell as she entered her private quarters. It seemed that the guard she asked to take her armor back to her rooms did just that, in the barest sense of words. Her training equipment had been dumped just inside the door and barely off to the side. She made a mental note to make sure that guard would be added to the warehouse cleaning roster for a couple of days.

As she had assumed the role as the new captain of the guards, there had been several minor incidents of disrespect like this. They didn't like her and resented her being there. Many believed that she was captain merely because Merik wanted to appease her because of her strength controlling people's bodies, and not through any real merit of her own. They would learn, just like the mercenaries who came with her. An example would more than likely need to be made out of a couple of them. It was unfortunate, but that was the nature of things.

She picked up the armor and placed it on the stand in the corner of her room. It would take time, but she would prove to all that she was more than capable of being captain of the guards. Hell, in the past, she was one of Kour's best officers in his group of marauders and bandits. Unfortunately, that all came to an end when she lost the duel and was exiled. Kour only accepted the best, and when an officer was challenged and lost, they were cast out. It was brutal, but his method served him well. The common mercenary was safe from exile, and it kept reckless ambition in check. Only those brave and strong enough to risk losing everything would rise to leadership with the group.

Quickly, her skill with the blade proved itself time and time again. Before long, she had made her way to squad leader. With a team under her, she really began to flourish, and her other abilities, besides psychic ones and blade work, began to show. She won her first duel for leadership before she was twenty. Kour had even begun to take notice of her and mentored her in the ways of command. That all came to an end with the duel. She would not let her past failures stop her, though. Merik gave her a second chance when others were too afraid. Each day, she did her best to repay him for that, and to make sure that she would not fail again.

Her clothes were still soaked with sweat. She left the front room and went over to the small room that she used for bathing. The large tub was steaming with hot water. She stripped down and stepped in. The water was nice and hot and did wonders relaxing her overworked muscles. She leaned back and took a moment to relax and forget about things. With the outside world forgotten, she could be just a woman. Just a plain ordinary woman enjoying a soak. Soon enough, she would have to get out of the tub and assume her roles. Her role as a warrior, as captain of the guards, as Merik's psychic thug. Tianna looked down at the water and saw her scarred face reflecting back at her. Never again, she thought. Never again.

CHAPTER 13

ASHA

Asha sat on the rooftop watching the sunset. Quietly, she cursed herself for her arrogance and foolishness. She had been observed stealing and almost captured by the guards. What a stupid move! It was careless stunts like this that was going to be the end of her. She was better than this, much better. Next time, she would be perfect. Next time, she would double check to make sure no one was watching her before she stole. For the next hour, as the sun finished setting, she continued mentally berating herself for the mistake that she made.

No one was as hard on themselves as she was. Her rough start in life with the harem left mental scars long after anything physical would have healed. Asha still believed, and probably always would, that she was not good enough and that each little mistake was a result of her inadequacy. She was overly critical of herself, and that kept her from realizing her full potential.

Of course, when she was doing great and succeeding, she was on top of the world. Everything was great, she was doing fine, and she believed in herself. That was until the next mishap. Things didn't even have to be her fault, or something she could have prevented. In the end, she nearly always found a reason to blame herself.

Long after the sun had gone down and the stars came out to dance in the night sky, Asha was still on the rooftop staring off at the horizon, lost in dark thoughts. Eventually, she stirred and got up. Her stomach growled in discontent, but she did not feel like eating. Slowly, she crossed the rooftops until she reached the abandoned building that was her home. Asha made her way to the couple of rooms that she used. She lit a lamp and went through the pile of skirts that she had until she found one that was suitable.

With very little thought, she sat down in her sewing chair and began making alterations on the outfit that would make it suitable for quick changes and fast escapes. It was a routine she had done dozens of times and would probably do hundreds more throughout her life if things did not change. The repetitive routine of each stitch provided her a bit of therapy and eventually allowed her mind to relax a bit. By the time the outfit was altered enough to satisfy her, the self-loathing she had for herself was muted enough to allow sleep.

CHAPTER 14

TIANNA

The room had started to fill up. There was nervousness in the air. Many did not know what to expect from their new leader. It was easy to spot who had come with the psylord and who was a part of the city's old governing body. Everyone who was a part of Merik's crew was calm and, if not relaxed, they were at least busy with something of importance. Tianna sat in her chair and observed people as they came into the room. No one was a threat, but you never know when some dissident had enough and was willing to risk their lives on the chance to harm Merik. Hurlt was standing nearby, should she need anything. Erlin was going through a stack of reports. Apparently, being chief herald and head of information kept him quite busy. Suval stood leaning against a wall in the corner with his hands steepled and stared at everyone as they entered the room. There was a discontented hunger in his gaze that made people hastily look away.

Members of the original counsel of advisors stood in small clusters, nervously chatting with each other. Their place in the grand scheme of things had yet to be figured out by them and, if Merik knew what he wanted, he had yet to let them know. They were happy to have been spared during the take over, as well as the rounding up that was still going on. It was their hope that the services they provided were important enough to warrant keeping them alive, or at least alive long enough for them to ingratiate themselves with their new ruler.

Merik was hard put to trust someone and kept his motives known only to a few, and then only when they had to be shared.

The heavy oaken door on the back wall quietly opened and Merik stood there surveying the room. For a moment, old council members did not know what to do next. Those who were standing tried to sit, and those seated tried to stand. Meanwhile, Merik's crew waited patiently for their lord to let this little drama play out.

"Please, find your seats so that we can begin," Merik stated in a firm voice.

Quickly, everyone found a seat at the table, except for Suval. More than one person gave a worried glance over to him, at which he returned a leering smile and muttered to himself. Merik leaned back in his chair and surveyed the people gathered in the room, one by one. Most failed to meet his gaze and would quickly look down. Merik loved to posture and was fond of such basic displays of dominance.

"Well, I don't know about you, but I think that my speech was a wonderful success."

There were several people nodding their heads rather quickly to agree with their new ruler. The room lapsed into an odd silence as the previous council members nervously shuffled their papers and gave furtive glances to one and another. There was none among their number who wanted to risk upsetting Merik by speaking out of turn. Merik let the silence play out and allowed the stress to build in the room before nodding to Tianna, to indicate that she should begin.

"Well, sir, we have had several citizens inquire with the guards as to how they could join. We converted a nearby warehouse to a barracks for the new recruits. Patrols have been increased, and I have made sure that each group patrolling has a mix of old and new guards. Two additional smiths and one tailor have been hired in order to make sure that we will have enough uniforms and arms for the new recruits, once their training is done."

"Excellent, but go ahead and double the number of smiths and tailors. I want to make sure each soldier, I mean guard, is properly equipped. After all, I want them to be safe."

"I will add that to my list of things to do. We had two more raids yesterday, both were a success with only minor injuries to report. I am still only using members of the new guard on these raids."

At that Erlin gave her a puzzled look and said: "But my people have gone through all of the old city guards and I can assure you that there are none left that can not be trusted."

"It's not about trust, or not in that way. The original town guards are a bit untrusting of those who fought alongside us. Several of the old guards have been removed from their positions, thanks to Erlin's assistance, due to outside ties that would make them disloyal. We have not finished rounding up the last of Djinar's loyalists. It is possible that there may be a loyalty conflict when they come across someone that they didn't realize was in hiding. Finally, their combat skill is subpar. I have instituted extra drills, but it will take some time before they get close to what our forces can fight like."

"They will never trust one another," Merik interjected, "until they have spilled blood together. You are being over cautious, Captain. I expect you to have them fighting alongside one and another at the next major raid, should there be one. If any of the old town guards gives you an issue, then discipline them immediately. Show them that things have changed and that they are expected to hold to the same standards as all of the other guards. Quite frankly, I am surprised that you haven't done this already. Perhaps you should spend more time with your men than attending to other duties."

Tianna reddened, whether with rage or embarrassment it was hard to tell. She cleared her throat and continued, but it was obvious to all that the captain's chastisement struck a nerve. "As to the city itself, there is not much to report. There have been no incidents of public unrest. Crime is currently down, but I expect that to change once the criminal element gets used to the new government."

"Why is that?"

"I think they are just playing it safe until they can learn the new rules. Once they know how you will govern, they begin to find ways to cheat the system again."

Merik gave an amused snort at this and leaned back in his chair. He did his best to stifle a yawn as he folded one hand over the other. "Other than the time of the Kysian Empire," he began, "there has always been a criminal element on the fringe of society. These vultures prey on the weak and the downtrodden. I tend to eliminate them completely. They will find the good people of Crestburn to be a much more difficult prey when the guards can transition into the role of Warden."

"Under Djinar's rule, crime was tolerated. Local street gangs ran their neighborhoods and the city guard was designed to be impotent. A clear message must be sent to let all know that times have changed. That the tolerances of the past will not be acceptable and that we will have new standards to live by. I have decided that a public example needs to be made so that all will know the price of being a criminal in Crestburn. Jenal Goldentongue is to be chained to the platform in the Merchant's Courtyard and his crimes announced to all present. He is to remain there for one week, on display."

There was a murmur in the room, and not just from the old council members. One of the braver ones raised up a hand meekly, waiting to be recognized... Merik stared at him and arched an eyebrow, "Yes?"

"Wh, wha, what are the charges?" the councilman stammered before hastily throwing in a "My Lord," as he looked down.

"The charges? Surely you jest. It has long been known that Jenal was an information broker. Therefore, he is being charged as a spy against the new government. He was even seen heading to this very manor on the night of my liberation of Crestburn. Had Suval not acted as quickly as he did, who knows how bloody things would have escalated had Jenal managed to get word to Djinar."

He waved an arm to gesture to Suval who was still in the corner quietly, but was now grinning like a dog pleased with himself. His almost shoulder length hair was unkempt and frazzled. There was almost a greasy sheen to his olive skin. How on earth such a man became favored by Merik was beyond everyone in the room, except for the few who were a part of Merik's inner circle. A few words with the man left a creepy feeling that stayed with you until hours later. Even Hurlt, the grizzled old veteran, felt uneasy in Suval's presence.

"Jenal Goldentongue had information that was most dangerous to our new lord and savior," Suval purred. "The man possessed dangerous information and threatened harm to Lord Merik. I testified to all this in a private hearing that Merik has set up to examine the remains of Djinar's court." This was met with murmurs. "Personally," he continued, "I think the man should be imprisoned in the lower holding cells until we can be sure that his information could cause no harm, but that's just me."

Several members of the room shuddered at what Suval suggested. No one dared try to guess what motives Suval would have, let alone might do with someone locked away and forgotten in a cell.

"No, I don't think so. He needs to be on display as a message to all, but you do raise an interesting point. Jenal could still cause harm with that golden tongue of his, so we will remove it before we put him on display."

Suval looked crestfallen, as if a parent had taken away a child's favorite toy. He looked out the window and proceeded to ignore the group for the rest of the meeting.

"Erlin, what have you learned about Djinar's whereabouts?" Merik asked.

"Nothing, sir. No one has seen him since the night you overthrew ..." Erlin coughed to cover his poor choice of words "Excuse me, my lord. As I was saying, we have not heard a word about Djinar since the night of your liberation of Crestburn. There have been rumored sightings of his Senechal, Botun, but nothing on Djinar. The two hareem girls we found pleasing each other on the couch were the last to see him."

Merik stared at Erlin, now leaning forward in a chair. His carefree and relaxed posture was forgotten. His fist clenched, released and clenched again. The room fell silent again, except for random mumbling coming from Suval as he continued to stare out the window.

"This is unacceptable," Merik said in a slow and measured voice. Each syllable came with a pause that barely contained the psylords' anger.

"I am sorry, my lord, but Djinar has vanished."

"He could not have vanished. Someone has seen something. Question every single person in the manor. Question those girls again and again. Make use of Suval. I have not saved this city only to have it ruined because Djinar got away. You need to spend more time with your telepaths. Make sure they are doing their jobs right! You don't want to be the reason this all falls apart, do you?," shouted Merik as he stood up.

Erlin tried to respond, but was at a loss for words. Merik's eyes locked on Erlin and the man began to shrink under his gaze. His body began to shake, and those seated near him could hear him mummer, "No, no, no,"quietly. Merik just stood there quietly, his eyes never leaving his herald.

His attention completely focused on the poor man as he became overcome with what appeared to be terror.

This lasted only a moment, but it felt much longer to everyone in the room, and probably like an eternity to Erlin. Merik sat back down, smiled, and asked one of the old council members what they had to report. The poor sod damn near jumped out of his skin and could not suppress a squeak of fear at being addressed. This made Merik smile and he leaned back into his chair once again, relaxed, as if nothing had happened.

CHAPTER 15

KERWIN

It was a warm day, but at least it was overcast with a gentle wind. It had rained in the early hours of the morning, just before the sun made its way across the sky. By the time breakfast had been served, the ground was dry again. With any luck, there would be another rain in the next day or two, for the land badly needed it. It had been a dry year in this region, and that would make for a rough winter if crops didn't get more water.

Kerwin sat on the back balcony of the inn. An open book sat in his lap, which was fine, because he had read it several times over the years. It was a work of fiction, a collection of tales inspired by legendary figures of the Kysian Empire. There were many similar tales, but this collection was his favorite. It was his way to escape and travel to a time when civilization had a purpose.

Downstairs, he could hear a commotion as several people entered the inn. From what little bit he could make out, it seemed like a group of traders had just come into town. Perhaps he could get a ride with them as they left the next day. It was always safer to travel with a caravan than by yourself. A lone person was easy picking for bandits, and few groups were organized well enough to try and take on a caravan. Or at least not to the best of his knowledge.

Kerwin picked up his book and started reading again. It was easy to lose yourself in the stories. The heroes of old seemed larger than life and their deeds were amazing wonders of impossible feats. Their lives had purpose, even if they did not know it at the time.

The only problem with the book was that it was fiction. While the people in the stories did exist, and the deeds were accomplished, somewhat, it was not done in the magnificent way it was presented. The important figures of the Kysian Empire had their deeds extensively chronicled. While the accounts had all but been obliterated when the empire collapsed, the stories were passed from mouth to ear, from one generation to the next. The deeds grew larger, the obstacles more daunting, and the sense of destiny more present.

"I don't know why you read those silly things," came an interrupting thought to his mind.

"*They give me pleasure, that is why I read them. These silly things as you called them are a temporary escape from the mundaneness of this world.*"

"*And yet you know that they are full of ridiculous, over the top events. The events and people have been blown way out of proportion. It amazes me that a man who is so grounded in facts of events, whose job it is to investigate things, can enjoy such frivolous fluff. Let's not forget to mention that you have read the actual accounts of all those events from the society's archives.*"

"*While all that is true, it changes nothing. These stories give me pleasure that I don't find elsewhere.*"

There was the mental equivalent of a snort, or the rolling of eyes. Kerwin stopped reading and looked around. Across the balcony, there were several people sitting down to eat. By the looks of them, they appeared to be traders and were more than likely the ones he had heard coming into the inn a little while ago. It seems that they were now all settled in and ready for a meal.

"*Such drama with you. Most would love to have our jobs. To travel freely in the world, seeing new cities and meeting new people. We are the lucky ones.*"

"*Lucky? To what end? I chase down leads and check on events that the society never acts upon and never will. We have been chasing our own tails since our creation. At this point, there would have to be a coronation of a new emperor before the society decided it was time to throw in their support.*"

"*You are not the only one who feels this way. There are a lot of people in the society who have been saying something similar.*"

"*I don't blame them. The society was formed to help rebuild the empire, but all it has ever done for hundreds of years has been sit and watch. Occasionally, they send out some poor bastard like me to risk their lives to investigate a situation more fully, but then they never do anything with the investigations. How many operatives have died for nothing?*"

"*If one day the empire does get rebuilt, then it will not have been for nothing.*"

"*If? You are not losing faith, too, are you? Joining the ranks of the faithless?*"

"*I ah… It doesn't matter. What matters is that you have a new assignment.*"

"*Oh, joy. Another dead end or false lead.*"

"*It doesn't matter if it's a dead end or not, you still have to go and check it out. The council wants this done quickly, too. We had to adjust our route to get to you so that you can be on your way as soon as possible.*"

"*What's the rush? The council won't even react to the report that I will give, except to file it away with all the others.*"

"*Apparently, one of the catch phrases was said.*"

"*And? You know this wouldn't be the first time I was sent off because someone said one of a dozen special phrases.*"

"*There are not a dozen of them.*"

"*Might as well be. Besides, the phrases alone are virtually meaningless.*"

"*I guess you're in luck, because this time it was said in conjunction with talk about rebuilding the wardens and reestablishing old laws and customs. Either way, you are to head to Crestburn. Djinar has been overthrown in a coup and Merik is the new lord in* town. *Nothing on his abilities as of yet. The observer is a young man named Jariek. He works as an apprentice falconer for Master Gerwald. Jariek will be able to give you more information once you get there. You are to go to Hungry Mind Inn where there will be a room ready for you."*

"Sounds like the empire being remade at last. All of our hopes and dreams are fulfilled at last." Kerwin thought, sarcastically.

"Hey, man, I just deliver the orders, I don't make them. Hopefully, this will turn into something the society needs."

The seriousness of the man's tone was enough to give Kerwin a pause. The second caravan member that delivered the orders, or message, was primarily based on who was close, and available. Over the years, Kerwin had interacted with the man several times, as much as any other second caravaner. While he didn't know the man, he did know his mannerisms and picked up that something was off.

"The society needs it? Explain."

"What? Oh, I didn't mean anything by it. Just a poor choice of words on my part, I guess?"

"Are you sure?"

"Yes."

"That's not what I was asking. Are you sure you want to lie to me? You know what I do. You know it's my job to find things out. I know you well enough to notice there was something off in the way you thought that. A level of tension with those thoughts that weren't there before. So, please, do explain."

"I, ah.."

"I can make you, you know."

"You wouldn't! It would be violating the rules of the Cashek Society!"

"That is true, but I have a feeling that the Cashek Society would be more interested in what you don't want to tell me than the infraction I would be committing to get that information."

Across the room, one of the merchant's paled and started shaking his head. His companions stopped eating and questioned him but were waved off. Kerwin gave him a moment to collect himself. After all, he had the advantage now. The man forgot that Kerwin survived by his ability to observe and ferret out information. Like other operators, he was good at getting to the truth and adept at social manipulation.

"How we proceed is your choice," Kerwin offered him.

"You're an asshole."

"I am told that most of us operatives are."

"You didn't hear this from me."

"Of course not."

"There is talk. A number of people within the society have a view similar to yours."

"What do you mean?"

"That the Cashek Society is useless. People are starting to say that the council will never find someone who they will assist in rebuilding the empire. Some even are starting to say that there is no point even trying to rebuild it."

"What is the council doing about this?"

"Nothing. They don't know about it, or, if they do, they have not let on. Those who think this way are cautious about who they talk to about this."

"Very interesting. Thanks."

"Screw you, it's not like I had a choice."

With that Kerwin went back to his book, although wasn't focused on it as he turned the pages absentmindedly. It was interesting news, but he wasn't sure how serious it was. More than likely, the council already knew about it and was not acting on it. The Cashek Society has existed for hundreds of years and this can't be the first time members have grown disillusioned with it. But, it was nice to know that others were feeling the same way as he did.

CHAPTER 16

TIANNA

It was in the middle of the night when Tianna received the summons from Merik. This was not unusual, as the man often worked late into the evening. She quickly got dressed and splashed cold water on her face to help wake up. Tianna glanced at the moon's position as she passed a window and figured she had been asleep for only an hour or two at best. When she entered Merik's private receiving room, reserved for receiving high ranking officials, Tianna could see Erlin was already seated across from Merik by the fireplace.

Merik tended to be nicer when it was just his inner circle. Still, there was always a chance of another outburst like the one earlier with Erlin. For his part, Erlin didn't seem to hold what happened against him. Not that holding anything against Merik did anyone any good. He would find out, and then there would be even more problems. It was just best to ignore the outbursts and keep your head down.

A side door opened and a pair of servants came in. One brought forth glasses and a decanter of dark wine. The other laid out a tray of spiced meats and cheeses. Without even bothering to glance at them, Merik waved them off and reached for the food. Erlin took a glass and leaned back into his chair, slowly sipping. "Say what you will about Djinar," Erlin said, "that hedonistic pig did have a wonderful selection of wine."

"Yes, he did. Of course, I am saving the good stuff for my most loyal. You guys work hard for me and deserve it, even if your work has been a bit of a disappointment as of late." If Merik's jab struck a note with Erlin, the man did nothing to show it. His ability to remain composed was amazing, but, as head of the information network, he probably had lots of experience keeping his feelings to himself, Tianna mused.

"It seems that there will be a rather large group of Djinar's loyalists that are attempting to leave the city soon. Right now, I do not have specific details as to when and where. Tianna, I want you to have your guards ready to deploy. A mixed group of old and new guards."

"If that's what you wish, then I will see to it that it is done."

"Good. I want these loyalists to leave the city. They will be more relaxed if they think they have gotten away, and it will make your job easier. Once they are a few miles out of town, I want them slaughtered. All of them, with one exception. The informant that provided me with this information is to be left alive. I want this young man brought back in for questioning; however, I want his identity to remain secret. I may have more use for him."

"That won't be a problem. I take it that this raid is to be kept quiet."

"Why else would I be talking to the two of you," Merik chided.

"I was just confirming, sir"

"This is why I like you, Tianna. You don't play games and you make sure you have understood everything."

"You know, it's been a while since we had a session together. I know you want answers, even if it is pointless, and I promised to help you find them. After the raid is successful, I will make time in my busy schedule, and we can go over things again. You really should consider giving this up."

"I can't, sir. I wish I could explain why, but I don't have a reason. I just know that something was wrong with that duel."

Merik gave her a dismissive wave of his hand and took a sip of wine before he responded. "It's not important. Either I or Erlin will alert you when the group tries to flee. Just make sure you are ready to go at a moment's notice."

CHAPTER 17

SUVAL

The wretched heap that once was Jenal Goldentongue laid on the cold floor of his cell. Moans emanated from his mouth and alternated with weeping. His mind was gone, and his ability to tell the difference between dream and reality was no more. Not that it really mattered, for both were horrid. He stank of piss and sweat, and his clothes had become filthy. It was fascinating, in a sick and twisted sort of way, how quickly his condition degraded due to lack of sleep.

Truth be told, it was more than just a lack of sleep that did this to him. Almost anytime he closed his eyes, and his body finally shut down in pure exhaustion, nightmares tormented his sleep. The dreams would only last a few minutes before waking him up in terror, and this was how he spent his days. Falling in and out nightmarish sleep a few times every hour.

Suval stood in the corner, like he had done most days, and watched his plaything. He was sad that Merik ordered him to be put on display. It had been a wonderful learning experience for Suval. Never before had he had someone at his complete mercy. He was able to try a few things out with Jenal and satisfy several curiosities. What surprised Suval the most was how Jenal's mind began to produce bad dreams without his influence. It was as if it had been trained to do so, and when Suval stirred up those dreams, they became much worse. Several times Jenal had awoken shrieking in complete terror. The guards hated that, but, then again, they didn't like Suval to begin with. Few people could stand being around him for very long; that was what made Lord Merik special.

Jenal's whimpering died down, and it looked like the man had passed out again. Suval studied the sleeping man and connected to his mind. It was a place of utter chaos. While he couldn't see dreams, he could feel them, kind of. The only way he could describe his talent to Merik was that he could stir up a person's dreams. They would go from ordinary to something disjointed and chaotic. This made sleep less restful for the victim. The experience was hard to describe, and there was no one in the world that was like him to learn from. It was this unique ability of his that made him special, and what attracted Merik to him. In return for his services, Merik promised to give him people to experiment on and test the limits of his abilities. Suval had learned a lot by playing with Jenal's mind. He looked forward to his next plaything.

CHAPTER 18

BOTUN

The servant's name was Vera, and she had been a servant in the mansion for almost five years. Thankfully, she was not pretty enough to have attracted Djinar's attention and become one of his harem girls. There was a sad advantage to being plain looking. While being a servant wasn't glamorous work, it did provide her with a roof over her head and a bed, one that didn't include Djinar or his friends, to sleep in. She had made sure to do a good enough job to keep the lord happy, but not too good to gain his attention. While she failed to be noticed by Djinar, she did get noticed by Botun.

After the attack, she had been surprised that Botun had requested to speak with her. When they met, he explained that he wanted her to act as his eyes and ears inside the mansion. There was a spot in the garden that could be seen from a nearby building. Every other day, Vera would wait there first thing in the morning so that he could contact her telepathically, and she could give her to him. This would guarantee her anonymity and his favor. Vera had been hesitant at first, since all of the staff had already been questioned by Erlin and Merik about where their loyalty lay. It had taken some convincing on his part, but eventually she agreed. He included her sister and family in the exodus out of town, which was about to happen if Liam showed up. Already, the kid was several minutes late.

There were little over twenty people in the crowded room, all of whom were starting to get nervous at the delay. Over the last several days, Botun had been busy meeting with people, trying to convince them to join him. It had been slow going at first. Most were unsure as to whether or not they wanted to take the risk. Staying was a risk, too, but it is easier for a person to rationalize a risk that didn't require drastic change. It had been several long days filled with clandestine meetings and late nights. Sleep was a luxury Botun barely received.

Even with all the hard work and long hours, he was thankful. Zahra had been a godsend. With her smooth touch and silky skills of persuasion, she was able to nudge several people to join who had been on the fence about the operation. She also made sure he managed to find a place to sleep, even if it had been in the back room of her brothel. With her hard work, the almost impossible task had a better chance of success.

The turning point of the week was when Lord Merik's herald brought forth Jenal Goldentongue to the stage that had been erected in the middle of Merchant's courtyard. A proclamation was read and sent telepathically by the herald, who listed the crimes that Jenal had committed and been found guilty of. It was a ridiculous list, and Botun was surprised that someone who could pull off such a successful overthrow would do such sloppy work with this. It wouldn't take the average citizen long to realize that the charges were ridiculous. How could a person commit treason against a government not yet established? Ridiculous or not, those were the charges, and poor Jenal was chained down to the middle of the stage like an animal.

It had been late on the first afternoon of Jenal's public display when Botun had dared to come and see him. The poor man was a disgusting wretch. He could not believe that was the same man he had spent years working with. His clothes were soiled and torn. He could smell his unwashed body from ten feet away. The man himself just wept on the stage and muttered incoherently.

Everyone who worked directly for Djinar knew Jenal and his position as an information broker. Having him placed on public display in that wretched condition, with trumped-up charges, did a lot to change the minds of those who Botun had talked with. Several even offered more money to aid in the efforts. They were afraid of what Jenal knew about them, and what he could or may possibly tell. Although, given his condition, Botun didn't think Jenal would ever be able to speak coherently again. Those who had thought themselves safe from Merik, now found themselves in the difficult position of possibly being found out.

Now, here they all were, crowded into the room in which they had met a week previously. Everyone was on edge. Several people jumped when the old door creaked open, announcing a new person or group joining the room. Long knives and short swords were openly worn and hilts fondled. It was a much larger group than he had originally expected, and he hoped that Liam was able to accommodate them.

As the night wore on, more and more people glanced over at the door, as if they expected either Liam or guards to come through it. Nervous murmurs gave way to angry comments and tempers were starting to show. Botun didn't blame them. At this point, he, too, was beginning to feel that Liam had betrayed them, or at the very least stood them up.

"This is getting ridiculous. Where is this Liam kid?" complained one the group. There were several nods of heads and murmurs of agreement.

"Gone is what I think. Sold us out," came the response from another. Zahra shot Botun a worried glance before making her way over to the upset man. "Oh," she cried out of shock and spun around, hand raised ready to slap the person who grabbed her ass. Her hand landed on the side of Liam's face, but his cocky grin never flinched. How on earth did she walk right past him without noticing him, she wondered? Furthermore, how had she or anyone else failed to notice when he came into the room?

"Aww, yous miss me. Don't worry, I missed yous too," he said as he gazed at her ample bosom. He gave her a wink and a quick kiss on the cheek and walked into the middle of the room, slowly spinning around. "Sorry if I had yous all worry a bit. Noting ta fear."

"You were sup," Botun began but was quickly cut off by Liam, who held out his hands palms up in a placating gesture. "Time fer business, eh? Given de size of de turnout, I take it most of yous has a good look at old mumbletongue on stage." Liam's comment brought everyone's attention completely on him. "I know I'm a bit late tonight but everyting is ok. Wit our new lord given everyone wine from Djinar cellar, I wanted te check de route, te make sure noting tat I had planned had changed.

"De last ting any of yous want is fer tis te go sideways. Tere is not enough room fer all of yous te be on tat stage next te yours buddy, so some would have te go in dank dark holding cells. Worst of all, my reputation would be destroyed. I mean talk about a travesty."

Liam's flippant talk was winning him no friends in the room. Two men went so far as to start to draw their blades, until Botun, who had managed to make his way behind them, put his hand on their shoulders. Their blades stayed in their sheaths as they spat onto the floor and cursed at Liam.

"So, we are all set then?" Botun asked their guide.

"I just said so, boss man. We's all good. Now, we will be taking a roundabout way. So please don't get yours panties in a bunch, everyone, when this takes a while. Wit all de extra guard patrols, and tonight's festivities, we's will have detours te take. Don't worry, I have it all planned out and you's will be safely outside the city walls and on yours way well before sunrise."

"Now, before you all leave," Botun began, this time uninterrupted by Liam "there are a few things I want to say. First of all, thank you. By joining us tonight you give us a chance to take back our lives. Once Djinar is found, I will help him reclaim what was once his. I will make sure that each of you is remembered and has a place here, waiting for you upon your return. After you leave, I will stay behind with a few others and continue our search for Djinar. He will be found in a short time, and we can then begin the next stage of our undertaking. I wish you all the best of luck."

With the end of his short speech, he left the room with Zahra at his side. They went to the room where he had the brute squad in waiting, should things have gone awry. The men were all heavily armed and armored, ready for trouble. The squad leader looked over from where he had been leaning against the wall and nodded at Botun. Botun closed the door before addressing Zahra

"Did you have any success in reading his mind this time?"

"No, not at all."

"Oh she read it all right, she just didn't want te admit te yous is all. I can't say I blame her, wat wit all tose dirty toughts I had about her running trough my head" Liam finished with a wink.

The brute squad leapt to their feet with weapons drawn and ready to strike in a heartbeat. Zahra stumbled back in seeing Liam right next to her when, just a moment before, she could have sworn the space was empty. Botun, to his credit, barely reacted at Liam's sudden appearance in the room.

"How?" Zahra stammered.

Hargod, the leader of the squad, looked at Botun to see how he wanted this to play out. It was obvious that he wished for a violent solution, especially after having just been surprised like that. If it had been an armed attacker, they would have taken serious losses before they could have put him down. Botun remained calm and walked past Liam, as if he wasn't there, and took a seat and pointed to the empty chair across from him. Casually, strolling as if he was in a park on a sunny day instead of a room with weapons drawn on him, Liam crossed the room and plopped down into the offered seat. Zahra stood behind Botun while two thugs stood right behind Liam.

"I hope it was worth the risk?"

"How do yous mean boss man?"

"Revealing your talent just like you did."

Liam just laughed loudly in response and shook his head with an amused grin on his face.

"Why?" asked Botun

"Does it matter why?"

"Humor me."

"A man as smart as you would figure tings out eventually. Kind of surprised no ones else has by now. You know it's amazing how many people actually buy de luck ting. Tat alone has given me an edge tat others don't have."

"True enough, but answer the question."

"No games wit you, huh boss man?" Liam replied, holding his hands out with the palms up. "Like I said, yous would have figured tings out sooner or later. So, I figured I might as well be upfront wi hings."

"Up front would have been you telling me."

"Nows, boss man, yous can't blame a poor boy like me fer a little bit of showmanship. After all, it's tings like tat which has kept me alive and help perpetuate de legend of Lucky Liam. Tings are changing in tis city. Changing in a bad way, I tink. Not saying I liked Djinar, but tis Merik ,well, I … let's just say I have seen someting that doesn't sit well wit me. Besides, tings are changing, and change is bad fer business"

"So, by letting me in on your secret, that was your way of letting me know I could trust you."

"You got it, boss man. Like Jenals, your best currency is secrets, and I just gave yous one hell of payment."

"Not much of a payment if it was something I was going to figure out eventually."

"Well, time is money and." Liam paused as Botun held up his hand.

"We will talk more in a few days. In the meantime, you have a job to do."

Liam nodded and stood up, the guards adjusted their grips, ready to swing at a moment's notice.

"A final kiss farewell me love?"

Zahra scowled at first, but then walked over and gave Liam a kiss, not on the lips as he had hoped for, but on a cheek. With a chuckle Laim sauntered off and, when the door was closed and guards sure that he had indeed left, Zahra sat in the chair and asked Botun, "How did you know?"

"I had my suspicions for quite some time. His little stunt in the other room supported what I thought, and was proven by what he just did here. The powers that people inherit are limited to what existed during the Kysian Empire. Over the centuries, no new power has ever been discovered. Liam is lucky because he is extremely strong at making someone not recognize he is there. The mind tricks the eyes into not seeing you, somehow. They just slide over you, as if you are invisible."

"So, that is how he got away from ambushes in the past."

"Partially. It is not foolproof, and someone with heightened sense can notice him, especially if they are strong in that power. Even a regular person can detect something as not being there without realizing exactly what is missing. If they started actively looking and focused, then they could find him. If Liam had tripped and fell, we would have heard the noise of him hitting the floor. Our eyes would fail to recognize him at first, but, if we took the time to search, we might have been able to see him. There is a limit the mind can be tricked into not noticing something. When someone is right there in front of you and you are actively looking, then it would take incredible strength to remain hidden that way."

"Liam is a lot more skilled than he lets on. He probably is very skilled at stealth, knows to stand in people's blind spots and how to move very quietly. Combine that with his ability, and he can almost disappear, provided you're not trying to find him."

"Then, how did he escape those ambushes?"

"More than likely, he has another skill. My guess would be clairvoyance. If he can see what people experience, it would make it easier to hide from someone looking for him. He would better know where their blind spots are and stay, literally, out of sight and then use his ability as a safety net.

"He was very smart to perpetuate the myth that he is lucky. If people believed he is lucky, then they would attribute his avoiding detection to luck and not his psychic ability."

Zahra smiled, getting what Botun explained to her. "So, let me see if I get this. If they think he disappears by luck, then they won't be searching, or searching as hard. This would make it easier for him to trick their minds into not noticing him."

"Exactly. The question is, why did he reveal this to us?"

"He said he wanted you to trust him."

"That's the problem. Liam has always been a loner. There is a reason for this change, and I am not sure if the reason he gave us is the real reason or, if it is, it's not complete."

"He said that Merik is bad for business and seemed like he wanted to throw his support with Djinar, but he didn't come out and say that."

"Yes. We still don't know where Djinar is, and I know from my informant that Merik does not either."

CHAPTER 19

MERIK

Merik sat alone in his study, a stack of reports cluttering his desk. It was a large flat top thing that was more like a table than a proper desk. Djinar must have used it because his bulk would have been uncomfortably crammed into a more proper desk. It was functional but not stylish. He would have to exchange it for one that was better fitted for a man of his stature. For now, it would do, since it was covered in various reports. The history books never mentioned all the reports and paperwork associated with ruling people. The attention they required was maddening at times, but it was necessary to make sure things happened the way he wanted them to. Perhaps, when things were all said and done, he would write about all the mundane tasks that a leader must put up with. It could be eye-opening to his subjects.

There was a soft knock at the door and, after a short pause, a servant came in and said that Erlin wished to speak to him immediately. Merik nodded and leaned back in his chair.

"Good evening, my Lord. I am sorry to bother you while you deal with these," he cast an eye at the stack of papers on the desk, "more unglamorous duties required of a leader. The informant has let me know that tonight will be the night. They should be leaving in a few hours. I thought you would want to know this immediately."

"Thank you, Erlin. Your dedication and efforts are much appreciated. Please, send in my servant on your way out."

"Of course, sir."

The door had barely been shut when the servant entered the room.

"Please inform Captain Tianna to see me immediately." Merik ordered.

Merik waited until the servant left before giving a weary sigh. He was exhausted and there was still so much to do. It would figure the dissidents would choose tonight, a night that he was already busy, to leave on. Today started off with a small ceremony at which he unloaded several caches of food and drink that Djinar had kept for himself. Then, there was the dinner reception with many prominent members of the city. Another speech in the afternoon, followed by a formal dinner with more city officials. This was in addition to all the other duties of ruling.

Merik got up, walked across the room, and poured himself a drink. The glass was almost finished when the servant knocked and announced that Captain Tianna had arrived. He downed the last of his drink and nodded that she should be let in.

"I am pouring myself a glass, would you like one?"

Tianna shook her head.

"Are you quite sure? It is quite lovely, even if a bit strong. That's why I don't have more than one a night."

"You wished to see me?" Tianna asks.

"Yes. I have just been informed that there is a large group of Djinarian loyalists trying to flee the city tonight. I want you to take your men and deal with them first thing when the sun rises. They should be only a few miles out of town and you should have no problems tracking them. Remember, I want the informant alive, but keep his identity hidden when you bring him in. I don't want other people knowing that he gave up their secrets."

"This shouldn't be a problem, sir"

"It won't be a problem. I will not accept failure on this matter. Also, I want to remind you to make sure you have a nice mix of old and new guards. We need them to form a bond so that there will not be any problems in the future. Remember, if you fulfill your duties I can set aside a little bit of time to go over the duel again, even if it is a waste of time. You may go. I am sure you have plenty to do now."

CHAPTER 20

LUCKY LIAM

Liam paused, allowing the rest of the group to catch up with him at the mouth of the alley. Liam surveyed the street and closed his eyes to see if anyone would be coming down the street in the next ten heartbeats. He kept focused, not on the street but how it would be a few seconds ahead in time. Liam waved his group across, one by one. He only had to pause twice for people walking down the street. Each time he saw them before they came within sight and had been able to halt the street crossing in plenty of time.

This was the key to Liam's success. While his ability to get people's eyes to slide off of him was strong, it was the strength of the precognition ability that allowed Liam to do the seemingly impossible. Most people don't even realize they have precognition. Usually, people only saw a second or two into the future. Often, this was not enough time for the mind to recognize that they were seeing into the future, and it appeared that the person had great reflexes or the knack of knowing what someone else was about to say. With practice, a person could meditate and see a few minutes ahead in time, but that required a lot of focus..

While Liam was able to do that, it required too much mental concentration to make it of use out in the streets. That is where his raw strength came in. He was able to see further into the future without concentration than anyone else he knew of. This allowed him to be able to function while using precognition. Liam could switch it on and off at the drop of a hat, and many of the daring escapes were due to knowing when it was safe to proceed and which locations would get spotted by a pursuer. To anyone else, it appeared as if Liam possessed an uncanny amount of luck, which was fine. As long as everyone was thinking that Liam was lucky, then they would be a lot less likely to figure out the truth. A precog was tough to catch, but not impossible, especially if you knew how far into the future they could see.

What most people didn't realize was that the future was not constant. Perhaps it was because most could not see as far into it as Liam could. They were not able to experiment and see how their intended actions would impact the future. While ten seconds was not much time, it was enough to make sure a door was unlocked or a window could easily slide open. Liam got really proficient at delving into how his actions could impact the near immediate future. This added greatly to the reputation of luck, by allowing Liam to proceed with actions that look dangerous or risky but he knew were going to succeed.

Through abandoned buildings, across rooftops, and down alleyways the group made its trip. The festivities in celebration of the new Lord had lots of people out in the streets. This was not necessarily a bad thing, since most were drunk and distracted by the party atmosphere. Still, there were times the group had to hold up as a large crowd staggered its way down a street. Much to the exasperation of the group, Liam messed with a few lone drunks, playing a dangerous game that risked their exposure. Not that Liam would get caught, since the outcome was already known to him. To those in the group who helplessly watched him risk their discovery with needless grandstanding, the experience racked their already frayed nerves.

CHAPTER 20

TIANNA

The sun had crested the horizon not even a half hour ago, and yet the city guard was assembled. They stood rank and file, fully armed and armored like a military unit. The clubs that they typically used when on patrol in the city had been exchanged for short swords. An air of nervousness hung about the courtyard while the morning dew glistened in the sun's first rays.

Captain Tianna was mounted on a large chestnut steed. She rode up and down the ranks as she surveyed the men. She had broken up the units and intermixed the men at Merik's insistence. This was met with disgruntlement from all around, and was also the source of this morning's nervousness. The guards knew they were about to do something alongside people they had not trained together with. The old guards didn't trust the new ones and they had a very low opinion of them. The ones who had come with Merik would do fine, it was the old guards that worried her. At being jackbooted thugs, they had plenty of experience. What would happen later, would require more than they have done before, especially if they never fought as a part of a group mind.

"Today we head out to deal with a group of sympathizers who still remain loyal to Djinar. Lord Merik has been gracious to those who once held loyalty to the former Lord of Crestburn. He has been kind to many and allowed them to stay in our fair city and continue with their lives, as they had been doing. These people who we seek have rejected his offer and seek to undo his efforts. Some of you have never faced a person in combat, and it will not be easy for you to draw a blade upon another. You must, though, for not only does your life depend upon it, so does our future."

Tianna was about to continue on, when she heard a soldier mutter something about why they had to listen to a marked bitch. She stopped, surveyed the crowd, and noticed several nervous glances.

"Which of you said that?" she asked the group. Her response was marked by silence. "I will not ask you again. This entire unit will be tossed in a cell and dealt with upon my return unless I get an answer."

Two men pointed towards a third who spat at the grown and cursed them.

"Aye, it was me and I stand by what I said. Why the hell should we follow some marked bitch!"

"Why indeed?" was her cool reply.

"We all know what that mark upon your face means. It means you were kicked out of Kour's group. He only brands those who can't lead and failed him. Maybe we should claim the bounty on your head. Why should we follow some dumb bitch who was not even good enough to lead a group of ignorant outlaws?"

His remark was not met with a murmur of approval like he had hoped it would. Still, she could feel everyone waiting for a response. She had been expecting something like this to happen, eventually. It was a shame that it had to happen now, when they had more important matters to deal with.

"You do as I say because I am your captain, and you follow the orders of your superior officers. You do it because it is the will of your Lord Merik for this to be done. It does not matter which officer gives an order, and any who do not follow an order will be charged with dereliction of duty."

"Sergeant Herlt."

"Yes, Captain."

"Arrest this man and have him put into a holding cell until my return. This goes to anyone who thinks that an order is something you have a choice in following."

Two guards next to the man grabbed him, stripped him of his weapons and followed Sergeant Herlt. The rest of the gathered men remained in formation, completely silent. Tianna waited until the trio was back before she proceeded again, which allowed what she had said previously to sink in.

"It may be difficult for some of you to draw a blade upon another for the first time. Let go of your fears and worries. Remember the man standing next to you, for it is he you will be protecting with each swing of your blade. It is his life you will prolong with each thrust. We will be marching double time until we get close to the loyalist. Once there, we break into a skirmish line.

"Those of you in the front line will be linked together. Do not worry if you have never fought a part of a group mind. It's not that much different than being linked telepathically. The group mind will allow you to warn each other much faster, as well as better perceive attacks. Everything your brothers in arms see will be filtered by the group mind, and your own mind, to provide you a heightened sense of what is happening. You will perceive much more than you normally would and be much more efficient at fighting."

She wheeled her mount around and headed out of the training grounds. Officers quickly called out orders and the units began to march out. There was a murmur through the ranks as the old guards tried to digest what she had told them. This was where having the units intermixed came in handy, for those who had fought with Tianna knew what it was like to be in a group mind. They reassured the others, and by the time they made it through the city gates they were all marching along silently.

Once they left the city, the trail was easy to follow. A squad of scouts on horseback led the way as they checked for signs of the Djiinarian loyalist. The ground was torn up at fairly regular intervals, whether the work of the informant or just happenstance from that large of a group, either way, it made it easy for the scouts to track them. A few hours after they left the city, a scout signaled that the group had been spotted resting at the edge of a clearing.

Tianna ordered scouts to flank the loyalist and gave them a half hour to get into position. This allowed her men to rest from the fast pace that she had them march. Soon, it was time for them to get into formation and linked the front row into a group mind. She did this only for a few minutes before switching to the second rank and then the third. It allowed the men some familiarity with being a part of a group mind before the skirmish started, and helped calm some of their nerves.

"Alright, men. The scouts should be in place by now and will handle those that try to flee. We will march forward as quietly as possible, so that we can get in close. They are camped at the edge of a clearing, which we will have to cross. I want only the first row to cross with me. The second and third row is to hold back until after we are engaged, then I want you to cross at double time and support our flanks. Mental commands in the group mind will take priority over any vocal command that comes from my mouth. Let's move out."

The men marched along quietly in a loose skirmish line. She hung back just behind the first group, in the middle. It took them only a few minutes to make it to the edge of the clearing. She dismounted, tied her steed to a tree, and ordered her men forward. They had made it only a quarter of the way across the clearing when they were spotted. Thankfully, the rebels had been asleep and, by the time they realized what was happening, her men were almost upon them.

Several of the loyalists grabbed their weapons and formed a defensive line between her men and the rest of the group. A few tried to run off into the woods, but quickly came back after they noticed the mounted scouts.

Perfect.

Tianna ordered them to hold back, while through the group mind she sent a series of quick thoughts: *act unsure, wait to press, ignore vocal commands.* Those who tried to flee now joined the ones who formed a line against her guards. Now, the loyalists outnumbered the guards and were emboldened by the guard's tentativeness. They started taunting and even a few dashed up and made quick strikes before dancing back to their line.

"Damn it, you fools. You are supposed to be able to fight not to stand around like children. Fight you, coward." Tianna shouted at her men while sending the commands: *fall back, halfway, hold, good job.*

"Stop giving up ground, you sorry ass excuse for guards!" The loyalists grew more courageous as her men started to back across the field. Several would attack and press for more than a few seconds before backing off. It appeared that they would succeed with driving off the guards. She turned and linked up with the second and the third row and ordered them quietly to proceed to each flank.

That illusion of the Djinarian loyalist success lasted a moment longer. With a thought, Tianna sent the command to assault and every one of her men pressed the attack. The men on the front line blocked strokes before they came close and returned strikes with fearsome proficiency. Three loyalists were cut down before the others realized that the tide had turned. Four more died in the span of the next few heartbeats. Their ranks quickly broke, and several more tried to run but were cut down. Her men on the flanks now pounced and took care of the ones who tried to run off.

In little more than a minute, every last loyalist who tried to escape the city was dead, except for one. A skinny young man who stood quietly in the field with his blade dropped at his side. He was surrounded by several of her men, who had their swords pointed at him.

Tianna ordered a couple guards to double check the bodies and make sure each was dead. It was more than likely an unnecessary order, but there was no harm being thorough.

"Captain," the young began, but quit when she glared at him.

One of the guards she had assigned to check the bodies came up to her and waited to be recognized. She looked at him and he snapped a crisp salute before beginning.

"Sir, all of the bodies have been checked. We slide a dagger into each heart just to make sure, even on the obvious kills. All are dead. Do you wish anything to be done with the bodies?"

"No, leave them where they lay, and thank you for being so thorough."

The man did another salute before walking away.

Tianna surveyed her men. Several of the original guards stopped what they were doing when they saw her look at them and give a polite nod. The success of the skirmish seemed to have the impact she was hoping it would. Not a single man was wounded, and every opponent killed quickly. Tales of the easy victory would spread to the rest of the guards and there should be fewer difficulties, now that the men respected her as a proven commander.

"Excuse me, captain?"

"Yes, guard?"

"There is a caravan along the roadside. I am not sure how much of the fight they saw. What are your orders?"

"I want the prisoner bound with a bag over his head. Lord Merik does not want him identified. Have him ride double with one of the scouts. Let's go have a chat with the caravan."

Tianna remounted her steed and watched as her orders were carried out. She even noticed, with surprise, that they even went a step further and wrapped one of their cloaks around the prisoner to further conceal who it was. They were improving, and today's skirmish went a long way to change their attitude towards her.

CHAPTER 21

KERWIN

Kerwin had been fortunate, he supposed. A day after he left the inn he found a caravan, a real one not a part of the society, that was heading towards Crestburn. With a little bit of haggling, he was able to convince Marv, the caravan master, to allow him to join for a nominal fee. The next couple of days had been a boring ride through the countryside. At night they made camp and he was welcomed to the fire circle. Small talk was made about weather and local news but it was obvious that they were merely being polite. This was fine as he was not in a sociable disposition.

The trip did give him plenty of time to contemplate what he had learned from the second caravan member. He was surprised that there was a large number of people within the society who were dissatisfied with the way things were. The big question was whether or not the council knew about it, or probably more accurately what they knew about it.

It was difficult to keep secrets in a group that had restricted access to the outside world and had its own telepaths. Any threat to the stability of the society would be dealt with by the council. For several hundred years, the Cashek Society has existed and very little had been done towards achieving the goal set by Emperor Palreon. Even for someone like himself, who got to go and do things in the world, it still felt like the same old monotonous routine.

The places that he visited were the same thing over and over again. Sure, the location was different, but the problems, the people, the politics, the downtrodden - they were all the same. Going to a different town and investigating a matter was as monotonous as choosing what outfit to wear. It was something you did in order to get through the day.

Once in a while, there were times that made it worth it, but those were few and far between. Even those rare instances didn't make it better, being a part of the Cashek Society, or further their grand mission. He was just glad to be able to put his skills to use so that he could help someone, like when he helped Lena.

Lena had been an observer stationed in the small city of Gorthsfall. She was an apprentice to a tailor and soon achieved journeyman status. Lena had requested to relocate to Kurst so that she could work for a different seamstress. The Cashek Society approved her request and even helped set her up in the larger city. Unfortunately, the caravan that she had traveled with had been hit by mercenaries and she disappeared.

Kerwin was sent to investigate the matter and see if there was any chance that she survived. After he interviewed the survivors of the raid, he rode out to the site of the attack. The ambush happened when the caravan had been fording a river. Searching the area, he was able to pick the bandit's trail back to their camp. He sat outside the camp observing for two days until he was sure that Lena was not among them as a prisoner. Kerwin returned to the site of the ambush and began to check downstream, to see if by chance she had fallen in and swept away by the current.

By the time Kerwin found her, a few miles downstream, she was in awful shape. Her leg was infected and her body was ravaged with fever. He had been able to find herbs nearby with which to make a poultice. Once the poultice had been applied, he set about improving the shelter. Leana's lean-to barely provided her protection from the weather and looked like it was about to collapse in a strong breeze. The shelter took some time to rebuild, as he had to tear down what she made to build something better.

With the poultice, her fever was brought down. By the second day, she was healthy enough to tell him what had transpired. During the attack, she had jumped into the river to get away. When she came upon some rocks, she was able to cling to them and pull herself up out of the river. As Lena tried to cross the rocks, she slipped and fell, which resulted in her broken leg. Luck was with her, for she was right by the bank and had been able to make it to the bank. For the next several days she survived on berries from a nearby bush and took shelter in the poorly built lean-to.

By the end of a week, she was healthy enough to travel. Even with her riding the horse and him walking, the trip back to town was slow and took an entire day. Lena spent the next several months in recovery. The society provided her a place to stay as well as money to live on while she healed. Eventually, Lena made it to her destination and was able to study under the seamstress as originally planned. To the best of his knowledge, she was still there, now with a shop of her own.

He sighed heavily as his thoughts shifted from Lena to the upcoming assignment. It should be pretty simple and routine, he thought. Get to town, check out the new psylord, see what changes he has made. More likely than not, the changes would not be indicative of him having a copy of the manuscript. He would then file his report and move on to the next assignment. Hopefully, it would be fairly quick, Crestburn had a seedy reputation and he didn't want to stay there too long.

He looked up from his thoughts as the wagons slowed and then came to a stop. Up ahead and to the right was a skirmish.

Several soldiers were driven back by a group of fighters, while others stayed behind. Two other squads were coming up to flank, but if they fought like the others their numbers would even things out and things would probably draw out to a longer and bloodier fight for both sides.

"How close to Crestburn?" he asked one of the caravan members.

"Not far at all. We should be there in a couple of hours, provided they don't take interest in us," came the reply from one of the drivers as he nodded to the fight.

He watched as the black and green uniformed soldiers were driven back. The group they were fighting were becoming more confident and their individual engagements changed from a few quick swipes to a series of blows. It was odd. There was a uniformity in how the soldiers backed up that didn't feel quite right. For all the good the group was doing, they didn't seem to actually wound any of the soldiers.

Then, in an instant, everything changed. Without a word, the soldiers went from backpedaling to assault. Before anyone realized that the fight had shifted, several of the warriors were dead and the rest were being cut down. It was over in seconds. The members of the caravan stood silent, jaws slack and eyes wide as their brains tried to comprehend the massacre that they had just witnessed.

Slowly, they looked towards the caravan master to see what they should do next. To his credit, the man did a good job of not showing much fear. He told his people to stay put and wait for the soldiers to decide what to do. There was a chance they wouldn't even approach them and, if they did, there was nothing they could do to stop them.

The seconds dragged out to minutes as soldiers went about their business of checking the field and making sure all who fought against them were dead. Well, all but one it seems, as a cloaked prisoner could be seen being placed on the back of a mount with a bag over their head. Then, without a command, the soldiers formed up and marched towards the caravan. A collective gasp could be heard from several in the group. One looked behind to see if there was a way to run, only to see several mounted soldiers blocking the road. They were trapped, it seemed.

The soldiers came up and formed a semi-circle in front of them. Their leader was a young woman, whose face had been scarred in a way that marked her as an outcast from Kour's mercenary group. That was a bit of a surprise. Normally, those with the mark don't live that long, due to the bounty associated with it, let alone become any kind of leader. He will have to make sure to ask Jariek what he knew about her. Kerwin watched the soldiers and noticed how well they moved together, how in sync they were with each other. Their commander must be linked with all of them in a group mind, a rare ability. It was the only way to explain it, as well as the dynamic shift in their fighting and the lack of audible commands. Given how close they were to Crestburn and the matching uniforms, this must be the force that Merik used to overthrow Djinar.

"Who is in charge of this group?" the scarred woman asked.

Heads turned silently towards Marv. Sweat began to form on his brow as he shakily raised up a hand in a combination of acknowledgement and greeting. Everyone around him backed away, as if afraid to be associated with him.

"What is the purpose of your visit to Crestburn?" the commander asked.

"We are," Marv stammered as he lowered his hand. He paused for a second and looked around at his group before continuing "are merchants with goods to trade and sell in your famed Merchant's Courtyard. I try to swing by Crestburn a couple of times a year as business is good here."

"Merik is the new lord of Crestburn, as he ousted the tyrant Djinar. You will find things have changed from the last time you visited the city. While the city is now at peace, there are still those who are dissatisfied with the change and wish to have things go back to the way they were. Their efforts, the futility of which I believe you all just witnessed, does require us to take a few extra precautions. There will be no issues with us checking your wagons? After which we will be pleased to provide you with an escort into town."

Merv nodded his head and wrung his hands as the guards began going through the wagons. His group stayed together in a huddle and barely talked to one and another. They didn't trade in illicit goods, but that didn't mean one of the guards might find something that the new lord would have an issue with. The minutes crept by slowly as the wagons were examined and cargo went through.

"Captain, we found nothing that would be an issue," said one of the guards.

"Fine. Form two lines along the edge of the road. We will march alongside them and make sure they reach the city safely."

At the command, the guards did exactly what their commander said. Once they were in place, she nodded to the caravan master and rode to the back of the group to join the other mounted guards - along with the one carrying the prisoner on the back of the horse. Marv sighed with relief and started shouting commands to his people to get back to their wagons and get moving. Their escort marched beside them, and Kerwin noticed that their steps were no longer in sync.

CHAPTER 22

ASHA

Hargod laughed with several friends as they enjoyed a few drinks on the deck of the Gate's View tavern. They sat at one of the smaller tables near the corner of the deck. The inn was close to the opening of the Merchant's Courtyard and the rear deck provided an excellent view of both the courtyard and the city's main gates. In the middle of the courtyard, chained onto the platform, was the prone form of Jenal. He laid there, moaning and whimpering - the shamble of a man was a constant reminder of how quickly a person's fate could change.

Their conversation was anything but intriguing or original. Stories were swapped and encounters were bragged about. Asha did her part to look impressed and entertained by it all as she sat on Hargod's lap. She sipped her drink and laughed falsely at a comment that was just made. Hargod grinned at her as she rubbed the back of his neck with her free hand.

Asha was bored and disappointed that there was nothing to learn from this group. Still, the day was young and there would be plenty of chances to learn more about the new guards and their routines, that is once she could find a good excuse to get away from this group. Hargod seemed to be really enjoying her company, and that would make leaving early harder, especially if she ever wanted to use him as a source of information in the future. Rumor around Crestburn was that he was a well connected thug. She sighed mentally and gave another false laugh, as if what was being said was funny instead of lame.

"So, you have not talked much about yourself," Asha whispered into his ear. He smiled and looked at her. "What do you want to know? There is…" the sentence incomplete as he stared off in the distance.

She looked over towards the gate, where Hargod's gaze lingered, and saw that a caravan came in with a contingent of city guards as escort. That was indeed noteworthy. From what she could see, the caravan group did not look like anything out of the ordinary.

"Excuse me," Hargod said as he pressed his hand on her back, indicating that she should move.

"Uh, sure."

Without saying anything else, he crossed the deck and went into the tavern. His friends paused their conversation and gave him a queer look as he abruptly left.

Asha made as if not to be left behind, but once she entered the inn she slowed her pursuit to a more stealthy manner. Hargod made his way across the room and down the stairs. When he got out onto the street, he headed towards the street that would lead to the main gate. He rounded the corner and made his way towards the caravan and guards. She was surprised at how well he managed to blend himself into the crowd. It seems there was a bit more to this man than she first realized.

The caravan didn't seem that different from any of the others that came into the city. She could perceive no reason why it would warrant the attention of the guards, especially that many. As she got closure, she noticed there was a nervous tension about the members of the caravan. A moment later, the two groups split and went their separate ways. She was positive the caravan members became more relaxed when the guards left.

Hargod paid the caravan little mind as they parted company from the guards. Even the guards were of little interest to him, those he passed by with barely a glance. It wasn't till he got to a group mounted on horses at the rear that his pace slowed and his focus shifted. There were several mounted guards, the captain with the scarred face, and a prisoner. That must be what he was interested in, but why?

Soon she was even with the group and was able to examine the prisoner better. She sent out a thought not to be recognized and proceeded to get a better look at the prisoner without being noticed by the guards and their captain. The prisoner was short and skinny, she judged by the way the cloak wrapped around them hung loosely. There was little she could glean, as the guards had the prisoner's head covered with a cloth bag. Whoever it was, the guards wanted to make sure no one knew the person's identity, but they could care less if people knew they had a prisoner.

CHAPTER 23

KERWIN

The ride into the city was a silent one. There was not the idle chatter or someone occasionally breaking into song as there previously had been, just the sound of the wagon wheels turning and the steps of the guards marching next to them. Even though the guards didn't find any contraband with the caravan, their presence added a level of tension that previously didn't exist. At the gates, they were questioned by a group of guards as to their business into the city. This was standard practice for Crestburn, but there had been some hope that the presence of their escort would have waived this, especially after they had their things checked. Apparently, the new lord was not taking any chances.

True to their commanders' word, the guards did not leave their side until they were through the gate check and all were safe in the city. Even then, they marched alongside them for a few blocks, until they turned down a different street and went their own way. Tension visibly evaporated from everyone in the caravan once the guards were out of sight. Kerwin rode with them until they reached the inn that the caravan was going to use. Wearily, he hopped off his wagon and made his way to Marv.

"Thanks."

"Yes sure," was Marv's reply. He was still on edge from the encounter.

Kerwin shrugged and went back to the wagon and gathered his belongings. As luck would have it, the inn that he was using was on the other side of Merchant's Courtyard. Just great. That meant he would need to find someone to help carry his trunks. Several young boys sat at the mouth of an alley nearby. They would do nicely.

"Interested in earning some easy coin?" he asked them.

They were cautious but interested, often offers of easy coin meant something dangerous or bad would happen. This was not the case, and they relaxed when he told them that he needed his trunks hauled to the inn where he was meeting a friend for drinks. Eagerly, the boys hopped up and followed him to the wagon.

He named the inn to the oldest in the group and followed them as they went down the street and then cut behind an inn. The shortcut came out behind a row of merchants' stalls. The boys went down a few stalls and squeezed between an even more narrow gap. From there, they weaved their way across the Merchant's Courtyard, although they gave the stage a wide berth where a filthy man was chained down.

That was new. From the distance, he could not identify the person on the stage, or tell if it was a man or woman. One of the boys noticed he was looking at the stage and shook his head, and then nodded in the direction they were headed to let him know that he should stop looking and keep moving. Soon, they were at the inn and, with a quick word with the innkeeper, he had his assigned room.

The boys were quick to carry up his trunks and put them in the room, and even quicker to hold out their hands for payment. He paid each one and then held out a few extra coins.

"The stage in the middle of the courtyard?" Kerwin asked.

"That was built for Lord Merik, long may he reign and rebuild the Kysian Empire," he added a little loudly. "From there, he addresses the people, as well as puts those who violate the laws on display."

"Who is on the display?"

The boy stared at him and then at the coins patiently. When he produced a few more, the young boy continued. "That trator is Jenal Goldentongue. He was found guilty of betraying Lord Merik by selling secrets to Djinarian Loyalists." Kerwin handed the boy the extra coins and the group quickly scampered off.

With the street kids gone, Kerwin went into his room and shut the door. He checked the locks on the old and worn trunks to make sure they had not been tampered with. Although there had hardly been a moment when the trunks were out of his sight, it was possible the kids could have swiped something. More than one operative had their missions compromised by underestimating the skill of a street urchin.

After Kerwin assured himself that his trunks had not been tampered with, he set about making himself at home in the room. Each trunk had a couple of hidden compartments that contained the things he might need to investigate matters for the council. Everything's from small blades and herbs for healing and poisoning, to black grease paint and rope. You never know what you need rope for, but it often came in handy and was often used.

Next came the books. Part of his identity was that as a trader of rare books and manuscripts. This allowed him access to the rich, as well as a solid cover story for why he traveled so much. While he possessed several rare and valuable books, there was nothing too noteworthy in his collection. Occasionally, he did sell or buy something, but that was the exception as opposed to the rule. Then, there was the special manuscript that contained a selection from Palreon's text on rebuilding the Kysian Empire.

Inside the manuscript, there were clues that, if noticed and steps were being taken to implement the ideas, would make a person strong and wise enough to start the process of bringing back the Kysian Empire. Of course, the society would be there to help, support, and guide them along the way. It was still foolish, but then maybe Kerwin was just a burnt out pessimist.

Tap. Tap. Tap.

Kerwin looked up from his trunks and saw a pigeon on the windowsill. Tap. Tap. Tap. He went over to the window and saw there was a small slip of paper attached to its leg. Kerwin opened the window and the bird did not fly off. Surprisingly, it hopped over the sill and into the room. It looked at him and cooed.

Slowly, Kerwin reached down and retrieved the slip of paper. It was a handwritten advertisement for Master Gerwald's aviary. Odd. He looked at the pigeon and swore it winked at him. The pigeon cooed once more and took off out the window.

CHAPTER 24

ASHA

Asha had tailed Hargod for over an hour. The man had doubled back several times and even laid up in a couple places to wait to see if anyone was following him. While a lot of people in Crestburn were cautious, the steps he took to make sure that he was not being followed spoke of skill beyond that of a typical thug or street thief. He was very good, but Asha was better. She made sure to stay back a half a block and kept out of sight. Naturally, she reached out to his mind to make sure his gaze would slide off of her unnoticed. Eventually, he turned down an alley. She crept towards the mouth of it and watched as Hargod knocked on a door. He waited and knocked again. Carefully, he looked down the alley to make sure no one could see him before giving a third series of knocks. The door opened and he slipped inside.

Asha backtracked a few blocks and then went down another alley. Carefully, she made her way down and scanned the garbage for anything she might find of use. Luck was with her, for there was a discarded cloak that was torn and heavily bloodstained. Quickly, she took off her skirt and reversed it, showing the stained plain cloth that was on the other side. Out of her bralette, she pulled out another shirt. Being small chested, men tended not to think twice about her padding her top to give the appearance of a larger chest. This allowed her to keep an extra outfit on hand for an emergency quick change, such as now.

She undid her hair and fussed with it to make it look unkempt. A couple leaves she found were threaded into it and a layer of dirt and grim was added to her face and hair. Someone had discarded food after only eating part of it and the leftover portion was starting to rot. She grabbed it and chewed it for a bit. It was hard not to throw up, but she managed. After a moment, she spit out the food but there were still bits of it in her mouth. Now she was ready.

A moment later she emerged from the alley looking like a completely different person. No longer she an attractive young lady looking for a night of fun, but a down on her luck street urchin. She stumbled as she walked and made her body shake in a way that was common to those who were going through withdrawals. With the end of Djinar's reign, also came an end to the majority of the Twilight Haze, and there were a lot of people who had the shakes nowadays.

She cautiously made her way down the alley that Hargod entered. When she neared the door, she staggered against the opposite wall. A few more steps and she fell on her side, right across from the door. To anyone observing her, it would appear that she was having a very hard time with withdrawal and was passed out.

Asha laid there in the dirt. Her body gave another shudder that conveniently positioned the cloak partially over her face. It was just enough to conceal the fact that she was watching the door. After a few minutes, she could hear someone talking. It was indistinct and she could only make a few words out. One of the voices she thought belonged to Hargod, but she wasn't sure.

Slowly, the door opened and a man came out. Quietly, he approached her and gently shook her. She moaned but stayed where she laid. He started to pat her down when she let out another moan and shifted position. The man paused and was about to resume when she croaked out, "Got any haze?"

He froze and looked at her. "Got any haze?" she asked again, this time with a cough. The man's face crinkled with disgust as her putrid breath hit him. She collapsed, again pretending to pass out. He backed away and opened the door. Hargod was standing inside. "Just some junkie passed out. It looks like you weren't," was all she heard before the door shut.

So, they had been worried that he was being followed. Good. It looks like she would definitely have to see Hargod again. There was a lot more to that man than she first thought. With all the changes that were going on in Crestburn, it would be good to know a new secret or two. She had a feeling that Hargod had more than a few secrets that might be valuable to know. Asha laid there for a couple of hours before rising and stumbling down the alley. Once she was a few blocks away, she changed again and cleaned up a little bit. Her first stop was down to a fruit vendor and bought several sweet tasting fruits. She had to get that taste of rotten food out of her mouth.

CHAPTER 25

TIANNA

There was a noticeable difference in the guards when they arrived back at the barracks. Their steps were more uniform and their back straighter. Those who were a part of the original city guard even saluted her and gave her the utmost respect. She had proven her capabilities as a leader to them, but that won't be enough. There were still plenty of guards left who did not go out with them this morning. They would have a hard time believing what they would be told by their comrades. That would not do. When the guards began to tell of their fight, she wanted to make sure their impressions would take hold in the others.

"Sergeant Herlt."

"Yes Captain"

"Transfer the prisoner to a cell and dispatch a messenger to inform Lord Merik of our success. I want all guards not assigned to the gates or on patrol to form up in the training grounds. In fact, let's have half of those out on patrol join us as well. I am sure that Erlin's heralds can help spread the word. Speaking of his heralds, I require four to assist me. See that this is done."

"Yes, mam."

"Oh, and one more thing, Herlt. I want the guard that was arrested this morning brought out to the training ground, as well, and make sure he has weapons and armor on."

Herlt nodded and began bellowing out orders. The guards started heading over to the training grounds while Herlt selected a few to help him escort the prisoner and get a message to the heralds. It would take some time for the Heralds to get word out to guards on patrol in the city. The time would allow the guards to talk while they waited, and it gave her a chance to refresh herself. What she had planned was risky, but would cement her capabilities in the eyes of all of the guards.

Tianna dismounted and headed into the barracks kitchen. A cook scrambled to get her some meat and cheese to eat and a flagon of water. She took her time eating, preparing herself mentally for the task at hand.

"You have my heralds quite busy, Captain," said Erlin. She had been lost in her thoughts and had not noticed that he entered the mess hall. Tianna looked up from her plate at Erlin and then offered him a seat. "Yes. There was a minor incident with a guard this morning and I am taking measures to make sure such a thing does not happen again."

"I take it your mission was a success."

"Yes. It went very well and the informant is yours to question."

"Excellent, although I know Lord Merik wishes to speak to him first."

They continued talking about more routine matters for almost an hour when Sergeant Herlt marched up and saluted.

"The guards are all assembled and waiting, Sir."

"Thank you, Sergeant. Erlin, would you care to join us?"

"I would enjoy that. I am curious as to how you plan to handle things."

The trio walked out to the training grounds. The place was filled with guards and a few curious servants. They had formed up along all four sides of the training ground, facing the middle which they left clear. Herlt, it seems, had anticipated what she planned. There was little that got past that old merc. Tianna walked out into clear space in the middle and surveyed the crowd. The men had been at ease and there had been a buzz of conversation. That quieted down as the trio entered the clearing. Over at a distant balcony, she could see Merik, with few council members, watching. She had not expected that, not that it mattered. Tianna wasn't sure if she rathered him to watch it first hand or hear it through reports.

"Marked bitch," she said in a loud and clear voice so that all could hear. "That is what I was called." She spun in a slow circle so that all could see her scarred face. Everyone was already familiar with it and knew what it meant, even if they never talked about it. "It was questioned why you should follow someone who was marked by Kour and cast out of his group. Hell, I bet there are some of you who even thought about claiming the bounty that goes with this mark." Tianna stared at the men and several turned away from her gaze for fear that she would see into them and know that they had possessed such thoughts.

"Well, here is your chance. For the rest of the day, I wave all sanctions against any guard who wishes to claim the bounty on me. I will accept all challenges, starting with the one that was offered this morning," she finished as she pointed at the guard who caused a scene earlier that morning. A shocked look crossed his face and he started to stammer a response. "I ah, ah, never issued a challenge. Um, captain," he added weekly.

"You said, 'Maybe we should claim the bounty on your head.' Now, here is your chance to do so."

"No."

"What's the matter, afraid?"

"It's not fair. You got them powers. You killed Bearus the Indomitable with them." There was a murmur of agreement from the guards. "You could make me lose without even trying."

"That is why I asked for the heralds to be present. When there was a duel for leadership with Kour's group, powers were forbidden. Each person chose a telepath as their second. The second would establish a link with their opponent and if they noticed a change in the person's thoughts that indicated that they were focusing on using an ability, then the second would call the fight and the cheater would forfeit. So, take your pick from the heralds, one for you and one for me, or, do you question the integrity of Erlin and his heralds?"

He was trapped and he knew it. There was no way out of this now without being looked upon as a coward. He picked two heralds, and the one assigned to her sent a telepathic message to let her know he was in contact with her mind.

"Pick someone," she said. Confused, he just gave her a puzzled look. "I said pick someone." He turned and looked at the guards and nodded to one that he often hung out at taverns with. The guard came cautiously forward, unsure what to do.

"Good. Pick a herald to be your second, I don't care which. It doesn't matter. I will choose Lar." Shocked, Lar strode over to her side and nodded at a herald.

"Oh, come on. This is ridiculous. Everyone one knows Lar is the best sword fighter in the guards. You can't beat me, so you are going to use him to do all your work," he angrily shouted as a murmur of discontent rumbled throughout the crowd.

Tianna smiled. "Actually, Lar will be fighting alongside you and your friend."

"What?"

"I said he will be fighting alongside you and your friend. It is three against one."

Lar gave her a dubious look, but she just nodded and gestured that he should stand with the other two. There was a general murmur from the guards watching, and many were shaking their heads. While they had no doubt that she could best the troublemaker, and might even take him and another guard, there was no way she could handle three at once, especially with Lar being one of the three. She was insane.

"As I said earlier, I waive all sanctions for this and any other duel today." With that, she drew her falcata and squared off against the trio.

They were unsure of how to proceed at first. The last thing any of them had been expecting was to be involved in a three on one match against their captain. The two trouble makers paced back and forth and kept looking at each other and Lar as if trying to figure out a plan. Lar just watched because he had seen her practice and was smart enough to not underestimate her.

"On me," he said to the others.

They each stood on a different side of him. "Spread out a bit," Lar said, having taken command of the trio. Good, the man knew better than to let the others get too close to him as they fought. An inexperienced fighter could get an experienced ally killed by getting in their way. People didn't realize how much room swordplay required and how easily a friend's blade could get in the way. By spreading out, Lar made sure that they could be free to strike at her without worrying about hitting one and another, or interfering with another's strike.

Still, it wouldn't make much of a difference. She was as comfortable with fighting against several opponents as she was facing one. Tianna knew how to move and keep them at bay until she could get a clean strike.

The first blow came not from the troublemaker, but his friend. It came in low on her left side, and she turned to block it, exposing her back to his friend. He took the bait and leaped in, stabbing at her exposed shoulder. She ducked low and whipped her sword around to slice through his stomach, only to meet Lar's blade. The man had seen her ploy and moved in to stop it. Quickly, she backpedaled and gave Lar a nod of approval.

A grunted reply was all he gave back.

"Watch it. She almost had you," he said to the trouble maker. "If it looks like an easy kill, then it is a setup. The Captain practices a lot. There is no way she would make a mistake like that unless it is a trap."

Tianna smiled.

The next several moments, the three danced back and forth with her. Strikes were coming in better, less overextended or sloppy. They took turns swinging at her, keeping her constantly moving from one attack to another. It was a decent plan. Eventually, it would wear an opponent down until they slipped up and someone could close in for the kill.

Descent was not good enough, not good enough by far. She let the charade play out a few moments longer, just long enough to make things entertaining. Afterward, most of the guards should realize that the fight lasted as long as it did because she let it.

Another swing came in from her left side, about shoulder height. This time, she leaped forward, getting in close when she blocked it. Once the blades clashed together and her attacker's momentum had stopped, she spun on her left foot, bringing her blade in a backhanded strike just under the last rib. The man grunted from the impact. As she finished her stroke, Tianna rolled her wrist to deflect an overextended lung from the trouble maker. She brought her blade back down against her first target, slicing a deep cut into the wounded man's right leg. As the guard shifted the weight to his good leg, Tianna shoved him with her free hand. The man toppled over and a quick kick to his hand sent his blade skittering across the training ground.

Fear shone in the troublemaker's eyes. Lar had no time to waste on such things. He was on her before the blade that she sent flying had stopped moving. His strikes came in quick and with power. Rapidly, she blocked several strikes while backpedaling as he pressed for advantage.

He paused. It wasn't much, but it was just enough for her to begin to stop when he came at her again. Lar had hoped the temporary change in momentum would be enough to trip her up. It wasn't. She managed to fend off his blows and keep her ground, although he did manage to score a nice shallow cut on her forearm.

His bladework was good. The strikes were powerful, and he was careful not to overextend himself. She wondered if his skills extended to other things besides swordplay. With a bunch of new recruits coming in, they would be in need of talented officers to lead them. She will definitely have to talk to Herlt about him after this was all said and done. For now, she needed to find a way to subdue him without too much injury.

While their blades danced back and forth, the one who started all this mess hung back. Most of the gathered guards were so wrapped up watching the duel between the Captain and Lar that he went unnoticed for several minutes. Finally, one of the guards happened to notice that the trouble maker was just standing by and letting Lar do all the fighting.

"Get into it you coward," he yelled.

The man pretended to ignore him.

"What kind of chicken shit are you?"

The guard elbowed a buddy and pointed towards the trouble making coward. He joined his friend in the taunts and soon others followed suit. Before long, a large group of guards were booing and catcalling the man. They hurled insults and threatened him.

Tianna heard the insults when they first started. It pleased her greatly to see the guards get upset with the man. The fight had gone on long enough as far as she was concerned. By now there should be no doubt that she could handle her own when it came to combat. The boos and taunts were getting louder and harder to miss. Lar kept at her with single-minded determination, oblivious to anything other than their match. That gave her an idea. Dirty, cheap, and totally underserving for it to be done to him, but it would allow her to end things cleanly.

Lar's strokes came like clockwork and she continued to block, but this time she paused after doing so and tilted her head as if listening to something. "Do you hear that?" she asked him. At first, there was no indication of a response from Lar, but then confusion spread across his face as he tried to figure out why he was hearing booing. At that moment, Tianna lashed out and struck his temple with the pommel of her blade. Lar's eyes rolled back up into his head and he dropped. Now, it was just her and the one responsible for this mess.

She smiled predatorily.

Terror showed in the man's face and his body began to shake as she slowly approached him.

"I yield," he shouted as he tossed down his blade. Oh no, he was not going to get off that easy. She shook her head and told him, "Pick it up." He hesitated, not sure what to do or if there was a way to get out of this alive. "I will have no problems striking you if you remain unarmed, so I advise that you pick up your blade." His eyes darted from her, to the blade, and back again. The reality of the situation hit him, and slowly, tentatively, he reached for his blade. His eyes never left her for a second, in case she should decide to strike as he recovered his weapon.

Tianna snorted and gave her head a half shake at his mistrustful gaze. What an utter fool. She could have struck him down the second he threw down his sword, not that his having a weapon would make much of a difference.

"Ready?" she asked.

Hesitantly, he began to nod and, before he had finished moving his head, she leaped towards him, her blade darting out to pierce his thigh. Blood had no more began to spread on his pants when her blade flashed forward again, this time drawing a nice crimson line across his shoulder. He staggered back, flailing his blade about in a vain attempt to stop her. She made a cut here, a slice there. Soon, he was bleeding from over a dozen wounds, none of which did any real or lasting harm.

His skin grew pale from the blood loss. The crowd had stopped their jeering and grew quiet. It was obvious to all that she was playing with him as a cat does with the mouse.

"Please," he moaned.

Tianna sunk the tip of her falcata into a knee as her response to his plea. The leg gave out and he collapsed, barely maintaining his grip. An overhand strike severed the arm at the elbow. He gave a half moan as his nerves overrode his brain with pain.

She looked over at the heralds who were monitoring the fight. "Were powers used by any of the combatants?" she asked loud enough for all to hear. All four heralds shook their heads and almost in unison replied, "No." Tianna looked back down at him, and then to the rest of those gathered before her. "Is there anyone else who wishes to claim the bounty on me? Is there anyone who is brave enough and skilled enough to face me? I will accept all challengers, so step forth and be the next!" Slowly she turned and scanned the crowd, staring down any who dared to look at her. No one dared to step forward. All were silent, and the only thing that could be heard was the ragged breathing of the doomed guard. Without even looking at him, she swung and sank her blade into his head.

Tianna turned away and walked towards where Sergeant Herlt and Erlin were standing. "Dismiss the men, sergeant," she ordered.

Erlin turned towards Tianna and complemented her. "Well done, Captain. Brutal, but effective."

"Men learn quicker when violence is the teacher. A lesson I learned well from Kour."

"Indeed."

"Thank you for the use of your heralds. It was greatly appreciated."

"You're welcome, and it was a creative use. I had not thought of doing that. You have given me plenty to think about. I take it that was something else you learned from Kour?"

"Yes. All of the duels for leadership were done without the use of powers. Kour believed that people with gifts tended to rely on them and they could become a crutch. He wanted his leaders to be strong warriors in their own right. If they were good with their powers, then even better. Also, it allowed for a few of those without abilities to rise in the ranks. Kour only wanted the best and the most daring as his leaders."

Erlin nodded then turned and walked away, musing about what she told him. His heralds followed behind him, silently. The heralds never spoke out loud to one another, always relying on their telepathy. It was just another way that Erlin's group stood apart from the rest of Merik's force. Tianna turned to find Sergeant Herlt waiting for her.

"Captain, the men have been dismissed. Those who were out on patrol are returning to their routes as we speak. Lar is awake and is currently being double checked by a physician. The other is getting sewn up and will take several weeks to recover."

"He may remain with the guards until he is fully healed. At that point, give an additional month's pay and dismiss him from service. He would not have been picked were he not of similar mindset as his friend. I will not have anyone like that in my guards."

"Yes, sir."

"As for Lar, what is your opinion sergeant?"

"Well, Captain, he is a damned fine fighter. The other guards look up to him, and not just because of his skill with a sword either."

"Is he intelligent?"

"Smarter than most."

"I think he can handle more responsibility. Find a place to make better use of the man and let's see what he is capable of."

"Will do. If you don't mind, Captain?"

"Go ahead and speak your mind, sergeant. You know damn well that I don't keep you around for your looks."

"I think what you did was foolish."

"The men needed to learn a lesson, sergeant."

"I agree with you there, and they did, but they weren't the only ones. There were many watching that fight, and I am not just talking about Erlin and his lackeys. You are a damn fine swordswoman, and after that display, your skills as a warrior are now made very clear. Additionally, you are a solid leader and, when you throw in your royal blood, you could easily be construed as a threat. If you shine too bright, others will get jealous, and there are more than one who might have serious issues with that."

She looked at him and the seriousness in his expression. He was old in a profession where people died young. Tianna would be a fool not to listen to his caution, and he gave her something to think over that she had not been concerned about before. Power and prestige were nothing that she had ever been concerned with. Respect and loyalty were much more important to her, and, because she gave both, she expected others to return it.

"I appreciate your candor, sergeant. Perhaps next time I will try and remember to use more subtle measures when dealing with matters, especially the public ones."

"With telepaths like Erlin, even the mind is public." Herlt replied.

CHAPTER 26

MERIK

Merik watched the duel with mild interest. He knew very well that Tianna was one hell of a fighter. He wouldn't have brought her into his group if she wasn't skilled. It took a special kind of person to survive with their face being marked up like hers. Everyone who saw it knew that she was not good enough to be a part of Kour's mercenary group. They also knew that there was a bounty on her head and that anyone who killed her could claim it.

Most people with the mark did not last more than a few months on their own. The open bounty on them made it hard to trust others for fear of being betrayed. Additionally, no one wanted to be associated with them and become collateral damage when someone eventually came to claim the price on their head. In the end, those bearing Kour's mark died alone.

Yet, Tianna was different. Her unusual strength in dominating someone's mind made a direct attack against her foolish. As Barius proved, there was no one strong enough to resist her ability to control their body. That had been a gamble on his part. He had not been positive that Tianna would be able to control Barius. Thankfully, he was correct in his estimation of her ability. Even without her psychic abilities, she was still a very capable warrior in her own right.

No one had been willing to give her a chance, and, once he did, he found a very hard working and dedicated ally. It did not take him long to realize there was a lot more to her than her ability to survive. Quickly, he began to entrust her with more responsibilities, and, once he had leverage on her, she became a part of his inner circle.

He was fortunate that no one else could see her worth. All everyone saw when they looked at her was Kour's mark. They couldn't see past that and the short violent end it promised. That was fine by him. Tianna was able to survive as a loaner but was at her best when working with others. He knew people wanted more than mere survival, and he had been able to offer it to her. It was a shame there weren't more people bearing Kour's mark for him to gobble up. Their loyalty would be bought by letting them live. Merik would have to keep an eye out for any others that bore the mark in the future. Sheltering them would put him at odds with Kour, but that could be dealt with.

It was odd that she was so obsessed with the duel that caused her to lose her position within Kour's group and gave her that scared face. He had been through that memory countless times with her and saw nothing out of the ordinary. And, yet, she still insisted she was missing something. For some reason, she could not believe she lost the duel. If he had to guess, false pride was the culprit for her obsession. It really didn't matter. As long as she was obsessed with that duel, he could hold that over her as leverage.

His thoughts turned to matters at hand as he entered the balcony where lunch had just finished being set. It was a large balcony that overlooked the lush gardens that were a part of the mansion. The view was very nice, and it was an excellent spot for entertaining guests. Servants had just finished setting up as he sat down at the table. Meats and cheeses, fruits and pastries, pastas and honeyed desserts. It was a bit extravagant, but the luxurious buffet often caught people off guard, and that made them all the more easy to manipulate and have their memories read.

Merik had spent years as a scribe for a bookseller. His days had been spent copying books and contracts in a quiet corner in the back of the shop. There was little excitement in the work, and he was often ignored. On more than one occasion, his master had completely forgotten about him. He locked up the shop and went home for the evening while Merik worked silently in his little corner. Those were long nights, usually without food. When the morning came, and his boss came in and unlocked the shop, he would fail to notice that Marik had spent the night alone.It often would be noon before he let his apprentice take a break to get something to eat.

During those long and lonely nights, he had nothing to do but to read and copy books. At first, he copied what his master had assigned him, hoping for some praise or recognition for getting work done early. What he got was another text to copy.

After that, he began to copy whatever he wanted. If a rare book came in, he would duplicate it to sell later when he had a day off. While this earned him extra money, it didn't ease the feeling of being so easily ignored. When there wasn't a rare book to copy for extra money, he would spend the nights reading everything from history to philosophy to military strategy. Even though the nights were long and lonely, he learned a great deal that, eventually, he was able to put to good use. This cycle of loneliness and self-education continued until, one day, he realized he was different from everyone else.

At that point, his life changed. He knew he was destined for greatness, and why not? No one else possessed a new psychic ability. Eventually, Merik would meet another like him, but the feeling of specialness, of destiny, never faded. Those years being neglected and overworked as a scribe allowed him an education that he otherwise wouldn't have had. It hadn't been much longer before the shop was gone and he had taken the first steps of his journey.

Merik pulled himself from his thoughts about the past and started eating when the prisoner whom Tianna had captured was brought in. He was a skinny young man and very nervous. The guards brought him in and then faded to the back of the balcony. He was no longer tied and bound, those had been removed once he was securely in his room in the mansion. With clean clothes and a hot bath, he looked refreshed and, judging by the way he eyed the spread on the table, he was very hungry.

"Please, help yourself."

"Thank you, my lord," the young man replied before hurriedly filling his plate with meat, cheeses, and pastries.

"Please, none of this 'my lord' stuff, just call me Merik." The young man paused in shoveling with a confused look on his face. "I owe you for what you did," Merik continued. "Thanks to you, I was able to take care of a large group of people who were still loyal to Djinar. They would have eventually been a problem, but, because of your help, I was able to have them dealt with before that could happen."

"It was nothing my lord, I mean, Merik, sir."

"I disagree. Like I said, you have been a tremendous help to me stabilizing this city. Now, I do have some questions for you."

"I don't know much, but I am glad to tell you everything that I know."

"That would be wonderful."

For the next hour, the young man talked about the secret meetings. He talked about Botun and how he was still looking for Djinar. That was good news. At least if Djinar was alive, he was still in hiding and not able to assist Botun and his crew in an attempt to take back the city. Each person who attended the meetings he had been at were listed or described in detail. He talked about travel arrangements and the path taken out of the city.

It was a wealth of information. The young man talked, and, occasionally, Merik asked a guided question or two. Merik maintained a link to the young man's memories while this was going on. As he brought forth each memory to answer questions, Merik was able to see it as well as make the memory more real for the kid. By the end of the lunch, the boy felt both pleased and impressed with himself over how much he remembered and how detailed his memories of recent events were.

CHAPTER 27

KERWIN

Kerwin had spent the afternoon visiting the various shops around Crestburn. He stayed away from the Merchant's Courtyard, going to the different sellers that were scattered around the city. These places tended to be higher end and didn't need a high volume of business to succeed. Getting a feel for the city, he took his time as he checked out the goods in each shop that he visited. Eventually, he made his way over to Master Gerwald's aviary.

The shop was a rather large set of buildings at the edge of the city close to the wall. It was a short distance from one of the city's few functioning lesser gates. This particular gate was set up to help move animals in and out of the city without people having to deal with the noises and smells of the beasts. Nearby were stables for horses, sellers of exotic pets, and Master Gerwald's place. Butcher shops, tanners, and dealers in common animals set up shop a little further down from the gate.

Gerwald's place was very clean, a lot more than he expected for a place dealing with birds. He remembered during training working with the birds at the society's sanctuary and their roost. While well maintained and clean, the society aviary was nothing compared to the shop. The floors were swept, the wood polished and cages clean.

"Anything I can help you with sir," a young man asked him. Judging by his age and appearance he was one of Gerwald's journeymen.

"Yes, I was wondering if you had any messenger birds that I could use?"

"We do, sir. Our birds are trained to fly to several of the larger cities. We also have birds that we return here should you wish to take a bird with you."

"No, that won't be necessary."

"Is there a particular destination you are looking to have a bird sent to?"

"At this time, no, but I might in the near future." After seeing a puzzled look on the journeyman's face, he added "I am starting a business venture with a friend in another town. We are looking for a fast way to keep in communication."

"Ah, well, that we can help you with." Thomas, as his name turned out to be, then began to tell him about how much it would cost to have birds sent and explained how their messenger service worked, just like all the other messenger services that already existed. Kerwin asked for more details and wondered if he could get a tour. He feigned interest as he was shown the birds of prey and the training area. There was no way he could count how many shop tours he had been on over the years. It was merely another step in the tedious sea of his job. During the tour, he kept an eye out for a teen matching the description of Jariek. As the tour wound down, the journeyman began talking about messenger birds and rates again.

"Excuse me, Thomas?" a young man asked, most likely an apprentice.

"Yes, Jariek?"

"Master Gerwald is requesting you. He said there are things he wants to go over with you before you join him on the upcoming hunt."

"Hunt?" Kerwin asked.

"Yes, sir. Master Gerwald has birds of prey that can be used for hunting. It is quite exciting to launch a falcon into the air and have it bring you back a rabbit." replied the new apprentice.

"Tell Master Gerwald that I will be there in just a moment, once I finish up with our guest." replied Thomas.

"Actually," Kerwin began, "I am finished here. You answered all my questions and I will be back after I talk to my partner. It sounds like your Master Gerwald has something important he needs you for. I am quite sure that this young apprentice can show me the way out."

"Yes, sir. I would be honored to show you the way out."

Jariek showed him the way out in silence. He could tell the kid was ready to burst but did his best to keep professional. This had to be his first time dealing with an operative. He felt sorry for the kid. Once his work was done, the situation debunked as another false claim, the kid would be left here to continue his work with the first bitter taste of disappointment. Oh well, better to get it over with sooner rather than later. At least this way he can spend his life focusing on his trade as opposed to focusing on the reports to the society. This way he could at least have a chance of a good career as opposed to hanging on the whims of the society.

When they reached the door, Kerwin left without as much as a goodbye. Kerwin could see the struggle on the boy's face as he stood there and watched him leave, trying to find something that would let Kerwin know that he was his observer. Kerwin ignored him not out of any sense of cruelty, but to see if the young man would risk speaking out to him. He needed to know if the kid would put him at risk or follow the rules. After several steps in silence, he was satisfied and paused then turned around. "Do you know of any good places one might find a decent place to relax this evening that is not a tavern and perhaps find good conversation?"

Jariek's face lit up with excitement. "I, ah, would recommend, let me see, no, wait. Hang on a sec and let me think of a place. Oh, I have it. Go to Cracked Carafe. I will meet, I mean, I wish you good afternoon, sir," he replied as he failed to keep the excitement from his voice.

Kerwin nodded and walked away. Once he was a good distance away, he started shaking his head. This kid had a lot to learn, but, then again, they often did. It was not uncommon for observers to get excited the first time a report got investigated. Had he ever been so young and hopeful? On his way back to the inn, Kerwin tried to recall the last time he had been excited about something and couldn't. It wasn't just his role with the Cashek Society where his passions had run dry. He sighed wearily and tried to remind himself not to be too hard on the kid. There were always things that could only be learned in the field, and conducting yourself when an operative came to investigate matters further was just one of those things. The society instructors could lecture their hearts out but those lessons were often forgotten, at least temporarily, with the first investigatable report.

CHAPTER 28

BOTUN

There was so much to do. At least now that Lucky Liam has delivered the people out of Crestburn, he was free of that concern. A large portion of the fee that he charged them had already been spent securing his group a new hideout. It would be a few days before he would shift things over there and make it his base of operations. While the new location was now his, he did want to have an emergency exit in place before he moved in. That would take time and more money.

Exhaustedly, he made his way back to their current hideout. If he was lucky, he could take a badly needed rest. Botun had found himself being up for almost an entire day again. While he never needed much sleep before, he was not used to working for days at a time with only four and five hours of sleep.

The most discreet way to build an emergency exit would be through the sewers. A nasty and filthy way to travel, but at least it gave you the option of traveling some distance from the hideout undetected before you needed to merge into a crowd on the streets. Plus, all the work to make the exit could be performed in the safety of the hideout.

Lucky Liam had given him plenty to think about. The young package runner had been operating in Crestburn for several years now and had never previously had any inclination of choosing an ally. Why now? Once the new hideout was secured, he would reach out to Liam and see what the young man had to offer. Zarah would be less than pleased about that. Liam seemed to have a thing for her, and she would be good to have around to keep his attention focused elsewhere. Liam was an enigma. Normally, he would enjoy an intellectual puzzle like Liam, but now he had too much to deal with and not enough time.

Botun gave the series of knocks that were required to enter the hideout. Once inside, he asked one of the men to get him something to eat, and he sat down at the table in the common room. He had barely seated himself before Hargod was in the doorway.

"Any luck boss?" Hargod asked.

"It depends on what you are asking about. If you mean my search for Djinar, then, no. So far, every place that I have looked has come up empty.

Still, there are a few places I have yet to check, several of which are out of the city. However, I have secured us another hideout. We should be ready to switch to it once we get an escape route in place."

"How long will that take?"

"Not too long. Time and money are of the essence, so we will go dirty and cheap with the escape route."

Hargod wrinkled his nose and said, "By that you mean a sewer exit."

"Unfortunately so."

"Then I suggest you have extra clothes for everyone."

"A wise idea, which I will take under consideration, but with my limited funds, money will probably be better spent elsewhere."

"Do you really think he could have made it out of Crestburn during the attack?" Hargod asked to change the subject.

"Highly unlikely, but still possible. If he had a secret exit or fast route through town, he could have gotten to the wall or gates a lot sooner than they would have expected and slipped out. I know they were mainly focused on the mansion and securing the key players; the gates and walls came second."

"Speaking of secret routes and exits, I have some disturbing news and if you don't mind I would like to give it to you in private."

The request was met with scowls from several of the people in the room. They were a tight-knit group whose survival depended on secrecy from others, not their own members. They had to trust one and another, for there was no one else they could trust. Needless to say, Hargod's request was frowned upon. Botun looked at him for a moment and then nodded. Slowly, they filed out one by one, each giving Hargod a dirty look as they left.

Hargod walked across the room and listened at the door for a moment to make sure none had lingered close enough to hear. Botun stared at him while he did this but didn't say anything. When he was convinced there were no eavesdroppers, he sat next to Botun and began to explain.

"I think something happened to the group that left town. This morning a contingent of guards came in with a prisoner. By the look of them, they had seen action, and that new captain was with them. They had a prisoner who was hooded and covered in a cloak, so I couldn't see who it was, but they were small in stature. I think Lucky Liam sold us out."

Botun sat there thinking a moment before speaking. "Liam only took them to the wall, he didn't leave town with them."

"We don't know that for sure. He could have joined them, or that sneaky bastard could have followed them and left a trail that the guards could have followed."

"You are sure the guards were in a fight?"

"Pretty positive. They had this look about them. Like they were champions. Soldiers only come back like that if they kicked someone's ass."

"The city guards have never been much in the way of fighters."

"True, and the old guards have no love for the new captain, so reports go. But, what I saw was men marching in step, like real soldiers. Also, it didn't seem like there was any problem between them and the new guards or the captain. Why else would they come in, and with a prisoner in tow?"

"No one else?"

"Well, there was a caravan, but the merchant's caravans come in all the time. Plus, they looked scared out of their wits by the guards."

"Liam has always been a bit of a wild card. I would be surprised if he sold us out, but, with a new regime in charge, he may decide his chances are better with them or was working for them all along. There were two other young men in that group who were close to Liam's size. This person could also be one of them."

"You vetted everyone yourself, boss. I don't think it would be one of them; they would not have much to gain since Merik isn't likely to trust them."

"As you said, I vetted everyone, and that includes Liam. You are right that Merik would be very hard put to trust any of them. He gave everyone a chance to declare loyalty to him when he took over. Liam, on the other hand, has no allegiances and would stand to gain quite a bit by earning Merik's favor. I am glad that you brought this to my attention, and you were right to keep this between us. I want you to go to the rendezvous site. See what you can find and report back to me.

CHAPTER 29

KERWIN

The Cracked Carafe was a surprisingly good location for them to meet. It was a fairly busy place with a constant buzz of conversation. People and conversation flowed from one table or booth to another. Often people changed places when they saw a new friend enter the place. There were people tucked in their own little group while the rest of the patrons flowed around them. This would be a great place to meet with someone and not be noticed.

It was, for the most part, a younger crowd, but youth was by no means a requirement here. Conversations ranged from all kinds of topics. Some discussed whether or not the old emperors were divine in nature while others talked about existential topics. While there were a variety of topics, none of them touched upon the new ruler of the city or his claim to being able to rebuild the empire of old. What they talked about was fluff that he referred to as mental masturbation, something fun and pleasurable but served no real purpose.

Kerwin had been there for about an hour and a half. He had joined a few conversations to blend in. Jariek came in, ordered a mug of something, and joined some friends of his. The kid didn't even look at him. It was good to see that he remembered some of his lessons and did not initiate contact right away. For the next half hour, they flowed to different groups until they were in the same one. The group was discussing myths from the old empire and it was clear from the get-go that most of them had never read anything reputable. Ridiculous claims were being made about the nature of the heroes of old, and he bit his tongue.

"You know, I was always a fan of the tales of Vetrius," Jariek commented.

"Those tales are lame and boring. The man didn't do much." said a young man with a neatly trimmed mustache named Auther.

"While his tales are more subdued than some of the others, they are a lot more believable than the others."

"Who wants believability? Mythical characters are supposed to be larger than life and do things that normal people can't," scoffed Auther.

"I disagree. I think it is inspiring that a common person can accomplish amazing things and have stories told about him." Kerwin rolled his eyes and the mustached youth chuckled. If Jariek really believed what he said, he could be a bit of a handful, as well as in for a big disappointment. The average person doesn't have stories told about them, or even get mentioned as a minor character in someone else's story. If he thought that his actions would become a part of someone's tale, then he might take more daring risks.

"What, you don't believe me, sir?" Jariek asked him.

"I agree with him. I think myths need to be larger than life, but I am willing to hear you out. I am willing to bet you a drink you can't convince me otherwise."

"Fair enough. Come, I see a table over there that we can use."

They walked over and, to his credit, Jariek began explaining in a very boring fashion his theory. A few people had joined them, but left fairly soon once they saw how dry Jariek's explanation was. He continued on for a few minutes after they left before winding down.

"Well?" he asked.

"Well, what?"

"I don't know. I was hoping you would tell me. You are the oper… um, lead on this."

"On this?"

"You know what I mean, man."

"I do?"

"Stop messing with me. I can't help it if I am a little excited. This is…"

"This is the first time you had an operative come to examine a report that you filed," Kerwin interrupted telepathically.

"Yes. Sorry if I am a little eager."

"It's not a crime to be eager, kid; just don't get your hopes up. The Cashek Society has been at this for hundreds of years, and the odds are that they will be at it for several hundred more."

"Yea, but there is a chance."

"That's the problem. There is always a chance. Those chances are extremely small. Don't feel bad. While a bit annoying, it is not uncommon for observers to get a bit zealous their first time. Soon enough, you will realize there is nothing to get excited about and that even dealing with operatives is just another routine."

The kid just sat there and drank from his mug. His shoulders were slumped, and it was obvious that his words hurt him. Kerwin didn't feel bad about it, well, maybe just a little. Jariek needed a taste of reality. Optimism really could taint a person's outlook on things and make them find connections that weren't there. While his feelings may be hurt now, he would be better off down the road.

"So, tell me about recent events."

"Well, like I ah, um, said. Merik took over the city in a single night. Barius was killed by a woman who later became captain of the guards. She was able to dominate him

and make him kill himself. Then, according to the reports, she did the same thing with his crew, and did it so fast that none of them left the table. Anyway, she is now captain of the guards and has a weird scar on her face."

"The scar is called Kour's Mark. I am not surprised that you don't know about it. Usually, people who have it don't live very long."

"How does someone end up with it?"

"By being tossed out of Kour's mercenary group. Anyone who leaves is branded like that. He also puts a bounty on their head. Needless to say, it doesn't take long before someone notices that mark and kills them for the bounty. If she is as strong in controlling people's bodies as you think, then that is probably why she has lived this long."

"Couldn't she have just dominated Kour and not got marked?"

"Not sure, since we don't have much information on Kour's group. The mark happens when you get kicked out of the group. As to how he managed to mark her, that is anyone's guess. I have heard that no abilities can be used on him. Now, I don't believe that, but he could have strong immunities to powers. That, or they drugged her and branded her when she was unconscious."

"Oh. Well, the attack was fast and clean. Very little in the way of people being harmed. Since Merik has been in charge, there has been an increased number of guards and some roundups of those who are believed to be loyal to Djinar. They say…"

Kerwin held up his hand to cut him off.

"I don't want to know what people say. I want just the details as accurately as you can give them."

"Oh, ok. Well. The stage was built in the middle of the Merchant's Courtyard and, eventually, Merik gave a speech where the phrase was mentioned. There was a lot of talk about improving the guards and extra training to make them more like the wardens of the Kysian Empire. Also, he had his chief herald, Erlin is his name, and he is a strong telepath. His unfocused thought could be heard throughout the entire Merchant's Courtyard. Merik definitely has several people who have some serious royal blood in their veins.

"Anyway, Merik gave people a celebration and provided food and drinks from Djinar's supplies. There has been an increase in guard patrols. The soldiers he used to take over the city are part of the city guards now. Also, the patrols are communicating via telepathy. They are catching a lot more criminals now. Of course, that is also because several of the old guards, which were corrupt as hell, are gone, so they aren't turning a blind eye to things anymore.

"The heralds make announcements about laws that are changed. All of them now report to Erlin. Also, it is now a crime to lie to a guard and they can use a telepath to figure out if you are lying to them. Uh, I have an idea, but it's not exactly a 'detail' as you put it."

Kerwin saw the hesitation in the kid as well as his willingness to please. It wouldn't hurt to let the kids tell him his idea. If anything, it would give him a better idea on how attuned to the situation Jariek is. He nodded his head for Jariek to go on.

"Well, I got thinking," he paused and then continued telepathically, *"if the head herald is a strong telepath, and he oversees all the other heralds, who are also*

telepaths, and Merik can use telepathy to find out lies, then that kind of makes this Erlin a spymaster. Or maybe the head of a group of secret guards, or something like that, and all of his heralds would be his enforcers. Not only do they tell people the news, but they can be used to dig out people's lies. They would control a lot of information, and that makes Erlin a very powerful person."

Kerwin was impressed. While the kid might be overly optimistic, he did have a good grasp of logic. If his observations were as good as his logic, then he would indeed have the potential to be a very good observer and possibly even get trained to become an operative. The society was typically short-handed when it came to having enough operatives. It was rare to find someone who was capable enough to handle the work as well as have the drive to commit to actions that needed to be taken. Operatives have a lot of responsibility and sometimes have to make quick decisions that cost lives. It was a lonely and hard path to follow.

Jariek continued, *"Everyone was surprised when the stage was not taken down. They were even more surprised when Jenal Goldentongue was chained there. A herald read off a list of his crimes, which are also posted by the stage. Jenal's charges are weak. They accuse him of treason against Merik, yet he disappeared on the night of the attack, probably taken prisoner, only to reappear for his sentencing. More importantly, they messed with him real bad. Jenal was an arrogant, wealthy information broker. He was close to Djinar and was his best information gatherer. The man was confident and lived lavishly. What is on that stage is a shattered mess of the man who used to gather everyone's secrets."*

"There have been some minor raids as the guards go after people who were connected to Djinar. At the onset of the attack, Captain Tianna told everyone they had till morning to switch their allegiance to Merik. These raids are taking care of those who did not switch their loyalty fast enough. This morning, the guards, and not just the new guards - it was both old and new together - were seen coming into town with a prisoner."

Kerwin nodded his head and replied, *"Word must travel fast if you already know about that."*

"Wait, didn't you get in town today? So, how do you know about that?"

"You tell me."

Jariek thought about it for a moment. *"There was a caravan that came in at the same time as the guards. You must have been traveling with them. Did you see anything?"*

"I saw several things, but nothing for you to worry about."

"So, what do we do now?" Jariek asked.

"What I will do is verify the report you filed. Namely, check to see if this Merik has a copy of Palreon's manuscript. If he does, then the council will need to make a decision on if and how they will support him. More than likely, the man just got lucky with his choice of words, at which point I file my report and move on to the next assignment."

"Don't you believe that he could have a copy of the manuscript?"

"Look, kid, it is not my job to believe. I investigate matters and see if they are of any value to or conflict with the Cashek Society. Most everything I am sent to deal with turns out to be dead ends and false leads. Once in a while, I do have to take steps to handle

things, but I have never seen anything that would remotely fall into the realm of the Cashek Society being able to help rebuild the Kysian Empire."

"Oh."

"You're not the first to get excited when an operative comes into town. Soon enough, you will realize how routine this all is and, eventually, even dealing with operatives becomes boring. The odds are that very little if anything will come from this. Don't feel bad about it. This is not the first time I have investigated a claim that a psylord has access to the manuscript, and it won't be the last.

"There is enough information about the Kysian Empire that motivated people are able to come up with something that happens to match what is in the manuscript. Then there is the fact that others have read the manuscript and said the words, and it is possible that he is merely copying them. Typically, it is this general information that gets unknowingly copied, and we are sent in to investigate. This doesn't make it a bad thing, but it doesn't mean the empire is getting rebuilt anytime soon.``

"Do you think the Empire will eventually be rebuilt?"

"I don't know, kid. It has been several hundred years since the last emperor went mad, killed his family, and drove the wardens insane. If someone was to rebuild the empire, I kind of think they would have done it by now. Even if they didn't succeed, the Cashek Society should have backed at least one, if not more, candidates by now."

"Then, why do you do it? Why investigate reports if you believe they won't lead anywhere or change anything?"

"You know, I have been asking myself that question a lot lately. I don't have an answer to that one either. I guess I do it because I don't know anything else to do."

They sat in silence. Neither talked or communicated telepathically with the other. Kerwin got up and ordered another drink and some kind of sweet cracker snack that the place served. When he got back to the table, he put the snack in the middle and offered some to the kid as a half-assed peace offering for bursting his dreams.

"What I plan on doing is trying to establish contact with Merik and see how knowledgeable he is about the Kysian Empire."

"How are you going to do that?"

"Normally, I would use subterfuge. But, with his declaration that people with knowledge of the old empire can come to him, I think I will do just that. I have a collection of manuscripts that were written ages ago. These will serve as bait and should allow me a meeting with him. There is enough in these that should pique his interest and open the door for more meaningful conversation"

"If not, then you file your report and go on to your next assignment."

"Yes."

"What do you need from me?"

"Right now, nothing. You have updated me on the current situation. Explained a few more details. With Merik requesting people to come to him, my job is unusually straightforward. If I need you, I will send for you. There are two scrolls that I have that will be of interest to anyone who has a copy of the manuscript. One teases information and would be enough to get their interests. If he picks up on those clues, then I will arrange a *second meeting. Then, I will have the more serious documents for him to look at. We can meet up after my first meeting with Merik."*

"Why do two meetings?"

"Several reasons. First of all, I want to know that I can trust him not to try to take it from me, not that such an act would do the society any harm. People aren't very trusting of someone bearing just what they are looking for. So, I will play coy and a bit hard to get. I will get him to trust me by not trusting him."

"Wait, what did you just say? Get him to trust you by not trusting him. That makes no sense."

"Sure it does. People are not very trusting by nature. If I come bearing gifts, he is not going to trust me. He'll be very cautious, because my behavior is unnatural. Now, if I go to him cautiously and keep secrets, that will reaffirm to him that my behavior is normal and he can begin to slowly trust me."

"That is messed up."

"People are messed up, kid. People are."

CHAPTER 30

MERIK

Merik had another pile of reports in front of him. Did the damn things ever end? Even with hiring a few new clerks, he still had a mountain of paperwork to go through. Merik swore that he never did this much paperwork, even when he was a scribe. Thankfully,he had started to resolve the problems of bureaucracy between the old city government and his new rule. Things were becoming more streamlined and clerks and officials were better at anticipating what he wanted. Still, it left a lot for him to go over.

A servant knocked on the door and waited to be called in.

"Sir, Captain Tianna is here to see you."

"Go ahead and let her in."

He sighed heavily. Tianna was here for the session that he promised her. These sessions had started to get a bit tedious. Merik couldn't figure out why she was so obsessed with the duel, but she was. Her obsession did provide him with excellent leverage over her. As long as she was determined to get answers that weren't there, she would do as he asked. Thankfully, she was stubborn and he didn't see her giving up on this matter any time soon.

"Please, have a seat by the fireplace, Captain, I am almost done." He continued with his reports for another ten minutes or so. It was good to make her wait. When enough time had passed, he got up, crossed the room, and sat down in the chair next to her.

"Well, I must say you did an excellent job with those loyalists. I hear that not a single man was wounded. Excellent work, Captain." She merely gave a polite nod of the head in acknowledgment. "The prisoner that you brought in provided a wealth of information. I also appreciate the level of discretion you took when bringing him in." Again, another nod. Her hands were clenched as they rested on her legs. He better not draw it out too much. The duel with the others must have gotten her blood up.

"Now, about the duel"

"I know it is something minor that we are missing. Perhaps if there was a way to go through the memory slower."

"No, not that duel. I am talking about earlier today. I saw your little performance. I really don't appreciate that you put yourself in such a dangerous position."

She stared at him blankly, for it took her a moment to realize what he was talking about. "What do you mean?" she asked him.

"The duel today. There was no reason for you to put yourself in harm's way like that. I mean, three against one."

"I was not in any danger. Two were cowards with little experience in blade work. While Lar is a good swordsman, he is no match for me."

"Still, one of them could have gotten a lucky strike. Besides, what kind of message does that send to the guards?"

"That I am not to be messed with. That, while I may be a marked bitch, I am no easy prey."

"Of course you are no easy prey. You are the captain of the guards. What you showed them was that you are capable of thrashing inexperienced fighters. Let's not forget to include that you view yourself in a weak enough position where you must fight off insults instead of ignoring them as someone of your rank should."

She sat there in silence, her jaws now clenched, like her fist. Hopefully, she will be so upset that she would not be able to focus on the memory well enough, and they can end this session early. Not that her ability to focus mattered, but he wasn't about to let her know that.

"If you don't mind, sir," she began, "I would like to begin."

"I don't mind at all. You know I am more than happy to go over any memory that you have. I have said it before, and I will say it again, I think this is utter foolishness. We have gone over that memory several times and yet we learn nothing new. While our abilities to recall a memory may change, the memory itself stays the same."

"We are missing something; I just know it. There was no reason I should have lost that duel."

"But you did. You should let go of your past mistakes and move on. Look at where you are now - captain of the guards of Crestburn. I have brought you into my inner circle. You have moved up in the world from where I found you - alone and fighting for your life. I gave you a second chance and really wish you would not be so hung up on the past."

Mcrik knew that she would not listen to him and would insist on going through the memory over and over again. This was as he planned. While he may be bored by the process, he was not about to give up his hold over her. She was stubborn, and he knew that if he told her that she was wasting her time, then she would dig in her heels and continue on with it.

"Please, sir."

He let out a loud sigh and replied, "Fine. Let's get on with it."

The nice thing with going through people's memories is that if they wanted to remember something it was really easy for him to pull up the memory. He didn't have to wander around their mind and look for a specific memory. Once he did find a memory, he could always go to it and pull it up, and then each time it would be easier for him to do so. It was as if they were becoming conditioned to experience that moment. Merik had only begun to test that idea out.

Tianna leaned back in her chair and closed her eyes, not that it mattered. Her mind was blank: a vast nothingness. She always started their sessions together this way. If it was something she wanted, Tianna had amazing focus and dedication. Not for the first time, he wished that she wasn't so obsessed with the duel. Their time together could be spent doing more productive things, like testing the boundaries of his abilities. Merik didn't know the limits of his power. When he first discovered he could go through people's memories it was by accident.

He had gone up to his employer to let him know that he had finished copying a book early and was wanting to know if it would be ok to take off a bit early that night. His employer was staring out the window at his desk. Merik watched his boss with disdain for a moment, and then something changed. He began to see in his mind a dinner with several guests seated around the table. Laughter filled a familiar room as someone finished a story. He could hear his boss speak and it sounded as if he was the one speaking. The storyteller turned to him and then the image shifted to the two of them at a tavern having drinks. Their clothes were different, and he looked much younger. Abruptly, the vision had stopped and his boss looked over at him and said, "What are you doing standing there boy? Don't you have a book to finish copying?"

It took him awhile to figure out what had happened, until the man came into the store and thanked his boss for dinner from the other night. Merik realized that he had seen his boss's memory. Several days passed before he had another opportunity. This time, he was careful to remain hidden behind a bookshelf a little ways off. He watched his boss carefully and eventually a few visions would emerge in his head. These would be fleeting and random things. Occasionally they would last for a few moments and often be about things from his boss' past. He realized that somehow he was able to view his bosses memories as he was remembering those moments, too.

It was different from telepathy. With telepathy, you were with the other person's mind communicating back and forth. Each thought appeared as the person formed them, and lasted but a moment. With memories, they lay hidden in the background and could be viewed over and over again. One memory would lead to another and then another, and he would ride along with no control just experiencing them voyeuristically.

Eventually, he was able to steer them and choose what a person was remembering. When he delved through someone's memories, both of them experienced the memories. Every now and then, someone, without realizing it, would wrestle control from him. As he grew more experienced, he could forcibly regain control of what someone remembered, but that left them feeling odd, as if there was almost a ghost in their mind. He even had a few close calls where he had almost been detected. As long as he was subtle when he steered memories, making sure there was a connection between one memory and another, he remained unnoticed in the other person's mind. This method took a lot longer but allowed him to explore their past without detection.

It amazed him how detailed people's memories were. He didn't realize how richly the mind stored details. His own memories were never as sharp and precise as what he experienced with other people. This puzzled him, until he discovered another aspect of his powers. Apparently, the mind captured everything and how much detail a person could remember was up to the individual. When he went through someone's memories, he found that they could experience the memory better than they could on their own. Over time, and with practice, he got to where a person could all but relive the experience. This became very handy.

Merik pulled himself from his reverie and focused on Tianna. She had waited long enough while he strolled through his own memories. Now was the time to work, even if it was boring and pointless.

As always, the memory started with her as she stood there in front of everyone as the sun darted in and out from behind clouds. Her second was seated next to Kour. A quick nod to Kour and she walked out into the middle of the circle. Argent stood facing her, a confident smile splayed across his face. He had risen fast through the ranks, faster than even her. There was no doubt in her mind that he would eventually be a part of Kour's council, but she was surprised, like everyone, when he challenged her for command. Her skill with the blade was well known and few lasted more than a moment against her.

"Begin," Kour said, and everyone in the crowd became deathly silent as they watched this young upstart take on Kour's favorite.

Not one for wasting time, Tianna launched herself at him in a flurry of blows. She swung aiming for his left shoulder but deliberately shortened her stroke. By the time he realized he did not block her strike, Tianna had already reversed her motion and extended her arm enough to knock his blade away on the reverse strike. She rolled her wrist and changed momentum again, this time coming at his thigh. Argent quickly back peddled and barely avoided having his thigh lacerated and blocked the strikes as they came at him. She pulled back and adjusted her stance; that was when she noticed her sleeve was wet. She looked down at the red line across her bicep where he had managed to cut her. When did he manage to do that, she wondered. Tianna didn't give it much thought. Several times in the past, she had failed to notice a wound during the heat of the battle and only later, after things were done, realized that she had been injured. The wound wasn't much and shouldn't slow her down, but she should be a bit more cautious.

She came at him again. This time her strikes were more measured and controlled. They would be easier to block or parry at first, but each would build on the last one and eventually wear him down. A thrust to the chest, followed by a faint at the leg. A block, repost, and another swipe at the legs, followed by a lunge at the ribs. Tianna backed off to catch her breath and could have sworn at least two of the strikes had met flesh, yet, once again, he had managed to block everything.

He staggered a bit and looked pale. Well, if she wasn't landing a hit at least she was wearing him down. She was beginning to think it was a shame that he would be kicked out of the group after the duel. His skill with the blade was better than she thought, and that would be missed in future raids. Tianna wiped her hands on her pants only to have her hands come up bloody. Scarlet billowed from a large cut on her thigh.

How in the hell did she miss getting that?

She put her weight on her leg and, surprisingly, it held. Judging by the amount of blood she was losing, she would have to end this duel soon, or else she would pass out from blood loss. Cautiously, she stepped forward. The dirt in front of her was soaked in blood. Did she really bleed that much?

Tianna attacked, rotating between strikes at his shoulders and legs, hoping to get him into a steady pattern of blocking before disrupting the routine and scoring another hit. She never had the chance, as this time it was he who broke off the engagement. Sweat beaded on his brow. It wasn't that hot out, the stray thought danced across her mind, especially with the clouds out. Tianna pressed the attack. This time she slowed her strikes to give him a small opening to swing back at her. The plan was to force him to overextend his counter strike and use his unbalanced footing against him. He ignored the openings and tried to break off again, but this time she stayed with him. Amazingly, her leg held. Blow after blow came at him and he managed to block them all. She slipped in blood soaked earth, and he took that moment to get away from her.

She steadied herself and looked to see if there was another wound that she didn't remember getting. This time, there was a long slice along her lower left ribs. Amazingly, she didn't feel dizzy. Argent looked at her with grim determination, his skin looking very pale for some reason. She wondered if the blood loss was making her look as pale, too. When he lunged at her, she barely brought her sword up to block. Argent backed away and started to circle her. He lunged again, and she blocked but was unable to return a swing before he backed away.

Soon, the tip of her sword began to sway, and her movements began to slow down. Exhaustion seeped into her body as her blood seeped out. She staggered and dropped to her knees, her blade off to the side from where he had apparently disarmed her. It was over. How could this .... Blackness.

"So was this time any different than the others?" Merik asked.

"No," Tianna said grudgingly.

"Look, I get it. You are one of the best when it comes to swordplay, but it seems like Argent was better."

"You saw the fight. He had no real form to his sword work. His moves were haphazard and sloppy."

Merik let out an exasperated sigh. "Did you ever think he was sloppy on purpose? That just maybe he did it to trick you. He was rising through the ranks quickly. Eventually, he would have had to deal with you. So he made it look like he couldn't sword fight and fooled you into a false sense of confidence. By the time you realized you had been had, you had already lost too much blood."

"I can't believe that."

"What else could there be? We have gone over that duel a dozen times. Each time we learn nothing new. I think he meant to take you out from the start and that he hid what he could do until it was time to take you down."

"I," Tianna was at a loss for words. This was not the first time Merik had made this suggestion, nor the second. She had seen Argent fight during raids, and his blade work had been barely average. It was hard to believe that he would put himself at risk on a raid with subpar swordplay in hopes to fool her and take her out at a later time. It made no sense, but then again nothing else did either. Not for the first time, she began to wonder if Merik was right. Perhaps she had truly been beaten by the better swordsperson, and yet something didn't feel right about it. Something inexplicable, perhaps it was pride and ego.

"Look, if you want to keep reliving this duel, I will be glad. Well, not glad, but I am willing to go over it with you again and again. What I would rather see is that my captain move on from this and get on with her life." This time it was her turn to give a heavy sigh. Merik got up and headed towards the door and paused. "The only thing I find odd with that duel is that you didn't land a single blow on him. Not one single scratch."

CHAPTER 31

KERWIN

It was mid-morning by the time Kerwin got to all of the addresses he had been given. After breakfast at the inn, which was decent if overpriced, he began his day by making discreet inquiries about old books and manuscripts. Kerwin went from one merchant to another but didn't really look at what they had. Most of their wares were only a few decades old or faux copies of imperial texts that had been often reproduced and sold. Each time he inquired if they had something that was older, or more stately, he kept his language vague but made sure to drop certain words to hint that he was looking for a private collection. Actual surviving artifacts from the Kysian Empire were rare, highly sought after, and often attracted the attention of a psylord.

It was amazing to Kerwin that anything of the old empire survived at all, and yet stuff did. There were times that he wondered how much influence the society had in keeping the memory of the empire and its records alive. He would not put it past them to plant copies of documents to be found by later generations to make sure that the empire was not forgotten and fuel the dreams of conquests so that one day a psylord would be able to reforge the empire. It was extremely cynical of him to think such thoughts, he fully admitted it, but he could almost believe that they would go to such a length to keep their purpose alive and validate their existence.

Since a lot of artifacts from the time of the Kysian Empire had been destroyed, any remaining relics were quite valuable: everything from elegant plates and vases to weapons and tools. Often, a psylord bent on conquest would collect these relics, as if owning Kysian artifacts give weight to their claim to rebuild the old empire. Djinar was said to have quite the collection of Kysian furniture. Although it was too early to tell, it sounded like Merik would be one of the rare people who were more interested in documents and records than items of daily life.

Collecting relics did come with a certain level of risk, and serious collectors kept their collection known only to a small group of friends and other pursuers of antiquities. The last thing they wanted was for a psylord to come and take their collection that they had worked long and hard to amass, especially when pieces of the collection could be handed over for preferential treatment. This secrecy created a hidden market for surviving artifacts.

It took time, but if you knew the right questions to ask and how to spot reproductions, you could find someone who could get you in touch with an actual collector. Judging by what the last merchant had, in a private room in the back of his store, he had gotten closer to finding one of the collectors in the city. He just hoped and prayed that they had not shut off communication out of fear of drawing Merik's attention.

The store was not very big and smelled of a blend of cinnamon, damp soil, and wool. To call it a store was almost an exaggeration, for it was a room with a counter and nothing on display. The man who sat behind the counter read a book. He looked up at Kerwin as he entered the room, smiled, and put down the book.

"Welcome, fine sir. How can I, Frazieer, be of assistance to you?"

"Well, I am not sure that you can," Kerwin replied.

"I am the finest incense maker in the city. Whatever lovely scents you wish to burn in your home or business, I can make. Floral scents with a hint of rain, or would you prefer a subtle musk?"

"Truth be told, I am looking for someone to reproduce a recipe I found in an old book."

"I can easily do that for you," Frazieer said with a smile.

"Maybe. The problem that I am running into is that the recipe calls for a few ingredients that the other shops don't have."

"That should not be a problem, my friend. As I have stated, I am the best incense maker in all of the city. If I could see the recipe, I could tell you how long it would take me to acquire the ingredients and have a sample ready for you."

Kerwin unslung the satchel from his shoulder and laid it on the counter. He pulled out a few old manuscripts and sifted through them as if he was looking for the recipe. The contact person for a collector could be almost anyone. They were typically a well off business person with a diverse collection of contacts. The recipe did not exist, not that it mattered. What was important was if Frazieer noticed one of the documents he was going through as he looked for the nonexistent recipe.

Kerwin went through one of his books, shook his head and laid it off to the side as he grabbed another, "Just a second while I find it. I recently received these and I am trying to remember which one it was in."

Frazieer smiled and nodded "Of course sir." Kerwin tilted the book he was going through a bit to partially block his view of Frazieer. This gave the incense merchant an opportunity to discreetly study the book he had put off to the side and see that it would be of interest to a collector.

"Well, I am embarrassed. It seems that I don't have it with me."

"No need to feel embarrassed sir."

"I recently acquired several old books, and I must have left the one with the recipe with the others. Would it be all right if I came back later?"

"That would be delightful, sir. In fact, I think that I can definitely assist you in what you are looking for," replied Frazieer as he reached over and handed the book that Kerwin was using as bait back to him. "Why don't you come back later this evening. I do have an appointment I need to keep in the meantime."

"That would be good."

"Excellent, sir. I will see you then."

Kerwin left the shop and shook his head. The cat and mouse game of finding a collector annoyed him. He didn't blame them for their desire for secrecy. If he had been in their place, he would have done the same. Although, he suspected it was now done just as much because it was now a part of the collector's culture as it was done for survival. It was just a pain to go through the routine of hints and clues, of teasing artifacts and waiting for a response. Frazieer was lucky, for it happened infrequently enough that it didn't grow old and wear them on him. To Kerwin it was just another repeated pattern that made his life feel like a cage.

CHAPTER 32

BOTUN

Word had reached Botun that Hargod was a terror. He had just finished inspecting the progress of the escape tunnel of the new hideout when a second member of his crew found him and pretty much repeated what the first one had said. Hargod was pacing back and forth and snapping at anyone who got near him.

This was not good. Hargod was normally not one prone to such violent moods. Word would spread quickly that something was wrong, and that would most likely scare off the new members that he had found. No one, besides Zarah, knew that Hargod had been sent to check on those that had fled Crestburn. If Hargod was in a foul mood, then the worst had probably happened. Someone would need to be blamed, and that blame, whether right or wrong, would fall on Lucky Liam.

He already had enough stuff to deal with. If they had been betrayed, that would be bad, but now he needed to get Hargod calmed down before he finished off the shakey moral of those still somewhat loyat to Djinar. A lesser man might have rushed over to calm an outraged subordinate, but not Botun. He had built a reputation of implacable calm and quiet demeanor. It was like a suit of armor that made it difficult to wound him socially, but like armor there were times it did slow him down.

Camly, Botun entered the hideout and, immediately, he could feel the tension in the air. He made his way over to the table and got something to eat. Before he could sit down, the door from the other room crashed open.

"We need to talk now!" Hargod growled.

"You have something to report?" Botun asked, even though he already knew the answer.

"Report, oh you could say that. Everyone, get the hell out of this room immediately!"

The dining area always had a few people hanging out. No one hesitated or bothered to glance at Botun to see if this was something he wished. They had no desire to risk Hargod's anger, or to flame it further.

"There are ways to conduct business, and this is not one of them," Botun said evenly.

"You have no idea," Botun raised his hand in front of Hargod and silenced him. Hargod stood there fuming, clenching his fists over and over again.

"Given your aggressive display, I do have an idea that the news you bear is not good. I do not appreciate being addressed in this manner, nor do I presume that the others like it much either."

"To hell with how they feel!"

"My friend, how they feel is important, but what is more important is the damage you have done."

"Damage? Me? What on earth do you mean?"

"Word reached me a little bit ago that you were upset, and that the others were worried by your behavior. While you paced back and forth and growled at everyone who came near you, others began to speculate what could cause you to be so upset. Thanks to your actions, there are dozens of rumors floating around. None of them good. You have undercut the morale of this group and have caused an already stressed and paranoid group to be even more so."

"I, ah." Hargod stammered, lost for words. Most of his rage had withered under the calm chastisement of Botun.

"Now, give me the bad news."

"Well, I went to the place as you told me, sir. I didn't see any signs that our people had been there. So, I made my way back to the city, weaving back and forth across the countryside trying to find signs of their passage. It didn't take long before I found their bodies. They were all cut down in a field a few miles from where they were supposed to lay low."

"Were there any survivors?"

"Not that I could tell. It looks like they were all there and made their best effort to make a final stand. Even the few young boys in the group died with blades in their hands. Most were cut down close to one another, and a few had wounds on their backs. I guess that once the fight turned against them they tried to flee and were cut down in the process."

"Any signs that the attackers were wounded?"

"Can't say for sure, but judging by how the ground looks, I didn't see any sign of blood other than right by the bodies."

"Was that the entire group?" Botun asked.

"I am pretty sure it was."

"Pretty sure?"

"I didn't stop and count the bodies, but I didn't see anyone that was missing, not that I can remember."

"I want you to see if you can find Lucky Liam."

Hargod grinned at that, "With pleasure, boss. I'll bring that little rat bastard in."

"Liam is not quite as lucky as he wants everyone to think."

"Oh, he definitely won't be lucky when I get a hold of him."

"That is not what I meant. Liam has the ability to make it hard to recognize him, and it is rather strong. This, combined with another talent, I am thinking clairvoyance, is how he has gotten away from everyone. So, if he gives you the slip, keep looking for him and double check your blind spots. He will probably be linked with you, and 'he'll make sure and stay out of your direct line of sight. Remember, he can't really disappear, and he has no luck powers."

"Got it, boss."

"A couple of things I want you to bear in mind. Liam has always escaped others' attempts at ambush. Don't spring your trap too quickly. Try to restrict his movements and limit his options. A warehouse would work well. Once he has entered, you can have your men surround it."

"That's been done before to no good."

"True, but this time things are different. You know he has no luck. You know he is clever and patient. He is not the cocky fool he likes everyone to think he is. Once Liam knows a trap is sprung, he will maneuver out of sight for his chance to escape. Limit how he can move. I suggest flour."

"Flour?"

CHAPTER 33

KERWIN

Kerwin sat in the corner of the balcony, facing the Merchant's Courtyard. A book sat in his hand, but he didn't read it. His mind wandered from the words that normally gave him comfort. Lately, it seemed even his books could not provide the refuge from life that they once did. More than once, he thought about picking up something more contemporary, yet he never failed to go back to the old myths and legends. Even his sanctuary was nothing more than a different form of unchanging repetition.

He had read them countless times. The stories were so familiar to him that he didn't even need the books themselves, for he had them memorized by now. Moreover, he knew the real stories behind them. He had read and studied the historical documents that were kept by the society, and he knew the deviations between fact and fiction. Some were of such divergence that it hardly seemed possible they were about the same story. Yet, cognitive dissonance aside, he delighted in the old stories.

Today, however, he could find no solace in the book. His eyes wandered across the crowd as they went from stall to stall, as they haggled and bartered where they went. It was not a great system, but it worked. In fact, it had worked for Crestburn for over a hundred years. The city was not unique in having an integral part of its foundation being so old. While it was common for a psylord to rebuild their domains as they saw fit, they often left large structures, such as the Merchant's Court Yard, alone.

Not for the first time did Kerwin wonder if there was really a need for the society. It seemed to him that people went about their day as they always had. Even during the Kysian Empire, the vast majority of people did the same as their descendants were doing at this moment. They ate, shopped, worked, played, and worried about their future. For the vast majority of humanity, it didn't really make that much of a difference if there was an empire or not.

He sighed heavily. Thoughts like these were definitely not becoming of a society member, especially one of their operatives, whose duty it was to find a candidate to rebuild Kysia. Kerwin looked down at this book, but closed it a few moments later. There was no point in trying to read it, at least now. He caught the attention of a serving girl and ordered another mulled wine. The drink seemed to settle his mind more than the book did.

Kerwin wondered if other operatives got this despondent about the job. He tried to think back to when he enjoyed his work. Other than when he helped out Lena, and, even then, it was not happy as much as feeling like he actually accomplished something that made a difference. The serving girl brought over the wine, and he took a healthy sip. He sighed and went back to watching people go about the various stalls looking for whatever it was that they were needing at that moment.

An hour had passed and the wine was finished. He contemplated ordering another but ended up deciding against it. In his current state, it would be too easy for one drink to turn into another and then another. With a heavy sigh, he got up and headed back to the inn where he was staying, just a few streets over.

The innkeeper smiled and greeted him as he came in.

"Good evening, fine sir. I hope your day was prosperous."

Kerwin was not in the mood for conversation and kept his reply short "It went ok, I guess."

"Very good, sir. I have a letter for you that was dropped off by a herald."

That was fast, he thought to himself as he crossed the room. The innkeeper reached down behind the counter and handed a sealed letter to him.

"It has Lord Merik's personal seal," the man informed him.

"Thank you," he replied and tossed the man a few coins for a tip.

Kerwin waited until he was back in his room, with the door securely locked, before he broke the seal. It was a personal invitation from Lord Merik. Kerwin was invited to come over tomorrow afternoon and discuss books and other subjects of antiquity. There was very little information in the invitation other than the necessary time and location of the meeting. It was a shame because he hoped for a few details that might provide more insight into Merik. He was a bit surprised that Merik had responded so quickly. Kerwin planned on having to deal with a few other collectors before he got to Merik.

He grabbed a cloak and headed out. While herald's worked for the local psylord, they also earned money on the side as messengers. Typically, a herald would have an assigned spot where they would give out the news and take messages for a few hours. After a few hours, another herald would come by and they would either exchange messages or the new herald would take the spot, freeing the other to deliver the messages he collected. Most cities had a network of heralds, and Crestburn was no different than the rest.

Thankfully, there was almost always a herald or two in most shopping bazaars. In the Merchant's Courtyard, the heralds congregated by the new stage in the middle. Their proximity to Jenal seemed to discourage people from coming up to them for messages to be delivered. This was fine with Kerwin, for that meant that he would not have to waste time waiting.

"Excuse me, but I would like to send a message."

"Who is the message to?" replied a bored looking herald.

"Lord Merik."

"I am sorry, but if you wish to talk to Lord Merik then you need to go to the manor and schedule a meeting. Our Lord is a very busy man, and we can not bother him with everyone who wishes to speak to him."

"I understand, which is why I brought this letter that I received from Lord Merik. I was hoping that you can inform him that I would be delighted to meet with him tomorrow afternoon, and I look forward to our pending conversation."

The herald studied the invitation that Kerwin offered him for a moment or two before looking back at Kerwin. "I see, sir. Let me apologize. I did not realize that you had official business with Lord Merik."

"That is fine, my good man. I understand that you were doing your job to prevent Lord Merik from being bothered by unnecessary messages."

A look of relief washed across his face as he responded. "Thank you for understanding, sir. I will make sure your response will be delivered to him soon. Please, might I have your name."

"Kerwin."

"Well, then, Master Kerwin, I will see that your message is sent right away."

With that, he turned and looked at the guards near the gate and must have engaged in a telepathic conversation for one of them turned and looked at him and nodded. The guard disappeared inside the gatehouse, only to return a few moments later accompanied by a young herald who set off running. These people were efficient, Kerwin noted. They were even working alongside the guard. While heralds often happened to have a decent relationship with guards, after all both worked for the same people, they tended towards more of a loose rivalry then actively working with each other. Merik was definitely shaking things up a bit.

He went back to the inn, where the caravan that he had come in with was staying. After a few minutes of searching, he was able to find the young boys who had helped him haul his belongings a few streets over, near the mouth of an alley. Their leader recognized him immediately and hopped up and ran over to him as he drew near.

"Hello, sir. What is it that you need."

"A message delivered," he replied as he held up a letter that was drafted before leaving his room.

"Do you know where Master Gerwald's aviary is?" Kerwin asked.

"That I do."

"Take this and deliver it to Jariek.e works there. Here are a few coins for your trouble."

"Thank you, sir. I will deliver it right away." He grabbed the letter, took the coins, and ran back to his group. After a moment of talk and a clout to the head of one of the younger kids, he handed the message and a coin over to one of his accomplices, who then ran down the street.

CHAPTER 34

JARIEK

The falcon soared in the early morning light. It glided from one thermal current to another, occasionally flapping its wings. It was a warm summer's morning and, if the weather held, it would be cooler this afternoon than it had been for several days. Fine weather for a hunt. The bird scanned the fields below and looked for a rabbit or other game. It knew that if it found something and returned it to the masters, it would be rewarded with something far tastier than what it found.

Silently, it flew across the sky as it scanned for prey. There, in the field, a movement. Not much, but it was something. There it was again. He circled back and carefully watched a small section of the field and waited for movement again. He beat his wings again, and just after his shadow past a tuft of trampled grass there was a short burst of movement. It was a foolish mistake, one that would cost the rabbit it's life.

Falsely, it had assumed that once the shadow of the predator had passed, it would be safe for it to move to another hiding spot closer to it's warren. It must have been a fairly young rabbit, for it had not learned the trick that the predator used to lure it into a false sense of security. The falcon swung around again, and this time honed in on where the rabbit was hiding. He waited until his shadow cleared the spot where the rabbit had moved to and then began his dive.

Sure enough, the rabbit once again dashed out after the shadow had cleared the spot and rushed to another hiding spot. He had only gone a few hops before claws sank through his fur and into his flesh. A shrill of terror and pain escaped from its throat as the ground receded.

The falcon scanned the land looking for the masters. They were not far away, just a couple of fields over by a clump of trees. An older one pointed and said something to the younger one in an increasingly raised voice.

Shit!

Jariek pulled himself from his link with the bird, turned, and began stuttering out an apology. He quickly reached into a sack and brought out a hood and binding for the approaching bird. Finrin, a journeyman, snatched it from him, shaking his head and muttered, "fool," just loud enough so only Jariek could hear him. He turned red and cast his eyes down.

Finrin rode over to Master Gerwald's side and awaited the return of the bird. There were several potential buyers nearby, who watched Master Gerwald and his bird. Jariek got the bird's cage ready to receive him and started to prepare the next one. He fumbled with the cage and nearly dropped it. Finrin watched him out of the corner of his eyes and shook his head in disgust before he turned his attention back to Master Gerwald.

Jariek managed to get the cages ready and waited patiently for Finrin to ride over with the falcon.

"Pay attention, apprentice, or you will never make it to journeyman," he scolded Jariek as he handed the hooded and bound bird to him. Jariek placed it in its cage, locked the door, and retrieved the next one.

"Sorry, I was lost in thought."

Finrin scoffed at him "You think? I doubt it. Just don't blow it. I am close to becoming a master, and I don't need you ruining things for me.

Jariek merely nodded and kept his head down as Finrin rode back to Master Gerwald. Why did he have to be paired with that jerk on today, of all days? He got along with everyone at the stable, except for Finrin. Then again, most of the apprentices and several of the journeymen had issues with Finrin. He was a pompous ass who thought he was better than everyone else. To hear it from him, he would be made a Master in no time and have his pick of cities to run his own shop. The truth, of course, was another matter entirely. If Finrin didn't have such a wealthy and well connected father, Master Gerwald would have probably dismissed him years ago. As it was, Master Gerwald chose to suffer with him, as well as made everyone else do so, too, because keeping Finrin's father happy was better for business.

When they got back to the aviary, he knew Finrin would tell the others how he botched up. The details would get exaggerated, and they would all have a good laugh at his expense. It wouldn't matter that most would realize that Finrin's account would be far from the truth. Things went smoother if people didn't buck Finrin's narrative. It was easier to allow him to harass someone else and be thankful it wasn't you this time.

Perhaps, he could go to his room early and catch up on sleep. Today's situation could have been avoided had he managed to get some sleep the night before. As it was, he had been too excited to fall asleep. His mind raced with the possibilities of what lay ahead.

Late yesterday afternoon, a street kid came by the aviary and delivered a message to him from Kerwin. The message said that he would like to see him again, but it would have to be early evening, as he had a special meeting that afternoon. It was vague enough that had anyone else seen it, they wouldn't have known what he had been talking about.

That was wonderful news. Now, Kerwin could see for himself whether or not Merik had the potential to be supported by the society. Things were moving along faster than he thought they would. His training made it seem that these events happened at a slower pace. Perhaps it was just coincidence, fate. If Merik was to be the one to rebuild the Kysian Empire, why shouldn't things move along a little smoother and quicker than normal?

Kerwin would be disappointed in him for that thought. He would say that Jariek's thoughts were foolish nonsense and that nothing would happen, like it always did. How did he manage to get stuck with such a burnout? Part of him was worried that Kerwin would be so ambivalent with his report back to the society that it would not accurately reflect the situation. It was possible that they would miss this opportunity because the wrong operative was sent. That was a scary thought.

This, and a dozen other thoughts, raced through his head last night, keeping sleep well away until almost dawn. Between the lack of sleep and the excitement of what could happen at today's meeting, it was difficult for Jariek to keep his mind on his job. Thankfully, Master Gerwald hadn't said anything yet, but that doesn't necessarily mean his lapse of focus escaped notice. Master Gerwald was not one to scold in public, unless it was a major mistake. Odds were that he would receive a lecture about focus and paying attention when they got back.

Jariek sighed and wished things were easier. Sometimes, it seemed life would be easier as an animal. The new bird, this one a hawk, flew across the fields. This would be the fourth and final bird of this morning's display. Jariek had just recently been allowed to accompany them on these hunts. Master Gerwald took the more experienced and senior apprentices to tend the animal cages, while the journeymen handled the animals. These outings happened whenever there were several potential buyers of predatory birds. Master Gerwald would send invites out to several people who had been by the shop recently and treat them to a morning hunt and display the birds. These outings usually ended with one or two birds being bought. Soon, today's hunt would be over, and they would be headed back to Crestburn, where Finrin would be sure to make everyone aware of Jariek's absent-mindedness.

The hawk swooped by again, and something seemed off. Jariek linked up with the bird and could feel something was wrong. The hawk was sick, something Jariek should have noticed earlier that morning as he got the animals ready. If it performed poorly Master Gerwald might notice that he slipped up and let a sick bird go out on the hunt. Jariek took over and flew the bird higher and began to scan for prey. He flew it in a wider circle, since the previous birds had probably scared most of the nearby animals into hiding.

Off in the distance, there came a gleam of several objects reflecting the sun. He flew over towards it, knowing that he would have a few moments before he needed to return. Several bodies were lying in a field. The bodies had started being picked over by scavengers. They must not have been there very long, for there was still plenty of meat left on the bones and the swords, which had reflected the sunlight, had not started to rust. There were over a dozen, and it seemed like they had died close together. This was odd and something he would definitely have to tell Kerwin, and then be scolded because dozens of bodies was just another part of the routine, he thought dejectedly.

He had the hawk swing wide around and began to search for something for it to bring back. While he was not as good as the animal left to its own instincts, he could hunt with most animals. Diving down on an unsuspecting prey was harder than it looked, and it had taken several tries for him to get the hang of it, much to the disgruntlement of the birds whose bodies that he had crash landed. Now, he was practiced enough that he could capture prey almost as often as the birds did themselves.

The only drawback to his plan is that once he caught something, then the hunt would end and the harassment from Finrin would begin. He saw them through the bird's eye, Finrin seated on his horse next to Master Gerwald looking smug. The bird's stomach quivered with discontent. Man, it was definitely not feeling well. Jariek smiled as he put the hawk into a dive. This would be tricky but if he pulled it off he wouldn't have to worry about Finrin for quite some time.

One of the potential buyers spotted the hawk coming in from behind them. He said something and pointed at the bird and everyone turned and looked, including Finrin. It couldn't happen in a more perfect way, well maybe Finrin's mouth could have been open. As the hawk drew near, Jariek pulled him out of the dive and let loose with its bowels, splattering Finrin who got a faceful as he turned into it.

The hunting party erupted with laughter at Finrin, who was busy screaming in rage. Master Gerwald's eyes got big as saucers and he took a quick glance at the potential buyers before laughing as well.

"I warned you, boy," he began, "that hawk would get even with you one day," he shouted at Finrin, who was next to him. His comment had the desired effect and the others continued to howl with laughter. Finrin stammered and fumed in rage, making unintelligible sounds.

"As I was saying," Master Gerwald addressed the others "these birds are highly intelligent. They are well behaved and well trained. Of course, if you happen to have done something stupid and careless with one and piss it off, it will get revenge. They are kind of like cats in that respect."

"What did the boy do to it?" one of the potential buyers asked.

"That my friend is one hell of a story, but I think the lad has had enough suffering today. Perhaps, I shall tell it to you later, provided you buy one of my fine birds." This sent a chuckle of merriment through the crowd. No doubt Master Gerwald had a story he could easily tell to whoever bought from him. The consummate businessman, Master Gerwald had no problem spinning a situation into something that could increase his chances of a sale.

Finrin rode over to Jariek, who already had a towel out to help him get clean. A few minutes and most of the mess was gone, although he would need a bath to get the rest of it once he got back to the city. With any luck, he would ride in sulky silence and say nothing about what happened. He was tempted to mention what happened to the others when they got back, but he decided against it. Finrin would retaliate against him and that would be the exact opposite of what he accomplished with the bird. Besides, it felt wrong to further Finrin's humiliation, since the incident was something that he had engineered in the first place.

CHAPTER 35

MERIK

It was early in the afternoon; a gentle breeze made the temperature quite pleasant. The balcony overlooking the gardens was set up with light snacks and refreshments. Merik had begun to enjoy this spot and started having a few of his lighter appointments out here. Compared to the tedious paperwork and endless meetings, this was a nice change of pace. Slowly but surely, each day's paperwork has gotten easier to get through. It still amazed him how boring and monotonous it was being a ruler. The history books always made it seem so exciting. A coronation here, a decree there, a few rousing battles, and none of the insufferable paperwork.

At times, he wondered if he could have taken over the city merely by having all the paper production stopped. Reports couldn't be filed, meeting notes not taken, supply requests went unanswered, and so on and so forth. The process would take longer, but he did wonder if such a thing were possible.

He leaned back in his chair and sipped his lemonade. A few minutes of peace and quiet, and then his meeting with, what was that man's name again. He shifted through his notes, once again using paper, until he found the sheet that he needed. Kerwin, that was the man's name. There was not much information about him. He recently came into Crestburn and, apparently, was a collector of Kysian artifacts. Yesterday, he had been informed that a stranger had been asking about private collections by an informant of his.

Merik had hoped to attract the attention of serious collectors. He figured it would be weeks before someone came forth. There were collectors in the city, but they didn't have anything that was of value to him. This was to be expected, since Crestburn wasn't known as a cultural center. It would take time for word to reach other cities, and even longer for someone to head to him, provided they believed his claim. Perhaps, he had gotten lucky.

He possessed a rare manuscript that was created by Emperor Palreon. The large volume appeared fairly straight forward, but, if you read between the lines, you could see that there was other information hidden within. The average person would miss this, but a scholar, such as himself, would pick up on them and go over the document again and again and dig out more information with each read through.

Even if others did have a copy, and he was reasonably sure he was not the first to find this treasure of antiquity, they probably didn't have a new power. That was a major game changer. For generations, powers varied with strength but never changed into something different. While others knew how to deal with the traditional powers, they could not prepare against something that they never dealt with, let alone had no idea existed.

Merik figured that there were probably dozens or so out there in the world like him. They had a new power and would keep that a secret. Some would remain in hiding, while others would do as he did and secure themselves a seat of power. The biggest difference between them and him is that he could find those who had new powers. He could go through the memories of anyone, and one of the first things he did was to look for their big secrets.

This was how he found Suval. Merik had been out scouting for people he could use. Once he realized what he could do with his power, he began collecting secrets. Everyone had secrets of some kind or another. After he learned what a person was hiding, he would extort them. The money earned from this allowed him to quit his job and start on his path. It was not long before he had started asking for favors in addition to payments. Merik came across Suval in a tavern. Taverns were a great place to scout out memories, for drink tended to cloud the fact that their memories were being steered. Not that he expected to be discovered, but it was better to play things safe.

Merik shifted through Suval's memories and discovered a horror of past abuse from his uncle. It was no wonder the man was messed up and creepy. It turned out that sexual abuse was not the only secret Suval had kept. He had the ability to mess with people's dreams. Suval couldn't actively control them, but he could make them chaotic and troublesome.

Merik studied the man and his memories for several nights before he approached him. Suval was poor, and the promise of a good meal and an offer for a job was enough to tempt him to a private meeting. The meeting was not exactly private, as Merik had two thugs in attendance as guards. They had stolen money from their boss, and knowledge of that secret forced them into his service. The guards were there to make sure Suval didn't try to leave before he was done explaining what he wanted.

It took very little effort to convince Suval to work with him, especially when Merik let him know that he too possessed a new ability. Judging by their facial expressions, the two thugs who he coerced in helping him did not like the fact that he could read memories. They tried to be discreet when they exchanged glances and signals, but Merik had half expected this. As promised, the meal was served and there was more than enough to go around. The guards helped themselves, not thinking twice about it. The meal was fine, but the ale that they washed it down with had a little something extra in it.

By the time Suval had finished eating, both thugs were dead. As a special favor and proof of loyalty, Merik requested Suval to dispose of the two bodies. Suval nodded, smiled, and agreed to do that. He now had someone with a new power under his control, and there would be more to follow. For his part, Suval was more than happy to do whatever Merik needed. He was thrilled to find someone that accepted him and let him be a part of something big. What was odd was that he could care less that Merik was like him, in the fact that he too had a new power.

His thoughts of the past fell away as a servant came onto the balcony with a stranger. This must be the antique collector. He was a bit older than Merik expected. Judging by his receding brown hair, his soft belly, and a bored look in his eyes, he figured him to be in his early fourth decade.

"Ah. You must be Kerwin. It is a pleasure to meet you." Merik said as he stood up and came over to shake the man's hand.

"Thank you, sir." Kerwin replied.

Sir, not my lord Merik noted. The man's grip was surprisingly strong. Merik pointed to the chair next to where he had been sitting. "Please, have a seat. Can my staff get you anything? Thanks to the former owner's sweet tooth, we have all kinds of wonderful delicacies."

Kerwin shook his head as he sat down in the chair that had been offered to him. "I think I will pass on the snacks, but I will drink whatever it is you are having." Merik returned to his seat and waited while a servant rushed about to get Kerwin his drink. Once that task was accomplished, she faded to the back of the balcony to allow Merik and his guest some privacy as they talked.

"I greatly appreciate you taking the time to join me on such short notice."

"It is my pleasure."

"My schedule has been quite busy dealing with matters of the city and cleaning up the mess that Djinar left behind. When I heard there was someone reputable looking for genuine antiques from the Kysian Empire, I knew I had to meet with you. As fortune had it, I was able to shuffle a couple of meetings around and clear a little bit of time to meet with you."

"You didn't have to go through all of that trouble. I was planning on staying in town for a little while."

"I am sure that, by now, you are well aware of the fact that Djinar is no longer in charge of Crestburn. I am sick and tired of seeing one tyrant after another take over somewhere and set themselves up as a dictator. A few even believe that they could rebuild what was once lost, but, in the end, they always fail."

"If you will excuse my question, what makes you different from any other psylord?"

Internally Merik wanted to scream at him and tell him all the ways he was different, all the ways he was better than the others. Outwardly, he kept a cool smile on his face and laughed. "Good question, my friend. The reason

I am different is that I have studied. I am not some brute, hell-bent on conquest. What powers I have are minor I assure you."

"Studied?"

"Yes. I come from a well off family and have always had a love and fondness for books and history. Over time, I managed to ascertain a small collection of manuscripts that came from the Empire. I know what you are probably going to say. There were dozens of people claiming the same thing before I heard about you. That this kind of claim has been made by psylords before.

"Well, I can assure you that I do have several manuscripts dating back to the Empire. They are the foundation on which I am building the new laws to govern Crestburn. I believe that, in order to rebuild the Kysian Empire, we must not conquer one another but live under the laws that the empire had. We must rebuild the empire from within. As we readopt the old laws and traditions, others will see our success and flock to join us."

"That is certainly a new approach, and I think I can assist you in that matter." Kerwin said cautiously.

"I take it that you have some books and records from that time?" asked Merik.

"Yes, I do. I even have a diary from a successful blacksmith's wife who talks about the time of the collapse."

"That might be interesting to look at. As I have said, my main focus is law and societal structure."

"In her account, she does talk about how things used to be and dealing with the changes. If nothing else, it might help fill in the blanks. Laws and rules are all well and good, but how the people dealt with them, how they lived. That will help color in the picture of what the Kysian Empire was."

"You make a good argument, my friend. I am definitely interested in seeing what you have. Of course, you are free to take a look at my collection as well. I am afraid it is of limited scope, but I am looking to expand and would appreciate any help with that. Now, Djinar did have a small collection of books as well. Most of those items I have no interest in. However, I can arrange for you to view them as well."

"That is most gracious of you, Lord Merik."

"Unfortunately, I am a busy man, and I have other appointments, but I had to see you at the first opportunity. My servants will show you out, and I will send a messenger to you at the inn about when I am free to meet with you again. A day or two at most, I assure you."

Both men stood up and shook hands before Merik turned and left. Once he was off the balcony, he smiled at the success of the meeting. As they talked, he probed Kerwin's memories. The man did indeed have books from the empire. Whether or not they contained anything of use to him was yet to be seen. Kerwin came to the meeting with very low expectations and figured it was another dead end. He was either not a very successful relic dealer, or collections were getting harder to find. Either way, the man's memories gave the impression of apathy and lack of hope.

Kerwin was a man who had lost his way and went on from day to day because it was a motion he knew. A man like him needed something. A place to belong and have value. If his books turned out to be worth buying, then Merik might hire him to find more. He could buy Kerwin's loyalty by providing meaning to his hollow life. Naturally, he would need to interview him further to make sure he was suitable for such a position, as well as find something he could use in case loyalty happened to falter.

CHAPTER 36

LUCKY LIAM

It was a simple run. Occasionally, those did come his way but more often than not it was because someone was trying to set him up. He couldn't blame them; there would be a certain amount of fame to the one who caught Lucky Liam. Not that they would. Everything went smoothly. He had no issues on the route, which is typically where they would ambush him. At the warehouse, he paused to see what the future held. If someone followed him in, it wouldn't be right away.

The warehouse manager was engrossed with paperwork and barely looked up when he came into the room.

"You Liam?" he asked.

"Lucky Liam ta be precise."

The man shook his head and replied, "Was told you were coming by. The man you want is Rony and should be in the back. Just ask the guys, and they will point you to him." With that, he turned back to his paperwork and Liam headed into the warehouse. He paused at the threshold and didn't see anything to be worried about, so he went in. There were a couple of guys nearby that had been stacking crates. He approached them.

"Hey, I am looking fer Rony."

"Rony should be over on the side, about halfway down. Can't-miss him. He is wearing a light brown shirt."

He said thanks and the man nodded and went back to handling the crate. Liam headed over to the spot he had been told, only to find another person who said that Rony was on the other side of the room and that he had gotten turned around. At this point, Liam was sure something was amiss. He paused for a moment and, when he looked ahead in time, he saw the manager stepping into the warehouse and calling all his men in.

It was a setup.

Someone must have figured out that he was a strong precognitive and waited a bit before coming after him. They might know he could see the future, but they would have no way of knowing how far he could see or how many potential futures he could look into. Liam waited until the last man had entered the office and then made a mad dash for the center of the room. From there, he climbed onto the crates and watched as a group of thugs entered the warehouse. Odd, each man was carrying a large sack except for Hargod, who had a nice sized club. Once the men had spread out along the front of the warehouse, Hargod gave a command and they began to coat the floor in flour behind them. They waited until every man had covered their area of the warehouse floor in flour before Hargod gave the command to advance and repeat the process. By the time they would reach the end of the warehouse, the entire floor would be covered in flour, which would make it easy for them to track Liam as he moved about the large room.

Hopefully, Liam could find a solution in the future, before Hargod and his crew got to where Liam was currently hiding. The problem with looking into the future, at least the way Liam did it, was that it took time. For most people, their foresight came in a quick flash, a sudden intuition or gut feeling. A few people were strong enough to use it in more than just a reflexive manner. With focus, they could see several minutes ahead in time. Naturally, the larger section of time a person looked over, the longer it took. Fortunately, the visions of the future happened at a faster pace. What most people didn't know was that you didn't have to be passive while looking into the future. There was no reason to sit and see what the future brings. If you wanted, you could see possible outcomes based on how you wanted to act. It amazed Liam that no one else had figured this out.

There were two answers that Liam had come up with that could explain this. The first was that the other precognitives could not see far enough into the future to experiment with other possibilities, let alone make it worthwhile. The other reason was simply, no one thought it was possible. The idea was as impossible as someone using their ability not to be recognized to make a random object not be noticed. Such a possibility was beyond their ability to grasp. Thankfully, Liam was not like others.

Exploring how different actions affected the near future required a lot of concentration, perhaps that was another reason why no one else did it. It also took longer. The more random variables, such as the thugs crossing the room, the more possible outcomes there could be. A person could react in a number of different ways to any given situation, and this got compounded by the number of people who were there to react to it. On top of that, each person also reacted to everyone else. With just a simple action, such as trying to leave a room where several people are looking for you, there are a vast number of possible outcomes. The number of possible outcomes grew to a staggering number when you needed to see past your first action to several steps further in time.

The men searching the warehouse grew closer and their leader, a thug known as Hargod, was almost on top of him. He didn't have time to wonder why Hargod was looking for him, that would have to be looked into another time. What he needed was more time. Thanks to the runaround the guys in the warehouse gave him, he still had the package. A quick scan forward and he was able to find what he needed, or so he hoped.

Liam turned slightly, leaned back and threw the package towards the front of the warehouse. As his ability showed him, no one saw it flying through the air but everyone heard it as it hit something. The men paused and looked back at where the noise came from. Hargod pointed to one of the men and told him to come with him as he checked out the disturbance. The others put their sacks of flour on the floor and drew their cudgels.

Now was his chance. Liam climbed down from his hiding spot and was about to head to the back of the warehouse, where he would have more time to plan, when a crazy idea came to him. Instead of moving away from them, he moved closer. Slowly and quietly, he crept up as close as he dared to one of the guards. He reached out to the man's mind and awakened a feeling of apathy. Liam gave a moment for those feelings to take hold, then focused on the man not recognizing him. The ability for someone not to recognize another person was like telepathy, and several other abilities, in the aspect that it had two forms. When you used it in an unfocused manner, then anyone you could see would be affected by it almost instantly. A person could focus on an individual or two and then it became much stronger and harder for someone to recognize you.

As stealthy as he could, Liam climbed on top of the pile the thug was standing next to. He did his best to stay out of sight and prayed that the overlapping of his abilities on the man would be enough to stay unnoticed. Once he was on top, he stayed flattened down as much as possible. Hargod would soon see that it was the package that was tossed and come back to order his men to continue with the search. They would suspect that Liam used the distraction to get further away and be more focused on the other end of the warehouse, rather than right on top of their current position.

A moment later, Hargod came back as the thug covered their tracks with more flour. "It was a diversion, men. Lucky Liam is still here with us and a bonus to the man who finds him. Keep an eye out because he is somewhere in the area we have not yet searched."

Excellent. His plan worked and soon they would be moving past him. Now, he would have a few minutes to plan his next move. Once they got to the other end of the warehouse without finding him, they would probably start to check the piles of crates and other things in the room as they made their way back. The odds of him getting past them a second time was not good. Slowly, he shifted his position so that he could see Hargod. Liam reached out and sowed frustration and anger in Hargod's mind. That should unfocus him a bit and make him careless.

It was kind of funny that everyone thought he never worked very hard to make his escape. The truth was quite the opposite. Sure his precognition was a huge help, but when you were trapped and surrounded it wasn't enough. Abilities had to be used together in creative ways to make a situation that he can use to slip away. All of his hard work and effort would go unnoticed because it would be attributed to his luck. Now, he needed to make more luck and somehow get out of this mess. Liam dove back into the vast collection of possible futures, but each time he got down from where he was hidden they spotted his tracks as they made their way back across the warehouse.

CHAPTER 37

KERWIN

Frata was an odd food but, according to Jariek, it was something to be enjoyed. It ought to be for the price he paid for it. Frata was a spiced nut that was coated in thick cream and then rolled in flour and fried. Kerwin still had his doubts but went ahead and ordered it anyway. Jariek was to meet up with him in a few minutes, and he was still hungry, even after eating breakfast at the inn. The food vendor was just on the edge of the animal vendor district. In fact, there seemed to be several such vendors in the area. Kerwin guessed that they prefer not to get any further in where the smell of the various animals became much stronger.

"I am glad to see you took my advice," Jariek said as he approached the vendor and took a seat next to Kerwin.

"I have yet to see if your advice was any good." Kerwin replied.

"Oh, it is pretty good, ain't that right Kreva?"

The vendor turned from him and smiled at Jariek "You are very much correct, Master Jariek."

Jariek laughed and replied, "You know that I am no Master and that I would catch a lot of grief from Master Gerwald and the others if they caught you calling me that."

"Then I suggest you keep sending me more business, my young friend, or else I will address you in such a high fashion that everyone will have to stop and take notice."

Jariek smiled and shook his head. It seemed that the verbal play was routine between the two. It was Kreva's playfulness as well as the frata that kept the kid coming back. Kreva placed Kerwin's order in front of him and smiled patiently. Kerwin picked up a still steaming frata and popped it in his mouth. The sweetness of the creme was nicely complemented by the spicey nut. If nothing else, the kid had good taste in food.

"See, I told you," Jariek beamed as he watched Kerwin eat.

"The kid may not know much, but he does know that I have the best fratas in Crestburn."

A false wounded expression splashed across Jariek's face before he burst out laughing. Kerwin quickly finished his order, thanked Kerva, and nodded to the kid to leave.

"Be safe, my young friend, and listen to you buddy. He barely speaks and a man who speaks very little will have something profound to say when he does so, unlike a man who talks all the time will say little of importance."

"If that's the case, why should I listen to you cause you never shut up." With a wink, Jariek got up and left Kreva, who was grinning at his retort. He quickly caught up with Kerwin, who had already moved on. Kerwin went down a few blocks, as he headed into the animal vendor's district, before he turned down a side street.

"You seem awfully cheerful today kid," Kerwin commented.

"Yea. I can't help it." Jariek replied.

"Why is that?"

"You're meeting with Lord Merik. How did it go? Is he what we are looking for?"

Kerwin shook his head. "I told you that this was probably going to be a dead end. If you keep believing everything is a sign that the empire is ready to be rebuilt, then you will wind up being killed by a psylord in no time."

"I don't think everything is a sign. I mean Merik said the words."

"And, as I told you the other day, so have others. This is not the first time I have checked on someone who said a phrase from Palreon's book. Nor am I the only operative to have investigated such matters either. My meeting with Merik was just to see if he was worth a second meeting."

He waited for a response but saw that the kid was looking fairly dejected after his scolding. "As it stands, we have agreed to meet again. This time we will have our collections with us and see if the other has anything of value. I will have a better understanding of Merik after that meeting. Even if he does possess a copy of the manuscript, it still does not mean he realizes what he has nor that he has the capabilities to rebuild the empire."

"He did successfully overthrow Djinar."

"Yes. That combined with the report was enough for the council to send me to investigate things further." That was a bit of a lie. It was standard practice to investigate anyone who quoted the manuscript.

They continued on in uncomfortable silence, winding their way down various streets lost in their own thoughts. Kerwin felt a little bad for the kid. He remembered at one time he had been optimistic and full of energy like him. Well, maybe not to the level that Jariek was. The optimism had faded as the years passed, and the futility of what they were doing became more apparent as time progressed. It was not the first time he wondered when he stopped giving a damn.

"Thanks for the information." Kerwin said.

A confused look appeared on Jariek's face. "Thanks? It was my job."

"Oh, so you do work for Kreva by sending an unsuspecting tourist to him."

Confusion was replaced by shock, then a smile, as he realized Kerwin had been talking about the frata. "Naw. That cheap old bastard doesn't even give me free samples when I send people his way." He paused. "I am glad that you liked them."

"Definitely. Even if this mission is a bust, I will definitely have to swing back this way for the frata if nothing else."

"Do you think..." Jariek started to respond but caught himself.

Kerwin shook his head. At least the kid had caught himself before asking the same question again.

"Like I said a little bit ago. I won't rule him out until the next meeting. Even if I don't rule him out, it may take some time and several meetings before I have enough information for the council to make their decision. Unfortunately, the better chance a person has of being chosen, the longer it takes for the council to decide. It is easy to tell if someone is an idiot and a fool with little to no chance in rebuilding the Kysian Empire. Someone who is capable takes longer."

"How long?" asked Jariek.

"That depends on the person and the council. If someone is of interest to them, they are watched and studied until the council finds something about them they don't like. The longest time I was checking a candidate out was four months."

"Why so long?"

"Well, the man was a psychic of mediocre strength. He had some connections and was fairly wealthy, but not in a position of real power either. There was nothing that made it easy to discount him."

"Why was he not chosen?"

"He was killed by a rival who was interested in the same woman."

"What!"

"Apparently, he and another man were pursuing the same lady. The other man didn't take kindly to this and murdered him."

"I don't get it. If he was a possible candidate, why didn't the council or you do anything to save him."

"We can't risk being discovered. The Cashek Society possesses a mountain of knowledge and there are many psylords who have killed for much less. Could I have prevented his murder? Probably. Would it have made a difference? More than likely not. If the man couldn't protect himself from a romantic rival, what chance does he have against a skilled psylord or assassin?"

"I..." Jariek paused, lost for words.

CHAPTER 38

LUCKY LIAM

Liam was pulled away from a myriad unvaried possible futures by Hargod's shouts.

"Do you still think you can get away from us kid? What, with your little tricks of throwing bags and playing with my emotions. They won't work. Make me angry as hell, and I will still find you. You have much to answer for. This time you won't get away. Surrender to me now, I will promise you Botun will not hurt you. He just wants to ask you some questions, is all.

"Alright, guys. Lucky Liam is still here. The little bugger was trying to mess with my emotions. I want you guys to switch places. I want no man walking back in the same spot he just was. Look at the floor but, more importantly, look at the stacks of crates and other goods. Our first sweep was just preparation for this sweep and the next one. In a very short time, we will be the ones to have caught Lucky Liam. We will manage what the others failed."

From his vantage point, Liam could see the men when they smiled and smacked each other on the shoulders as they swapped places with one another. Hargod opened up one of the loading doors and the messenger boy came in with new sacks of flour for each guy. Quickly, he handed them off and ducked back out. Hargod shut the door and gave the order to proceed.

No matter which future he looked at, the thugs always saw his tracks. Liam also knew that, if he did nothing, they would definitely see him, one and sometimes two guards. Unable to see a better option, Liam got down and made his way quickly over the front of the warehouse. He cut around a stack of crates and scooped up some flour. Carefully, he walked backward and retraced his steps.

Liam was about half way back to his hiding place when one the men yelled out that they had seen his tracks. It was now or never. Liam lepted towards his left and then started walking backwards again, slowly as he used the flour to cover his new tracks. Hargod could be heard as he gave orders to his men to hold their positions. Slowly, Hargod made his way along Liam's initial tracks as one of his men trailed behind him. Good. Now there will be a gap in the line. Liam scrunched himself to be as small as possible and willed them not to notice him.

Once Hargod and his thug passed him by, Liam crept forward and stealthy made his way through the hole in the line and towards the back of the warehouse. At the back door, the future showed him getting spotted and being chased down the street. While not a great future, being on the streets would provide him with more opportunities. Steeling himself, Liam yanked the door open and dashed down the street.

A cry immediately went up and more shouting could be heard from inside the warehouse. Liam set a frantic pace and had gone maybe a block before he could hear people chasing him and calling out where he was.

Shit!

They had realized he could make it difficult to be noticed and whoever saw him made sure to aid the rest of his pursuers. With all that attention on him, it would all but impossible for him to avoid notice. Liam ran for all he was worth. He changed directioned at every intersection, dashed around food vendors, and slipped through knots of people. There was an alley up ahead and, at the other end, were people that would defend him if he ran into them. He didn't waste time to wonder who would defend him in this city. Liam ran down the alley and made sure to aim for the pair that was heading down the street.

CHAPTER 39

JARIEK

They had meandered through the streets since they left Kreva's food stand. Kerwin updated Jariek with news about the other cities and what had happened in them. He told of the various psylords who have come and went in power in the last several months, as well as the state of the society, which was unchanged. He even told Jariek about a few of his missions that happened years ago. Jariek appreciated the news and did his best to politely follow along with the stories. He figured Kerwin was telling him these because there were lessons that he could learn from each one.

His mind was a bit distracted. Once again, Kerwin had berated him about getting his hopes up. Why did the society let someone as burnt out as Kerwin remain an operative? Why didn't he retire and find something more suitable for his disposition, like working in some forgotten dark corner of the archives? Those old records never changed, and that should suit Kerwin just fine. He sighed heavily. His first chance of doing something important for the society and little will come of it, because he was stuck with him. Too bad there was not a way to make sure that Kerwin reported the situation in Crestburn with the gravity that it was due.

Jariek was pulled from his thoughts as a young boy crashed into them. The kid panted as he looked frantically over his shoulders. A group of five men raced towards them yelling at the boy.

"Please sirs!" the boy begged. "Tey will kill me. I have done noting wrong. Please, help me!"

"Back away from him, or you will be hurt," shouted one man who was probably their leader. "I said back away. This little thief is ours to deal with."

"Sirs, I have stolen noting," the boy pleaded and turned out his pockets to show that they were empty. Jariek felt great sympathy for the helpless young boy and anger welled inside of him at the thugs, who had slowed down now that their target had stopped fleeing.

"I won't tell you again. Step away from..." the sentence never got finished. Kerwin lashed out with a fist and struck the man on his jaw, sending him tumbling back where he fell onto the street. Another thug was stuck with several blows to the head and chest and dropped before the others could react. Just like that, the odds shifted, and it was now only three on one, with the three still out of breath from their pursuit.

They eyed Kerwin wearily, not sure if they wanted to engage the man. He didn't look like much, but he had quickly dispatched two of their group. The remaining three weren't positive that they could take them out as well. Kerwin, for his part, stood there calmly, fist raised, not saying anything.

Jariek checked to see that the kid was ok before he came alongside Kerwin. The society had made sure that anyone who would be out in the real world was trained in fighting. Granted, it was only the basics, but informants were able to use blades and bows as well as their fists. Operatives like Kerwin received a lot more intensive training. Now that Jariek had joined the fight, the numbers were almost even, which should put the odds into their favor.

Figuring him to be the weaker of the two, one of the thugs lashed out with a three punch combination. He blocked the first two and dodged the last one. Then countered with a kick to the shin and his own three-punch combination, all of which landed. The man staggered back, and the other two looked at each, then at their downed commander, who was starting to stir.

"I suggest you all leave" came Kerwin's steady voice.

The men grabbed their leader, who had just started to rise. Their leader was getting back onto his feet, all the while clutching his jaw that had a bruise rapidly forming.

"This is far from over," Hargod said.

"I disagree," replied Kerwin.

"Disagree all you want, but Lucky Liam is mine and I will take him."

"Then, I suggest you bring.."

" Were you going to say more men? As a matter of fact, I do have more men."

Their leader smirked as he looked over his shoulder while several more men came jogging down the street. They huffed and puffed as they tried their best to catch their breath. These must be the ones who couldn't keep up with the others. This changed things drastically.

Jariek scanned the area, looking for something, anything, that could help them. A man rode a horse and was heading in their direction. The thought of using his special ability around Kerwin made him sick to his stomach. What if he noticed something was amiss and reported it back to the society? He looked down the side street and saw that the new group had almost rejoined their leader. What they would do to him and Kerwin would be much worse than anything the society would do to him if they found out about his ability to influence animals.

He reached out to the horse and took control. Jariek let it continue on until it was half a block away, then he made the horse let out a loud whiny and begin to buck. The rider was quickly thrown from it. Jariek made the horse charge towards them and, at the last moment, had it turn down the alley.

Before they realized what was coming at them, Jariek had the horse amongst them. He made the horse rear up and lash out with both hoofs, knocking two guys down. The horse leaned forward and tried to bite their leader on the face. Jariek made the horse buck and snort while it spun about, preventing anyone from moving past it.

Jariek broke the connection and grabbed Kerwin by the sleeve, who was staring dumbfounded at what had transpired. "We need to leave now," and gave Kerwin's sleeve a hard tug. Kerwin turned and nodded absently at him before he headed down the street, setting a quick pace. Jariek was about to take off right behind him, but he paused for a moment when he noticed the kid was looking at him with amazement. He took off after Kerwin and, out of the corner of his eye, he saw the kid give one last look down the alley where the now frightened horse, back in control of itself, was dealing with an angry group of men. Kerwin set a quick pace and kept at it for a long while, until he was sure they were not being followed. Surprisingly, the kid was still with them. Jariek had figured he would have ditched them after they were a fair distance away.

"I do not appreciate what you did back there." Panic filled Jariek as he thought Kerwin was talking to him and about his ability. Before he could respond the boy spoke up. "Sorry about tat, boss man. Tem tugs were after me, and I was out of breath. Couldn't have run any furter. I knew yous were a fighting type. Yous are stronger tan yous look."

"Well, that may be true, but you still had no right to mess with my emotions."

"No, yous are right sir. I wish I could say I was sorry, but yous handled tem nicely and now I am safe. I owe yous my life."

"You don't owe me anything."

"Tat is only because my meager life is not wort anyting." He finished with a bow and flourish. "Look, I know tis city well. Better tan anyone, I say. Let me be yours guide. I can help the two of yous around the city and carry anyting you buy. You're new in town, ain't yous? I can tell tat about you. Let Lucky Liam be yours guide."

"Kerwin, I have heard of this kid before", Jariek thought at Kerwin. *"He is supposed to be a famous package runner and errand boy. Never been caught and has amazing luck."*

"So?" Kerwin replied telepathically.

"Well, you have to meet Merik again right?"

"Yes."

"Well, you have a lot of books and manuscripts to bring to that meeting. Liam can help with that. It would be odd for me to be there, since I am an apprentice of Master Gerwald. No one would think twice if you hired a street kid to help you. It will also make you look a bit better in Merik's opinion if you have enough money to hire a servant."

"Not a bad idea. Is he reliable?"

"Probably more so than most street kids."

"I do have a need for a porter, and you will do as well as anyone, Liam. Now, I will warn you that I will be meeting with Lord Merik. This will be a rather important meeting. Can I count on you?"

"Yes, boss man. Yous can count on me. Just let me know when, and I will be tere."

"Good. Let's see about getting you a new set of clothes. Even though you will be functioning as a porter, I want you looking presentable."

"As you wish, sir. I should inform you that there will be no need to worry about etiquette instruction. I can easily behave like a proper servant with the correct mannerisms of one befitting the class and station of your choosing." Liam spoke properly for the first time while executing a formal bow and then stood silently with elbows held in and his palms up.

"Since you can play the party of a house servant so well, I bet you have your own set of clothes."

A wounded look splashed across Liam's face. "Now, boss man, I'm just a poor street kid. Tis is de only set of clothes tat I own. I have ta wash tem in de dark of de night cause I have nothing else ta wear while tey dry, and I don't want anyone to see me unclothed, " Liam said and then turned to Jariek with a smile and added "Cause if the ladies saw me naked tey wouldn't be able to resist me."

Kerwin gave a shake of his head, and a smile almost came across his face. "Fine, I'll give you a new set of clothes. Deal?"

"It's a deal, boss man. Let's get shopping for those outfits?"

"Outfits?" Jariek asked

"It's fine, Jariek. I can afford a couple of outfits for Liam. In all honesty, I was probably going to have to buy them anyway, because there could be several meetings with Lord Merik."

CHAPTER 40

BOTUN

One of the hardest things a man can do is wait patiently when he is upset. News of the chase of Lucky Liam had reached Botun over an hour ago. Still, he had not headed back towards the hideout. While Hargod more than deserved his ire, it would not do for others seeing him upset. The calm, controlled demeanor that he displayed was more than just control over himself, it was control over others. Since he never reacted to anything, his opponents could never figure out if their plans upset him or tore his plans asunder. An additional benefit was that people took it for granted that he already knew things before they reported it to him.

So, Botun sat and waited in a run down tavern smelling of sweat and disappointment. While it was only early afternoon, the place was busy with tanners, fullers, and other odorific laborers. They took their breaks in the early afternoon when the heat of the day made their jobs more unbearable. Due to the lingering odors of their profession, these kinds of men rarely socialize with others. Not one of them would know what the former sensechalt looked like, and probably not his name either. It made for an ideal spot for him to sit in a dark corner and glower for a while, or at least until he came up with a solution to the mess Hagod made.

It was too early to have any of his crew be noticed by the guards. The new hideout had just been finished, and he had planned on starting to move everything to the new location that night. That could still happen, but without Hargod. While Hargod was a fairly dependable man, he needed to distance himself, at least until he could see what kind of attention the chase with Liam attracted.

Hargod's mistake was not the only thing weighing heavy on his mind. There was still no clue as to Djinar's fate. If Botun had to, he could become the face of those resisting Merik's rule. As it was, he was sliding fatally close to that as it were. Power and popularity were fleeting things that he never cared for. They were often gone shortly after you had them. Few things lasted more than a couple of years. There was always a power hungry psylord who would gladly destroy what you made so that they could make their own stamp on the world.

Despite the various rulers that Crestburn had over the decades, the one thing that remained constant was the Merchant's Courtyard. It had been in place decades before he was born and would more than likely remain there long after he was gone - trading and selling goods for countless generations with a longevity that psylords could only dream about. How he wished that had been his brain child. While the others wanted to rule, he wanted to make something that would not only last but become an accepted part of the way of life. Without Djinar to deflect attention, there was little chance he would be able to do that.

As his anger faded, Botun eventually left the tavern and made his way towards the hideout. There would be little good that could be done about dwelling on things that were out of his influence. For now, he had to focus on the tasks at hand, and that meant cleaning up Hargod's mess.

The first thing he noticed upon entering the hideout was how subdued the attitude of the place was. Several of the crew were nursing injuries, and Hargod was asleep on a cot. His jaw on his right side was covered with a nasty dark bruise that almost made him feel sorry for the man. Botun let him sleep and headed into the kitchen. Now, more than ever, he wished Djinar was here. That man had a talent for finding the best chefs. As it were, they had to make due with what they had, and after about an hour he managed to cobble together a somewhat tasty stew that was a bit heavy with garlic.

From the common room, he could hear several of his men moving around. He brought out the stew and sat it on the table. By the time he came back with the bowls and spoons, several of the men, Hargod included, were already seated at the table quitely. He stood there as he looked his men over and then laddled himself a bowl. Then sat down across from Hargod.

"I prefer to know about the success or failure of an operation from my people first, rather than hear about it from multiple sources on the street. We can not afford to have incidents like today. Too much attention was drawn when you chased Liam down the street. Then, to top it all off, there was the fight with the horse." Botun stated codly.

"Botun, I am sorry, but I almost had Liam. If not for ..." Hargod started to reply.

"It would not have made a difference if you had caught Liam or not. Too much attention was drawn by your actions and, by now, I am sure that Merik knows about it. Success is a good thing, but it does no good if early success leads to a large failure."

"I didn't expect the horse."

"That surprised even me. Of all things that could have gone wrong, a horse attack? I do not blame you for that, not in the least bit. What I am mad about is the charge through the streets. You should have known better. There should have been another plan to keep him from leaving the building."

"With that bastard's luck, I figured that no matter how well I planned things, there would be a chance that he would slip out of the building. All the other attempts focused on trapping him and making sure he didn't get away, even though he always did. I had a plan that had a contingency for if he slipped out. One that was working."

Botun sighed and nodded in agreement. "Yes, your plan was a good one. Had Djinar still been in charge, I wouldn't even care about the chase down the street. That kind of scene would have been noticed, but, more importantly, no one would have cared. Also, people would not have given it much thought if Liam escaped you. That young man escapes from everyone. They will, however, give your chase some thought, and right now I can't afford to have people thinking about members of our crew."

Hargod nodded as he stared into his bowl. Botun then began to explain his plans for moving to the new hideout to those gathered, as well as updated them on the search for Djinar.

"I have been thinking." Hargod stated.

"Thinking is good," Botun replied.

"My actions have drawn attention to me, not this group. I need to make sure that it stays that way."

"And, how will you accomplish that?"

"By hiding in plain sight."

A puzzled look crept on Botun's face. "Do explain, Hargod."

"Right now, there are a lot of people clamoring for Merik's attention, especially after that speech he gave about bringing back the wardens. Already, there is an increase in people wanting to join the guards, and a lot more who are thinking about it. Leaders are going to be needed, but getting noticed can take a while."

Botun nodded "Unless you do something that gets you noticed."

"Right. Like catching the impossible. As you have said, it doesn't matter that I didn't catch Liam. What matters is that I did it in a way that got noticed. After all, if I had caught Liam, then I would easily stand out when I went to join the guards. Of course, now I am too embarrassed, due to being beaten up by a horse and letting Liam slip through my grasp. Sure, people will laugh about what happened but that will be only for a little while. Eventually, it will fade from focus as others try their attempt at getting some fame and notoriety before joining Merik's forces. What I have done will be lost amongst the other harebrained schemes."

"I am impressed. That doesn't happen very often, Hargod. I expected you to sulk a bit and probably have to distance yourself from our operations until enough time had passed. However, you listened to what I said and managed to find a way to spin a defeat into a salvageable situation. More importantly, you are able to set your ego aside and let others think less of you so that you can control the situation. You figured all this out in a very short time."

"Thanks."

"What I want you to do is go out and have a few drinks. Get drunk. Let people see you drunk, and let them know you screwed up and that Liam got away, and thus ruined your plans. If need be, get into a fight, after all, you do have a wounded pride and that wouldn't be out of character. Just make sure you don't get into too much trouble for brawling. Here, take these coins. Have a long nap and rest up, and then, tonight, go out and put your idea to work."

Botun tossed him a small pouch that had several coins in it. It was more than enough to get drunk and drown any sorrows that he might have. Hargod's head will probably hurt tomorrow morning as much as his jaw currently did. It'll be worth it if he could salvage what happened.

CHAPTER 41

TIANNA

Tianna set a steady pace. She had been up earlier and gone to bed later these last couple of days as her duties increased. The city guard was growing and with that came more responsibilities. At this rate, she was going to have to start delegating more things to officers under her. She didn't mind doing that, but she still liked to see for herself how everything was coming along. It provided her with a better feel for things than just getting the information from a report. As it was, she was on her way to see how the healers were doing and if they needed anything.

The change with the city guard was a fairly dramatic one. More people volunteered for special details, morning muster was quicker, and there were fewer complaints about combat drills. That last of which caused Sergeant Herlt to shake his head and mutter that soldiers not complaining about drills was unnatural. Tianna just smiled and reminded him they still complained, it was just to a lesser degree. "Still not natural" the old sergeant had replied as he shook his head.

Between the skirmish and the duel, she had shown everyone that she had earned her position and not gotten it through other means. It was sad that such a thought was possible, but it wasn't the first time people attributed her success, in what was predominantly a man's occupation, to underhanded means. She was not foolish enough to believe that her display would mean an end to any disregard towards her. Eventually, people will forget, or there would be someone new who would doubt her ability to lead and suggest that she got her position through other means.

Thanks to Merik's speech and the new stories that have started circulating about her, there was an increase of new recruits. They had scrambled to get the one warehouse converted over so that they could have a place to put all of them.

The old guards and the mercenaries that came with Merik were getting along better. Still, she wished that there would be more time before she started dividing the new guards into all the units. Merik wanted to make sure that every unit would have one of the mercenaries that came with him. He said it was to make sure that he had a loyal man in each group, but she thought he had another reason. No one could take control of his mercenaries if they were spread out amongst the guards. The guards would be harder to turn because they were tied to the city and could care less about who was in charge. To them, one psylord was just as good as another for the most part.

Even with a lot of things that were going their way, there were still issues that slowed things down. The increase in citizens joining the guards meant that they had to divert more resources into getting new barracks up and running. Potential officers had to be picked and trained from the guards they already had. Additional supplies, as well as another healer, needed to be found. One of the local apothecaries was willing to join up and spent her time making salves and ointments for healers, which freed them up to take care of more wounded.

For the most part, the guards had minor cuts and bruises with the occasional sprained ankle. The city guards of Crestburn never saw very much action. In the past, they were more likely to get a bribe than a wound when they dealt with a criminal. There had been a few fights the first several days after Merik took over, as bribes were turned down and criminals were forced to defend themselves against the guards. Word quickly spread that the new guards were serious. Already, there seemed to be a drop in petty street crime. Tianna knew that wouldn't last, that it was more a matter of the criminals adjusting to the new system of laws and figuring out how to exploit it.

She entered the building that the healers used. It was rather crowded today. Several guards were being bandaged up or waiting their turn quietly. When the guards noticed her, they grew very quiet and cast their eyes down to the floor, like children who knew they had been caught doing something they shouldn't have been doing. The healers were both busy tending to guards. Tianna scanned the guards and found two who didn't shy away from her gaze.

"What is your name guard and what happened?" she asked the tall lanky guard who had already started to go bald despite his young age.

"Well, Captainm, uhh."

"We got into a fight at the tavern," interjected his friend.

"A what?" she replied.

"A fight."

"Like Dake said, we got into a fight at the tavern with some people. Oh, yea, and my name is Jylan," said the balding guard.

"Why?" she asked.

"They were bad mouthing you, Captain. I couldn't just let them say bad things about you," replied the thickly built guard named Dake.

"What kind of bad things were they saying?"

"Well, they said you were Merik's whore, and that you couldn't have dominated Bearus and must have poisoned him or something like that, and…"

"Your duel the other day was rigged," chimed in Dake who was still grinning.

"So, I told them to knock it off," continued Jylan. "They didn't stop, so we went over to where they were and told them the better stop or else."

"Or else what?"

Dake smiled. "Or else I would knock them off their chairs." Dake sat there with a childish grin on his face. Looking at him, Tianna had no doubt that Dake could do just that. The man was almost as wide as he was tall.

"And he did too," resumed his friend. "They didn't stop saying stuff about you and good old Dake knocked one right off his chair. That didn't go over well with his friends, and…"

Tianna held up her hand to silence him. "Let me guess. His friends jumped up, and then you joined in, coming to Dake's aid. So, more of them joined, and then more of the guards, until the whole place was fighting."

"Yeah, that about sums it up, Captain."

"I take it these men, who were insulting me, were drunk?"

"Uh, yeah, probably."

"What is our job as guards?"

"To catch the criminal and make sure the city is safe."

"Where does fighting the people we are supposed to be keeping safe fall into that?"

"But, they were insulti…" He stammered to a stop as Tianna raised her hand.

"People will always talk. I could care less what some drunk says about me. I have had much better people say worse things. When you are a person in power, there will always be people who will talk bad about you. Ignore them, or else you are going to be wasting too much of your time caring about what other people think. Those people won't make a difference in your life unless you let them.

"The last thing we need is a bunch of city guards getting into a drunken brawl with the people they are supposed to be protecting. Thanks to your actions, I now have several men who won't be fit for duty for several days. I won't have my guards fighting like common thugs. Perhaps, if you don't have any drinking money, then you won't need to be going to the taverns. All involved will have their pay docked by a quarter days worth. Now, as for you two, the next time someone insults me, ignore it. Since you started the mess, you are to go to the tavern and pay for any of the damage done by the fight."

Tianna turned to leave and was surprised to find Sergeant Herlt standing silently behind her. "Yes, Sergeant?"

"Sorry to bother you, Captain, but you requested to be informed of any incidents, and there was a chase through one of the warehouse districts a little while ago."

"A chase?"

"Yes, mam. Several armed men were seen chasing a young lad for several blocks, and then they got into a fight with some people. The fight ended when a spooked horse crashed into the group and broke up the fight."

Tianna just stared at him for a moment and then shook her head in disbelief. "I have another matter to attend to, Sergeant. Accompany me and give me the details."

Herlt fell in behind her as she left the room. He continued his account of the incident with as much detail he had, which wasn't much.

"Crestburn is a strange place, Sergeant. So, how much did you hear about the tavern brawl."

"Pretty much all of it, Captain."

"Your opinion, Sergeant."

"Well, mam, soldiers and guards, they will always be some that brawl. At least they did it for the right reason."

"It was nice to hear that they did it on my behalf, even if it was pointless."

"You have made a strong impression on the guards."

"Yes. I don't want to discourage acts of loyalty, just recklessness."

"If you want, I can have a word with them later. Let them know that they really lucked out because typically the punishment is much worse than what you gave them. I'll tell them they got off easy this time because their acts were of loyalty, and that is something you strongly believe in."

"Thank you Sergeant."

"No problem, Captain, but it won't be much of a stretch of the truth. You did let those men off easier than they deserved, in my opinion."

CHAPTER 42

ASHA

There were times that Asha wondered if she should become an information broker. Her current associations provided her access to a great deal of information. If she was willing to do a little bit more, she was sure that she would be privy to even greater information. That little bit more was something she was unwilling to do. Growing up being groomed to be a part of Djinar's harem left a huge distaste for physical pleasures. The thought of laying with a man made her nauseous. Thankfully, she was skilled enough at other things that didn't force it to be an option.

It was best not to dwell on those things. As it were, she had been able to get by. More importantly, she was, as far as she knew, unnoticed by those with power and influence. Being anonymous was a far more important thing for her than money or power. Asha was afraid that if more people knew about her, there was a greater chance that someone would realize that she had a unique ability, no matter how hard she tried to keep it secret. After all, if she had a new ability, that meant others could too, and someone might have an ability that made it possible to find others such as her.

Things might be different if she had a power that could be used in a fight. She could see what powers a person was using and their relative strengths. That would give her an edge on the unsuspecting, but it wasn't the same as being able to stun someone with a thought or possess their body.

Since Merik took over the city, Asha had avoided her wealthier contacts. A change in leadership made people quick to seize opportunities that they normally wouldn't consider. The last thing she wanted was to end up as someone's opportunity to gain favor with the new lord. For now, she played things safe and kept to places that were frequented by working class people. While the working class people were just as opportunistic as the wealthy, they lacked the resources and connections that could make real trouble for her.

The first tavern she entered was half empty, but that was because there had been a brawl between the city guards and some drunks the night before. The owner had not gotten around to replacing the broken furniture, yet. Asha stayed just long enough to hear what happened then went elsewhere. After she visited several taverns with little learned, Asha was about to turn in for the night when Hargod came staggering through the door. His face had a massive bruise, and he was favoring one leg. From the looks of things, he had been drinking pretty heavily for a good while now. He sauntered over to a table, collapsed into a chair, and flagged a serving girl down.

Asha waited till he had his mug half finished before she slid over to his table to join him.

"How you doing, love?" she asked.

Hargod looked up from his mug and stared at her for a moment. She could tell he was trying to get his inebriated brain working to figure out if he knew her. Asha smiled coyly and waited to see if there would be a spark of recognition.

"Hey. You're that... that girl from the other day."

"That's right, love. You're Hargod, right?"

He let out a large wet belch before nodding. "Yup, that's me, not that anyone else would want to be me."

"Oh? What's wrong, sweety?"

"What you haven't heard?" He laughed weakly before staring off into his mug. For a moment, she thought he was about to pass out but then raised his mug with a jerk and took a long pull from his mug.

"Shit, I thought everyone had heard by now how that little shit got the better of me?"

"Who's that?" she asked, but she already knew the answer.

"That little cocky bastard, Lucky Liam. I almost had him. Had real good plan. It was working too."

"I am sure a smart man like you did," she consoled him.

"Not my fault the little sshit sshuh lucky. I was prepared for him to sneak out of the ambush, had the way I planned it." He paused and wobbled in his chair a bit. "Had things going the way I planned it. First, the ambush, and if he got out I was set up for a chase. Couldn't have expected it to go the way it did. Who knew his luck was real."

"Sounds like you planned for everything."

"Well, the horse was a surprise."

"Excuse me, did you say horse?" Asha asked.

"Yeah. Liam and his cursed luck. Some damn horsse went berserk and ended up hurting me and ssome of my crew. By the time it was calmed down, Liam was gone."

"Well, darling, no one could have planned for that."

"Of course not, that's why they call that basstard Lucky Liam," he shouted. The tavern got real quiet all of a sudden as everyone turned to look at him. "That was goin to be my chance to make it good with the new lord. Wanted to prove to him I was worth something by catching the uncatchable Lucky Liam. If I had done that, Lord Merik would have had to make me one of his new wardens." At that several patrons shook their heads while others chuckled and turned back to their drinks and conversations.

"I am sorry it didn't go the way you planned. No one could have planned for a horse. I know Liam had to be just as surprised as you were." Asha reassured him.

Hargod snorted and drained his mug. He looked around for a serving girl and flagged her down for another mug. His face was bruised, and he was favoring a leg when he came in, but it will be his head that will be bothering him tomorrow. Asha slipped away and wasn't sure if he even realized that she left.

CHAPTER 43

MERIK

Merik left the meeting feeling frustrated. All the city officials did was whine, complain, and make excuses. It amazed him that they got where they were, because they did so little. If they had ever been motivated, it was definitely before they had the positions that they currently held. Had they been like this for Djinar? If so, then it was no wonder why the man loved to drink so much.

The thought of the city's former ruler soured his mood a bit. There was still no word as to his whereabouts. It was safe to say that by now he was either dead or managed to make it out of the city somehow. He will have to hire some people to start searching the nearby villages. More than likely, Djinar would not go to a city where another psylord ruled. He was too weak and would have nothing to offer in the way of an alliance. As it was, there were several rumors about Botun being spotted in the city. He would have to put out a reward for the man's capture.

As for the other psylords, he had drafted a letter and offered them a formal alliance. Naturally, they would turn him down, and he was fine with that. The only reason he had done so was so that the history books will show that when he first started reforming the Kysian Empire, he tried to be a man of peace and was pushed towards conquest.

There was so much to do before he was ready to expand his empire. He had always wondered why, in the history books, various psylords would hold up in an area for several months to a few years instead of keep pushing forward their conquest. The list of things that needed to be done was immense. Even though they were a bunch of lazy complainers, it was easier and more efficient, at least in the short term, to keep the city officials. He could replace them later, when he found someone more deserving of the position. As it was right now, his main concern was getting a couple of clerks to handle his mountain of paperwork.

Even that mountain was slowly becoming manageable, bit by bit. He started getting a feel for which reports need to be read thoroughly and which could be skimmed over. The latter of two he saved for the next day and read as he went about his rounds going to various meetings and receiving local people of prominence who were curing for his favor. He barely had any time for himself nowadays.

Merik left the room and headed towards the gardens. A few minutes stroll along the flowers would soothe him. The little bit of relaxation was not the reason he was going there, it was just an added benefit. There were several rooms that looked down upon the gardens, and from one of them would be his informant within the heralds. He trusted Erlin as much as he trusted anyone, which wasn't very much. Merik made sure to have a select group of informants that reported only to him. There was always someone who was willing to work for him in hopes of special privileges later on.

"I am ready to give you this week's report, my Lord," came the telepathic communication.

"You may proceed."

"There was an incident with the city guards the night before last at a tavern. Several members of the guards got into a fight with some of the people there."

"So, the guards are getting a bit rowdy. I will make sure Tianna is informed and gets after them."

"She already knows about it and has dealt out discipline."

"Then, why are you bringing this to my attention?"

"The reason that I mention this is because of how she handled the matter. Tianna docked..."

"Captain Tianna. You will remember her title and the respect that it deserves."

"My apologies, my lord. Captain Tianna docked the pay of the guards involved by a quarter day's worth and made the two who started the fight pay the tavern owner for any damages."

"That seems reasonable, even if they did get off a bit easy. Once again, I ask you why bring this matter to my attention."

"The reason they got off light was that they were fighting on behalf of her honor. Apparently, several people in the tavern were bad mouthing her, and the guards took offense and started a brawl with them. Since they were fighting out of loyalty to her, Tianna, I mean Captain Tianna, let them off easy. Sergeant Herlt disagreed with how she handled the matter."

"I see."

"I doubt that Erlin would mention this kind of thing to you in his reports, and I know how important it is for you to keep informed on people's loyalties."

"Thank you. You are proving yourself to be a valuable asset, and it will not be forgotten."

"You humble me, my lord."

CHAPTER 44

KERWIN

Any doubts that Liam could handle his part had been quickly laid to rest. The young boy arrived a few minutes early and carried himself with manners befitting a servant. A complete change from the brash young man he met on the street. If he performed as well in front of Lord Merik, then he will have to make a note in his report that Liam could be a useful asassest if anyone in the society needs to hire a local guide or porter. As it was, Liam rode next to his trunk in the back of the cart that he had procured. Thankfully, the trunk wasn't heavy or else he would have had to hire someone with a bit more muscle to help him carry it.

They had gone shopping for clothes for Liam shortly after their bizarre meeting. The kid definitely knew his way around Crestburn. Kerwin noticed that several of the shopkeepers noticed him, so the young man had some notoriety. Given the group that had been chasing him, his notoriety could cause a bit of a problem, but he could cross that bridge when he came to it. As it was, he didn't think that he would be in town long enough for anything like that to happen. He was serious when he had told Jariek that he would probably be there for only a few more days.

It was a shame that the society's rules forbade him from hiring an outsider as an ongoing assistant. Liam would make for an amiable traveling company, and it might even get the kid out of the trouble he was in. The young man was adept at pretending to be someone else and would be very useful. He sighed mentally and shook his head. Despite all his talk, he did possess a soft spot for street kids. Had it not been for members of the Second Caravan picking him up and bringing him to the Cashek Society, he would have ended up like the rest of the orphans. This was one of the reasons why he tended to hire street kids. Most of them had no parents and were desperate for money. They also tend to know the local area a lot better than most people, and they could easily disappear into the background if things went bad. He paid them a little better than average, but not enough to draw attention. Besides, new clothes and extra meals went a long way with kids like Liam. Liam even talked him into buying a nice messenger satchel, which he now wore, which held the document he would use to see if Merik was indeed looking for more clues from the Palleion manuscript.

Other than the heat from the late afternoon sun, the ride to the mansion was pleasant, and they were there in no time. Liam hopped off the cart and slid the trunk to the end to help him carry it. A pair of servants came out to receive them. The first, and the more sharply dressed of the two, greeted Kerwin and asked to show him to a receiving room where Lord Merik would attend to him in a little while. The other servant grabbed the end of the trunk and helped Liam carry it.

They were led to a reading room of fair size. One wall was lined with books and, across from it, a large fireplace. Opposite of the room entrance was a large window that took up most of the wall. That many panels of glass must have been a great expense for Djinar. It filled the room with natural light. The furniture in the room, couch and a couple of chairs, were small and fragile looking things with decorative trim. A small desk sat next to the window with a stack of books and parchments.

"Lord Merik bid me to inform you that he is, unfortunately, running behind schedule due to affairs of the state. He hopes that you would forgive him and has set aside some books from the previous occupant's collection for you to browse should you choose to. If you need anything, please ring the bell on the mantle and a servant stationed outside will attend to your needs." the servant said.

"Thank you, that will be all," Kerwin replied.

The servant bowed and quickly left the room. Liam had brought the trunk over to the wall by the desk and stood quietly off to the side. Kerwin sat down at the desk and looked at the books. Several of the titles were known to him, and he sat those off to the side without a further glance. He skimmed through the rest, giving them a quick once over before going back to the chosen ones for a better look. Not that these books had anything to offer. More than likely, they were left as a test by Merik to get a feel for his abilities as a dealer of antique books.

He was pretending to be reading one when Merik showed up a short time later. He smiled at Kerwin and greeted him warmly.

"Thank you for waiting. I do apologize. City council members tend to run on and on, but, if I want things to transition smoothly, it helps to listen to them." Merik said.

"It is quite alright. I know you are an important and busy man, Lord Merik."

"Thank you for understanding. I see you had a chance to go through the books on the table."

"I glanced at them, but there was nothing really of interest in them."

"What a shame. I must confess, I had not had the opportunity to look through them myself and hope that you will forgive me for using you to sift through them for me," he said with a smile.

That was not something he had been expecting. Regardless, whether or not what he said was true, it did show that Merik had a level of resourcefulness that he had not expected. Resourcefulness didn't mean the man was any more suited for the Cashek Society's backing than the other people he had investigated over the years. He gave a polite laugh and replied: "Well, I will make sure to send you my bill for the research I did for you."

Kerwin gave Liam a small nod before he continued, "Since we both have several manuscripts to inspect, I hope you don't mind if we skip the small talk and get straight to business." He turned towards the trunk and was pleased to see Liam had it already open and proceeded to get out several large volumes. Merik smiled, walked over to the fireplace, plucked the bell from the mantle, and gave it a ring. A moment later a servant appeared.

"Yes, my Lord."

"Please, have those books removed from the desk and the stack that I have prepared for our esteemed guest brought in for his inspection," Merik said.

"Right away, sir. Where would you like those books placed, my Lord."

"On the desk will be fine."

The servant disappeared and a few moments later a new servant came in and gathered up the books, while two more came in with large stacks of books. Merik sat down on the couch, and Liam brought him the books from the trunk. The next hour and a half were spent pouring over the books. Kerwin found it difficult to concentrate and kept letting his memories take him back to other collections that he had seen and books that he knew were better than what he had brought Merik to see. His mind had wandered so much that Merik had to speak several times before he realized he was being addressed. He must really be getting burned out for him to lose focus like this.

"I hope my books aren't putting you to sleep."

"No, my mind had wandered a bit." Kerwin replied.

"Ah, yes, I find mine does as well, especially when reading the rather dry texts. Unfortunately, I have not seen anything remarkable in the collection you presented to me. I would guess by the way your mind wandered you were less than impressed with my collections.

"Well…"

"It's quite alright. I half expected this. Too often collectors dance around one another, doing their best to get the other to show their hand first. We both brought books that, while interesting and very old, are not what the other is looking for. I would like to see what it is that you really brought for me to see, and then I will show you what I have."

Kerwin nodded and snapped his fingers. Liam came forward and opened up his messenger satchel. Carefully, Kerwin reached in and brought out a bundle and gently laid it on the table. He unwrapped the cloth and laid out several sheets of ancient paper. Merik came over and began to examine them. After several minutes, he took a step back and said, "This is a lot closer to what I am looking for. I do wish we had started off this way, but I understand how cautious collectors are of their possessions."

Merik got up and rang the bell for the servant and ordered that the other part of the collection be brought to him. They waited in silence for the servant to return with a small ivory cylinder capped in bronze. Merik nodded towards Kerwin to indicate that the servant hand him the document. He waited for the servant to leave before he uncapped the cylinder and slid out the parchment.

Slowly, his eye devoured what was on the page, along with the supplemented notes on other pages. It was no accident that he said the phrase during his speech. There it was in his notes. This was what the society was looking for. He would have to see how much more Merik knew and then file his report. It looks like he would be staying in Crestburn a while longer.

This was no guarantee that the council would even agree to support Merik. At times, it seemed that the only thing they were good at was resisting change. It was how they survived for years, since the collapse of the Kysian Empire. They have existed in secrecy all this time, waiting for the right person who could restore the Empire.

Palreon had decided to create a massive archive and repository for the Empire to preserve its knowledge. Originally, they were merely the custodians of the repository. They were just librarians and archivists. It wasn't until near the end of his life that Palreon decided to expand on that idea. The records would do little good if there wasn't someone to understand them and put their knowledge to use. Changes were made and the place underwent a massive expansion. A group of wardens was added as guards. The staff increased in size and a new purpose was added for their existence.

By the time Zharn took his father's place as Emperor, the transformation from archive repository to what they now were was almost complete. All this was still kept a secret from the rest of the Empire. Contact with the outside world was highly regulated, and only a handful of people besides the current Emperor knew of its existence.

Kerwin looked up from the page and out the window in an effort to clear his thoughts. Why on earth was he thinking about basic society history? His mind should be on pages before him and not what was taught to young children within the society. It was not like him for his mind to wonder such. Through the window, he could see the sky was already darkening and on the pane of glass he could just make out Merik's reflection. Thankfully, Merik was engrossed in either the book before him or his own thoughts. Either way, he probably had not noticed him reminiscing.

"This is very intriguing, Lord Merik," Kerwin said.

"That, my good man, is just a few pages of a much larger document," Merik replied.

"You have more?"

"Yes, several pages in fact."

"I would pay a good deal to see them."

"Unfortunately, we are out of time for this evening. The last piece you handed me was much more in line for what I am looking for. Do you have more?"

"Like you, I have several pages. I left them behind in my room because I was unsure of how serious of a collector you were."

"Well, now you know. How about we meet again in a few more days. I can provide scribes, and we can split the cost of having each other's documents transcribed. In fact, I can order a copy of mine done and have it waiting for you once you bring me yours."

"I don't know what to say," Kerwin said.

"A simple thanks will suffice. As I have said many times, and I know I will undoubtedly say many times more, I am serious about my belief in rebuilding the Kysian Empire. The more we share our knowledge of the Empire, the easier it will be for us as a society to rebuild it. I am just one man and do not possess the means to do this alone. I need others to share in my vision."

Kerwin nodded and said, "Thank you, Lord Merik. This will be an opportunity of a lifetime." He turned to Liam and was surprised that the kid already had his trunk repacked and ready to go. He gave another nod to Merik, who summoned a servant to help Liam with the trunk.

CHAPTER 45

MERIK

He waited several minutes doing his best to keep composed. The meeting with Kerwin went very much in a different direction that he thought possible. It started off with the surprise of Lucky Liam being Kerwin's servant. He didn't expect to see him here in the mansion. After what happened to the loyalist that he led out of town, Merik expected Liam to keep a low profile. Botun must not have realized what happened to the group. Either that, or the kid had nerves of steel.

Other than Liam being present, the meeting started off as planned. Kerwin had browsed through the books that the servants had laid out on the table, as Merik hoped he would. He had been honest in telling Kerwin that he had yet to go through them. It was good to have his suspicions confirmed that they were of little value. With so much going on these days, he hadn't had much chance to browse Djinar's personal library. He hadn't expected much since Djinar was more of a man of physical pleasures as opposed to intellectual pursuits.

He glanced over the books that Kerwin brought, but he wasn't really interested in them. It was a common ploy for an antique trader to slowly show his collection piece by piece, each one better than the last. Truth be told, he hadn't expected much from this meeting other than hoping to get the details of the more valuable books from Kerwin's mind.

Things that people experienced became memories immediately after they happened. While Merik could go through someone's memories seconds after they formed, it was wise to wait a little bit before delving into them. When he pulled up someone's memory about something they had just experienced, their brains had trouble dealing with the recent perception of an event that had just happened. Often, they ended up in a trance-like state that seemed to slow down their ability to react to things.

If he went back a few minutes into their memory, this effect didn't occur, although if the memory was too similar to what they were currently doing, they would have a feeling like they had already done this once before. Merik had planned to ride Kerwin's memory from a few moments in the past and then shift through his memories to find details of his book collection. That knowledge would provide him with a much better bargaining position.

He was shocked to find out that there was a secret society dedicated to rebuilding the Kysian Empire.

Merik was stunned by this revelation and almost lost his composure and control of Kerwin's memories. Thankfully, Kerwin, it seemed, was also shocked that Merik was on the verge of figuring out some of the clues that Palreon had left. Merik was able to reassert control of the memories and had been able to learn a little bit about Palreon's manuscript as well as the hidden society. It wasn't enough, not by far, but it was a beginning. His dreams were going to come true, for he was on the right track. He will do what many had sat out to do before, only to fail. This was no longer a foolish egotistical quest, as several of those who served him believed. He was on the right path and soon would be getting the kind of help that he never would have dreamed was possible.

What to do next, he wondered. He could wait until their next meeting and take things from there. It was a risk, but he could show his hand a bit and let Kerwin know that he knew about a secret society, or that at least he believed there to be one. The only problem with that is what bit he did tease out from the manuscript wouldn't support that idea.

Merik had to be careful. If he made a mistake, he could lose his one chance at getting their help. From what he did pick up from Kerwin's memories, it did seem that the council that ran the society were so used to denying their support they could easily deny him out of habit. He really couldn't blame them. After all, there had been countless people before him who had strong psychic talents and claimed to rebuild the empire. If he knew more about them, then he could make sure they saw him as someone to take seriously. To do that, he needed Kerwin's memories. They would provide a wealth of information, worth more than anything he currently had access to. Merik doubted that Kerwin would freely share what he knew about the Cashek Society.

Kerwin would have to make a report. If he didn't, the Cashek Society might investigate eventually, and that would buy him time. He could use the time to go through Kerwin's memories and learn everything he could about this secret society. This would give him a great advantage when he dealt with them. An advantage he could not afford to miss. Merik got up and rang for a servant.

"Yes, my lord," the servant asked.

"I want Suval here immediately. After I am done with him, I need to speak with Captain Tianna."

"Right away, my lord."

"Have my guests left yet?"

"I don't think so."

"Good. Delay them a bit. Nothing drastic, just find a way to slow them down a bit."

A worried look crossed the servant's face, but then he calmly replied, "As you wish, my lord."

Merik paced back and forth, his mind racing. It would be a sacrifice, but nothing great came without sacrifice. He would lock up Kerwin before he could make his report. Then, he would be free to dig through his memories and learn as much as possible about the Cashek Society. Eventually, they might send someone to look for him. At that point, he would be much better prepared to deal with this secret society. It was even a possibility that Kerwin would be very cooperative with him. Of course, he could dispose of him if he chose not to assist.

Merik rang for the servant and, this time, ordered stiff drinks to be brought in. The servant quickly reappeared with a small cart with several decanters of strong drink. He downed the first glass quickly, not evening tasting it, but felt the burn warm his throat. The second he drank more slowly and had finished it when he heard a soft knock on the door.

"Come in," Merik said.

Suval crept in and slunk towards the couch, where he sprawled out.

"You wished to see me, my lord?" he asked cautiously.

"Yes. I was about to have a drink. Would you like one?"

"No thanks, my lord. I prefer other things," he purred.

"Yes, I know about the things you like to pollute your body with." Merik poured himself a third drink and began to sip it. "I was just in a meeting with a man named Kerwin. He claims to be a dealer in antique books, but he is much more than that. I need you to follow him and, when he returns to his inn for the night, I want you to send word back here."

"That will be no problem, my lord. Might I inquire where he is now."

"We just got done with our meeting. He had with him a trunk that his manservant was carrying. I told a servant to delay them a bit, so hopefully you can catch them as they are leaving."

Leaping to his feet Suval bowed gracefully and smiled. "At your service, my lord." He quickly left and the door shut for only a moment when it opened again and Captain Tianna entered the room.

"You requested to see me, sir?"

"Yes. I have a need for you and a squad of my best guards to bring back a man to me. I don't know if he will have any trouble, but be prepared, for he is a lot more than he seems."

"Understood. When is this man to be brought back here?"

"Some time this evening. Word will be given when he, Kerwin, returns to his inn. Once he is turned in for the night, you will go and retrieve him. I want this done with as little attention as possible."

"No problem sir. I will get a squad ready, and we will be waiting for the order."

CHAPTER 46

SUVAL

The man, Kerwin, and his servant boy had just left the mansion property when Suval found them. Whoever it was that was supposed to delay them did a poor job of it. Not that he was worried, as he could find out who was at fault and pay them a visit later. Merik frowned upon him messing with the mansion staff, but he could give a little lesson now and then. Hopefully, Merik would not mind, especially since he would be dealing with a staff member who had failed in the task that Merik had assigned them. As it was, he was getting bored without having someone to play with. Merik hated it when he used that term, even though he did the same thing, although Merik called it experimenting. Experimenting or playing, either way, it is the same thing. The end result was they learned more about how their special powers worked.

Suval reached out and made himself hard to be noticed by all those near him. He was quite good at that. Kerwin was in the front of the cart, next to the driver, while the young man, what a pretty young man he was, sat in the back next to the trunk. Their ride through town was a silent one, and Kerwin seemed lost in thought. It wasn't long before the cart stopped at an inn. Disembarking with the trunk, the two quickly headed into the inn. They were only inside for a few minutes before returning to the streets, minus the trunk. The cart, having been dismissed when they got off, was already gone.

The two headed away from the inn, and Suval followed quietly behind them. At first, he listened to their conversation but was quickly bored by their bland chatter. They talked about the city and the different sites that could be seen. The boy was acting the part of a tour guide. He must be some local street guide, hired by the man to assist him during his visit to Crestburn. Eventually, they picked a place to eat. Sighing in frustration, Suval grew annoyed. Why couldn't they return to the inn and call it a night? There were more important things for him to do, like find out who failed to delay them properly and visit them while they slept.

Suval found a place on the street where he could watch them without being bothered. He could have gotten much closer if he wanted to, but his mind was distracted with other things. Why was Merik making him do such a banal task as shadowing someone? There was also that insult about the drugs he used. Who was Merik to chastise him? After all, the man had started to do more than sample Djinar's alcohol supply. If these people had been important then he could understand why Merik would need it to be him, but it was just some book merchant and a street kid. What a waste of his talents. The merchant, or antique dealer, or whatever he was, was bleah. The man was dressed nicely but not too nicely. His looks were average, his demeanor was subdued, pretty much everything about him made Suval want to ignore the man.

His young companion was the total opposite. While he wore boring nondescript servant's clothes, his actions and manners were anything but. His motions were exaggerated, as if to make sure everyone's attention would be focused on him. There was a gleam in his eyes as if he had a big secret and it was right under everyone's nose. The longer he watched them eat, the less despondent he grew about the job. As the meal concluded, he had become intrigued with the kid. Merik had told him his name but he had barely paid attention. What was it? He thought for a moment but couldn't come up with anything. Oh well, it didn't really matter.

Following them as they left, and headed back to the inn, Suval decided that the servant might make a good plaything. Stopping just outside the inn, Kerwin turned to the boy and talked to him for a moment. More than likely, he was giving him a set of instructions for the next day. Looking around, Suval saw a guard patrol coming down the street. Perfect timing. He rushed over to them and waited until he was almost upon them before letting go of his ability to make nearby minds not recognize him. He took a perverse pleasure in the startled reactions as he all but appeared before the startled guards.

The guard's hands were going for cudgels before recognizing who was before them. Merik had made sure that all the guards knew his inner council by sight and to follow any orders given by them. Eyeing him wearily, the lead guard was no doubt unsure what Suval's intentions were. He gave the man a moment to ponder and let his mind dance through the rumors that were circulating about him.

"Behind me, by the entrance to the inn, is a man talking to a young boy. Do you see him guard?" Suval asked.

"Yes, sir."

"Good. I need you to keep a discreet watch on him. Once he has turned in for the night, I want word sent back to Lord Merik."

"Consider it done," the guard replied.

"If asked, let Lord Merik know that I decided to follow the boy."

The guard did a poor job suppressing a shiver when Suval said that. He grinned at the guards' reaction. Let them think whatever they will about him, so long as they do as they were told.

CHAPTER 47

TIANNA

The order came to them that it was time to retrieve the merchant after only waiting a couple of hours. Tianna had two squads ready and waiting. The first would surround the inn, with a few members coming inside with her. The second squad would be a few blocks away, but in telepathic contact the entire time. She took Merik's warning to heart and was ready in case the man had a surprise waiting for her.

Merik had not given her much detail about the man. He was new to town and was supposedly an antique book collector. Kerwin was his name, and he had just finished his second meeting with Merik. Talking with a few servants who had seen Kerwin on his visits to the mansion provided her with little to offer in the way of information on him.

Why was this stranger important enough for Merik to have her bring him in personally? While talking with Merik, he seemed excited, even though he did his best to suppress it. Could it be that he found someone else like him, someone with a new ability? That would make sense and explain his warning for her not to underestimate the man. If he had a new power, then there was a chance that he could catch her by surprise before she had a chance to dominate his mind.

Kerwin was a decade or two older than Merik, which meant that if he did have a new ability, then he was very good at keeping it hidden or cleaning up after someone discovered it. Either way, it was better to have overkill on something like this. As it was Suval, would be on site to lend a hand if need be. Tianna shook her head in disbelief that she was glad the creep would be around.

It took effort to keep two squads of guards from being noticed as they moved through a city. Each guard went without armor or uniform, but they had switched out cudgels for swords. She made sure that right after they left the mansion they broke up into smaller groups and went down parallel streets to hide their numbers. Unless someone was really paying attention, they would have no clue the guards were there.

Noticing a group of guards nearby who were watching the inn, Tianna gave a signal for her squad to hold up. Approaching the other guards, Tianna took down the hood of her cloak. Upon recognizing her, the guards quickly snapped to attention and their sergeant quickly came forward with the start of a salute which she quickly cut off with a shake of her head.

"I need to keep a low profile. What is your squad doing here?" Tianna asked.

"Watching the inn as instructed by Suval," replied the guard.

"Where is Suval then?"

The guard was hesitant to answer her. Finally, he said, while looking down at the street, "He said that he was going to follow the boy."

A sense of nausea hit her as her mind came up with several implications as to what that could mean. She would need to bring this up with Merik. Tianna knew Merik favored the creep because he had a unique talent. Still, something needed to be done about Suval. It was obvious that the guards were disturbed by him, and so was she, truth be told. His presence could be detrimental to Merik's efforts.

"I take it that Kerwin is inside."

"Yes, ma'am. He has not left since we have been out here, and I have two more guards watching the back. I have no clue if he is in the common room or has retired to his own room for the night."

"Thank you. I want you to pull your men back two blocks and wait there. More than likely, I won't need you but be ready just in case."

"Permission to speak frankly, Captain."

"Permission granted," Tianna said.

"There ain't nothing that anyone can do to touch you if you don't want them to. Not saying that I have a problem with waiting as your backup, but, to be honest with you, there won't be anything for any of us to do."

Tianna managed not to blush. Praise from subordinates was something she was not used to.

"Even someone as good as I am can still be taken by surprise. If something happens, I need you to fix it and set things right."

Swelling with pride, the sergeant started to shout his order to his squad before remembering that they were to keep a low profile. Noticing that the sergeant had a swagger to his step as his group left the area, Tianna realized that perhaps she had overdone it a bit. The guards were a lot more receptive to her, especially after the duel, than Kour's group had been. She would have to work on being more subdued with her praise or else she may have a group of fanatics on her hand, and that won't bode well.

Turning to her squad, Tianna singled them. Slowly, they made their way down the street and around the building. Two guards had remained in uniform that was concealed by their cloaks. These would be the two who would come into the inn with her and retrieve Kerwin. She was hoping that seeing two uniformed guards at his door would be cause for less reaction than two strangers.

After her team was in position, she waited a few minutes longer to make sure they were settled in. With a nod of her head, Tianna headed in with the two uniformed guards following right behind her. It wasn't very busy inside. Several of the tables were empty in the common room. Walking over to a tired looking woman behind a bar, Tianna addressed her.

"I am Captain Tianna of City Guards. I need your assistance."

The woman looked at and her two companions wearily. "What can I help you with, Captain."

"I am looking for a merchant named Kerwin. He came into town a few days ago."

"He's here. Up the stairs, turn right, and go down five doors. That's his room."

"Thank you," Tianna replied.

Nodding to her escort, Tianna stayed put as they turned and headed up the stairs. A quick survey of the common room didn't reveal anything amiss before she started following. Slowly, she ascended the staircase, giving the two guards a chance to get into position ahead of her. Once she could clearly make out the doorway, she stopped and waited for the guards to knock on the door. Two loud sharp raps on the door followed by sounds of someone stirring inside.

The door creaked open a sliver, not enough for her to see the man behind it and link up with his mind.

"What do you want," came a sleepy voice.

"Sir, we just need to ask you a few questions about a young street thief named Liam. A merchant was robbed early this evening and claimed it was Lucky Liam. We have found Liam, and he said he was with you at Lord Merik's mansion, of all places." The guard gave a snort of disbelief as he finished his rehearsed lines.

"Liam told you correctly. I had hired him as a servant, and we were both at Lord Merik's mansion earlier this evening. I am a dealer of rare books, and your lord was looking at my collection."

The door hadn't opened any further since the conversation began. She had hoped that once he realized it was not a serious matter, he would relax a bit and open the door far enough that she could see him and dominate his mind. Hopefully, one of the guards would be able to get him into her view without having to shove the door open. Such a move would draw attention, and it was possible for him to jump further back into the room, out of her sight but still be able to see the two guards. If he had an undiscovered power, who knew what he could do to the guards.

"Sir," the guard began again.

Kerwin yawned loud enough that even Tianna could hear it at her place on the stairs. It effectively cut off the guard and gave him an opening to speak without needing to interrupt the guard. The man was good, she gave him that much.

"I am certain you have more questions, however, I have had a long day and another meeting with your Lord Merik. His staff can confirm that I was there with a servant. I have already told you Liam was with me, so, unless this is somehow a pressing matter, I need to get back to sleep. The last thing either of us wants is for your questioning to cause me to oversleep and not get up in time to meet Lord Merik. If there is anything else you need, I can answer those questions tomorrow. Ok?"

She was surprised at how well he took control of the situation and managed to derail any further questions. At this point, any more attempts from the guards would arouse suspicion. If something didn't change fast, they were going to have to force the door open and, even though there were few people down in the common room, someone was bound to notice the commotion.

A flash of insight hit her and she wrapped herself up in her cloak but kept the hood down. She went up the rest of the steps and down the hallway, weaving back and forth as she headed towards her guards while caterwauling a bawdy tavern tune.

"What do we have 'ere? You boys looking for fun?" she called out as she staggered into one of the guards. Pretending to get tangled up with her, one of the guards stumbled back into his partner, who crashed into the door forcing it open just enough where she could see Kerwin. Reaching out with her mind, Tianna took control of Kerwin. His body was hers to do with as she wished. Immediately, she had him drop to his knees and spread his arms out wide.

When dominating someone's mind, you had control of their body until you chose to let go, or were knocked unconscious. It was difficult to control someone's body and your own at the same time. The mind has a difficult time giving orders to two different bodies. With practice, a person could have someone they are dominating walk alongside them. The problem with this is that typically both bodies moved identically, and that could be noticed. Tianna had one of the guards escort Kerwin ahead of her by a few feet while the other stayed back with her. She hoped that, to anyone watching, it looked like Kerwin was walking under its own control. Once outside, they went down the street and met up with the other guards. A wagon arrived, and Kerwin was loaded in the back.

"What about his belongings?" asked a young sergeant.

Tianna turned to her and replied, "Get them later. It would be too suspicious if we got them now. Tomorrow, Lord Merik can draft a letter stating that this man is his guest at the mansion and requests that his belongings be delivered there."

"As you wish," the sergeant said and turned and joined her squad as they escorted Kerwin away.

CHAPTER 48

SUVAL

The young man certainly knew his way around the streets. Suval had to maintain a steady pace to keep up with him. The youth moved with grace, weaving in and out of crowds without a second thought. More than once, he paused at a vendor to check behind him in case he was being followed. Suval wasn't worried about being spotted, for he was quite adept at using his abilities, as well as being stealthy. It would take some serious searching on a person's part in order for their eye's not to slide right off of him.

Whoever this kid was, he definitely had a way about him. There was a grace in his movement and an almost feminine beauty to his face in the right light. Suval was definitely intrigued and couldn't wait to learn more about his new plaything. Oh, they would have such a fun time together later that night. It will be a shame that he couldn't have him back in the mansion's basement. There, in the basement, he would have a lot more freedom to do as he pleased. Wherever the boy slept, Suval would have to be cautious to avoid detection. Even if people didn't notice him, they could hear the boy's cries as his dreams warped and stormed about while he slumbered. It would be awful if their play time together would be interrupted by someone checking in on him.

All of a sudden, the kid just vanished. Suval's heart raced in panic as he began to look around for the boy. He could not lose his new plaything before they had their fun. He let out a growl of frustration. How on earth could someone disappear out of thin air?

Suval started chuckling as he realized what had happened. The kid was like him, strong in the ability to make people not recognize you are there. Suval stopped looking around and focused on the spot where he had last seen the boy. People often look everywhere other than the last spot you were standing at when you disappeared like that. They assumed that you used the ability and are now getting far away as quickly as possible. What they don't realize is that, by standing in the same spot, you are in the one spot where no one is looking. Well, most of the time, anyway.

Sure enough, the kid stood where he had been as he watched the street to make sure no one was watching him, before he crossed it and headed into an alley. Whoever this young man was, he was definitely skilled. Suval had to work to tail him, and that was pleasing. It had been too long since he found anyone worthy of his attention. Most people were clueless about their surroundings and could be easily followed without the use of any psychic ability, but not this one. No, he was different. He was special. Suval grinned.

For the next half hour, the kid led him across town, through back alleys and side streets. Eventually, he came to a stop halfway down an alley and sat there for a few minutes before scurrying up the side of a building and going through a broken window on the second floor. Suval waited in the shadows nearby, watching the window. Sure enough, he could barely make out the kid's form as he gazed at the alley below. Very good, double checking to make sure no one was following you, Suval thought.

He waited for what seemed like an eternity, then slowly crossed the street and made the climb up the side of the building, being careful to place his hands and feet where he saw the kid had placed them. Cautiously, he peered over the lip of the window and could see the room was empty. Carefully, he pulled himself up and slipped inside the room. He crept silently across the room and down the hall. The building was old and most likely abandoned. A path in the dirt and dust showed where the kid regularly walked. He followed the path up a flight of stairs to the top floor.

There was a large pile of garbage blocking the hallway. It looked unstable and would likely fall, making a loud noise if someone bumped into it. There seemed to be a path going through it, but the longer he looked at it the less sure he was that someone could make it through without bumping into the garbage pile. It had to be a setup, designed to catch someone trying to sneak in. The path was just wide enough to catch your eye, but he would bet that it would become deceptively narrow once you got far enough in. By the time you realized you couldn't make it through, it would be difficult to turn around. If this was designed by the kid, then he was definitely impressed. There was a lot more to the boy than first appeared.

Suval grinned like a child with a new plaything, and, in a twisted sense, he was. There had to be another way. He began to look around, but the only other things were two large wooden doors. Both had swelled and cracked and warped considerably. Even if he could force one open, the hinges looked so rusty that they would probably let out a loud screech as the parts grind upon each other.

He was missing something. The garbage pile looked like there was a path through it, but that was wrong, or so he believed. It was not what it seemed, and the same could be said about the boy. While he appeared to be just another street kid down on his luck, he was much more. Street kids didn't have his level of caution or strong psychic abilities. He was more than what he seemed. That seemed to be a theme with him.

Suval took a closer look at the doors. The one on the right looked like it could break apart from the force it would take to get it unstuck. The crack ran from the middle of the top to down about halfway. He could peer through it, but only darkness greeted his eyes. The hinges were definitely covered in a thick layer of rust. He crossed the hall and took another look at the other door. This one looked about the same, only the crack ran across it at a diagonal in the lower half. While the hinges were rusty, there was a faint smell. Suval leaned in and sniffed the hinge. Oil. He bent down and took a closer look at the bottom hinge. It was covered in rust but where the pieces met had been scraped clean and oiled. The top hinge, upon inspection, had not been touched. Carefully he slipped his fingers under the bottom of the door where there was a bit of a gap and gave a tug. The bottom half, up to the crack, opened. Clever.

He opened the door further, allowing him to peek through into the room. It was empty, and he carefully slipped through. He paused to listen. Someone was moving in another room and, from the sounds of things, it seemed like there was only one person. Cautiously, he crept forward. Thankfully, there was a ragged and holey curtain separating the two rooms. Pausing again, Suval double checked the curtain. As he figured, he could see several small metal pieces hanging from the other side that would clink together when someone brushed against them. Suval moved the curtain, just enough to see into the other room, which was large and mostly dark. There was a lamp on a stand next to a bed. He could make out a table off to one side that was just at the edge of the lit area. It looked like there was a pile of clothes, maybe dresses on it. The boy yawned as he tugged off his boots and placed them next to his bed. He stretched and then took off his shirt. A shiver ran down Suval's spine. Not from any pleasure at watching the young boy undress, but at the memories of his uncle it evoked. His uncle had liked young boys and had quite the fondness for him, a special fondness that left him feeling hollow afterward. He was about to look away, not out of modesty, for flesh was a source of misery to him, but something caught his eye. The boy's chest was wrapped in a bandage. Odd, he had not moved like someone with a chest injury.

The boy began to slowly unwrap the cloth bandage. His back had been turned towards Suval, and he began to coil up the long bandage. That was when he turned, and Suval saw two small breasts. The cloth was not for a wound but to bind the breasts down and allow her to pass as a male. Suval was stunned and pulled away from the curtain so he could collect his thoughts.

Why on earth would she do that? He could see little advantage to it, especially when you considered her psychic ability and her skill at naturally avoiding detection. She could have easily made a career working with a street gang as a top rate thief. Regardless, she was a find. He smiled at the thought of his new play toy. Tonight would be their first night together: the first of many. Suval waited patiently for the light to go out in the other room. Then, he waited a while longer until he could hear her breathing become regular. He crawled under the curtain, and then walked over to the side of her bed. It was very dark in the room. What little bit of moonlight there was came from a window in another room.

He gazed at her fondly. She was definitely better than punishing whatever servant had failed to delay her and Kerwin from leaving the mansion. Hopefully, Merik wouldn't need him for several nights, and they could be alone together. Suval wanted to reach out and stroke her cheek, but he was afraid it might wake her up. More than likely, she was a light sleeper. He checked the stand next to the bed, and the only two things on it were the lamp and a dagger. It looked to be quite ornate, yet the blade appeared to be very sharp. Whoever made it was a master craftsman. The jewel in the pommel alone would cost a high price. How did she get it? So many mysteries with his new toy.

To his knowledge, his unique ability was the only one that worked on an unconscious mind. He couldn't control anyone's dream, at least not yet, but he could alter it. When they linked, it was as if he was the person dreaming, except he knew it was a dream and there was no emotional attachment to any of it. His manipulation of a dream had been fairly limited. At first, he could only remove things from a dream. As time went by, he could make things speed up or slow down or adjust how much sound something made.

Over time, and with practice, he got quite adept at dream manipulation. The person could have a dream about sitting on a porch, watching the sun go down. Suval could speed up the setting sun to make it night. All sound would be gone except for the noise of the wind, which he made louder. The stars would stop moving in the sky. Then the empty chair next to the person would be gone all of a sudden. This would be more than enough to get a person's mind racing to dark and scary thoughts. If the dream was too much, he ran the risk of them waking up from it and discovering him before he could use his ability to get their gaze to slide off of him.

After a few close calls from people waking up in fright, he learned to back off on the intensity of their dreams. Suval became more subtle and began to change things up enough that it confused the mind but didn't frighten it. Being in a state of constant juxtaposition wore out their mind when it was supposed to be resting. They would wake up feeling tired and emotionally stressed. He, on the other hand, would feel very refreshed, as if he had a great night's sleep.

So, he stood there a moment, avoring the view and purity of her slumber. In the morning, she would awaken exhausted, and the morning after that. Each night of chaotic sleep would wear down her mind bit by bit. She would be different, changed, and not in a good way. Something would be taken from her without her realizing what it was until it was too late, and by then she may not even care. It was interesting, the different ways a mind could snap when it got extremely deprived of rest.

Suval reached out with his mind and caressed hers. She was dreaming of dinner at a restaurant. There were lots of people laughing and joking. It was a happy dream, but it wouldn't stay that way for long. His mental caress turned into a stranglehold and night eventually gave way to the dawn.

CHAPTER 49

BOTUN

"*I was told that you had something to report,*" Botun began.

"*Yes. Last night Lord Merik sent Suval to follow some people.*" Vera replied.

"*Who were they?*"

"*The one was a merchant, named Kerwin, who is new to the city. He had met with Lord Merik a few days ago. Kerwin is staying at an inn near the Merchant's Courtyard, but I am not sure which one. The other was a servant who I am guessing was hired to help carry the trunk that was brought to the second meeting, which was yesterday.*"

"*Any idea of what was in that trunk?*"

"*Books, scrolls, and other old papers. Kerwin is some kind of rare book dealer. He had brought a trunk full of books for Lord Merik to look at. I do know that Merik had a stack of old books placed in the room where they were going to meet.*"

"*Do you remember any of the titles or what they were about?*"

"*Unfortunately, I didn't get to see the books myself. I happened to see another servant carry a stack of books earlier that day. Later, when I went to clean a room, the books were there. I was told that this room had already been cleaned and that I should go somewhere else. I lucked out and found a couple of rooms in that wing of the mansion that needed cleaning. I took care of them and was able to keep an eye on who came and went on that floor. One of those rooms had a stack of books and manuscripts on a table, and I did get to look at them a bit. They were old books about the Kysian Empire. The manuscripts looked like records of trials that were held during the time of the empire. Nothing exciting, and pretty common stuff, such as a young girl who seduced a merchant, both were found guilty of adultery and sentenced to death. An awfully harsh sentence for fooling around, if you ask me.*"

"*I am told that betrayal of any kind was sternly dealt with by the empire. Since the merchant betrayed his spouse, he forfeited his life, or so it seems.*"

"*Anyway, I set about cleaning that room. I made sure the door was left ajar so I could hear anyone coming down the hallway. A short while later, Kerwin and his servant arrived. One of the other servants was helping his servant carrying the trunk. I know this, because I peeped out the door after they had passed. About an hour later, a servant came into the room as I was about done cleaning and took the stack of books and left. I waited a bit, then followed, and saw that they went to the room with the other books. I am guessing that's where Kerwin was.*"

"*How long was the meeting?*"

"A few hours. After they left, a servant fetched Suval. I was starting to leave when another of Lord Merik's servants saw me and ordered me to delay Kerwin and his servant. I ran off to do as I was told, but I had slipped going down the stairs and fell, hitting my head along the way. By the time I had recovered enough to walk, they were already on their way. I was about to head back into the mansion when Suval came out at a swift pace. When he saw that they had left, he swore under his breath and then headed out after them."

"So he was sent to follow them?"

"I think so," Vera said.

"Did he try to hide?" Botun asked.

"No. He walked down the middle of the road and then… you know, I am not sure. I remember watching him walk away, and then I was looking at something else at the side of the road. I must have hit my head harder than I first realized. I am sorry that I can't remember any more."

"That's fine. You did well to bring this to my attention. We know very little about Suval and why Merik keeps him close. Given what I have learned in the few reports I have heard about the man, it makes very little sense for him to be held in such regard."

"Well, I can tell you that none of us servants like him one bit. He is creepy as hell. Several of us have seen him watching us from a distance. One servant said she overheard Lord Merik tell him he can't use his powers around us."

"Do you know what powers he has?"

"Not a clue, but, then again, I try to avoid being around him at all costs."

"Things are getting more intense, and I will be having you report to someone else in the near future. I will bring them along the next time I collect a report from you, so you can be familiar with them."

"Ok."

"The work you are doing is important. Keep it up."

"Thanks. By the way, some of the servant's were talking this morning. I doubt if it is important, but one of them said the young man, who came with Kerwin, was called Liam."

"Liam? Describe him."

"Young man in the middle of his second decade. He was thin, and slight of frame, with short black hair. Is he important?"

"Maybe. Let me know if he comes back."

"Ok, I will."

Botun headed down the street away from the mansion. Vera's report was troubling. There was very little known about Suval. He didn't seem like the rest of Merik's inner circle. Captain Tianna and Erlin were both unusually powerful with their psychic abilities. More than likely, Suval was powerful in something, too. He probably had the ability not to be recognized, which would make sense why there were few reports about him. It would also give credence to why Merik wouldn't let him use his powers in the mansion, since Suval could use that ability to spy on or assassinate Merik. There was an account that was given to him that said Suval was seen walking down the streets of Crestburn with Jenal. The two were walking together, and Jenal appeared to be drunk or disorientated.

Jenal had stopped meeting with people right before the takeover. Botun had grown suspicious of the man and started having him watched, more than normal. It took a while to find someone he could trust not to go running to Jenal, after all the man paid very handsomely for information. He thought that Jenal had been plotting something behind Djinar's back. Botun had decided to make some changes with the guards as an added precaution. Guards were moved to new and less familiar areas to watch and patrol. Nobody would find this suspicious, as it was done a few times each year. Extra guards patrols were placed near the mansion and, when the attack happened, they were able to get to the mansion quickly. It was this thinking that probably saved his life on the night of the attack. If only he had realized the Jenal was not betraying them but had become compromised, things might have gone better for them.

As it was, somehow, Suval managed to compromise Jenal. There were several rumors that Suval had a new undiscovered power, but those could be dismissed immediately as flights of fantasy. Claims of new powers have been around for hundreds of years. The people who made the claims were either outright liars or fools. Occasionally, some were clever enough to use things to make it seem like they had a new power, be it an accomplice or simple misdirection. Those who were successful at convincing others that they had a new power were usually dealt with by a neighboring psylord who viewed their new power, real or imagined, as a threat.

It was not surprising that people claimed that Suval had a new power. The man had managed to go unnoticed by Jenal's spy network. More than likely, he was just extremely powerful at not being recognized. It would fit with the others of Merik's inner circle. With strength in that ability, he could have gotten close to Jenal and done something to him. Poison him? If Suval was a skilled herbalist, he could have gotten close and slowly drugged Jenal with something that took time to take effect. Such an idea was a stretch but not impossible.

Regardless of his powers and their strengths, Suval was dangerous because there was so little known about him. Other than taking out Jenal, Merik had not used Suval. Meanwhile, Tianna and Erlin were busy handling day to day operations of running the city. There had to be something special about this Kerwin fellow for Merik to summon Suval. He could check with a street beggar that he knew, who was an excellent source of information. Jenal used him as one of his main sources of information about what was happening around the inns, because the man was good at getting the street kids to tell him things. Often, the kids would be hired by visiting merchants as guides and porters, and they were familiar with who was coming and going. They would report what they learned to the beggar, and he would pay them for their information. Jenal figured the man made more money begging and collecting information than half the merchants did selling their wares in the Merchant's Courtyard.

Botun made his way down alleys and through side streets until he got close to the inns that ringed the Merchant's Courtyard. After a couple of minutes of searching, he found a group of young boys hanging out near the mouth of an alley. As he approached them, he made sure his head was covered by the cloak despite the day's heat. The boys' conversation drew to a halt as he neared them. He drew out a coin and tossed it to them.

"I need to speak with the old beggar," Botun said.

None of them touched the coin, and they looked at him silently. "There are lots of beggars in this city. Which one do you want? I can bring back a beggar or two."

Botun tossed down a couple more coins. "There is only one beggar who I want. He has a scar across his temple and he's missing the little finger on his left hand. Dark gray matted hair."

"I think I know who you are talking about," the street kid replied.

He held out another coin and said, "Get him and it's yours."

The boy nodded to one of the others, who scooped up the money and then took off down the street. Botun waited silently, and the boys eventually began to talk amongst themselves but not loud enough for him to make out what they were saying. After several minutes, the boy came back and held out his hand. When Botun placed the coin in it he said, "He is on his way." With a nod to the other boys, he turned and left. They followed behind him, probably to take up their residence for the day at a different alley. Once again, he sat and waited.

As quick as the boy had been, he thought his wait wouldn't belong. For almost an hour, he stood in the alley sweating under the hood of the cloak. It was much too hot to be doing this. He had to start trusting others to gather information for him. Eventually, he was going to get spotted. Someone would either recognize him or get curious why a cloaked man was walking around on such a hot day and report it to the guards. There was a nice reward for anyone who turned him into Merik, a reward that had been increased again.

"Nice day," croaked a raspy voice from behind him. He turned and saw the beggar hobbling down the alley.

"Took you long enough."

The man snorted. "I see the heat has made you irritable, my friend." He gave a ragged cough and slouched against a wall. "What do you want?"

"Information about a recent arrival to Crestburn. A book merchant, or antique dealer, named Kerwin. He was staying at one of the inns near here. I want to know which one, as well as anything else you can find about the man."

The beggar gave a toothy smile and nodded. "That won't be a problem. I can have the information that you need in a couple of hours. This day will only get hotter my friend. Will I be giving this information to you or a friend, or would you rather wait till the evening when being all cloaked up won't be near the issue?"

"The early evening will be fine with me. I have other affairs to attend to." He dropped a pouch of coins on the ground and walked away. The man was right; it was indeed going to be a hot day, and he had to get inside before he died under this cloak."

CHAPTER 50

MERIK

"Where the hell is Suval?" Merik shouted at Tianna and Erlin. Tianna just shrugged her shoulders, which infuriated Merik even more.

"He was gone by the time my men got there. The guards watching the inn said that he had left right away to follow the boy Kerwin was with," she replied.

"Why didn't you try and find where he went, Captain?"

"Sir, we tried. Suval is good at avoiding detection. It was one of the reasons you chose to work with him."

"I know why I work with him. You don't need to tell me why I do things. I know perfectly well why I do what I chose to do."

"My Lord," Erlin interjected. "Suval will show back up, eventually. I have alerted all of my heralds to report any sightings of him to me immediately. They are also instructed to tell him to report to you immediately. I know that Captain Tianna has done the same with her city guards."

"Her guards? Is she the ruler of Crestburn?" Merik asked.

"No, my lord. You are the ruler of Crestburn. I only meant that they serve under her at your pleasure. No offense was meant."

Merik stared at him, before he turned and stomped across the room. He fixed himself a drink in hopes it would help calm him down. Thankfully, Djinar had an unmatched supply of drinks. Most rooms had several crystal decanters filled with something strong and tasty. Since moving into the mansion, he started drinking more, and why not. He was the Lord of Crestburn, and there was a lot of pressure in running a city and preparing for the next phase of his plans. Besides, the whiskey was strong and smooth, and there was no sense in letting the fine liquor go to waste.

He finished a glass, poured another one, and took a long pull from it before he turned around.

"The guards have several prisoners in their custody, correct?" Merik asked.

Both Erlin and Tianna nodded, but not before sparing the other a quick concerned glance.

"What are they guilty of?" Merik inquired.

"Right now, sir, they are not guilty of anything. In the holding cells, we have a suspected pickpocket, a couple of smugglers, and a guy who beat up someone in a tavern last night." Tianna responded.

"Wasn't there a couple of people who got into a fight with my guards at a tavern the other night?"

"Yes."

"Why weren't they mentioned?"

"Because, it was our guards who initiated the conflict. The guards who were involved have already been disciplined," she replied.

"I want those people found and brought to justice. I will not allow my guards to be attacked and the people get away with it."

"But, sir, those guards were off duty. They were…"

"I don't give a damn if they were patrolling or at home with their families!" Merik shouted. He took another drink and slammed the glass down on the stand next to a chair. "During the Kysian Empire, a warden was always on duty. We are trying to rebuild the Kysian Empire, so it seems to me that our guards should be considered always on duty."

"Excuse me for interjecting, my Lord Merik, but I thought you were going to select a group of the best guards to become the new wardens. It would stand to reason that those people would be considered always at work," interjected Erlin.

Merik stared at him until he stopped. "I know what I said, Erlin. I know what it is that I wish to do, what I need to do in order to reestablish the Kysian Empire. The law of the land must be respected. A clear message must be sent out to all of those who oppose me. " he shifted his gaze to Tianna as he continued, "That none will challenge what I am doing here. I will accomplish what no one else has been able to do. I believed that this was possible, but I now know that it will be a reality. I learned something the other night. Something great, and I will make sure that everything is done in order to preserve my rule of this city, for without me they will not come."

"They?" inquired a puzzled Erlin.

"Don't worry about them. You will learn in time. As for the men involved in the tavern brawl, I want them rounded up and their punishment dealt with publicly. I want this done as soon as possible. Also, I have been informed that our men were fined for their involvement in the fight. That will not be happening. Our guards were fighting to preserve our reputation and our good name. Captain, I want you to apologize to each one and make sure they get a bonus. Let them know that I personally appreciate their hard work and loyalty."

Tianna stood there, not saying anything.

"Do we have a problem with this, Captain?"

"I," Tianna paused and responded, slowly choosing her words carefully, for she knew she was in danger of challenging his authority "am concerned that reversing their discipline would undermine our authority."

Merik laughed. "It would only undermine your authority since it was you who gave the order to fine them. Normally, that is how things are done, but, as I have told you many times, my ways are not the traditional ways. I greatly value loyalty, and those loyal will always be rewarded. Those who challenge my authority will be punished. Somehow, you have forgotten that. Perhaps being in charge of the city guards is too much of a responsibility for you?"

"No, sir," she growled.

"Then do as I say, and let me know once all of the dissonances from the bar fight are rounded up. I will make sure that everyone in Crestburn knows that I mean business."

CHAPTER 51

JARIEK

Jariek had been waiting for an hour and was beginning to get worried. Neither Kerwin nor Liam had shown up at the appointed time. Not that he was expecting Liam to be there, but he wouldn't have been surprised if the youth found a way to get himself included. He would stick around a little longer, then head over to the inn where Kerwin was staying. Hopefully, there was a reasonable explanation for him being late. Kerwin would chastise him for being paranoid and thinking that his tardiness was due to more extreme reasons. The meeting time was fairly early, and it was possible that things went late into the night, especially if Merik had something worth catching the interest of the Cashek Society. There he went again, thinking that Merik was indeed what the society was looking for after all these years. He would receive an earful from Kerwin if he knew that he had entertained such a thought.

The next several minutes passed slowly as he tried to curb his imagination. There were no signs of Kerwin, or even a message that plans had changed. He didn't have much more time to wait until he had to be back at Master Gerwald's aviary. If he hustled, he could go to the inn and check on Kerwin. Normally, that would be frowned upon, but he could always use an animal to do his checking and no one would be the wiser.

Thankfully, they had chosen an outdoor cafe as their meeting spot. He searched the area and found a bird resting on a gable. Possessing the bird, he had it hop off the roof and fly to the inn. He was there in no time and landed near the room. The bird hopped over and peaked in the window. Two men he had never seen before were busy packing everything into his trunks. Kerwin didn't have much. It wasn't long before they were done packing and hauled the trunks out to the street.

Jariek had the bird fly off to an eve across the street, which provided a better view of the front of the inn. The men loaded Kerwin's trunks into the back of a wagon and drove off. Taking flight, he followed the wagon as it headed through town. He cast his gaze about and saw that they were heading straight towards the mansion. This was not good. Thankfully, he had been able to get to the room before they had it cleaned out. Hopefully, Kerwin was an invited guest at the mansion and not a prisoner. This hope died as the carriage was let in without question and the trunks were unloaded in a rear door.

It was possible that he was jumping to conclusions, but his instincts told him otherwise. Letting go of control of the bird, his own senses greeted him. He got up and set a quick pace for the aviary. It would be late afternoon before he would get free time to check out the mansion for signs of Kerwin. He prayed that he was overreacting to the situation as Kerwin had often chastised him about.

If Kerwin had become compromised, then he would have to alert the Cashek Society right away. They would send a warden to remedy the situation. That was the last thing he wanted, because their solutions tended towards the terminal side. Wardens existed to keep the society safe, and that meant removing anything that threatens the Cashek Society's secrecy. That thought sent shivers down his spine and was the main reason he decided to hold off for a day or two, until he could find out what exactly happened to Kerwin. If he contacted the Second Caravan now, they would send word back to the society and a warden would be immediately dispatched. Even if Kerwin turned out to be ok, the warden wouldn't return until they were satisfied with the situation.

He could wait a day or two. If Kerwin was a prisoner, then help would eventually come and rescue him. Operatives were trained to handle being a prisoner and deal with questioning. The nice thing was that they knew they would eventually be rescued, and that lent them the strength to hold out. Shortly after Kerwin arrived in town, several members of the second caravan took up an extended residence in the city as well. They would stay until Kerwin moved on, and then go onto their next assignment. Their sole purpose was to quickly relay messages from the operative to the society, should time be a crucial factor.

Another apprentice greeted him as he entered the aviary. Jariek gave a curt nod as a response and immediately set to work. The others tried to engage him in small talk, but his meager responses served as his message that he wished to be left alone. At supper, he ate swiftly and was back to work before the rest. Once the last of his chores were done, he washed quickly and headed out.

The sun was setting, and he had to hurry because most birds didn't have great night vision. He found a quiet alley,went down about half way, and began to scatter seed about. Jariek retired to the mouth of the alley and waited. It wasn't long before a bird came by to enjoy the seed he had laid out. Just as it landed, it took off, but this time it was under his control. Quickly, he flew over to the mansion and began to scout the grounds. For the next hour, he had the bird dart from branch to windowsill and back to branch again. He couldn't find any sign of Kerwin at all.

CHAPTER 52

ASHA

Asha struggled to get out of bed. She was exhausted. Her dreams had been very strange last night. They weren't bad dreams, per se, but definitely messed up. It was very fitful sleep, so she woke up exhausted. She tried to go back to sleep, but every time the dreams would start up again. Eventually, she gave up and got out of bed. She could function with a night of bad sleep. There had been many nights in the past, when she was first living on the streets, where she had gotten little or no sleep at night.

She grabbed the wrap that she had used the day before and began to bind her chest. Her breasts were by no means large, but they were still more than a young boy possessed, if just barely. Once that was finished, she grabbed the second set of clothes that Kerwin had bought her and got dressed. A quick glance out the window and the sun's position let her know that the day was well on its way to noon. She had slept later than she thought.

Asha grabbed a few more things, left her room, and went to the floor below. At the large open window, she scanned the alley to make sure no one was around to see her and scampered down the side of the building. Her hands and feet knew which bricks to move to from memory. Once, she did it with her eyes closed, just to prove to herself that she could do it.

Her stomach grumbled, and she stopped at a fruit merchant to grab a quick bite to eat. She kept it light, because she knew she would be able to talk Kerwin into buying her lunch, even if he didn't have a need for her that day. That was why she suggested that they meet at noon. It also gave him time to meet with the young man from the aviary. She wasn't sure what their deal was, but she knew they shared a secret, and she was determined to find out what it was.

She made it to the inn early, sat down in the common room, and waited. Asha had chosen a spot where she could see the front door so she could see Kerwin when he came back from his meeting with Jariek. The innkeeper scowled at her, but didn't say anything. He knew that she had been hired by Kerwin as a porter, and he would tolerate her presence if she kept quiet and to herself.

Patiently, she waited. Eventually, people came in and started ordering meals for their lunch. Asha got up and went upstairs to knock on Kerwin's door. No response. She waited and knocked again. Nothing. She tried the handle, but the door was locked. He must not have come back from his meeting with Jariek, or whatever business he had that day. Damn, so much for a free lunch.

Asha went down the stairs and asked the innkeeper if Maester Kerwin had left any messages for her. The man shook his head and asked if she intended to order anything, since she had been sitting there for so long. Toying with the idea of asking if she could put a meal on Kerwin tab, she decided against it. Most likely the grim innkeeper wouldn't go for it. She left the inn and found a place a few buildings down where she could watch for Kerwin to come back.

It was a hot day, and a few times she started to doze off. She would jerk awake with a start as bizarre dreams came again. Most of her afternoon was spent watching the inn and fighting off sleep. When the merchants began to make their way home, she decided to go back and try Kerwin's room again. Perhaps she had dozed off longer than she thought and Kerwin had gone back to his room unnoticed. The inn was busier than when she had been in earlier. She crossed the room, went up to the stairs, and again tried the door without any luck. Well, she would have to try again tomorrow.

Her stomach growled in discontent. All she had eaten that day was a small piece of fruit. There was a shop not too far away that served spiced noodles with chunks of meat and vegetables. She ate at the counter, slurping down her noodles. Today was a bust. When she got back to her place, there were a few outfits that needed work done to them. Her Lucky Liam clothes needed a good cleaning after the sweat she had worked up while trying to avoid Hargod. It was flattering that he tried to capture her as his claim to fame with the new psylord.

Her escape would form another set of stories about Lucky Liam's incredible luck. Who could have imagined that a horse would have gone wild and attacked? She was surprised by that too, but for different reasons. The horse had a psychic cloud around its head. It had taken a moment for the shock to wear off for her to realize and accept it for what it was. She had looked at her rescuers and saw that the young man had a matching cloud around his head. Apparently, he could control animals.

He was like her. Jariek possessed a new ability. Perhaps that was why Kerwin was in town meeting with him. If so, then how did Merik fall into the mix? Did he have a new ability, too? She did check, when the meeting started, but after they had started reading their books, she dropped the ability and focused on not being noticed by him. Perhaps that had been a mistake. During their next meeting, she will make sure to use her power to see if he had any new abilities the entire time. She would do the same with Kerwin. It was a shame that she could only see abilities when people used them.

As for Jariek, Asha wondered what she should do. A part of her wanted to reach out to him and let the young man know that she was like him. That he wasn't alone and could have someone to share his secret with. Then again, that might already be known to him. It was satisfying to know that there was someone else like her in the world. Someone with a new power, and the burden of keeping it a secret.

She knew Jariek could control animals, but could he do it with other powers, too, if he had any others, that is? A lot of powers would be useless with animals, but some, like clairvoyance, could be pretty amazing. Telepathy would be weird, because how did an animal communicate with a human's mind? It was no wonder that the young man chose to work at an aviary. Asha would definitely give any bird watching her a second look to see if they acted human. Then again, what would a human acting bird look like? She shook her head and decided she needed to get some sleep. Such bizarre thoughts were probably a product of lack of sleep. Even though she had plenty of work that should be done on her outfits, she could always do them tomorrow. Besides, if she got to bed early then she could catch up on her sleep, wake up early tomorrow, and get the outfits taken care of before she checked in with Kerwin at noon.

Asha made her way back home. Once there, she began to lay out the outfits that she would be working on in the morning, as well as the needles and thread to sew with. She stopped several times to yawn but eventually got everything laid out. This would save her a good deal of time tomorrow. Sewing required precision that she just didn't have tonight, but laying out clothes, even as sloppy as she did, was doable. She stripped down, got into bed, closed her eyes, and was once again chased by her dreams. All through the night, she tossed and turned. A few times she almost woke up.

CHAPTER 53

SUVAL

Asha, as he learned her name to be from her dreams, had two main types of recurring dreams. In one, she was lost on the streets with nowhere to go. Cold. Abandoned. Alone. The other one, which she was currently dreaming about, was about growing up in the hareem. In these, the figure of her mother haunts her and tells her she is not good enough - not woman enough - and that no man would desire her. Occasionally, her mother would ignore her but, more often than not, she would constantly disapprove of Asha.

It took Suval very little effort to stir up her dreams. She had enough horrible experiences that her mind and sense of self were a wreck. At first, he just watched and let her own subconscious do her harm. Through this, he was able to learn a good deal about her. She was like him in so many ways. They both suffered abuse from the hands of family members, both did not get along with their peers, and both were outcasts and loners. While he had been sexually abused, Asha had been trained at a young age to seduce and please others. There were times her dreams almost made him sick to watch.

Eventually, he grew bored with just watching. When she dreamed about her training, Suval made sure to make her mother appear a bit larger, brighter, and harder to ignore. Her mouth's voice would be loud and seem to resonate from everywhere at once. Whenever Asha looked at her own body, Suval would make her skin duller in color and her voice softer. With the abandonment dreams, he would darken things and increase the volume of rats and roaches as they moved along the streets. He would make people move slower and their faces less visible.

Now, she was dreaming of her mother. Asha was sitting at a table, trying to sew a pocket inside one of her new skirts. It was orange, something that wouldn't stand out, but nice enough that she would look good in it. Suval leached the color from it, until it was a faded, greyish peach color. As she sewed, her mother stood behind her, scowling down at her. Suval made her taller than normal. She towered over Asha as she pointed out her mistakes. He dimmed the light around the table and brightened it behind her mother, so that her shadow darkened the table even more. It became a real, oppressive weight over Asha.

She pointed down at a stitch that Asha just finished.

"Look at that, stupid girl." Her voice boomed across the empty room, echoing off the walls, so it was the only thing Asha could hear. "That will never hold."

The crooked stitch was bright orange, like the original skirt, and stood out in stark contrast to the faded material around it.

"You're pathetic. You can't even sow a simple pocket. No wonder you could never please a man. Who would want a worthless soul like you."

Tear drops left dark splotches on the fabric as Asha cried in shame and frustration while she stared at her failed sewing through blurry eyes.

How many times had he cried in his dreams, too, Suval wondered. He knew it was far more than he could count. It amazed him that their trauma was so similar. His was because his uncle wanted him for physical pleasures, while hers was because she was told that she was not wanted and desired. Their desires, or lack of, for their bodies was the cage that tormented them. Two different sides of the same coin.

CHAPTER 54

KERWIN

The room was cold, dark, and windowless. So far, they had left him alone. The only time Kerwin saw anyone was when a group of guards came in to give him his meals, twice a day so far, as well as emptying out his chamber pot. Kerwin wasn't sure why there were four of them whenever they came. Perhaps they thought he was dangerous. Two always stood guard at the door while one brought him food and water and the last took care of his chamber pot.

They never spoke, nor did they acknowledge his presence in any way. Their behavior was odd, to say the least. Over the years, he had been captured and made prisoner a few times. Only on one of those occasions had a warden been called in to rescue him. The other times, he had waited until an opportunity presented itself and then made the best of it.

His calm, patient demeanor typically threw off whoever was holding him captive. Most prisoners begged, talked, or something. It was unnerving to have a person just sit there, calmly waiting, or so he had been told during his training. The Cashek Society had made sure he was ready for most situations, including being a prisoner. Kerwin had spent several weeks as a mock prisoner, being beaten, tortured, and humiliated. It had been awful, but he survived and was grateful for the experience because it made being a real prisoner a lot more bearable.

In a way, he never had it so good as a prisoner. His food was bland meat, bread, and cheese with a pitcher of water. The room was bare, but he did have a straw mattress and a blanket. By now, Jariek had probably alerted the second caravan members of his disappearance and a warden would be soon dispatched.

Kerwin occupied his time by reviewing his last meeting with Merik over and over again, trying to find out if there was some kind of clue for his capture. His words had been careful and he was sure that his expressions were controlled. Each time he replayed their meeting, he couldn't find anything that would have caused Merik to react with his imprisonment.

Merik's notes that he had taken on his fragment of Palreon's manuscript showed that he had started to figure things out. It was possible that Merik knew a lot more than he was letting on. The manuscript didn't possess enough material to give away the Casheek Society's existence. If the man had dealt with another operative, then it was possible, even if unlikely, that he had pieced together enough of the clues to know that there was an organization out there waiting to help rebuild the Kysian Empire. It was a bit of a stretch, but Kerwin couldn't come up with a better explanation.

If that was true, then what was the reasoning behind his imprisonment? Why didn't Merik reach out and try to inform him that he knew of their existence? It seemed foolish to imprison a messenger of a group you were seeking help from. Maybe he wasn't seeking help. What if Merik was planning on going against the Cashek Society? Then, he could use him for information, or so he thought, to gain an advantage over them. It was foolish to wage war against someone you didn't know. If Merik wanted to take Cashek Society on, then he would be in desperate need of information.

Kerwin couldn't blame Merik for not trusting the Cashek Society's intention. The world was home to psychics who used their abilities to subjugate those around them. Psylords took what they wanted and stayed in power until someone stronger or more clever eliminated them. It was survival of the deadliest, and a bit of paranoia and mistrust went a long way with helping a person survive. Most alliances only lasted only as long as one couldn't betray the other.

It was possible that Merik was saving him as a hostage. That would explain why he was being treated in a tolerable manner. He might even believe that the act of capturing and imprisoning a member of the Cashek Society would serve as a warning to them, that he was not a man to be trifled with or possibly even used as a bargaining piece. There had been psylords in the past that had traded people who were important to them to another psylord to serve as both hostage and a promise to keep an alliance.

The Cashek Society would not hesitate to eliminate people who stumbled upon their existence. If Merik knew about them, then it was possible that those who served him knew as well. There was no telling how many people under him knew. It was possible that enough people knew of the society that the act of eliminating them could expose their existence. The society would have to be cautious with how they handled Merik, and that would give him more time and chances to deal with them from a position of power. They definitely would want to know how much he knew about them before they acted against him.

None of his ideas mattered anyway. There were just too many unknown variables right now. Soon, a warden would rescue him, and then the Cashek Society would have to decide how to deal with Merik. That is, if the warden doesn't straight out kill Merik for knowing about their existence. It would be their luck that they finally found someone who would eventually meet their criteria for rebuilding the empire, only to have a warden kill him because he knew too much about them before they could make that decision.

Kerwin wondered how many times a similar scenario played out in the past, only to have the Cashek Society cover up their mistake. It wouldn't surprise him if this wasn't the first time. He tried to recall from his days of training if there had been anything from the histories that might have hinted at such a thing. Nothing came to mind, but that really didn't mean much. Kerwin was quite sure that the council's zeal for secrecy would apply to its own members, especially given how they controlled what was taught.

If he got out of this mess, he may have to do some poking around in the archives for old mission reports. The council recorded everything and, at this point, there were almost more volumes about the Cashek Society than there were about the Kysian Empire. Granted, most of the collection were reports with little value to most people. If the society had been in this situation before, then there would be a record of it. All he had to do was find it. For as long as he could remember, there had been rumors of a hidden archive that was only for the council. He had dismissed it as paranoid fantasy but, lately, had begun to entertain such thoughts himself. His disillusionment with the society and its purpose had caused him to question a lot of things over the last several months.

CHAPTER 55

TIANNA

It had been no problem for her guards to round up those involved in the bar fight. As to the guards who had been a part of it, she had Sergeant Herlt give them the news that they were not going to have their pay docked - by order of Lord Merik. He had not taken the news well. Herlt thought she had been too easy on the guards in the first place. When he had been informed of Merik's orders, he let out a string of profanity and colorful word combinations that made her mind balk that anyone could come up with such unique obscenities. As it was, he would probably find out that she had Herlt tell them the news instead of doing it in person, as Merik commanded.

Eventually, he stopped and stood there, waiting for her to continue. As she told him about Merik's other order, to round up the citizens who had been a part of the fight, he looked like he was about to burst. She was surprised that he hadn't snapped a tooth or two with how tightly his jaws had been clenched. He had asked permission to speak freely, which, naturally, she granted, but Tianna doubted there was anything he was going to say that she didn't already agree with or could change. Herlt just nodded and, for a moment, she thought she detected a bit of sadness in his eyes.

"I told you a while ago to watch yourself, Captain. If you weren't careful you might find yourself in a position where Merik deemed you a threat. Those men were fighting to protect your name, not his," he told her. She replied with a curt nod and dismissed him. There was no fear that he would betray what he felt while carrying out her orders. Sergeant Herlt was a man who took his job, and it's duties, very seriously. She was a bit surprised at the bond the two had formed and wasn't quite sure why he had chosen to be at her side. He could have easily obtained a better position with Merik than what he currently had.

Tianna wished she had listened to him better. He had been dead on with his assessment of Merik. It seemed like Merik took it as a personal insult that guards had been willing to start a brawl over her honor as opposed to his. The funny thing is, had the drunks in the tavern been bad mouthing him instead, the guards probably would have done the same. Now, he was upset and doing what he could to curry favor with the guards and remind everyone what she was.

Tianna stared down at the orders on her desk. Merik had decided what to do with those who took part in the bar fight. He was going to use them as an example not to be critical of his rule, and, as an added bonus, she would be lowered in the eyes of not only the guards but all of Crestburn. If people weren't already whispering things about her behind closed doors, they definitely would after today.

Not for the first time, she wondered if it was all worth it. Perhaps Merik was right, and her obsession with the duel was pure foolishness. His ability to pull memories was the only reason she was with him. No, that wasn't true. He had given her a chance when everyone else saw a disgraced bandit with a bounty on her head. Loyalty was something Tianna had always believed in, and it was hard for her to let go of that, especially with Merik. At times, it angered her that she was so loyal to him when he berated her or openly used her. There had been a time when she thought about walking away from it all and being on her own again, even though the idea terrified her. Then, he would meet with her and somehow restore her sense of loyalty to him. It didn't hurt that he could go through her memories so that she could finally get to the bottom of what happened with the duel.

Now, she was in a position of power, and she had responsibilities. The people who served under her meant something to her. At first, she was just another mercenary that Merik had found, but she had quickly shown her skills as a leader. Those who were in the city guard before Merik's take over had finally started to not only respect her but like her as well. Never would she have guessed those guards would be willing to get into a bar fight over her honor. It was hard for her to fine the men, but she knew that it was more important for her to set an example than to feed her ego by letting them off easy. Thanks to the guards' loyalty to her, things have gone from bad to worse, and there was no way out of it without opposing Merik.

She survived as a marked person because of her unusual strength in controlling people's bodies. Tianna hadn't tried to fool herself. That wasn't the reason, at least not the only reason, she had been able to survive while all others had succumbed to the bounties the mark represented. Now that she knew there were new powers, she was afraid. For the first time, she was afraid, and she didn't like that feeling. She didn't like what Merik's orders made her feel, but that was better than death, which was a possibility for her if she struck out on her own. It was possible that someone with a new power would be able to eliminate her. Without knowing what kind of new powers existed, there was no way for her to prepare against them. She could be killed and never see it coming.

True, someone with a bow could just as easily end her life, but her reputation had made assassination attempts extremely rare. If the arrow missed, the person who fired it was as good as dead. Before they could draw another arrow, she would be in control of the assassin's body. There would never be a second chance against her.

Once, a group in another city had tried to ambush her. They thought that several archers on the rooftop would be all it took. She had spotted one of the attackers, who hadn't kept out of sight very well. As soon as she spotted him, she took control of his body and made him jump off the roof. Tianna continued walking down the street without missing a step while he found himself back in control of his body mid-jump. At that point, there was nothing he could do but scream as he fell to the street. People turned to look just in time to see him hit. The other assassins were startled by the commotion and, by the time they realized that she was on to them, Tianna had already disappeared into a shop. It had taken practice, but she had become very fast with domination. People often assumed that in order to be effective at controlling another's body, they had to stay in possession of it for more than a second or two. Sometimes, all it took was a few seconds. A dropped weapon or a jump, and what was set into motion would take longer to correct than the initiating action. Tianna's proficiency made her quick. Often, it happened so fast that people didn't realize what was going on until it was too late.

When the archers missed her going into the shop, their fates were sealed. Tianna had snuck out the back of the shop and went down a few streets. Once she was a safe enough distance away, she climbed up to the roof. Carefully, she crept along the rooftops, making sure that she didn't make the same mistake as the man now laying in a broken heap in the street. A few buildings over, she found another assassin. Tianna drew her blade and hid in the shadows.

She was just barely able to see the assassin. Not for the first time, she wished she had clairvoyance. If she could see out of her subject's eyes, then she would have had a much easier time aiming his bow well enough to have him shoot his allies. Even with not having the best of aim, she still used the bow to her advantage. Carefully, Tianna had made the man draw his bow and shoot down into the street near a stall selling baskets. The arrow had embedded itself into the wooden pole by the vendor's head. It had been closer to the innocent man than she intended.

The pottery vendor screamed and ducked down. People near him looked around and, upon noticing the arrow, screamed as well and started to run to safety. Others quickly joined them in panic, and the street erupted in chaos. Her assailants peaked from their hiding places to look down at the streets to see if they could find her, believing that their ally had taken a shot at her. She made the man she controlled point down to the streets and the others leaned over for a better look.

She counted four more. Tianna let go of the man she was controlling and, one by one made, each of the others jumped off the building. It was boring and unimaginative, but it worked. When the first one was screaming as he fell to the street, the second one had already started to jump. The third tried to get out of her line of sight, but he wasn't fast enough. The fourth found safety, but she repossessed the guy nearest her and had him fire arrows in the vicinity of the one who had hidden. The arrows didn't come close to striking him, but it was enough to unnerve him and caused him to flee from cover to get away. He, too, jumped from the roof.

Tianna stood up and walked to the last man. She made him turn so that he faced her. Even though she controlled his body, she could see the fear in his eyes.

"Tell everyone you see what happens when you try to claim the bounty on me. Let them all know how quickly I dominated them and made every one of your team jump from the roof to be broken on the streets below."

Then, she made him jump too. Unlike his friends, he was lucky, for he had a message to deliver and, for that, she needed him alive. He landed in the booth of a basket merchant, which helped break his fall, along with several bones. Tianna took her leave of the city that night and hid for a while. The survivor had talked and, before his wounds had healed, word had spread wide about what had happened. While it did reduce the number of attempts to get her, the ones who did try were much more skilled.

Tianna pulled herself from the memories. That night had been quite some time ago. Life with Kour's mark had hardened her quickly. While she had never been opposed to violence and death, they became a way of life - no way of survival. That wasn't life. What she had here in Crestburn was life, but Merik was about to change that for her. After today, she would again be an instrument of death, and it would probably stay that way for quite some time.

CHAPTER 56

ASHA

Asha got up from her bed and staggered across the room. She couldn't remember the last time she had been this exhausted. Normally, she didn't recall her dreams in the morning. This was not the case today, and she wished desperately that she could forget about them. Although, she wasn't sure if that would make any difference. Her bed was in disarray from all the tossing and turning that she had done. She had the sinking feeling that even if she didn't recall the dreams, she still would not be rested from her sleep.

Ever the paranoid one, she searched her place for signs that someone had been there. After her search turned up empty, she chided herself for being a fool. There was no ability that could mess with a person's dream, let alone affect them in their sleep. Sometimes she wondered if she was extra worried about new abilities because she had one. What if there was someone else like her and they saw her using her detection ability. They could then... she shook her head and cleared her mind of paranoid thoughts.

Abandonment and living on the streets were more than enough to give anyone issues. Though, on top of that, the burden of keeping a new ability secret, as well as being a gatherer of other people's secrets, it was like adding more wood to a fire. More like a whole cartload of wood. Granted, she did other things for income but gathering secrets would keep her with money long after she quit being Lucky Liam.

As a young girl out on the streets, there had been few opportunities for her to earn money. Having been raised in Djinar's harem, she had been trained in the art of seduction, even if she hated using those skills. She detested the idea of selling herself for physical pleasure, and that reduced her options for earning money. Still, hunger had driven her to make use of her skills. Eventually, she learned how to steal, but that had its own dangers. It was quite by accident that she came into package running.

She had been squatting in the mouth of an alley when a man came up to her and asked her if she wanted to earn some quick coin. Asha shook her head and started to back away before the man snorted and said the coin was package delivery, and that he wasn't into young boys. It took her a moment to realize what he had called her, and he took her pause as her willingness to consider his offer.

"This is your lucky day boy," the man continued. "I need this letter delivered to a friend across town, and I need it done in a hurry. Give him the letter and wait for a response and then hurry your ass back here. Do this quickly and you will get paid nicely."

Asha had been so relieved that he didn't want her for her body, she hadn't bothered to correct him about calling her a boy. She took the letter, and he told her where to go. Soon, she had been running down the streets. Thanks to her strong precognition skills, she had been able to weave the crowds without missing a step. The other man merely raised an eyebrow at her as she handed him the letter. She could see him grow angrier as he read and was able to see the backhand coming before the man started to move.

Missing her infuriated the man even more, and she skittered back several steps to stay out of range. She could tell he was contemplating coming forward and taking his frustrations out on her.

"Sorry sir," she pleaded. "I'm just the message boy," hoping he, too, thought of her as a boy and would be less likely to find her later if he wasn't looking for a girl. "The man said you were a friend and just to give you the letter. Please, I am sorry."

"You tell that no good son of a bitch I will see the empire reborn before I will give him what he wants. You tell. . ." The rest was lost to her, for she had taken off down the street. He had said enough for her to give the man who hired her an answer. It wasn't long before she was back at the alley where he had met her. She wasn't sure what to do at this point, other than wait. It turned out to be a short wait.

"That was fast boy," the man had said.

Asha was afraid to speak for fear of giving away that she wasn't a boy, so she nodded.

"Well, what did he say?"

Doing her best to match the man's voice, she replied "You tell that no good son of a bitch I will see the Empire reborn before I will give him what he wants. There was more, but he was angry and had already swung at me once. I figured the rest of the words wouldn't be much different than what I already heard," Asha said.

"He hit you?"

She shook her head. "No, sir, I ducked and backed away."

"You are lucky. His fist is as quick as his temper. You did good. Faster than I expected, so here are a few extra coins. What's your name, boy? I may want to use you again in the future."

"Liam, sir. Lucky Liam," she replied, giving him the name that she had come up with on the run back.

He laughed at that. "You indeed are lucky, Liam." That was the first of many jobs as Lucky Liam. The money from package running paid little at first. With her strong precognition and other abilities, she had been able to stay out of dangerous situations, which added to her reputation, which then allowed her to charge more. Soon, the reputation took on a life of its own. She had always been able to stay one step ahead of an ambush. Hargod came closer to catching her than anyone else. He had known enough about Liam to be prepared for his abilities, and he almost caught her.

Asha had considered having Liam retire. Recent events would definitely suggest now would be as good a time as any. A lot of people tend to disappear when a new psylord takes over and, now that Merik was in charge, hopefully there would be fewer people who would look into the disappearance of Lucky Liam. She would have to wait until Kerwin was done with his business with Merik, but that shouldn't be an issue. It wasn't the job, or the money Kerwin paid that made her want to finish the job, but Jariek.

It was a bit of luck that she had run into them. She had seen far enough into the future to know that they would at least stand up to Hargod's crew. It had been enough for her to choose that path. What she hadn't expected was Jariek to psychically control a horse. Like everyone else, she had been surprised when the horse had bolted and charged into the alley. Well, everyone except for Jariek, who had been calm and focused. It had been quite the shock to see a domination cloud around both Jariek and the horse's mind. No one could affect animals, and yet here he was doing so.

He had noticed her looking at him, but, hopefully, he didn't realize she knew his secret. Since that encounter, she had very little time around him and no other chance to see him use his abilities on other animals. Jariek was probably very cautious about such things. She would be if she was in his place. No one was able to tell when she used her detection ability, but even a nonpsychic could potentially realize that he was controlling an animal, if they paid attention.

Kerwin and Jariek never said how they knew each other or what their relationship was. Asha knew they worked together but weren't close. It was an odd dynamic, but she had been able to piece together some information about them from comments they made and how they conducted themselves. Kerwin was definitely a traveler, while Jariek was from Crestburn. That was great news, because she could take her time to observe him and get to know him. From there, she might be able to get him to talk about his ability to affect animals with his psychic talents.

It was weird knowing that there was someone else like her. Someone with a new ability, or at least a new way to use an old ability. Did Kerwin have a new ability as well? Was that how he knew Jariek? Perhaps there was a group of people with new abilities. She really must be exhausted if she was thinking that there was a collective of people with new abilities. Anyone with a new ability was either hidden, or else they would be a target for any powerful psylord.

Asha yawned again. She took one of the outfits that Kerwin had bought her and began to make alterations to it. The changes weren't anything major, just a few hidden pockets, but even that took a lot longer than it should have.

More than once, she had miss stitched or poked her finger with a needle. Asha wanted to take out one of the seams and replace it with something that could come undone with a quick pull. It would make it a lot easier to get out of the outfit in a hurry. Another yawn escaped her lips, and she decided to hold off on the seam. The outfit was nice enough that she had to be careful with any alterations or else they might be noticed.

She got up and paced back and forth, stretching her legs a bit. If she didn't get a good night's sleep tonight, she would definitely be in bad shape tomorrow. The last thing she needed to do was lose another day due to sleeplessness. Early that morning, she had checked the inn, but Kerwin was not there, nor had he left any messages for Liam. Asha had returned home and tried to take a nap but had no luck. Every time she dozed off, her dreams grew weird and fitful. A few hours later, she woke up feeling not much better than when she laid down.

Something needed to change. The only reason she could think of for her lack of sleep was her discovery of another psychic with a new ability. Her mind must be racing with all the implications about what it could mean to both her and the world at large. When she tried to think about it when she was awake, it all but overwhelmed her. That had to be it. If that was the case, then perhaps she could shut her mind down a bit.

Her knowledge of herbal tincture and powders was very limited. She had learned a handful of recipes that could help her out. Itching and blinding powders to help her get away. A healing salve that fought infections, a tincture that was supposed to prevent getting pregnant, and another one that would take care of things if the first one failed to do its job. Finally, there was a sleeping draught that made sure you didn't wake up for a good long time. Asha had tried it once, shortly after she learned how to make it, so that she could better understand how it affected a person. She had slept very deeply for several hours and awoke in a fog.

Hopefully, it would work and she could finally get some rest. Once rested, she would have to check in on Kerwin and then make plans to talk with Jariek. It would be risky, but there would be some relief in letting someone know that she had a unique power. If she wasn't so tired, she probably would be frightened at the thought of revealing her big secret to someone, and a stranger no less.

Asha started to get dressed, only to realize that she was already dressed. She had forgotten that she had already been out once this morning. She yawned then made her way out of her building and out into the streets. The shops that she was looking for weren't too far away. Thankfully, she didn't have to go all the way over to the Merchant's Courtyard to get what she needed.

Was it her sleep deprived state or were people more on edge this afternoon? The first herbalist that she visited was rather curt to her, instead of gossiping like she usually did. Asha stifled another yawn and made her way down the street. Off in the distance, she could hear a herald announce that there will be a public sentencing in a little bit at the Merchant's Courtyard. What was that about?

As she neared the second shop, she saw Hargod with a small group of men. Quickly, she turned away from him and hoped he didn't see her. Asha shook her head at the amateur mistake that she just made. The quick movement often caught people's attention. It was far better to turn slowly and naturally, that way your movements blended into the crowd. It was all a moot point because she could have reached out and made them not notice her. She had to get some sleep.

Hargod passed by without a second look at her. She had been lucky, or so she thought, until she realized that she was dressed as herself and not Liam. There was no reason to believe that Hargod knew the truth about Liam. Asha shook her head and quickly went down the street to the next merchant on her list. Mistakes like that would be the end of her. She had to get some sleep, or else she would be in real trouble.

CHAPTER 57

TIANNA

It was a slow, quiet ride across Crestburn. The orders that she had received from Lord Merik were very clear. Shortly after she had gotten her orders, heralds had started announcing that there was to be a public sentencing today. Merik was wasting no time with this. He knew she would protest this if given the chance, and that would probably only widen the crack that was starting to form between them.

Sergeant Herlt was the only other person who knew the full extent of the orders. Tianna had shown him right before they left. In her opinion, it wasn't fair to blindside the old man about what was about to happen. Herlt's disposition was generally stoic, but his jaw clenched so much as he read that she was afraid he might break it.

"If I may suggest, it might be wise if you were to retire early tonight. I can make sure your quarters are ready for you when you get back, Captain. Any duties that you had planned can wait till tomorrow or be delegated to other officers," Herlt said.

"Thank you," Tianna replied.

"It's my job."

"No, it is your choice. I appreciate it and the advice that you give, even if I don't always listen to it."

"Will there be anything else, Captain?"

"You and I both know that there will be plenty of anything else after today. I have dealt with bad times before, and this wouldn't be my first time being unpopular and disliked."

"Yes, but we both know this is more than being unpopular. He is making an example out of you and giving the people someone to hate instead of him while he stabilizes his control of Crestburn. The citizens can get mad at you instead of him, and that will keep them distracted as he makes more changes and strengthens his position. Soon, it will be too late for anyone to oppose him, short of an invasion."

Herlt was right, as he often was. Now, here she was headed across town to do Merik's dirty work. It was unjust and unfair, but she could not see a way to change things. If she was to refuse, she would be removed from her position as captain of the guards and someone else, who was more obedient, would take her place. At least this way, she would be able to do some good. Would it be enough to let her sleep at night?

She was no stranger to acts of violence and brutality. With Kour's raiders, she had killed her fair share of people. Combat was different. At least then the other person had a chance to kill you first, not that anyone really had much of a chance against her. Still, the raids had been done for the group's survival, as well as profit. Kour was as much a psylord as any of the others, he had just chosen not to rule over people. He was satisfied with raiding and attacking. At least then people only suffered when they raided, as opposed to other psylords who made their people suffer daily.

It seemed like there was no good choice. Those with power took from those who didn't have it. Once you had power, you fought like hell to keep it until someone finally took you down. It was violent and brutal, but it was the way people were. Perhaps they didn't deserve to have the empire rebuilt. Kysia was so long ago it was starting to seem like a myth to people, a dream to give them hope so they could get from one day to the next until their time is up.

Her escorts stopped and she looked up to see the stage before her. They had arrived at the Merchant's Courtyard and the place was packed. Jenal had been taken down from his place on the stage and had been replaced with the men who had been in the bar fight with the guards. There was a ring of guards around the stage, which was good because they probably would be needed. Tianna dismounted and made her way up to the stage. It wasn't that long ago that she was up here with Erlin and Merik as he addressed the city. She looked over the crowd and could all but feel the dark emotions brewing. This will not end well, she told herself for the dozenth time that day. Tianna took a deep breath, stepped forward, and addressed the crowd.

"Crestburn is a city of law. It is what makes us different from the rest of the world. We choose to adhere to these laws for the greater good. We do not pick and choose which laws we obey, for all must be followed equally. Our Lord Merik is attempting what no one before has done. He is introducing us to the old ways of the Kysian Empire. He will bring about a new era of hope and prosperity.

"I am here to see that Lord's Merik vision will come into being. I am determined to do what is necessary to make sure he can build a better world for you. An attack on my guards is an attack on Lord Merik himself. They are here to keep the peace and enforce the laws, so that Crestburn can become the city that he believes that it can. Unfortunately, there are some among you who have problems with this. They decided to lash out and attack the guards. They hurled insults and, when asked to back down, they struck out. People were hurt and property was damaged.

"Since an attack on a guard is an attack on Lord Merik, I decree that those involved shall be punished as if they struck Lord Merik himself." A murmur rippled through the crowd like the rumbling of thunder from a summer storm off in the distance. "Therefore, it is my decree that those involved in the fight with the guards will be put to death. To harm Lord Merik is to harm the future of Crestburn and, in turn, harm yourselves. It is fitting that those who raised a hand against Lord Merik now will raise a hand against themselves."

Tianna hated those words. They were designed to inflame the crowd's emotions and make them resent her. Merik had chosen the words carefully, so as to make sure the anger and outrage at what was about to happen that day landed directly on her. She knew he had a dark side, what psylord didn't, but she didn't realize how far he would go with someone who was loyal to him. It wouldn't take much for people to believe that this was her interruption of the law, and not necessarily Merik's will.

She nodded at a guard who unchained the first prisoner and noticed how quickly he averted his eyes from her. Tianna drew out her knife and handed it to the condemned man, who just looked at her confused. Reaching out to his mind, she had him grip the knife firmly and face the crowd. Slowly, he held the blade up before plunging it into his chest. The crowd gasped as the man dropped to his knees. His body swayed a bit then tumbled the rest of the way to the stage.

Tianna turned back to the guard, who already had the next prisoner unchained and ready for her to take control of the next condemned man. This one she marched out onto the stage. He grabbed the body of his predecessor and slid him off to the side before pulling the knife out of the man's chest. A few short steps and he was standing where the other man had just been. Once again, the knife was held high for all to see before being plunged into his own chest. This process was repeated with each prisoner, each one dragging the previous body to one side of the stage or the other. When the last person plunged the knife into his chest, the front of the stage was lined with their corpses.

Tianna could hear several people in the crowd weeping.

CHAPTER 58

MERIK

He looked out over the balcony and enjoyed the splendid view of the gardens in the early morning light. Songbirds sang as they embraced the dawn.

"You asked to see me, My Lord," came a voice from behind him.

Merik turned and smiled at Tianna. It looked like she barely slept. Thinking of barely sleeping, where the hell was Suval? He must find that man, and soon, but that can be handled later. He had important business to deal with right now.

"Yes. I need you to bring up Kerwin from his room. I want him brought here to the balcony. I want to have breakfast with him and see if perhaps we can't start a dialogue."

Tianna nodded in response and started to turn to leave when Merik spoke again.

"Are you alright, Captain? You look rather exhausted."

"I am fine, sir. Just didn't sleep well last night, was all."

"That's too bad. Thankfully, it takes little effort for you to control people. Oh, and one more thing. Since you did such a good job yesterday, I will be willing to go through your memories of the duel again."

Tianna left and Merik looked at the table filled with pastries and selected a few. Originally, he was going to get rid of the chef that Djinar had, but he had become quite fond of the man's cooking, and he had developed a bit of a sweet tooth. This morning, as he got dressed, he noticed his clothes felt a bit tighter. If he didn't watch himself, he would end up getting as big as Djinar. He would have to have a word with the chef to make more robust meals, and he had to stay away from the pastries and cakes. This was something he could do tomorrow, for today he was celebrating.

The execution went exactly as planned. Captain Tianna had done her part well, sticking to orders she had been given. It had taken Merik half the previous night to write the speech that she gave. He wanted to make sure that everyone's anger would be directed at her. After such a blatant display of her ability to control others bodies, there was no doubt in anyone's mind that she was a ruthless killer. It was good to remind everyone, as well as her, that Tianna was around because of her royal blood.

True, she was a good commander when it came to matters of combat, but such a thing was not unique. He would have to think about who he wanted to replace her as Captain of the Guards. The men looked up to her, or they did before yesterday's display, and that could lead to problems in the future. It was best, he decided, to use her as his own personal blade, to have her kill when he needed a clear message to be sent. This was not anything he needed to do right away. According to several reports, when Tianna got back from the execution she retired to her room and stayed there all night.

Hopefully, he had broken her spirit and, judging by how she acted a few minutes ago, it looked like his plan was successful. It annoyed him to go through those same memories over and over again, but that was a small price to pay to retain her service. Now that he had punished her, he would reward her for following directions. Soon enough, she would learn her place and not draw attention to herself. If not, well, he could get rid of her. He would, of course, make sure her death had some meaning. After all, she was a valuable resource, and he didn't want to waste her.

It wasn't long until Kerwin was brought in, with Tianna following close by. Merik gestured towards the table laden with food.

"Please, help yourself," he told Kerwin.

Tianna backed away to give them some privacy but still be able to keep an eye on Kerwin should she need to take control of his body again. Kerwin looked over the food and filled his plate with sausages, eggs, and fruit, then sat down across from Merik. They ate in silence, which was fine for Merik because a person with a full belly was more continent and more prone to let their mind wander in memories.

"I bet you are wondering why I had you brought in?" Merik began.

"Not really," Kerwin said.

That caught Merik off guard. Usually, the first thing a person did was plead their innocence or ask why them?

"Oh, why is that?"

Kerwin looked at him and asked "Do you mind if I get more food?"

It took Merik a moment to realize what the man asked before responding. "Yes, of course. Help yourself to as much as you wish. If you have any special requests, please let me know and I can have the chef make it for you. Djinar had a wonderful chef, as you could imagine. Needless to say, I have kept him on, although I will have to get him to back off on the sweets."

Without another word, Kerwin got up and got himself another plate of food, this time fried potato, and eggs with a few muffins. He sat back down and started eating again, without another word.

Merik leaned back into his chair and watched the man eat. This would prove to be interesting. Normally the man's actions would have angered him to no end, however, since he belonged to a hidden group, Merik wondered if it was because of his training with them. Did they have contingencies in place for when one of their members was captured? Was this a part of the plan or was it merely the man's unique behavior?

Kerwin finished the plate, pushed it away, and looked over at the serving table, contemplating another plateful. Instead, he slid it back and stared at Merik. Merik smiled and stared back at him, as if playing a game of look away but instead jumped into his immediate memories.

The food was good. Real good in fact. Here it comes, the question and now his turn to reply. Good, Merik was puzzled. The nonchalant reply always threw them off. More than once this had worked. He remembers back in the society when they started to teach them how to deal with interrogations. Those times in class with Nilton going over the different techniques of questioning someone for information. The hours spent practicing with each other, honing their techniques at getting information as well as withholding it.

It wasn't much information, but it would be a start at least. The usual tactics would probably not work with Kerwin since this Nilton had trained him and others. Merik had hoped to get the conversation started before bringing up this hidden society, but it looked like he would have to lead with that.

"We can play this staring game," Merik began "for as long as you like. I am quite sure we will be here staring at one another like lovers come supper time. Nilton did do a wonderful job training you guys." At the mention of Nilton's name, Kerwin reacted. It wasn't much of a reaction, but enough to know that he had been startled to hear it. Kerwin leaned back in his chair, doing his best to keep his composure.

"Yes, I know quite a bit about you and your organization," Merik said, practically cooing.

The best way to get information, Merik found, was to act like you already know the information. People were much more likely to tell you things if they thought you already knew. That provided him with a starting point he could use to dig through their memories, or he could choose to acknowledge one of their theories as correct, thus devaluing the secret. Kerwin was no different.

How on earth could he have learned about the Cashek Society, the man had thought? The council had not mentioned anything in their report about Merik, other than he was a new psylord. Had another operative investigated Merik before he took over Crestburn? He had to get word to the council as soon as possible. Hopefully, Jariek has done his part and already notified them of his disappearance and help would be on the way. He hated being saved by a Warden, but it would be a small price to pay.

That was long enough in Kerwin's recent memories. Already the man had a spaced-out look to him. Hopefully, between a full stomach and the shock of what Merik had just revealed to him, he wouldn't notice the side effect of a recent memory being brought up so close to its creation.

"Please, let's talk and be civilized about this. I don't want to hurt you," he paused "or Jariek, but I will do what I must to protect Crestburn and rebuild the Kysian Empire. It will take some time before a Warden comes to try and free you, so let's talk, my friend."

Merik could see Kerwin visibly pale at the mention of Jariek and he almost shook when he acknowledged the warden's presence. Good. This was working out wonderfully. The great thing about secrets was, the bigger the secret, the bigger the shock when someone thought you knew what the secret was. People were so predictable.

"What do you want?" Kerwin asked.

"I am not sure. What I would like is for us to work together, but I am not sure that is possible. It would take quite a bit of work on your, well your society's part to rebuild my trust. Now, you can help speed that up by being open and honest with me. Why don't you take a moment or two and think about it?"

Merik got up and went to the table to pick out some more food to eat. He wasn't hungry. It was to give Kerwin some space so he could come to terms with what he had just learned.

CHAPTER 59

KERWIN

Kerwin's mind spun in a dozen different directions at once. What the hell happened. It was too much to process all at once. Thankfully, Merik had left the table so he had a moment to collect himself. Kerwin wanted to get up and walk around a bit, as walking helped him think, but he wasn't sure if Captain Tianna would allow that. The last thing he wanted was her taking over his body again.

He took a deep breath, and another. Each one he let out slowly. It took a few more repetitions, but he began to calm down. Whatever was going on, he was definitely not prepared for this shit storm. What on earth did the council do to piss off Merik? His briefing from the Second Caravan had next to no information on Merik. If they had dealt with Merik before, then why did they send him and not a group of wardens? Why, unless they thought that sending wardens would be tantamount to a declaration of war with Merik. Then why him? Was it because he happened to be close by, or did they think he could do something to bridge peace between the two? No, if that was the case, then they would have informed him of what was going on so that he would have been better prepared. It was more likely because he was an operative that could be sacrificed easier than some of the others.

He was in deep and, unfortunately, Jariek was involved as well. Could the kid be the reason that Merik knew so much about the society? Jariek was very optimistic about Merik being the one the Cashek Society had been waiting for. The kid was young and a bit naive, having only been out in the real world for a few years. It was quite possible that, after hearing Merik's speech, Jariek jumped ahead, confronted Merik, and told him everything he knew about the society. The more he thought about it, the more he disliked the idea because it sounded very possible.

There was one thing that bothered him about this notion. How did Jariek know Nilton trained him about interrogation? Nilton died about ten years ago, which would have been before Jariek was even ready for that part of his training. It was possible he could have found out somehow, but the odds against it were very high. The society made sure its instructors were able to teach multiple subjects and rotated them often. It would have to be a set

214

of unusual circumstances for Jariek to know who the particular instructor on interrogation was for the operative that ended up being sent to Crestburn.

Nitlon had not only taught him how to handle being questioned, but also the lectures on how the Cashek Society operates. The Cashek Society was governed by a council. Each council member was in charge of their own area of influence such as records, supplies, training, and whatnot. The head of the council, who was currently Kaia, was not the ruler of the Cashek Society, merely the person to guide the council and keep them on task. A first among equals. The reality was something else, even if no one dared acknowledge it.

Within the Cashek Society, there were three groups that dealt with the outside world. The first was the Second Caravan, which handled the supplies and information network. Next, were the informants, such as Jariek, who worked as the eyes and ears of the society. They kept the council abreast of what happened in the world by reports given to the Second Caravan members. Then, it was operatives such as himself who investigated the reports and looked into matters more fully to see if there was a possibility of the society throwing in their support to a psylord. Finally, there were the wardens who served as their guards, enforcers, and clean up crew. The goal of the Cashek Society was to…

Kerwin shook his head and looked around a bit, confused as to why his thoughts had drifted to his training all those years ago. He glanced over at Merik who was over at the other tables, getting more food for his plate. Tianna stood across the room and watched him. It was odd. There was no reason for him to think about his training, especially in his current situation. He had been thinking about Jariek and whether or not the kid could have known that Nilton trained him and then… Well, it didn't matter. Kerwin would have to make sure he was more focused on matters at hand. For him to get lost in thoughts like that was as good of an indication as anything as to how shocked he was to find out Merik knew about the Cashek Society.

His two biggest concerns right now were to figure out how much Merik knew about the Casheek Society, as well as try to find a way to open negotiations between Merik and the society. Right now, he was at a huge disadvantage, but the situation wasn't hopeless. Unless Merik already intended to kill him, then he was screwed. That would be his luck, though. Finally, after all these years, he would come across the one psylord the society had been waiting for, only to be killed by him because they had already pissed him off.

Merik returned to the table, his plate laden with pastries and fruit. He smiled pleasantly at Kerwin and began eating without a word. Good. He was willing to give Kerwin some more time to wrap his head around the situation. He had to find some kind of common ground, some form of neutral territory where they can slowly build trust in one and another.

"I do have to admit, the food is delicious," Kerwin began.

Merik paused his eating and smiled, "Yes, quite so. I am going to have to have my wardrobe altered if I don't learn a little more restraint with breakfast. Thankfully, lunch is a more bland affair, but the quality is no less," Merik replied.

"I now see how Djinar got to be as big as he was. With the Cashek Society, our food is good, but we don't have a lot of variety."

"I am quite sure that everything has to be on schedule and rationed out, with your people living in seclusion and all."

"Yes. They keep everything pretty orderly; it is how we have survived since the collapse of Kysia."

"Now, as an operative you, as well as the informants and Second Caravan, get to sample some of the world's splendors. I bet that makes it harder to go back to the Society's fixed routines."

"Not really. There is comfort in the routine. Besides, we are busy with our tasks when we are out, so it is not like we have time to sit back and savor things."

"What a shame."

This was good. He had begun to find some rapport with Merik, and he found out a little more about what Merik knew. If he could keep him talking, then he could wheedle out more information. Kerwin looked down at his plate and saw that it was empty. He was full, but he didn't want their conversation to end. He should have paced himself better, but after several days in captivity, with only mediocre food, it was hard to do, especially with such a splendid display before him.

"If," Merik began, "I allow you to make contact with the Second Caravan, what would you say to them?"

Kerwin did his best to conceal his surprise at the question and hoped the moment he took to do so made it appear as if he was gathering his thoughts on how to best reply.

"Well. I would let them know that I was your," he paused just a bit for effect "guest. I would let them know that you had some rudimentary knowledge of us and that you are willing to talk. As an act of good faith, I am staying here until a more formal sit down can be arranged."

"How would they react to this? I know you guys have been kept secret for hundreds of years. I can't imagine that your council will be happy to have their secret society discovered after all these years."

"Honestly, I am not sure. It will cause an uproar within the council. They will probably even blame me for telling you too much about them. This will be their initial reaction. However, knowing the society, I am sure that they have a protocol for dealing with a situation like this."

"What is that protocol?"

"I don't have a clue. Something like that would be above my access level. I am sure whatever they decide to do will be based on something that was planned when the Cashek Society was first founded."

"No original thinking then," Merik chidded.

"Oh, we are free to think as we wish. The protocols that they follow are more of guidelines than rules. Very strong guidelines. They have kept us safe and undiscovered all this time. Well, until now that is."

"Until now," Merik replied.

"Who would they send?" Merik asked.

"I honestly don't know."

"Then, make an educated guess."

"Well, they could send someone who is trained for this moment. Who that could be, I have no idea. The other option would be to have one of the members of the council come out and talk to you. Either way, more than likely, the person would be accompanied by several wardens."

"Yes, I know you have wardens of your own. I wish to know more about them. You probably already know that I am in the process of recreating them myself. Anything you can tell me about your wardens would help me refine mine and make the eventual transition of our two groups smoother. I won't harass you for details. Please, just tell me a few things."

This was not going the way he thought the conversation would go. In a way, it was much better, but there was something off about the situation. He couldn't quite figure out what it was. It was as if there was almost an artificialness to Merik's words. This set Kerwin on edge. It didn't make any sense for Merik to be this cordial to him after keeping him in a cell for several days following his late night abduction. By allowing him to choose what to say about the wardens, Merik had given him control of the conversation and information. Kerwin couldn't quite explain it, but it felt wrong.

Merik wanted to know about the wardens. Kerwin couldn't blame him, and, had roles been reversed, he definitely would be trying to figure out what the society's military strength was. Not that they had a military, just about a hundred or so highly trained fighters. Wardens were trained in combat from a young age. They took the most physically fit of the children and gave them extra physical training. Those who excelled at it would then go on to martial arts and weapon training. By the time they became a full fledged warden, they had over a decade of training and sparring matches. They were supposed to be some of the best warriors on the continent. Although it was hard to say how good they really were, since they rarely saw action other than ambushing intruders who wandered onto their land or cleaning up mistakes from operatives and informants.

The wardens were divided into ten person units, known as patrols. Each patrol would be led by the senior most warden in the group. They were called patrols because that was what they mainly did, patrol an area. There would be one patrol assigned to the base, one just outside it, and three more further out at the edge of the society's territory. Another patrol, made up of the best wardens, would be assigned to go out on missions into the world. The other patrols would be at their barracks, in the society home, and would be off patrol, which meant training and taking it easy, not that a warden ever really took it easy.

Kerwin paused in his reflection of his days in the classroom being taught the structure of the wardens. Once again, his memories became rather specific. It was not like him to get lost in his thoughts like that. The first time, he could excuse it but, twice during the same dinner? The odds were against something like that happening. Like all operatives, he had been trained to guard and control the flow of his thoughts. It was mental discipline designed to keep them safe in a world filled with psychics.

"Something amiss?" asked Merik cordially.

Kerwin looked at him and thought he detected a hint of frustration. "Sorry, I was lost in thought."

"It happens to us all. And, I am sure you have a lot of things to think about, now that you know your society is no longer a secret."

"Yes, it is a lot to take in. I am not trying to stall, it's just," he paused before continuing, "a lot for me to come to terms with. Your knowledge of us has changed everything. We aren't exactly ready for something like this. I am sure there are protocols and procedures for what to do, but that is not the same as being able to accept the reality of the situation."

"I can understand that. I am sure the last thing your society expected was for me to figure out they existed. Hopefully, we can move forward and be able to work together. After all, they have been waiting for someone like me to appear."

"Yes," Kerwin replied.

A servant appeared and waited for Merik's signal to approach. He whispered into his lord's ear, and Merik nodded to what was being said. Merik had slipped up a bit. The man went from being angry at the society to acting hopeful that they could work together. It was too rapid of a change. Then, there was how he kept getting lost in thought. The conversations felt as if Merik was being fed lines as to what to say. It was as if Merik had been reading his mind while he was thinking.

No, that wasn't possible, not even with telepathy.

He looked up, and Merik was still conferring with his servant. If, and it was a big if, Merik could somehow read his mind while he remembered things, then it would explain a lot about their conversation. In theory, the society believed it was possible for new abilities to exist. When they tested their members to see what powers they possessed, they even asked if the person felt like they had any abilities that were different from what was documented. It was possible, but the odds were against Merik having an unknown power. However, there was a way he could find out..

CHAPTER 60

MERIK

The servant stood at the edge of his vision, waiting to be recognized. Merik gave a mental sigh and nodded that the servant should approach. Hopefully, whatever this important matter was, it could be handled quickly and without him leaving the table. He had managed to pull out a lot of useful information from Kerwin. Unfortunately, the man was good at recognizing when his mind had wandered too deeply in his memories, and he would take back control of his memories.

He only half listened to what the servant had to say. Apparently, the families of people executed by Captain Tianna wanted to know if they could have the bodies so that they could be buried. He was half tempted to deny them this but decided against that. After all, the whole purpose of the execution was to turn people against her. They could have the bodies back, he decided, later this evening. There was no real reason for the delay other than not giving them what they wanted right away. The servant nodded and backed away.

Merik turned and looked at Kerwin who was once again lost in thought. Excellent. This last interruption was enough to stop Kerwin's attempt to stall. Perhaps now he could get somewhere. He reached out, touched Kerwin's mind, and immersed himself into the man's memories

Kerwin was walking down a dark hallway. A young man with black hair was walking beside him.

"Things have changed a bit since you have last been back," the young man said.

"Things change, yet they always stay the same, Ardric. Odd how that happens," Kerwin replied.

"Such a pessimist, Kerwin. How have your assignments been?"

"Different cities and different psylords but nothing worth our time."

"More change and, yet, all the same," the young man laughed.

"Yes."

"Did you hear that Prian is now in charge of the wardens?"

"Prian is now a member of the council? How did that happen? I thought Dovgrin was going to live forever."

"It was an accident. He was sparring with a couple of younger wardens when his bad knee gave out causing him to drop. Unfortunately, he dropped into the path of an oncoming blade, which crushed his throat. The council had the incident investigated and it was ruled as an accident."

"Councilman Prian. That will take getting used to."

"That isn't the only thing that will take getting used to."

"What do you mean?"

"He is pushing to increase the number of wardens. Right now, he has about a dozen new recruits that have been selected to train. He plans to do the same next year, as well. Rumor has it he wants to double the number of wardens."

"Sorry, I didn't realize you were done with your servant," Kerwin addressed Merik.

Merik blinked as reality came back to him. "It's quite alright. Like I said before, you have had a lot to take in. I understand that you need to collect your thoughts."

"Yes, well. The wardens are grouped into units called patrols. Each patrol is led by a senior warden. Councilman Daveter runs the wardens."

Merik raised his hand to cut Kerwin off. "I have been quite generous to you," he began, as he felt his anger rise, "but I do not appreciate being lied to. As I have already told you, the society has already screwed up with me before, for not being honest. I will not tolerate being lied to again. You don't realize how extensive my knowledge is of your society. I know that Prian is the council member in charge of the wardens."

"So, it is true," Kerwin stated.

"What is true?" asked Merik, a bit confused.

"You can read people's memories. I wasn't sure at first. Didn't really believe the rumors, I mean who would," Kerwin lied. "No one has seen a new power since the fall of Kysia. Somehow, you happen to be able to read people's memories."

"What are you talking about?" Merik said, raising his voice to almost a shout.

"That memory you jumped in on was from years ago. Prain hasn't been in charge of the wardens for about three years now. Daveter took his place. I noticed my memories were rather vivid. Kind of odd, and so I figured the rumors had to be true."

"What rumors?"

"That you can experience people's memories. I wondered how you had such detailed, yet limited, knowledge of us. You plucked my memories and then used that information to appear to know about us already."

Merik slammed his hands on the table and stood up. "You will…"

"Hold that thought, Merik. While you may have a new ability, did it ever come across your mind that we had abilities that you never heard of?"

Merik's eyes widened as he realized the implications of what Kerwin had just said. He sat back down, seething with rage.

"We have existed before the Kysian Empire fell. When the final emperor went insane, and the wardens descended into madness, well, our wardens were spared that. When Emperor Palreon created us, he made sure there were special safeguards in place. Didn't you wonder why I was so calm while you had me chained up in the holding cell? Jariek has already been in contact with them, and they are aware of the situation."

"Your bluffing."

"Maybe, but how will you know? Sure, you can go through my memories, but, as I just demonstrated to you, I am aware of when you are in my head. I should also point out that we are highly disciplined. I will be keeping a close eye on my thoughts and will make sure my mind is only focused on the present."

"Get him out of here now!" he shouted at Tianna. Kerwin went rigid and then slowly got up and walked away from the table. Tianna followed behind him, just a few short paces. How in the hell had things gone so bad that quickly? Kerwin had to be making that all up. Somehow, he figured out Merik had a new ability and bluffed. That had to be it. He had been too careful making sure no one knew of his special ability. Where the hell was Suval?

"Attend me, now!" he shouted.

Quickly, a servant, who had been stationed on the other side of the door, came running up to him. Merik didn't even bother to look at her as he commanded her. "I want Suval found immediately. I don't care what it takes. I want him ferreted out of whatever hovel he is hiding in and sent to me immediately."

She dashed out the door and Merik strode over to the balcony edge. He needed Suval to be found as soon as possible. Suval could work his magic on Kerwin and, after a few days of no sleep, he wouldn't be able to control his thoughts. Then, he could find out if he was telling the truth or not.

As it was, there were plenty of things he could do in the meantime. Extra guards could be put on the city gates. Merchant's could be kept from leaving for a few days. No, that would seem like he wasn't in control. The guards could switch from cudgels to blades, though. Drills could be doubled. He was panicking. Merik took a deep breath and then another. He closed his eyes, leaned his head back, and basked in the sun. When he began to feel calm, he opened his eyes to see a large hawk flying overhead. How he wished that he could be like that bird, free of the pressures and stress of being a ruler and just free to fly as he pleased in the sky without a worry.

He was calmer now. Kerwin should not have gotten to him as he did. Kerwin would pay for that. No one could withstand Suval's ability. A few days of no sleep, and there would be no secret that he could keep from him. Until then, he would keep things running just as they had been. If Kerwin had been telling the truth about being in contact with Jariek, then they would be watching him for any changes in his routine. If it was all a lie, then they would have no clue that Merik was on to them. As it was, he would have to find out who this Jariek was. Erlin can handle that task. The man was great at finding out things. His heralds served not only as Merik's voice, but his eyes and ears as well.

CHAPTER 61

JARIEK

Shit! Shit! Shit!

Jariek hurried up to his room, grabbed several outfits, and put them on one after the other. He covered himself in his cloak, drew the cowl about his head, and left. Guilt surged through him as he made his way down the street. He hated that he had to abandon Master Gerwald, but he couldn't risk staying. Hopefully, Lord Merik wouldn't punish Gerwald for having employed a spy.

This was as bad as things could get. He sweated profusely with all those layers under the cloak. Swiftly as he could, he made his way down side streets and back alleys until he got close enough to reach out to the second caravan.

"Ouch that burns," he sent out as an unfocused thought. It wasn't long before the correct reply came back. Jariek used all his willpower not to cut the man off and jump in with the explanation.

"Operative is a prisoner of Lord Merik. Merik is aware of me. Need help immediately!"

"Is the operative compromised?" came the response from the Second Caravan member.

Jariek hesitated, because he didn't want to get Kerwin in trouble

"You paused, so I am going to assume yes."

"I am not really sure. Kerwin disappeared after his second meeting with Merik. He was gone for several days, until he was spotted with Lord Merik this morning."

"What were they doing?"

"Having breakfast," Jariek responded

"Are you sure that the operation is not compromised?"

"Pretty sure. I have clairaudience. I heard the entire conversation with Merik and Kerwin."

"How, then, did Merik learn who you are?"

"He doesn't know who I am, but he knows that a Jariek works with Kerwin. It won't take him long to figure out who I am. I need shelter."

"Ok. We can set you up with a room at an inn not too far from here. Find a place to lay low until we can get back in touch with you. Did you grab anything before you left?"

"Only clothes. I grabbed several outfits and put them on along with a cloak."

"Man, you must be dying with all that on in this heat. That was good thinking on your part, but go ahead and ditch most of the clothes. I have enough coin to get you several outfits. Besides, you will want clothes that no one is familiar with."

"Ok. How will you get in touch with me?"

"I will send an unfocused thought where I am cursing at a horse."

"Uh, ok."

Jariek felt a little bit better now that he had made contact with the Second Caravan. It was a good thing the Cashek Society always made sure they had a couple on hand whenever an operative was investigating something. He retreated down an alley, ditched an outfit, and then headed to a different alley. Jariek made sure it was empty before shedding another layer and moving on. It took longer to do it this way, but a discarded outfit wouldn't draw attention like a pile of clothes would. Before long, he was done, back where he started, and the first discarded outfit already was gone. Some street kid probably snagged it shortly after he left. It was hot under the cloak but at least it was a lot more bearable.

He was lucky. He had awoken a little earlier than normal this morning and decided to take a bird out to scout the mansion in hopes of seeing some sign of Kerwin. Hurriedly, he had gotten dressed, grabbed a bird at random, and sent him aloft. Jariek had the bird race over to the mansion and spent several minutes scanning the area. He hadn't seen anything, at first. He was about to quit when he noticed food being brought out onto the balcony. A few minutes later, Merik came out and soon after that the scared lady, the captain of the guards - who was now Merik's executioner, joined him. She had left and returned with Kerwin in tow a few minutes later.

Carefully, he flew closer and landed on the roof, not far from the balcony, and listened in on the conversation. He was as shocked as Kerwin when he learned that Merik already knew of them. Jariek did his best to focus on what was being said and not to worry about the implications of it all. There were several levels in the conversation, and he contemplated having the bird take off to see what was going on. Eventually, the conversation would resume, and he realized that Kerwin was trying to figure out what to say. He didn't envy the man one bit and realized that sometimes this was the price of being an operative. It shocked him to hear his name get mentioned, but not nearly as much as when Kerwin confronted Merik about his ability to see people's memories.

Another new power. Someone else like him. He wondered at the implications and was only brought back to the present when he heard Merik shouting at the servant to have Suval found. Jariek had the bird take off and circled about the mansion. Kerwin was gone and Merik was alone on the balcony looking up into the sky. The man was much calmer now and, for a moment, Jariek swore he was looking directly at him and that Merik knew it was Jariek in control of the bird. It was nonsense, but the man's gaze had spooked him, nonetheless. Quickly, he had put the bird back in its cage, grabbed his stuff, and fled. Now, all there was for him to do was sit and wait.

A few hours had passed before the second caravan agent sent out his unfocused telepathic thought swearing at a horse.

"Now what?" Jariek asked nervously.

"You are all set with a room at the Crestview Haze," came the response.

"There?"

"Yes. I know it is probably a lot nicer than what you were thinking we would get you."

"Definitely. I would have been happy with a small room in a run-down inn."

"The problem with those kinds of places is that's where they will look for you once they realize you have left Gerwald. You are an apprentice falconer; you don't have much money. A place like Crestview Haze would be way out of your price range, so they would probably dismiss it as an option, at least for now."

"I see your point. That is something I would never have thought of."

"It's ok, kid. There are several outfits waiting for you in your suite. They are different from what you are used to wearing."

"That's fine."

"You haven't seen them yet."

"Ah, ok, I guess."

"Anyway, you are booked as Jorin, and you are here to meet a master smith who you are planning to work with. The master smith will be the warden that the Cashek Society will send to clean up this situation. Your cover story shouldn't be questioned too much because it is no secret that Merik has been hiring blacksmiths."

"Yea. It looks like he is starting to gear up for something big, or at least be ready for an attack from someone else."

"We will get word to the society, and they will send someone quickly. Stay safe, kid."

CHAPTER 62

SUVAL

For several days he had kept company with her, although she hadn't yet realized it. They very rarely did. He learned to keep his distance and wait patiently for the time to slink in closer to them. By now, the lack of sleep was visibly starting to show on her body. Her eyes developed bags under them. Each movement seemed to take more and more effort. It was delightful to watch this decay. At night, and now in the day time, her dreams were naturally growing more and more chaotic. The stress of not sleeping was affecting her mind and producing a natural effect that was almost a compliment to what he did. This did not stop him from playing with her dreams.

Right now, Asha was awake and trying to get stuff done in her place. Suval could care less about her mundane tasks. When he was confident that she wasn't going to try taking a quick nap right away, he snuck out to find something to eat. While his ability reduced his need for sleep, it did nothing for hunger. Thankfully, he was a fairly inactive person and his body required very little food to keep it going. As much as he hated being away from his prey, he could use a break. Were she to fall asleep while he was gone, it wouldn't be enough to give her any real rest. If anything, it would give her a little more strength to keep going a little longer, which meant they could be together longer.

Suval wasn't sure what he wanted to do with her just yet. Jenal was a fun plaything, and he learned a fair amount from their time together. For one thing, he had a much better idea of how long a person could survive with little sleep. He wished Merik hadn't taken him away, because he would love for the man to have a chance to rest up and then start all over on him. This time, there would be no downtime between their time together. Suval wouldn't have to wait for the man to come home from work and try to keep up the appearance that everything was normal. He could have played with him non-stop until the man broke again.

Suval was curious to see how fast he could bring someone to insanity through lack of sleep. Who he wouldn't kill for a set of twins to experiment with. One twin could be done only at night and, with the other, he wouldn't take a break. Of course, he would have to do these one at a time because he couldn't affect two people's dreams at the same time. It would be fun to see how different use of his powers would affect such similar people.

Merik would have to give him people to play with to make it happen. It annoyed him that the staff at the mansion was off limits to him, and he wasn't supposed to go searching for someone to play with. There was too big a chance that he could get caught, or so Merik claimed. The man was too worried about people learning that there were new powers. Eventually, people would find out and, as far as he was concerned, it was pointless to worry about the inevitable.

Suval found a vendor selling spiced noodles and ordered a bowl full. He sat and watched the people in the street as he waited patiently for his meal. Even without using his ability, people tended to ignore him. He was very used to being alone. Even before his powers developed, he spent a lot of time alone. Other kids had made fun of him, and he was bullied a lot. His uncle would stand up for him and chase off the other kids. Suval thought it was because he cared for the boy, but it was for his own dark desires that he did it.

Even without Merik's help, Suval could remember his uncle's touch all too well - how his arms, wrapped around him in a sheltering and comforting manner, had shifted to forceful and dominating. He was too young to fight back. Eventually, he would learn ways to cope with it, and he told himself that the bullies wouldn't be bothering him with his uncle always around.

The vendor placed a bowl of spiced noodles in front of him, but he was no longer hungry. Memories of his uncle tended to obliterate his desires for anything. He listlessly picked at the noodles, occasionally taking a bite as he slouched in his seat.

"Suval."

He sat up upon hearing his name and looked around. Standing in front of him were several city guards. Shit, they found him. This was the last thing he wanted. Now, he would have to report to Merik and, in the meantime, his new plaything would get some rest and recuperate while he was gone. It was possible that she could even move from where she lived before he got back to her. The thought horrified him. He enjoyed having a plaything that had a secret. It made him feel connected to her in a way that he never had with any of his other playthings.

"Suval?" the guard said again, questioningly, when he hadn't answered.

"Yes, I am he."

The guard looked both relieved and disgusted to have found Suval. The rest of the guards fanned out as if Suval was planning on causing some kind of trouble or escaping. He couldn't help but smirk at their futile gesture.

"Sir, Lord Merik requires your presence at his mansion immediately. There is an important matter that requires your attention."

Suval sighed. Just what he feared. "I will be there in just a little bit."

The guard shook his head and said, "I am sorry, sir, but Lord Merik said that it was of the utmost importance that you present yourself to him right away. My guards and I will be escorting you there to make sure that you don't run into any difficulties returning."

"Fine, let's get this over with," Suval said as he hopped off his stool with a yawn and started making his way down the streets. The guards formed a ring around him and the ones in the rear position made sure to keep their attention focused on him. They arrived at the mansion in very little time. Everyone on the street had made sure to stay clear of the guards and the man they were escorting. He had hoped that once they arrived at the mansion his personal escort would leave. Unfortunately, they stayed with him, even when he entered the chamber that Merik would receive him in.

A short while later, the door banged open and Merik strode in angrily. "Dismissed," he shouted at the guards without bothering to look at them. No sooner than they had left, Suval felt two strong hands pushing down on his shoulders.

"Noooo," Suval moaned. "Please don't, I am sorry.!!!"

"Where were you?" Merik asked forcefully.

"With the boy."

"What boy, you deranged monster?" The sensations of hands on his shoulders intensified and he could swear he felt a hot breath on the back of his neck.

"The one that was with the man you had me follow."

"You were with him the whole time?"

"Yes, my lord!" pleaded Suval. "I saw him leave the man you wanted me to follow. Since the man had gone into his inn for the night, I found some guards nearby to watch him while I was tracking the boy."

"The guards already told me. The ones you got to do the job I told you to do."

"I am sorry, sir! I thought that the young man might lead me to some valuable information. I knew that your guards were capable of handling a sleeping man."

The sensation of hands on his shoulders lightened up but was still there, lingering.

"What did you find out about the boy?"

"Very little, sire. He lives in an abandoned building. The kid would go back to the inn and see if there were any messages from the man."

"Did he see anyone else? A young boy by the name of Jariek perhaps?"

"No, sire."

"That is fine. Still, you said you followed the kid, Lucky Liam, back to his place and watched over him undetected for several days."

"Yes, my Lord Merik. I swear to you that I didn't go anywhere else."

"At any point in time did Liam realize you were there?"

"No," Suval whimpered.

"Are you sure?" Merik asked.

"I am positive. The first night I messed with his dreams, just a little bit, so that he would be a bit groggy. I didn't know who he was, but I knew he had to be important if he was working for the man."

"Kerwin," Merik interjected."

"If he was working for Kerwin. I didn't want to take risks, so I stirred up his dreams only a little bit."

"You are lying to me, Suval."

Suval started to shake and tremble with fear. A low moan started to escape his lips and a lone tear trickled down his cheek. He flinched in anticipation of the memories that were about to become as real as anything else in the room.

Merik just looked at him and smiled. After a moment he continued. "I know you are lying to me about using your ability on the boy. We both know what a sick monster you are. You can't resist the temptation of a new plaything. I just hope you haven't messed him up too bad. Lucky for you, Suval, you have managed to do the impossible."

A look of confusion crept across his face.

"You managed to learn where Lucky Liam lives. Liam is perhaps the most famous, or rather infamous, street kid in all of Crestburn. No one has managed to learn anything about him or even come close to capturing him. Just a few days ago, there was a group of thugs who tried to make a name for themselves by capturing this Lucky Liam. Apparently, they thought the notoriety they would gain by doing this would win them favor with me. The only thing they managed to accomplish was to make a spectacle out of themselves and add to this boy's reputation. A reputation that will come to an end now that you know where he lives.

"Since you managed to find out where Liam lives, I will look past your mistake of not reporting back to me. However, there will be repercussions for you trying to lie to me a few minutes ago. Right now, I need you to do your thing on our special guest. While you were out stalking Liam, our good Captain Tianna brought in Kerwin. The man is a lot more dangerous than I realized. Apparently, he is a part of some secret society dedicated to rebuilding the Kysian Empire, or something along those lines. His mind is quite disciplined and you may have a hard time breaking him."

Suval squealed with delight and a perverse gleam hit his eyes as he smiled. He bobbed his head up and down repeatedly in a half bow, half nod gesture. Finally, he was getting a playtoy that would challenge him. Liam was special but, if what Merik said was true, this Kerwin would be a wonderful distraction until he could get back to Liam.

"See to it that Kerwin breaks. I have no doubt that it will happen eventually, but I will be sorely disappointed in you if it takes longer than I think it should. Consider this a speed challenge. How quickly can you break a strong mind? You are dismissed."

CHAPTER 63

BOTUN

Botun quickly checked his surroundings, even though it was late at night. No one was around, besides Hargod standing right behind him, so he knocked on the back door of the building. After a few minutes, the door slowly opened. Zarah waved them into the room. It was barely big enough to be called a room. With all three, it was a bit crowded, but she didn't want to risk one of the other girls seeing them. Even though Zarah trusted her girls, for the most part, there was still a chance one of them might betray her.

"Sorry about the cramped quarters," she said.

"It's fine," Botun replied as he removed the hood of his cloak. Hargod just stood in the corner, silently. Botun began taking him along as a bodyguard; the man's night of drunk complaining about Lucky Liam worked well to defuse attention. Things had started to get tense in Crestburn after the Captain of the Guard executed several townspeople for getting into a fight with the city guard. It was rumored that Merik was upset with how she handled the matter and almost removed her as captain. Whether that was true or she was merely Merik's scapegoat didn't matter. People were upset about the incident and fights were starting to break out.

"So, where do we stand?" Zhara asked.

"Pretty good. Our numbers are starting to grow. The recent executions have upset a lot of people. Unfortunately, the number of new guards recruited has increased, as well."

"Why on earth would that happen?" came the reply from Hargod.

"Now, people are too afraid to raise their voice to a guard, let alone their hand. There are people who would like to shelter in that fear backed power. I am not surprised he's getting more recruits. He pretty much sent a message that if you are with me, you will be untouchable.

As it is, I am going to need another location to host a meeting."

"I will see what I can do. One of my girls has a regular who is a bit upset because one of the people executed was his cousin. He owns a few warehouses you might be able to borrow," Zarha suggested.

"Good. See if you can't get him willing to host a meeting at one."

"I think I can manage that. What kind of time table are we talking about?"

"In the next couple of days, if possible. If things calm down in the city, it will be more difficult to start any kind of movement."

"I will see what I can do. He is a regular and should be in later this week."

"Since you want him to host, I take it you plan to make him a figurehead."

"Something along those lines. It is good that we are growing, but I am worried that we will get someone whose loyalty is for sale, yet, we would be foolish not to tap into the anger that is starting to build."

"In other words, we are damned if we do and damned if we don't," grumbled Hargod.

"Hargod, I see you have recovered from your exploits." Zarah teased.

Botun raised his hand to halt the conversation. "Hargod did what was needed to fix the situation. From the looks of things, everyone believed that his intentions were to gain a reputation by catching Lucky Liam. Liam was seen working for someone who had a meeting with Merik. That was a few days ago. After that, no one has seen the kid. Of course, that's not unusual because Liam has been known to disappear for a few weeks at a time. He was reported to be working at a porter for an out of town merchant, named Kerwin, who deals with antique books. I have the name of the inn he is staying at here in town. Liam might show up again if he is still serving as this book merchant's porter. Let me know if Liam is spotted. There are answers that I need from him."

"I can do that." Zarah said.

"Do you still have guards coming to visit your girls?"

She laughed at that. There were always guards interested in women for hire. "As if you had to ask that," Zarah replied.

"How do the guards feel about the recent events?"

"For the most part, the officers could care less about what happened. There are a few who think that Captain Tianna got a bad deal in this. Originally, she had fined the men involved in the bar fight and made the ones who started it pay for the damage done to the place."

"That seems more than reasonable to me," Botun replied.

"Reasonable or not, Merik had an issue with it. The fines were dropped and the citizens who were in the fight rounded up. The speech that the captain gave sounded off too."

"How so?"

"That decision to execute those people was pretty harsh and, when you look at the method of execution, that is something a fanatic would do. She was rather dry in issuing the proclamation, not at all like a devoted follower. I would guess that she had been following orders from Merik."

"I find that kind of hard to believe. She was able to control Bearius, so why doesn't she do so with Merik."

"I have no idea. The original city guards have no clue about what Merik's abilities are, and the ones who came in with him won't talk about him. The few times one of my girls asked, the guards would change the subject. One thing one of my girls did hear was that Captain Tianna was obsessed over a fight that she lost."

"That would probably be the fight that got her the scar and kicked out of Kour's group. I don't know much about them, since they operate several days away from here and never showed any interest in Crestburn.

"I can't help you out, either. What about you Hargod?"

"Not much to say about them. They are raiders who have a strong leader. He's harsh but inspires loyalty. Bounty on the ones who get a mark is supposed to pay well, but they rarely make it to Crestburn.When they do, there are so many people after them here that it's not worth the headache to try and claim the bounty. I can ask around a bit and see what I can come up with for you, if you want, Botun."

"That would be good."

Hargod nodded and then started to say something, but then fell silent. Botun merely raised an eyebrow at him and waited patiently. The thug fidgeted a bit before meekly speaking.

"I do have an idea."

"What is your idea," Botun asked.

"Well, it's not a good one, and I am not sure you are going to like it."

"Botun doesn't have to like an idea if it works. Even bad ideas can be built upon to make them better,"Zarah chimed in, trying to put Hargod at ease.

"Well, it's not so much as a bad idea but one that is rather brutal. That's why you might not like it, boss."

"Working for Djinar, I have dealt with many such plans. Your's won't be the first, nor the last, should we all be fortunate to live long enough."

"Merik is all about cementing his power and cracking down on those who oppose him, right?"

"Yes."

"What about giving him people to execute? If there are more displays like the other day, it will widen the wedge between people who like him and those who don't. It could give us opportunities that we can make use of."

Zarah frowned, obviously not a fan of his idea. "There is no guarantee that he will publicly execute them. All we would be doing is wasting the lives of our allies."

"Merik would publicly execute them if we gave him reason too. Besides, who said they had to be allies of ours? It wouldn't matter who we blame, so long as it's someone Merik would believe had something to gain by opposing him. The early raids took out those who didn't declare their loyalty fast enough. That speaks of a man who is a bit paranoid. Quite frankly, I ain't never heard of a psylord who didn't have a bit of paranoia."

"It's not a bad idea. The problem I see with it is Erlin and his heralds. From what I have learned, they are very good at finding lies. If they believe the person is telling the truth about not knowing about whatever evidence we plant, then our work would be for nothing," Botun countered.

"True, but what if they were to meet with you."

"What?" exclaimed Zarah, who realized that she had said that too loudly. There was silence as all three waited to see if Zarah's raised voice had woken anyone. After a few tense moments, Hargod began again.

"Botun, you are the most wanted person in Crestburn, next to Djinar that is. You could find someone to meet with secretly and ask for their help. Make it worth their while not to turn you in right away and agree to a second meeting. When Erlin and his heralds question them, they would have to lie about meeting you. That would be enough for Merik to remove any question about the legitimacy of their betrayal."

Botun ran the idea over in his mind, looking at it from various angles. "It's not a bad idea. The arrest or execution would have to be witnessed by lots of people in order to force a wedge into the people of Crestburn."

"Then, what about that warehouse guy," Hargod asked.

"What?" replied a shocked Zarah.

"What about him?" asked Botun.

"Well, instead of using his place for a hideout, or whatever you were planning, why not have him hold a meeting there and then let Merik know about it. The meeting will have a reason to happen. We could even make sure there is evidence planted for Merik to find. Of course, we then spread the word about how easy the guards happen to find the evidence that we plant. Odds are, there will be a few people who escape and spread word of the roundup."

"I am impressed, Hargod. It's complicated, but it could work. This could help destabilize Merik's hold on Crestburn before he destroys the city's culture. Zarah, go ahead and see if you can get this man to hold a meeting. Let him know that there are others who are upset over the recent events and that it could be very advantageous for him to host a meeting."

"I will do as you ask," Zarah replied reluctantly.

"Good. Then I suggest we part ways, and I will have Hargod check in with you in the next couple of days."

Zarah nodded and then opened the door. It was obvious that she didn't like the plan at all. Hargod slipped out first, to check and make sure there was no one around before letting Botun know it was ok to step out. The ground was wet. It must have rained just a bit while they talked. A thin bit of fog clung to the ground. The little bit of rain dropped the temperature a good bit, but, if it rained anymore, then tomorrow would become very humid.

They strolled along in silence for several blocks before Botun spoke. "Your plan is a good one, but there is one problem that I didn't want to address in front of Zarah." Hargod paused and turned to look at Botun.

"Whoever Zarah has planned to host this meeting will know that she was the one to suggest it. I know she is a clever woman, but we don't have enough time to make it seem like it was his idea. We need to make sure that he doesn't make it to questioning."

"No problem. I can have one of my people make sure it looks like a guard kills him as he tries to flee."

"Good. The plan is not perfect but it should work, especially if we can find out which warehouse before the meeting starts. We stand a better chance of making sure people get out if we know the layout of the meeting place and the surrounding buildings. I can see if, perhaps, I can arrange for a diversion in the street to provide cover for the people escaping."

"Looks like we have a lot of planning to do, boss."

"That is the one thing that has not changed in all this mess. When Djinar ruled, I made plans so I could build something lasting. Now, I make plans to take back the city in hopes to preserve what I built. There are times I wonder if it was all worth the effort. Would my life have been any easier if I just acted like a normal psylord, hell bent on conquest and power, instead of trying to build something lasting?"

"It might have been easier, boss, but it definitely would have been shorter. At least with Merik, the people of Crestburn were relatively unharmed in his takeover. Had you been in charge, you would not have been surprised and lots more people would have been hurt in the battle for the city. It's not much, but at least it's something."

CHAPTER 64

SUVAL

Kerwin had proved to be more difficult than he had anticipated. While the man's dream was easy to mess with, it appeared not to bother him. Whatever society he belonged to must have hardened him psychologically. It usually didn't take much more than controlling the various sounds in a dream before people's unconscious minds started taking over and allowing their fears to seep into the dream. Kerwin, on the other hand, didn't seem phased by Suval's usual tricks. Normally, he would have enjoyed a challenge as Kerwin presented him, but he was in a rush to get results so that Merik would let him go back to Liam.

This man's mental fortitude prevented him from spending time with his new plaything. Each hour, he grew more frustrated and angry. Suval lashed out and amplified the sounds into an overwhelming crescendo of noise. Colors faded and brightened only to fade again. How long this went on, Suval wasn't sure, but, eventually, he pulled himself from Kerwin's dreams and he felt drained. He wasn't tired, or in need of sleep, but he felt wiped out, as if he had just gotten through a trying ordeal.

Suval looked over at Kerwin and saw the man had tossed and turned a bit. His skin was a bit paler, and his breathing had picked up a bit. A slight moan escaped his lips, causing Suval to smile at the sound. He reached out with his mind again and entered Kerwin's dream. It was wild and chaotic but not the torrent that Suval had made. He withdrew and pondered.

In the past, he always had to be subtle because he feared discovery. It was also fun for him to see his victim's gradual decay into a wretched, sleep deprived state. Here, he had no fear of discovery. Kerwin was locked in this room. There was nowhere the man could go and no one he could tell. Suval could go all out and overwhelm the man's senses with a torrent of noises and sounds. If the man couldn't be induced to fear, then perhaps overwhelming his senses would work.

Another smile splayed across his lips as thought about this. This was definitely a new approach to things, and he couldn't wait to see the results. Perhaps this new way would cause the mind to degrade faster. A giggle escaped his lips. He had gone from nothing to having two new playthings and a new method to try out.

He delved back into the dreams, this time with gusto. For the next several hours he ramped up Kerwin's dream, alternating, at random, which things he would increase in intensity. It was a new experience for Suval, and he tried different combinations of sounds and colors to overwhelm his victim. Several times throughout the night, Kerwin would startle awake and set up, looking around the room confused. Eventually, he went back to sleep. Around mid-morning, Suval left to go find Merik. He gave orders to the guards to make sure Kerwin didn't sleep for more than a few minutes at a time.

Merik happened to be in the middle of a council meeting when he found him. While he had always been allowed to attend, it was rare for him to do so. He knew that Merik only allowed him to attend the meetings because his presence made the council members uneasy. That was fine by him. A quick glance around the room showed a couple of empty chairs. Quietly, he walked over and sat between a corpulent man with a greasy beard and a young woman fiercely taking notes. The man did everything he could to shift his bulk to the side of the chair away from him. It was comical to watch, and he wondered if the chair would break with such an uneven distribution of weight sitting on top of it. The woman was so focused on her notes that she didn't notice that he occupied the empty seat. He toyed with the idea of asking her for some paper and a quill but decided against it. Merik was not thrilled with his disappearing act and it would probably be best that he behave himself, for now.

Suval tried to listen to the report being given, but the man kept droning on and on about the market and impact on merchants. He was about to doze off when Merik turned and asked him to report. Well, that was unexpected. Never had Merik bothered to address him during a meeting. The woman next to him froze when Merik said his name. He took a moment to compose himself before speaking.

"Things are going quite well with the special assignment that you gave me," he all but purred.

None dared murmur, but there were several who gave furtive glances around the room in hopes to see if anyone might have an idea what the special assignment was.

"My work has led to the discovery of a new technique that should yield some interesting results."

"What kind of time frame are we looking at?" Merik asked.

"It's hard to say. I have only just begun, however, the new technique looks promising," Suval replied.

"You can tell me the details later, then. Now, I believe the next report is on farms in the surrounding countryside."

Suval ignored the report being given by a well dressed middle-aged man, whose skin was heavily tanned from long hours in the sun. He turned to the woman to his left and said, "Shouldn't you be writing this all down."

She jumped and her knees hit the table with a loud thump. Several heads turned to look at the commotion, and Merik raised an eyebrow. Suval just leaned back into his chair and closed his eyes. Most people thought he slept a lot. The truth was that, when he used his special power he got as much rest as if he had been asleep. He could go days without sleeping, which was good because often he dreamed of his uncle when he slept. It was a cruel twist of irony that he couldn't alter his own dreams. So he would just close his eyes, ignore what was happening around him, and be lost in his thoughts or embraced in the caress of a drug he had taken.

Eventually, the meeting ended and, once the last council member had left, he opened his eyes and began with a more detailed report for Merik.

"Kerwin seemed unfazed by usual methods. Nothing I did seemed to bother him the least. So, I tried something different. Instead of being subtle with changes, I was blunt and overwhelming. I would temporarily increase the color of things, as well as sound. This would get changed randomly and constantly kept his senses reeling. He woke up several times but would go back to sleep in short order."

"You are sure this will work?" Merik asked.

"Pretty sure. Each time he went back to sleep, I saw that his dreams were more chaotic. I have guards checking to make sure he stays awake."

"This is nice, but I want him broken as fast as you can."

"I understand, my lord, but if I were to dedicate my entire time to him, you would miss another opportunity."

"Let me guess. You want to go visit Lucky Liam."

"Yes, please. I can wear him down. Eventually, he will be so tired that your guards could walk right up to him and grab him before his luck kicks in."

Merik snorted at the mention of Liam's luck.

"I can do both. You know that I don't need to sleep when I change people's dreams. I can do Liam at night and Kerwin during the day. The guards can keep Kerwin awake at night and get him on a different time schedule."

Merik frowned as he thought it over. Suval did his best to wait patiently, but he was never one for subduing his passions or showing restraint.

"Please, my Lord," he whined.

"Very well. You can go to Liam this evening, but only after you have several more hours with Kerwin. I don't want you to overdo it with Liam. Only mess with his dreams a little bit. Breaking Kerwin is your top priority. I don't want his luck to kick in because you are messing with his dreams too much." Merik smirked.

Inwardly, he groaned, but this was better than nothing. Besides, he could always sit and watch her. That wouldn't be against what Merik commanded.

"You said that your normal methods didn't work on Kerwin. Any idea as to why?"

"I am not sure, sire. You said that he belonged to some secret society. Perhaps his mind is more disciplined than most. Some people's dreams are easier to influence than others. Usually, I don't bother getting to know a person too much before I join their dreams. I had to study Jenal before messing with his sleep because that was what you wished. The man was very disciplined and his dreams took more finesse than most. I would guess that the stronger the will a person has, the harder it is to mess with their dreams. What I do is something new. We will learn more as we explore other memories and dreams. At times, I wish there were more people like us."

"There is no one like us Suval. We are unique, and that is why I will rebuild the Kysian Empire. Now, go back to Kerwin and continue your work."

Suval nodded and left. It had taken Kerwin several hours before he went to sleep. The man was tougher than most and the lack of sleep the night before didn't seem to bother him much. He would see to that. Things would change for him soon.

After several hours, he felt that he had done enough and slipped out. He ordered the guards to keep Kerwin awake until he returned. Hurriedly, he left the mansion and made his way to where Liam lived.

When he first arrived at her hidden home, she was nowhere to be found. Panic had welled up inside of him. He had paced back forth, frantically, and it was all he could do not to go out and look for her. Merik had agreed he could go out and visit her, but he didn't give Suval a lot of time. What would happen if she didn't come back before he had to return to the mansion? The thought made him ill and he had begun to feel nauseous. He sat down and tried to calm down.

Where could she be? It was already late at night and she should have been home fast asleep when he arrived. He had figured that she would have been catching up on all the sleep that she had missed with him. Liam, or whatever her real name was, was nowhere to be found. It made no sense.

His mind raced at different possibilities until he heard a faint sound. Reflexes from years spent skulking around others kicked in and he immediately froze in place and wrapped himself up in a mental shroud that made it very hard for anyone to recognize that he was there. Suval focused on his hearing, and he was able to pick up more sounds than before. Once again, he heard a floorboard creak, slightly. Even with his enhanced hearing, he had barely noticed the sounds. It must be her coming back.

Slow and steady, steps made their way closer and closer. Soon, the person was inside the front room. Light flared briefly then began to flicker steadily. A moment later, she was standing in front of him holding a lamp and looking tired, but not nearly as exhausted as when they had parted ways. When he was sure that it was just the two of them, Suval switched to focus

Empire Remembered

his psychic ability on just her. Finally, they were together again. It would only be for a little while, but at least he could have time with her.

She went over to a pile of clothing on the floor and went through it, searching for several different pieces. Liam, it was weird to think of her with a boy's name but he hadn't learned her name yet, then moved over to the table and sat down and began to cut and sew the pieces she had brought over. It was confusing to watch but, eventually, he realized that she was making alterations to the garments she had selected. Some things she added extra pockets to, others she sewed together to make them reversible. What a clever girl she was. Truly, she was the most fascinating plaything he had ever come across.

For the next hour or so, she worked on the clothes. Suval was continent to sit there and be adrift in his own sea of thoughts as he watched her sew. It had taken some work but, eventually, he had convinced Merik that it was in his lordship's best interest for Suval to keep seeing Liam. Somehow, Liam was considered extremely lucky and no one had been able to capture the lad. Of course, Suval was now beginning to understand that a lot of this luck was simply clever misdirection. He wasn't sure what other secrets she had, but he was definitely looking forward to finding them out. As it was, Liam was a valuable prize and, if Merik was to bring in the uncatchable, then it would do a great deal for his status in this city.

It was very late into the evening when she finally finished with her handy work and went to bed. She tossed and turned a bit, and he wondered what her name was. It seemed odd to think of her as Liam, especially now that he knew her secret. Eventually, he would learn what her name was. It was amazing the things someone would tell you when they had barely slept for days. After a bit, he could hear her breathing become steady. Now was his time to share the intimacy of her dreams. He would watch the dreams for a bit before messing with them. There were things he could learn as he watched her mind unfold the dreams. Soon, he would start but, for now, he would just be a voyeur.

239

CHAPTER 65

MERIK

Merik stood on the balcony and looked up at the nighttime sky. In the clear sky, an unfathomable multitude of stars shone. He smiled as he gazed up at the heavens. A cool breeze blew. On nights like this, it was easy to believe that he was destined to greatness, to be the one to reforge the empire. He would do what others had tried but failed. There was a lot of work to be done, but in the end he would accomplish something that others only dreamed about.

The city had already started to turn against Tianna. That was good. The executions that he made her perform, along with the speech that he had written, angered the crowd nicely. Eventually, he would have to do something about their anger but, for now, it made them easier to control. The upside to the executions was that such a blatant show of power increased the number of street youths looking to join the city guard.

That was good, too. Instead of being at the mercy of other gangs, they would become untouchable, as well as be in a position of power and authority. Eventually, he would have to go to war with his neighbors, and it was far better to send young boys off to war than old men. There would be enough time to get them trained before any fighting started. For now, they left their street gangs and homes for the promise of being a part of something bigger than themselves. They wanted to be a part of history.

Still, there was a lot of work to be done. Meetings and reports followed by more meetings and personal audiences. To say that it was tedious was an understatement. Then, when you think you got things figured out and a good hold on the situation, something unexpected happens. Kerwin and his secret society were one. Thankfully, Suval had been found and started working on him. Even that came with its own surprise, since Suval had managed to find out where Lucky Liam lived. He was leery of letting Suval visit the kid. There was something wrong, a twisted gleam almost, in his expression when Suval talked about the young boy.

If the man didn't have such a useful unique power, he would have had him killed long ago. As it were, he realized that he would need to keep a closer eye on Suval and maybe reign him in a bit. Perhaps he should find a few peasants Suval could experiment with. Djinar had several rooms in the lowest levels of the mansion that had been converted into cells. It would be easy to round up a couple of people who weren't loyal to him and turn them over to Suval. This way, he would be able to keep an eye on him as he tested the boundaries of his dream meddling power.

Merik looked up into the night sky again and smiled as he saw a shooting star streaking its way across the heavens. This was destiny, he reminded himself. Soon, there will be others like him and Suval. Those with new powers who joined his ranks wiould make it harder to dispute his claim to reforging the empire. He was no fool and realized that he would have to face down a few people like himself who have the misguided belief that they are the ones chosen by destiny. It was a pity, but an unfortunate part of life. He wouldn't blame them. After all, they must think they are special and thus singled out by fate. Of course, they wouldn't have the ability to find others as he could, nor would they be able to learn a person's secrets as well as he.

It was possible there could be another person that could pull memories, but that was highly unlikely. The odds of two people having the same new ability would be beyond counting. If anything, there might be someone with a similar ability as his or Suval's, someone who could stop people from dreaming or alter memories or...

Merik whirled about and yelled for a servant, who came running in. "Get me, Captain Tianna, now," he yelled. No, it couldn't be. The chance of that being what happened was too great to even consider as a possibility. Yet, such a thing would explain why she was so obsessed with the dual. Even if it wasn't what he thought, it could possibly be something else. He never thought to look at the structure of the memories. Merik wasn't even sure what to look for, even if there was something there. The next several minutes he spent lost in thought as he tried to think about the possibilities and implications that Tianna's memories of the duel were false. If not, then he had just wasted an evening on a foolish notion. However, if he was right...

Tianna arrived a little while later. Merik waved her over to a chair and took his time to sit next to her, so that he could regain his composure. The last thing he wanted was for her to realize why he wanted to go through her memories again. If he was wrong, then none would be the wiser to his motives. Without bothering to look at the young man, he waved the servant off.

"Captain, thank you for coming so quickly. My plans for the night had unexpectedly changed," he lied. "I know it has been a while since we have gone through your memories of the duel and thought that we could do so again."

"That would be fine," Tianna replied cautiously.

"I am sorry if my servant made it seem as if it was some kind of emergency. They still have some bad habits left over from serving Djinar."

"It's quite alright. I just thought it was something of importance and was surprised when you offered to go through my memories again."

"Oh, this is important, at least to you, but it wasn't anything serious, such as an attack on the city or rioting in the streets. Now, if you don't mind, I would like to begin. While I do have time for you, I don't have all evening. Ruling this city has been quite tedious, and there are so many things that I must do to make sure everything goes along smoothly."

"I am sure, and thank you for doing this again with me, sir." Tianna closed her eyes and relaxed a bit. He gave her a moment or two to focus her memory of the events before linking up with her mind. The memory started just before the duel. He let Tianna direct the memory while he remained a passenger. This time, he didn't pay attention to the details of the fight. Merik focused on the nature of the memory, looking for a clue that would give something away. To be honest, he wasn't sure what he was looking for, or if there was anything to see.

The fight began, and he did his best to ignore what was happening. Luckily, he had seen it dozens of times already and knew every move the two combatants made by heart. She would attack only to fail and come back with a minor wound, and then the experience would repeat. As he watched the blow land on her, there was an odd sensation or feel to the memory that was hard to describe. The feeling soon passed as Tianna moved forward to engage Argent. This time, he was ready for it and noticed right away that something felt off again. Tianna backed off from the engagement and saw another wound on her body. She hesitated for a bit before engaging yet again and the sensation was gone.

Merik took control of the memory and started back at the beginning of the duel. This time, he was ready for the odd sensation when it began, shortly after Tianna and Argent started exchanging blows. Try as he might, he couldn't see anything wrong. Each time she engaged and took a hit, the feeling was there only to disappear for a moment before the next series of blows began. He watched the scene over and over again, and he quickly grew frustrated. Tianna would realize something was not normal with his replaying one specific bit from the duel. He started the duel over again but was barely watching as his frustration mounted.

Then he noticed something. The sky went from partly cloudy to all of a sudden clear. As the duel went on, he watched the sky change back and forth. Every time the sky became clear, the memory had that odd feeling about it. He stopped the memory, got up, went over to stand next to the wall, and poured himself a drink.

"You found something," Tianna said excitedly.

Merik downed the stiff drink, poured himself another glass, and took a long pull from it before turning around to address her.

"Maybe. I got thinking. What if there was someone kind of like me out there? Someone with a new power. More than likely, they would be ambitious because this new power would give them an advantage over everyone else. They would seek out a position of power. Then, I remember how insistent you were about the duel. You are a smart woman and very focused. I didn't want to say anything at first, in case I was wrong. It wouldn't be fair of me to get your hopes up. After watching the duel, I noticed the sky kept going from partly cloudy to clear and back again. There was not much to see, because you were so focused on your opponent, but there was just enough sky in the background over his shoulder that I saw the change. It happened too many times in that short duel for it to be just the clouds blowing away."

"There was a fair amount of cloud cover that day. I remember because I was disappointed. The sun was behind me, and I would have had an advantage of the sun being in his eyes."

"Let's go through the scene again. I want to study it, now that I know there is something off." Merik sat down and took another long pull from his drink, nearly finishing it.

This time, he watched the sky. He waited for the clouds to disappear and halted the memory. The moment was frozen. As he studied it, he began to notice other things that were off. Argent's shadow was off just a little bit, and he held his sword at such an odd angle that it would be difficult to strike with any kind of force. Merik allowed the memory to proceed and stopped it when Argent's blade struck Tianna. Blood sprang from the wound as it should have, but Argent's blade was pristine. The fight continued on and Merik noticed how the blood would drip from her wounds but the ground never had any red stains.

Merik stopped the memory and focused on the things that were wrong. Then it happened. The memory began to split in half. No, that wasn't correct. It was more like it doubled, like when two pieces of paper stuck together. One memory of the duel as it happened, and another that appeared as a ghostly image, parallel to the first, but the actions of the two duelists were different. Then it was gone. When the sensation happened again, Merik stopped the memory and pried apart the alternative image. He resumed the memory and, again, it faded. This time, when the memory had that odd feeling, he let it continue as he pried at it. It was much harder but he was able to separate the two just before the false memory vanished.

Merik started the memory back from the beginning, and, this time, he could see the false memory as a faint silhouette around the original. It took very little to push them apart, and he was able to watch what really happened in the duel. This time, when Tianna attacked, it was all Argent could do to defend himself. Eventually, she backed off and started again. This happened each time they fought until, finally, Tianna just stood there and Ardent walked up and punched her in the head with his pommel.

Control of the memory was ripped from him as it replayed yet again. This time, there was more of a separation between the two images. It seemed that each time he pulled them apart, they didn't go back together again as well. He wondered: if he pulled them apart enough, would the false memory fade away, since it had nothing to cling to?

Lost in his own thoughts, he failed to realize that the memory was over. A low growl-like sound was what brought him to the present moment. He looked over at Tianna and saw her staring straight ahead at nothing, her fist clenched, her jaw tightened. The noise was coming from her.

"Tianna," he said as gently as he could. "Tianna."

She turned and stared at him, her gaze cold with fury. "It was all fake. That son of a bitch tricked me into losing the duel. He cheated and used a power to make me think that I had been wounded. I will kill him!"

"I agree. You must have justice, and I will see to it that you will have the means to do so. Right now, you need to take some time to cool down. You don't know the extent of his manipulation powers, and he could have you believing whatever he wants before you even laid eyes upon him. Take some time to deal with this revelation. Once my position here in Crestburn is secure, we can go after him. It would be a win for both of us, because Kour's mercenary group is something I would have to eventually deal with. I can have Erlin gather information on Kour's group, as well as Argent."

"Ok," she replied numbly.

"In the meantime, why don't you take a couple of days off. What you just learned was a lot to take in. Not only were you cheated out of your rightful place, but there is a maniac in a position of power that has an ability to alter people's memory. If I were you, I would be questioning everything I experienced from the time I met Argent to the time I was cast out. So, please, take a couple of days off. Think things over and come to terms with what you just learned. That will give me a chance to implement things here, and we can deal with Argent together."

Slowly, Tianna nodded her head and got up. Her fists were clenched as she left, but some of the anger was already seeping away. Merik had fed her mind with emotions of peace and hope, which seemed to be working for now. Once she was away from his influence, the anger would return, but, by then, he would no longer care. He had been honest when he said that he would question everything involving Argent. Now that he had solved her obsession over the duel, he could use the idea that there could be other false memories to keep her bound in service to him for a while. The nice thing about that is, there would likely be more memories that Argent altered, and he could drag out the process of finding them for quite some time. Eventually, he would find them all and, at that time, she would no longer need him, which would make her a threat to him. There was still plenty of time before he needed to decide how to handle that situation.

Merik waited a few minutes and finished his drink before retiring to his office. One of the clerks was busy going through a stack of reports. Good to see that they were doing a competent job. The man looked up as he heard the door open.

"My lord, I am almost done with the report for tomorrow, however, I can give you what I have done now, if it so pleases you."

"That won't be necessary. I have to deal with something else. Could you summon Erlin, please? There are some private matters that I need to discuss with him. I am sure a cook could whip up something for you in the kitchen, since you have been working so diligently late into the evening."

"Uh, yes, sir. Thank you, my lord. I will see that Erlin is notified right away."

Once the clerk hurried out, Merik sat down at his desk and began to draft a letter. He was almost done when he heard a knock on the door.

"Come in."

Erlin entered the room.

"You wanted to see me, sire," Erlin said.

"Yes. It turns out that our good Captain had reason to be obsessed over the duel, after all. Argent has the ability to make people remember something other than what really happened. I want you to find out all you can about this man. Also, we need a way to counter his ability."

"Given what you just said, I advise that you take lightly any information I find about him, since it could be false details planted by him."

"Good point," Merik replied.

"As to the other problem, I will need more information. You said he could change people's memories?"

"Yes. It turns out that he made Tianna believe that he was landing blows on her during the duel instead of barely being able to defend himself from her onslaught. Eventually, she thought she had lost enough blood to be on the point of passing out, then he just walked up and knocked her out."

"This could be a serious problem."

"If I wasn't around, then I would agree with you. As it were, I can detect the false memories now that I know how to look for them. What I need for you is to develop a way for other people to realize that he has altered their memories or is using that power."

"This is quite the difficult task and it will take some time to come up with a few solutions. The biggest problem is, we may not know which will work until after an attempt fails."

"I am sure you are more than capable of figuring this out. As you try each method out, I will double check to make sure it is working."

"How did you detect the false memories, if you don't mind me asking?"

"There was a feeling that something was wrong. I noticed a few details that were inconsistent from one moment to the next. After that, I just pried apart the false memory from the real one. Once apart, I could easily see both at the same time, but the false one was more of a ghostly image that overlapped the original. After that, the false memory never completely joined the original and was even easier to detect and separate."

"Fascinating," Erlin commented.

"Quite."

"I am thinking that we could have a telepath link with his mind, like when they have a second for a duel."

"Tianna had a second with her during the duel and that didn't help her," Merik replied.

"Hmm. Then we need a backup to the telepath. Perhaps a second telepath, who is unseen, linked with the first. Although, I am not sure if that would work. Well, I will come up with several possibilities, and we can decide how to proceed. It will be some time before we will need to deal with him."

"It may be sooner than you realize. I want this top priority."

"As you wish, my liege. Will there be anything else?"

"No, that was all. I did give the captain a few days off to let her deal with the revelation of what really happened."

"That was wise, and I know the guards will do just fine without her for a few days. If that is all, then I bid you goodnight."

Merik got up and poured himself another drink as Erlin left. He sat back down, sipped it slowly, and looked over what he had written. It was good, but there were things that could be said better. Over the course of the next several hours, he wrote and rewrote the letter several times. Eventually, he was satisfied with what he had. He placed the letter in a scroll case and sealed it with hot wax. He burned the rough drafts in the fireplace and then stirred their ashes.

The clerk was asleep in a chair just down the hall from the room. Apparently, he had finished his meal, came back, and waited for Merik to finish up with his business. Good man, he thought. It is rare to find a servant who was diligent about his work and yet able to maintain his lord's need for privacy. This was the kind of behavior that should be rewarded. He will have the head housekeeper provide him with his own bottle of something nice from Djinar's stash. There was plenty in the storage rooms, so it's not like it would cost him anything. As it was, he ought to learn the man's name. Servants tended to be deeply honored if their name was remembered by their master. Naturally, this was something he would only do occasionally; there was no reason to give the man an ego for just doing his job. Merik made his way down the hall and out toward the stables. A few soft knocks were all it took to rouse the stable boy.

"I need the stable master. Get him for me immediately," Merik ordered.

The young boy was in shock at seeing his lord stand right before him, let alone directly speaking to him. He stood there dumbfounded for a moment and then disappeared, slamming the door in his haste. A few minutes later, a half-dressed man opened the door.

"Sorry about my appearance, my lord, but I didn't believe the child when he said you were here. What can I do for you, sir?"

"I need this delivered. It is very important that it is delivered quickly and discreetly. The courier will wait for a reply and then come back and see me directly. He is to speak to no one else. I am sure you can find someone who can handle this matter."

"Yeah, I have a rider in mind."

"Good. Wake him up and send him out to me."

"Now?"

"Yes, and you and the boy don't bother coming back out here. What I have to say to your rider is for his ears alone."

"Ok, my lord, as you wish." the man said as he bowed and scraped, before he grabbed the stable boy and dragged him back inside with him. Merik waited in the cool night for several minutes before the door creaked open and a lanky young man came out. "You have need of me, my lord?"

"Yes. Yes I do."

CHAPTER 66

JARIEK

Jariek felt ridiculous in his new outfit. The shirt was two pieces. The bottom was a dark blue that fit tight across his chest, while the second piece was a bright yellow thing with a low cut neck and sleeves that had so much extra material at the end that they dropped down. The pants were split up the front to the knee and showed his lower legs, as well as the striped socks, every time he took a step. Then, as an extra precaution, he shaved his head. Supposedly, this was fashionable in Terbaria.

While he might have gotten a few strange looks at the inn, no one bothered to do more than just glance at him. When he got back to the Cashek Society, he was definitely going to look up Terbaria, where the second caravanner said this style was from. If this wasn't the style, there would be serious payback, not that he wasn't going to pay the man back as it was.

His room had been booked for a fortnight, and he was registered as Jorin, a younger son of a prominent merchant from Terbaria. There had been several outfits waiting for him, unfortunately of the same unbearable style. The inn had a fine kitchen, and he could eat his meal, which was already paid for, in his room or in the dining room by the kitchen. There was even a lounge and a walled courtyard. It was a very nice place, and it would be the last location Merik's guards would come looking for him. Even if they did come to Crestview Haze, there was a high chance that they wouldn't recognize him in the ridiculous outfit he was wearing.

The hardest part of staying at the inn was finding something to do to pass the time. He didn't want to talk with the other guests for fear that one of them might know of the region he was pretending to be from. Odds were good that wouldn't be the case, but it was a risk he was not willing to take. There were several books in the lounge that he could borrow, but he couldn't focus on any of them for more than a few pages at a time. Eventually, he gave up reading. Jariek began to grow restless from being confined to the inn.

He had been sitting in the courtyard, enjoying the afternoon sun, when a bird flew overhead. In a heartbeat, he took control of the bird and was aloft above the city. For several minutes he was lost in the thrill of flying and being free of the inn. Now that he had a body to control, he could go about the city as he pleased. Slowly, he adjusted the posture of his body to make it look like he fell asleep whilst reading and then focused back on the crow.

The first place he went to was Master Gerwald's. He landed the crow on a roof across the street. From his vantage point, everything looked normal. Jariek flew the crow over to a windowsill on the building that served as quarters for the apprentices and journeymen. A quick peek in the room told him that his bed was cleared and the trunk where he kept his clothes were gone. More than likely, his trunk was placed in some dark forgotten storage closet on the off chance he returned.

He took flight again and circled the roof looking for a location where he could sit and watch the aviary. Apprentices were going about their chores while a pair of journeymen worked with a bird of prey. Quickly, he landed again, so as to remain out of sight. It wouldn't do to have the journeymen notice the crow and send the hawk after it as a training exercise. Slowly, he walked up to the peak of the room and over near the ledge. In addition to a nice view of the training yard, he could see the front office and the main office on the floor above through windows.

The day passed slowly, with little excitement. Only someone very familiar with the daily routine of the aviary would notice the slight change as the chores were being divided up by one less person. Everything seemed fine, and Jariek was both pleased and a bit hurt by that. He was happy because he liked Master Gerwald and felt bad about abandoning his job, but it was sad to see how little he was missed by those there.

A herald, accompanied by several city guards, entered the shop. This was not good. He could see the head guard talking to Gerwald's oldest son, who was manning the front desk. Nertson nodded his head several times before holding up his hand to the guard and left the room. A moment later he appeared upstairs in Gerwald's office. Seeing that the training yard was empty at the moment, Jariek had the bird fly over to and balance on the edge of the window.

Several footsteps could be heard, as well as Master's Gerwald's voice, as he greeted the guards. The officer began right away with the questions to Master Gerwald about Jariek's employment. Gerwald told the guard that he had worked there as an apprentice but ran off a few days ago and had not been seen since. There were several more questions about his whereabouts, which Master Gerwald answered honestly - that he had no idea where his missing employee ran off to. The guard didn't seem happy about the responses he received. There were a few questions about recent visitors that he might have had and if there had been any unusual customers. From the line of questioning, it seemed as if they were looking to see if Kerwin had been there to see him. Gerwald answered their questions and then offered to let them walk around his establishment and talk to his apprentices and journeymen. Once the guards left, Gerwald returned to his paperwork.

Jariek made the crow take flight again and circle the aviary, trying to find the best spot to watch the guards as they searched the grounds and talked to the employees. With luck, the guards would leave satisfied that he was nowhere to be found and leave Gerwald and his people alone. It made him sick to think that they could suffer merely because he worked there. As it was, there was very little he could do other than just watch from afar.

A window opened up on the second floor of the building where the birds were kept. Thomas was inside cleaning the hawks' cages. The guards, having just left the kitchen and dining hall, were heading across the training grounds, straight to the building where the birds were kept. This was not good, for Thomas was the one who Kerwin first talked to. There was a small chance that he might remember him and relate that to the guards.

The crow swooped down and landed on the edge of the open window. Thomas was off on the other side of the room and Lucius, the apprentice who had opened the window, had his back towards Jariek's crow as he crossed the room. With a quick flap of his wings, he glided over to the cages. A hawk, startled by having a crow land on its cage, let out a cry. He hung on to the side and used his beak to open the latch as quickly as he could before the hawk could do more than cry out. Leaping from the cage and gliding over to the next one, he repeated the process. The boys were so focused on their tasks that they hadn't, as of yet, noticed the crow and so far ignored the little bit of commotion from the hawks.

With two cages unlocked, he went over to a third cage, whose occupant started making a racquet the moment he landed on the cage. Once unlocked, he nudged the door open and dropped to the floor. Thomas looked up just in time to see the cage door open and the hawk fly out. He shouted to his partner, who raced over to block the window. Jariek hopped slowly across the floor and made his way across the room. While the two were trying to grab the freed hawk, Jariek let another one out of its cage. At the sight of the second bird being airborne, the others began to stir in their cages. As the birds moved around in their cages, the first two that he had unlocked bumped their door which, now unlocked, swung wide open.

Now, the freed hawks outnumbered the men two to one. The door opened to a pair of guards with bewildered looks on their faces as they tried to comprehend the scene before them. Thomas managed to grab one of the birds and hood it quickly. With the hood on, the bird settled down.

Seeing the guards, Thomas called out to them. "If you don't mind, I could use a hand here. Just slowly walk this way and that will help push the remaining ones to me." The guards just stood there watching as Thomas nabbed a second bird.

"What's going on here?" came a voice from behind the guards.

Thomas was busy trying to get the remaining two birds while his companion kept the window blocked. The two guards and herald entered the room. The herald looked at the chaos and then went over to Thomas. "I have questions that you need to answer."

"Excuse me, sir, but, as you can see, I am a bit busy right now," Thomas replied.

"Those birds can wait. I can't. Your friend is blocking the window so it's not like they are going anywhere as it is. Now, give me your full attention, or I can take you in and we question you more formally," the Herald demanded.

Thomas dropped the hood in his hand and looked at the officer. "What are the questions that I can help you with, sir?"

"When was the last time you saw Jariek," the herald demanded.

"A few days ago. He up and disappeared without saying a word."

"Before he left, did he have any special visitors?"

"No, he didn't see anyone. He was just an apprentice, and Master Gerwald works his apprentices hard. They don't have much time for a social life. Even us journeymen don't get out that much."

"Did he speak out at all against Lord Merik?"

"Not that I ever heard."

"What about the previous lord of the city? Any connections to Djinar?"

"No."

The officer ducked as a hawk flew by him and landed on a cage nearby.

"Any changes to his schedule in the last several weeks?"

"Not that I know of."

"Uh, the same goes for me with all your questions, sir. I know it's not much, but I hope it helps," piped up Lucius.

The herald turned and looked at the two guards who nodded, turned, and left, with the herald following behind without bothering to close the door.

Thomas swore and went over to shut the door. Now was his chance. Jariek hopped the crow closer to the window and paused to make sure the young man was focused on the two remaining birds before he lepted into the air and flew straight at Lucius. He was caught off guard and Jariek was able to fly right under his arms and out the window. He could hear cursing behind him as he flew off. There would be quite a bit of confusion as they tried to figure out which bird flew off.

Jariek had the crow fly across the street, where he could watch the front entrance. A short while later, the guards and herald left. He followed behind them for a while, hoping to hear them talk about their search for him. Unfortunately, he was out of luck as they remained silent all the way back to the main guard house. Jariek thought about sticking around and seeing what he could learn, but the odds were too great that he would be noticed. With Merik knowing about new powers, the last thing he wanted was to risk exposing himself. Granted, he couldn't think of how that would be, but it was better to be cautious.

He flew the crow up and over the city, and he enjoyed being aloft in the breeze. Now was the time for freedom and an escape from the confines of the inn. At least he didn't have to worry about Master Gerwald anymore. The guards had questioned them and there was nothing to be learned from them. Jariek couldn't believe how lucky he got with his timing. And, he could rest easier knowing that there wouldn't be any repercussions to his former mentor.

Eventually, he grew bored flying over the city and took the bird out into the countryside. Farmers worked in the fields down below, while game moved through forests and the tall grass. Despite the recent upheaval in Crestburn, the countryside was going on as it always had. That may change if Merik tried to resurrect the Kysian Empire. At some point, he would wage war on his neighboring psylords, and that would be the end of the peaceful countryside, for a few years at any rate.

Something shiny caught the crow's eye. In fact, there were several objects that were shining in the early afternoon sun. He swooped in and, as he drew near, Jariek saw several bodies that had been picked clean by scavengers. This was the aftermath of some carnage that he noticed the last time he was flying in the countryside. Jariek had meant to come back here and examine the scene, to try and figure out what happened, but, with the excitement of recent events, he had forgotten all about it.

He circled the scene a few times, taking it all in. It looked like some kind of battle happened here. Several of the bodies were in a rough line, although he could tell that a few had been moved as scavengers tried to make off with choice bits. A swarm of flies gathered around the remains as their offspring feasted on what was left. Between the heat, humidity, and animals, the bodies had been reduced mostly to bones.

A crow cawed a greeting to him, which was repeated by another in the murder that picked at a pair of corpses. Normally, he would let the crow take back more control to return a greeting, but he had work to do. The crows cawed again and waited as the newcomer remained unnaturally silent.

He examined one body, then the next. It was hard to tell how they died, since most of the skin and organs were gone, but here and there were pieces of bones that were cut or broken. Most had wounds on the front while a few had them on the back and shoulders. If he had to guess, it looked like a battle was fought and some were cut down as they tried to flee. The bodies were too far gone to get more information out of them.

He hopped from one body to the next and looked for anything that might give him a clue about who they were. The scraps of clothing were of different styles and material but of good quality. Blades were still in hand or close to the body. It was hard to tell, but it looked as if all the bodies belonged to the losers of the fight. The winners' ether took their dead with them or didn't lose a person. Too much time had passed to get an idea of how many attackers there had been. If he had to guess, it would seem that these people encountered a trained group of warriors and were quickly beaten. The bodies were pretty far gone but not complete bones so whatever took place happened within the last month, right around the time Merik took over. It was quite possible they were killed before the take over, as Merik's forces made their way to the city. Or they could have been a scouting party from a neighboring psylord. A few corpses later and that theory was gone as he gazed on the body of a young kid. Another psylord would not have included someone that young in a patrol, or so he hoped.

While the bodies had been picked over by animals, none of their belongings had been touched by looters. Either no one had discovered the scene or were too afraid to mess with it. Several packs were together and in a loose pile. They had been moved around and opened, but the rips and tears suggested animals and not people had gotten into them. He wished he could switch from animal to animal so that he could take control of a critter more suitable for rummaging through people's belongings. Perhaps he could come back in a day or two, either in person or with a host more suitable for pilfering.

He flew up to a branch on a nearby tree to get a better view of the whole scene. Packs near the treeline, bodies in a ragged line with the ones wounded in the back closer to the packs. Yeah, it was beginning to look more like a one-sided battle took place. That means it was probably Merik's forces. The bodies were between the packs and the city which means that they were probably fleeing Crestburn. Could this be Djinar's group? If Djinar was among them, then, no wait, there was definitely nobody large enough to have been Djinar. They were probably people who had been loyal to Djinar, or failed to swear allegiance to Merik, and tried to flee but were killed a short ride from the city, just far enough that no one would notice.

It was a shame that there was no way to find out who they were. That information could be useful in the right hands. He sat there on the branch and pondered a bit. What could he do about the scene before him and what good would it do for those who were massacred. If this was Merik's handiwork, then he wouldn't be the first psylord to butcher people. The Cashek Society would definitely want to know about it, especially if they are considering backing him. Down on the ground, two crows squawk at each other over a piece of gristle. Was this what they were all to become, food for the crows?

He took flight again, to get away from the carnage and the morbid thoughts in his head. The other crows forgot their fight and looked up as he flew by. Down on the ground, something caught his eye, something he had missed before. Circling down in a quick spiral, he landed by what had captured his eye. There was a silver necklace on the chest of one of the corpses. The image was two upturned wings and, where they joined, three talons descended downward, the middle being the longest, that clutched a black oval-shaped stone. It was beautiful. He reached down, bit the leather cord to sever it. Then he grabbed the cord and took off with the necklace. Taking flight, he headed straight back to the inn with his memento clutched in the bird's claws.

CHAPTER 66

ASHA

Asha did her best to stifle a yawn. Her sleep has been horrible lately. She supposed it was due to stress. Kerwin had disappeared without a trace. When she went to look for Jariek, he was no longer at Master Gerwald's aviary. Something was definitely amiss, and she had assumed they left Crestburn until she saw a crow with a necklace clutched in its claws. She wasted no time to look and see if Jariek was in control of the bird and was pleased to see that it had a psychic cloud around its head. Jariek had to be somewhere nearby, and, if he was around, there was a chance Kerwin was, too. Normally, she could care less if someone disappeared. Here in Crestburn, it happened all the time, or at least it did under Djinar's rule. Jariek was different; he was like her.

The horse that interrupted Hargod and his thugs had gone by her so fast that she was caught by surprise when she saw the psychic cloud around its head. She didn't have a chance to study it to see if there was a new cloud along with the traditional cyan color associated with controlling someone. Originally, Asha had planned on doing a little information gathering, since she had been out of it for a few days with the bad dreams. If she wanted to make it in the information business, she had to stay on top of things. The crow had changed that. Unfortunately, its head was too small and far off to make much detail out, other than it had a cyan cloud around it.

Asha took off and did her best to keep up with the bird as it flew across the city. The crow flew along a straight path that was parallel to the street she was on. That made following it easier, but she knew that in another dozen blocks the street would end and she would lose sight of the bird. Quickly, she reached out to the nearby minds and made them not focus on her. A tug at a stitch in her dress and it loosened and fell to the ground, revealing thin brown pants and light blue shirt. She leaped up on top of a vendor's table, knocking down some of the merchandise, and scrambled up the pole that supported an awning. From there, she leapt to the wall that the shop sat against. Barely clinging to the rough side of the building, she was able to reposition her hands to be able to pull herself up and onto the roof. Down below, the merchant yelled at a customer who he thought had knocked some of his merchandise off the table.

The bird was several yards ahead of her, but at least now that she was on the rooftops she had a better chance of not losing it. She took off at a sprint and relied on her ability to see the future to make sure she didn't miss a step. Asha leaped from one roof to the next as she dashed her way across the city. A stitch in her side had begun to form, but she pushed herself. The last thing she wanted was to lose the crow, which had started to get further ahead of her as she was wearing down.

Finally, she could run no more. Asha collapsed on the rooftop and watched helplessly as the bird flew on. While she was in decent shape, her lack of sleep played hell with her energy level, and she had become winded sooner than she thought. She was just starting to curse her luck when the crow landed up ahead. She couldn't make out exactly where it had gone, but at least she knew the area. Slowly, Asha got back up to her feet and slowly made her way in the direction that the bird had landed. By the time her breathing was back to normal, she could see a rather posh inn up ahead. This had to be where it went. The guys must have rented rooms here. Kerwin had no problems paying for several outfits and meals for her when he needed to hire Lucky Liam, so he probably could afford a place like this.

There was no sign of the bird, but it could have easily flown into one of the rooms on the upper floors. Several of those rooms had balconies as well as their windows open. If the bird came in, then it would eventually have to leave. She could sit here and wait for it, patience was something she did excel at. It was tough to not nod off as she sat in the late afternoon sun with the day's heat reflecting off the roof. Asha had to focus in order to stay awake as time progressed.

"Well, well, what do we have here?" came a voice from behind her.

Asha spun around and popped up into a crouch. Several men stood behind where she had been sitting, each one armed with a club or long knife. The thugs looked a little familiar, but off the top of her head, she couldn't place them. A quick glance to the street below and she saw several more thugs watched with keen interest.

"We wondered when you would show up again. You laid pretty low after the last time. Then, you were spotted running across the roofs in broad daylight. Well, your luck is not going to save you this time, Liam."

Liam? Saw her running? Asha remembered making people not notice her when she started her climb. Then, she switched to precognition to see where to avoid stepping on her mad dash across the rooftops. In her exhausted state, she stopped using the one ability when she switched to the other. It was a stupid and amateurish mistake that was about to cost her. She never would have done something like that if she weren't having trouble sleeping. The clothes that she had picked out under her dress were rather masculine. No wonder they thought she was Liam. Well, she was Liam but hadn't planned on being Liam today. No problem. She could adapt. How much makeup did she put on this morning? She couldn't remember; damn those bad dreams. Well, she would have to keep her face down. The last thing she wanted was for these thugs to spot makeup on her face and get the idea that Liam dressed as a girl to go around in disguise, even though Liam was really the disguise.

"How da you know t'was a mistake that I made? After all, you clowns aren't de first ta try and catch me fer a bit of fame. I am sure tat Lord Merik would be very impressed if you had actually captured me and not da oter way around."

"What do you mean?" the thug asked hesitantly.

Asha brought up her arm as if she was wiping sweat from her forehead. She glanced down to see if any makeup had rubbed off on her arm. None. Good. For once, forgetting something actually came to her favor. Now, to mess with their heads and create an opportunity for herself to get away.

"Come on now, you're a smart fellow. Well, no your not, but we can pretend you are. Haven't you noticed de change in Crestburn since Lord Merik took control? More guard patrols, which are more efficient tan de old guards could ever have dreamed ta be. De execution of tose who oppose Lord Merik and his forces. Come on now, it doesn't take a smart man ta figure out tat Lord Merik is cleaning up this city. Getting rid of the rough and unlawful elements of the city."

"You're no upstanding citizen yourself, Liam" the thug threw back feebly. "Why, just several days ago you were running a package to a warehouse."

"Hey, I tought I recognized you," she said with a smile. "Nice try, by de way. I was really impressed. Did you happen ta bring your bags of flour wit you tis time? No? It's ok, it didn't work last time."

Several of the men grumbled, and she could tell she struck a nerve with the comment. One of them shouted out, "It didn't work because of that damn horse."

She let out a hearty laugh "Well, boys, I am called lucky Liam fer a reason. Now, ta our present situation. Remember how his Lordship talked about rebuilding the Wardens? Well, I went up ta him and offered my services. I explained ta him tat tere was no one better who could help him round up da criminal elements in Crestburn. So, he came up with a plan. I do business as usual, and de next time tey tried to catch me, he would round tem up. Yous see, my route was preplanned, and I knew tat someone foolish enough would tink tey could use de opportunity ta catch me. Guess wat, boys, it's you who are caught."

At this proclamation, several of the thugs grew nervous and started to look around. Fear crept into their expression, and one even started to back away. Good. They believed her. A quick glance at the street showed the ones down there hadn't moved, but she wasn't surprised by that. While the men weighed in the threat that she had just made, Asha took the time to look at the outcome of several possible actions. Charging them ended up with them reacting quick enough to knock her down. Jumping to the building across the street ended with her missing by several inches. Flinging a loose ceramic tile at one of them ended with a gash on his head and an opening that she was able to get through. It wasn't much, but at least she could have options after that.

From her crouched position, Asha grabbed a loose roof tile and, with a snap of her wrist, she sent it spinning at the thug just right of the center. The tile smashed into his forehead, cutting it pretty good, and got blood in his eyes. The man grabbed his head and yelled in pain and shock just as Asha leaped forward. The others were too startled to react quick enough as she skimmed by the wounded man. Now, there was just one ahead of her, who had started to back away when she threatened a trap. Her mind raced forward in time and saw that if she went to his right he would have just enough time to lash out with his leg and trip her up, so left it would be.

She charged the last man, feinted right, and dove to the left as his leg lashed out into empty air. Using her forward momentum, Asha turned the dive into a somersault and landed with a roll, banging her shoulder a bit on the rough edges of the ceramic roof tiles. In a moment, she was up and running. Having just traversed this area a little bit ago, she was familiar with the layout and had already formulated a plan to escape. The thugs were pretty stocky men and would have a harder time chasing her on the rooftops if she picked buildings with a large gap to jump over.

Asha leaped off the edge of one building and landed deftly on the next. Behind her, she could hear the men curse as they came to a stop. She risked a look and glanced over her shoulder. She saw one of the men, who had backed up, run at the edge and just barely made the jump across. He took a moment to regain his balance and then started after her. Another had started his jump, as well. Her pursuers lost a lot of ground in the time it took to make that jump. Losing them would be a piece of cake. A few more jumps like that and she could get down to the streets and disappear from sight.

Another leap and this time she didn't bother to look back as she heard the thugs cursing at her. There was a loud thump as one of them made it across the second gap and came down hard on the other roof. Up ahead was a nice gap and, after that, she should be in the clear. She picked up her pace to make sure she could clear it easily and hit the other side at a run. She heard cursing from behind her and, from the sounds of it, one of her pursuers was hanging on the edge after a failed jump.

Asha launched herself into the air again and felt a sharp pain in her calf. Her leg gave out the second it touched the roof, and she did her best to tumble through the rough landing. She looked down at her leg and saw an arrow jutting through it. One building over to her left she could see an archer, who had crouched down out of sight behind a chimney. This was not good. She had been so focused on ditching her pursuers and, with no one else in sight on the rooftops, she got sloppy and careless.

The archer whistled loudly and a moment later he was joined by three more thugs. Slowly, they advanced and, from behind her, the first of her pursuers had finally arrived. She scanned the future but several possibilities showed her being shot with another arrow. Pain throbbed from her calf where the arrow protruded from both sides. It looked like it went through cleanly, but, having never been shot before, she wasn't exactly sure. Her calf did hurt like hell, though.

"We gotcha yah, Liam."

Asha just groaned in pain but didn't say anything.

"Figured you would escape the first group, so we made sure to make that a bit easier for you. Once you got away, then you would let your guard down, and we would have our chance. Looks like the plan worked. We hoped that your luck wouldn't have much to work with if we shot at you mid-jump with no one around to accidentally mess it up."

The only thing she could do was laugh. Between the pain in her leg, the frustration of finally being caught, and the lack of sleep, the response she had was mad laughter. Had she not been lost in the moment, she would have realized how much her laughing unnerved her capturers. Eventually, they got over whatever was bothering them about her response and approached her.

Two of the thugs tossed her onto her stomach and held her down while another one tied her hands behind her back. Her feet were tied together with about a foot length of rope between them. She could walk, but she wouldn't be able to run. The archer came over and grabbed hold of her leg. He reached down and snapped the arrow in half. Pain shot through her leg.

"Hey. What are you doing?" asked one of the thugs.

"Removing the arrow."

"Like hell. Just leave it in and put a bandage on. If he escapes, it will slow him down a bit. I ain't taking no chances with Lucky Liam. You're new to Crestburn, so you have no clue about his luck abilities."

The archer scoffed, "Doesn't seem that lucky to me."

"Trust me, Jaxus, he is Lucky. Damned bastard got away last time cause a horse went mad and attacked us. He can walk with that in his leg, can't he?"

"Yeah," Jaxus replied.

"Good, then leave it in until we get where we are going. You can take it out later. Ok?"

"Sure."

She felt the pressure as he bandaged the wound that he had made. "There. That should be good. You definitely are still lucky. That shot was a clean one and you should heal from that in no time. You probably won't even have a limp."

"Yeah, I feel totally lucky ta be shot by yous. Thanks," Asha replied.

Jaxus just shrugged and looked at the others. "Now what?"

"Let's take him to the hideout. Botun will be thrilled with us, and Hargod will be jealous as hell. It was about time someone showed that thug up."

As Asha was pulled to her feet, she looked long and hard at the archer. He was young, perhaps her age, with a soft face with the beginnings of a thin beard and mustache. His brown hair was fairly short, and his eyes were a deep gray. She made sure to remember his face. One day, she would pay him back for this she thought as a hood was lowered over her head.

CHAPTER 67

TIANNA

She had left Merik in a kind of a daze. Her mind reeled from the shock of the revelation. The truth of what had happened to her was overwhelming and was difficult to cope with. In the past, when she was stressed and needed to work through an issue, she would practice her sword forms and drill herself to exhaustion. Focusing on the poses and forms allowed her to get lost in the rhythm of the moves and find serenity. With her mind cleared of distractions and her body worn out, she would often find a solution to the issue shortly after practice.

Not this time.

Each slice of the blade was off just a bit. Angles would not be true and moves would be too slow. With each mistake, her frustration mounted. It was Sergeant Herlt who came up to her and bayed her to stop. The old merc could tell right away that something was seriously wrong with her. When she hesitated to tell him, he told her to follow him. Herlt led Tianna to her office and pointed to her chair while he poured them a stiff drink.

"I know you are not one to lose themselves in the bottle, but you are too worked up to think straight at this point. I'm not sure what it is, but I would guess Merik has something to do with it. Now, drink and then tell me what is going on," he said.

So she drank and, when the first shot was done, he poured them both another. The sense of unrealness began to fade as alcohol kicked in. She told Herlt about how her memory had been altered, that she had been cheated out of her position. In the end, she just broke down in tears and cried. Herlt sat there patiently waiting until she had cried herself out.

"I have heard and seen a lot of things in my years. From time to time, a warrior gets a head wound bad enough they forget their past, but what you just told me." he paused to shake his head "To not be able to trust your own memories. That's worse than most of the things I have seen. You usually find peace with practice but that is not going to work this time. It won't ever work unless you can find some way to deal with this to one degree or another.

"Me, I can't imagine what must be like to not be able to trust my own memories. I can run things for a few days. Take the time Merik gave you and drink yourself half out of your mind. Then, when you only have half a mind, deal with things and try to find a way to come to terms with it all. I know it is one hell of a task, but it is the only way you will survive. Too many people get drunk to hide from things, don't. Drink enough to cloud your mind so that you can start to handle dealing with it in a numbed state. When you start to get a handle on things, then sober up a bit and deal with it a little more. Remember, you survived with Kour's mark when no one else could. You turned that thing from something people see as an invite to quick money into something they should be afraid of. It will be rough, but I believe you can get through this."

So that was what she did. Tianna went down to a storeroom and took a few moments to look over Djinar's stock. There were wines, ales, whiskeys, twilight haze, and other more illicit stuff. Not having been one to drink much, she grabbed several bottles of wine and returned to her room. For perhaps the first hour, she just sat at the edge of her bed and stared off into space. As the numbness of shock wore off, she began to think about what happened to her and what it meant.

It was overwhelming.

Grabbing the nearest bottle, Tianna popped the cork and took a long pull. It didn't help, so she took another, and then another. Time began to slip away from her and, at some point, there had been a knock on the door. By the time she staggered over to the door, whoever it was gone but there was a plate of food and several more wine bottles. She brought all of it into her room, ignored the food, and opened one of the new bottles of wine. For the next day and a half, she stayed drunk. At one point, she even forgot why she was drunk until she looked into the mirror and saw her scared face.

She broke down crying. Sobs wracked her body, and she cried for hours until there were no more tears left to give. Then, drive heaves shook her body. Why had her face been ruined? Why had she been reduced to nothing more than a prize that was worth a few pounds of coin? Why had her future been taken from her? Why was she the victim of something she couldn't possibly have prevented?

CHAPTER 68

MERIK

Merik sat at the large desk and drummed his fingers on the oaken table. Not for the first time, he thought about having this bland monstrosity of a desk swapped out for something more fitting of a ruler. While Djinar did have a collection of Kysian furniture, most of the day-to-day furniture was fairly simple in style and rather large in order to fit his bulk. The desk where he did his paperwork was an example of the banal furniture that filled the mansion. He made a mental note to himself that he really needed to change the desk, especially now that he was meeting more people.

As it was, he was annoyed at possibly having to reschedule his meeting with the mayors of several of the small towns near Crestburn. Now that the city was stabilized, he wanted to secure his influence with the nearby towns. Most of those towns weren't big enough to make much of a difference as far as which way their loyalty went. Eventually, he would expand his territory, and those towns could be wonderful staging areas. If they were supportive of him, it would make things that much easier. Naturally, he would crush any that would dare to oppose him, but now was the time to see where their loyalties lie.

Erlin had said that the heralds discovered something big and that Merik would want to look into it personally at his first opportunity. Merik hoped this was something that could be handled very quickly and not force him to meet the mayores at a different time. It wasn't that he was opposed to making someone wait, after all, there were many times he scheduled meetings too close together so that the latter would be forced to wait for him. What bothered him was that they may see his delay as sloppy leadership. Even though he had perhaps the greatest takeover of a city since the collapse of Kysia, he wanted the records to show that he was a capable leader and not some fool who got lucky and bungled what he had taken.

Merik sighed heavily and thought about getting a drink. The stress of running a city was piling up on him, and he needed to find some way to relax before he made a mistake. He knew he was not infallible; no one was. There were countless accounts of leaders who couldn't handle being in charge. It was one thing to take over a city or defeat an opposing army in battle and another thing entirely to rule a land you conquered. Thankfully, unlike most of the other psylords, he was well read. He knew good and well the follies of a leader and would not make the same mistakes they had.

Merik leaned back in his chair and longingly looked at the liquor stand. He was about to get up and pour himself a drink when the door opened to the room. Quickly, he sat back down and grabbed a piece of paper to make it look like he had been doing something. Erlin entered the room, followed by a skinny young man with brown hair and mustache, or more accurately an attempt at a mustache. They sat down in the chairs in front of the desk and waited patiently for Merik. After he drew out the time just a little bit, he did have another meeting he hoped to make, he decided that they waited long enough, put the paper in a drawer, and looked the young man over.

"Well, Erlin, you have yet to waste my time, so please inform me why you requested I meet with him."

"My lord, this young man knows the location of Botun's hideout, as well as Lucky Liam," Erlin replied while just barely suppressing a smile.

Merik raised an eyebrow at this bold claim but said nothing. Erlin turned to the young man and continued. "Jaxus came to one of the heralds a few hours ago. When they realized that he had probably told them the truth, they sent him to me. I questioned him and, when I did not detect any dishonesty, I requested this meeting, because I know how important it is that you find Botun."

"How is it that you know where Botun is?"

The young man leaned forward with a nervous smile. "They took me to him. I was the one that shot the Liam fellow everyone was talkin about."

"You shot Lucky Liam?" Merik asked in disbelief.

"Yes," then after a pregnant pause, he added a cautious, "my lord."

"Please, tell me how you managed to pull that off."

"Well, you see, I came to Crestburn to see if them rumors were true."

Merik held up his hand. "What rumors?"

"That you are tryin to rebuild the wardens, and that you wanted people to fight for ya. Anyway, I came here to see if the rumors are true. Well, I don't know no one, so I have been livin at an inn for around a week or so. I started to get to know a few street toughs, and then this mornin I am with a guy, and a friend of his tells us that he saw Lucky Liam running across the rooftops. He swore, and several more of his friends gathered, and they talked about goin after Liam. As I listened to them talk, I realized this guy is hard to catch, so I decide to use an old hunter's trick. They gave my plan a try, and we ended up catchin Liam, and took him back to their hideout."

"What was the trick?"

Jaxus gave a guilty smile. "Hunters sometimes use dogs to drive animals to them. So, I had them guys act like the dogs and drive Liam to where I hid. Ya see, I gots two strong abilities. I can make it so people don't realize I am there, wished it worked on animals so I would have an easier time huntin. I can also enhance my senses. That comes really handy with shootin. Of course, I am a good shot on my own without the enhancement.

"Anyways, they talk to this Liam fella, and he manages to slip past them and starts runnin away. I stayed hunkered down behind a chimney and, when that boy jumps from one roof to another, I fire off a shot and wing him in the leg. He comes tumblin down, and the rest of the group are on him before he can get back up.

"Now, everyone's happy that they caught this Liam guy. They hood him, and bind him, and off they go to deliver him to their boss man called Hargod. I get to tag along because, after all, it was my plan and my arrow that got him. They were all secretive about deliverin Liam but that didn't concern me none. Until they mentioned Botun, and I remember hearin about how he was a wanted criminal. Well, they lock up Liam and a runner gets sent to go get Botun. He comes back after a while and says Botun will be in later, that he is busy. The men start to celebrate and, after a few drinks, I found my chance to leave.

Since I wanted to be a warden, that's why I came to Crestburn, I thought that if I told your men where this Botun was holed up that it might help me become a Warden for ya. Didn't think I would be actually talkin to ya myself."

As Jaxus told his story, Merik linked with his mind and saw the memories of the event unfold. The young man had spoken truthfully, as Erlin predicted. This was excellent news. Now he can deal with Botun and quite possibly Djinar, as well, or at least get an answer about his fate.

"Erlin, I have a meeting with some of the leaders of the nearby villages. Can you please see that they are informed that the meeting will be canceled? Also, I need the city's guards ready to move out on short notice."

"At once, my lord." Erlin gave a quick bow and left the room. Jaxus watched nervously as he left. Merik got up and slowly walked over to the liquor cabinet. He grabbed two glasses and began to pour. He put the decanter back, took a long pull from his glass, then topped it off before turning around to Jaxus. The young man appeared to be nervous at being left alone with him.

He walked back across the room, this time choosing the chair that Erlin had vacated, and handed the young man the other drink that he made.

"Here, Jaxus. You know, I don't blame you for being nervous. It's not every day you get to be alone with a ruler of a city, let alone someone who is about to make serious history."

Tentatively, Jaxus reached for the glass and sniffed it before downing half of it in a quick gulp. He coughed a bit as the liquor burned his throat. A moment later, he took a much smaller sip and only gave the barest of coughs.

"I know you said that you came to Crestburn to see if the rumors are true. Well, I can't attest to all the rumors that must be circulating, but I can say this: the necessary steps are being implemented for me to bring about the wardens of old again. Needless to say, I am looking for talented individuals to be amongst the first. Not only will these select people need to have strong talents, but they must be smart and resourceful. Psychic ability will only take a person so far. Look at me. I have a few abilities but nothing powerful or out of the ordinary, yet here I am the ruler of Crestburn. It is through my other skills, my education, and hard work that I am able to achieve what I have done.

From the little bit that you told me, it sounds like you are a resourceful young man as well. There could be a bright future for you at my side, if you are capable and loyal."

"Really? I would like that very much. There was not much for me in my village."

"What village do you come from?"

"Trevon."

"I am not familiar with it."

"Not surprised. It's a tiny little village just south of the Emperor's Forest, right off the river. It's just a couple of dozen houses. Farmers, fishers, and a few hunters, like myself."

"You hunt?"

"Yes, my lord. I am a very good hunter. Never got along with other kids, so I would go slip off into the woods to be alone. My uncle and dad taught me how to use the bow, and I got really good with it, and that's without enhancing my senses."

"You must be an excellent shot then," Merik said as he sent the feeling of pride to the young man.

"Well, I did shoot that Lucky Liam fella. From what I heard, he was uncatchable," Jaxus replied.

"I am curious. How did you manage to pull that off?"

"Nothin to it. Like I told ya, it's just like huntin an animal. I found my place to hide and sat and waited for the prey to be flushed out and driven towards me. Once he was midleap I shot and hit him in the leg as he was about to land. Nothin serious just enough to slow him down. At that point, the others caught up and took care of him."

"I bet Liam was none too happy with you."

"He didn't say much but he did stare me down, or at least try to. Like I said I am used to not gettin along with other people so it's a look I have seen before and could care less about."

"What abilities do you have?"

"Well I can make it so people don't realize I am there, I can enhance my senses really good, see what others see and stun people."

"You are just full of abilities, and, on top of that, you are a good shot and stealthy."

"Yes, sir. I can survive on my own, although I am not sure that's a skill."

"Don't underestimate the ability to survive on your own. It is perhaps the most valuable skill a person can have.

"The information you have brought me was a great service, one that I will not forget. Your actions will allow me to resolve an issue that I have been wanting to take care of. Now, I am planning on eventually rebuilding the wardens, however, that won't be for some time." Merik waited a moment to allow a little bit of despair to work it's way into Jaxus' mind before he continued. "That being said, there will be other opportunities for people such as yourself who prove themselves worthy."

"I am willin to do whatever it takes to be one of ya wardens sir."

"That's just what I wanted to hear. You do realize that, given your narrow set of skills, I will be limited on the type of jobs I can give you, that is, until the wardens are formed."

"Yes, sir. I realize I don't have much to offer."

"You got me all wrong. I think you have plenty to offer, and a lot of good could come of it. With you, I could save countless lives." Merik added a sense of hope to the words he spoke to Jaxus.

"Really?"

"Absolutely."

"How? I am a good hunter, but I can't see how that can help save lives."

"What would be better, two armies clashing with countless people getting maimed and killed, or one well-placed arrow at the right time?"

"One arrow, but psylords have many powers, and they can see the future, and see a shot coming before it is fired."

Merik chuckled "We are not all powerful. In fact, I am very limited in my abilities. I won't bore you with the details, but you are probably stronger in psychic abilities than I am. I got where I am because I have other talents not handed down from an Imperial bloodline. Resourcefulness, determination, scholarly study. Those are what make me what I am. Not all psylords can see into the future, and the ones who can only see a short distance into the future. If I were to send you to take care of a rival, after all attempts of a peaceful union have failed, I would make sure it was someone whose powers can't counter yours.

With a well-placed shot, battles can be averted and lives saved. I am not foolish enough to believe I can rebuild Kysia alone. I have read too many historical records. Things will get dirty and innocents will die. Personally, I would rather a few corrupt and overbearing tyrants fall as we reforge Kysia than a bunch of innocents who now can live to see the dream come true.

"It pains me greatly to ask, but I will need someone who is willing to kill for me. If this is something you can't do, then I won't hold it against you. I realize that I am asking you to do something horrible. To murder in cold blood and dirty your hands while others are kept clean. It is possible you might even die doing this, but I can promise you this. Once Kysia is rebuilt, I will have the record set straight. There will be a recording of how I accomplished everything, so that, should the new Kysia someday fall, the people won't have to wait as long to see it rebuilt. In those records will be the accounts of the unsung heroes who sacrificed and got their hands dirty so others may keep theirs clean.

"I don't need an answer right away. I realize that this is a lot to ask of you. It is even possible that I won't ever need someone to eliminate a rival and save innocents from the horrors of war. I want you to stay as my personal guess here at the mansion. A room can be made for you. There is ample room on the grounds to practice your archery, and a pass can be given to you so that you can leave the city to go out and hunt if you should choose to. I am sure a man such as yourself probably does his best thinking when he is alone in the woods, with nothing to distract him. Stay for a month, By that time, I will be a lot closer to setting up the Wardens and we can talk then."

Merik stood up and offered his hand to the young man. Jaxus looked a bit shocked at the offer but quickly recovered. He stood up and excitedly shook hands with him. They headed towards the door and Merik walked him down the hall until he found a servant.

"Excuse me, miss."

The servant turned and, upon realizing who was before her, she bowed her head and asked, "What do you wish my lord?"

"Vera, was it?"

"Yes, my lord."

"Jaxus is going to be staying with us for a while. I need you to see that he gets a room to himself, as well as a pass to leave the city whenever he wants.

"Right away, my lord. If you will follow me, sir?"

CHAPTER 69

TIANNA

She woke up on the floor, her body stiff and sore, and her stomach rumbling with hunger. There were several plates of food on the table. Most of the plates had been picked over, but there was still a fair amount of food left. None of the servants had bothered her over the last couple of days. Each day, food was left outside her door. It was never anything fancy, mainly dried meats, cheeses, and bread. All stuff that would be fine if left out for hours at a time. Although it was servants who left the food, she was sure it was Herlt she had to thank for it. After she picked through the plate, Tianna began to feel better.

She groaned as she stretched, her muscles stiff and sore. Her head ached and throat was dry. There was a bottle of wine on the table, but she had lost her taste for it. Slowly, she made her way to the door and flinched at the groaning sound that it made as she opened it. Had it always been so damn loud, she wondered? The hall seemed incredibly bright compared to her dimly lit room. Tianna did her best not to lean on a wall for support as she made her way down the hall. It didn't take long for her to find a servant.

"Excuse me," she said.

The servant turned and looked at her and did her best to hide that she was wrinkling her nose, "Yes, Captain."

"I need a pitcher of water and someone to draw hot water for a bath."

"Of course, Captain. I will make sure it gets done right away."

By the time Tianna made it back to her room, there was already a pitcher full of water and another full of juice, as well as a tray of fruits. The tub was in the process of being filled. Tianna snacked on the fruits and drank the water and juice.

"Captain," the servant who had been filling her tub addressed her. "I took the liberty of adding some salt as well as a few oils, such as lavender, marjoram, and eucalyptus. Djinar favored these when he needed to recover after several days of drinking. I hope that you will find them as beneficial as he did."

Tianna murmured her thanks as the servant walked towards the door. She didn't bother to wait for the servant to leave before she stripped down and got into the tub. The hot water stung at first but then began to loosen her stiff muscles. The last several days had been a blur. At first, she had been in shock, but, once that wore off, she cried. Tianna couldn't remember the last time she cried. When the tears had run out, there had been anger and rage. Several shattered wine bottles and dried stains on the walls were a testament to that.

The last couple of days had been exhausting and emotional. Now, she just ached and wanted her head to stop hurting. What had happened to her was not her fault, nor was it something she could have prevented. It had taken her several days and countless bottles of wine to work through the torrent of thoughts and emotions before she came to this realization.

She wondered how this revelation would affect who she was. Would this truth destroy her sense of identity? It was almost a silly thought, because deep down she knew she was a survivor. Despite all that had happened to her, she was a survivor, and she would survive this, too.

Even though she had a ruined face and a price on her head, she had managed to earn a place with a powerful psylord. It wasn't just about Merik's power either. Even if Merik didn't reforge the Kysian Empire, she believed that he would be the catalyst for change, and that was something she wanted to be a part of. Although she would barely entertain the thought, she really hoped that she would find meaning to her life.

Merik was the first person to give her a chance, to believe in her after she had been cast out. Even though he didn't believe in her obsession with the duel, he had been willing to repeatedly go over the memory with her. She owed him greatly for that and the opportunity he gave her.

Her muscles were no longer stiff and the ache in her head had greatly receded. Soon, it would be time to go back to work and show Merik that he had every right to put his trust and faith in her. She would take the city guards and turn them into something much stronger than Crestburn ever had. Although, she had to be careful not to put herself in a position where Merik would see her as a threat. It wasn't that she was weak or afraid of Merik. The idea of ruling and being in charge didn't really appeal to her. Besides, who would follow her anyway? It was one thing to run a mercenary team or city guard; it was something completely different to run a city and the surrounding lands.

There would be a lot for her to do in the near future, the first of which would be getting out of the tub and getting dressed. Now that she was clean and had some food in her stomach, she was ready to deal with the world. First, she needed to get a hold of Merik and Herlt to let them know she was back and ready. As she headed across the mansion, she came across a servant escorting a young man.

"Excuse me, do you happen to know where Lord Merik is?" she asked.

"Yes, ma'am. We just left him. I believe he was heading back to his receiving room on the next floor," replied the servant.

"Thank you."

Excellent. If he was just done with a meeting, he should have just a few minutes before his next appointment to see her. Tianna quickened her stride and was soon knocking on the door.

"Come in," came the muffled voice from the other side of the large wooden door. Merik was standing by the liquor cabinet pouring himself a drink. He turned to look at her as she entered the room.

"Ah, Captain, I see that you have recovered," Merik said.

"Yes, and thank you for giving me the time to deal with the revelation," she replied.

"Of course. I am sure it was quite a shock. Sergeant Herlt has been doing a fine job of running things while you took some time for yourself. Your timing couldn't be better, by the way. I have just learned where several Djinarian loyalists are holding up. There is a good chance that Botun may be there as well."

"I can have a squad ready to raid the location in short order, sir."

"No. I don't want to risk this by getting ahead of ourselves. While we may know the location of the hideout, we don't know if Botun is there or not. We can wait, but I do want your guards on standby."

"Understood. I can have a team ready in less than an hour. Do you have an idea when we will need to clear them out? If I have an idea of a time frame to work within, I can better be prepared. It is about time we caught Botun, and I don't want him slipping through our grasp."

"Unfortunately, I don't, but I can't imagine it will be long. I am going to have Suval watching the place. He will alert the heralds when he sees Botun entering."

"Then, with your permission, I shall go get the guards ready."

"You are dismissed."

Tianna smiled as she turned to leave. This was wonderful, a chance to show Merik that, even though she no longer needed him to go over the memory, she was still willing to work for him. As she reached for the door, Merik spoke up again.

"One more thing, Captain," Merik said.

"Yes?"

"I am told that the loyalists have Lucky Liam in their possession. I do believe he is a prisoner, however, given his reputation for unbelievable escapes, I would recommend having a contingency plan on dealing with him. Although Liam's escape is an acceptable loss, I don't want Botun escaping with him or through a distraction caused by him. Understood?"

"Yes, and thank you for that bit of information. I will definitely see that Lucky Liam is accounted for in my plans."

"That was all. Carry on, Captain."

The stakes just jumped with that bit of information. Lucky Liam had quite a reputation in this city. Odd that Botun's people had managed to capture him. That means they probably had someone strong with royal blood with them. She would have to get a special squad together to be ready for this mystery person. There were a few ideas she had been wanting to try out, with regards to an unknown psychic with the opposing force. Maybe now she might be able to test one or two of those ideas out.

CHAPTER 70

SUVAL

Over the last several days, Suval was immensely busy, with two playthings to work with. He was so thankful that he didn't need sleep when he used his special gift. Suval did have to admit to himself that it was very weird to be conscious almost nonstop for days on end. People need sleep to not only rest their bodies but their minds as well. His mind got no rest as it ran ceaselessly for the last several days. This was the first time he had ever tried something like this. He spent only a few hours each day in the waking world. The rest were in the dreams of Kerwin and Lucky Liam, or Asha as he discovered her true name to be.

His body had been holding up pretty well. This was due in part to the fact that it remained stationary while he played with people's dreams. While it wasn't the true rest of sleep, it was better than nothing. With such a sedentary habit, he didn't need much food, either. Typically, he ate on the go as he went from one plaything to the other. First, he cursed the distance between the two, and the unnecessary time it took to walk from one to the other and back again. The walks, however, did his body much good as it allowed him a little bit of exercise. Originally, he sat at the end of the bed but, having to deal with two people for longer periods of time, he started laying down on the ground next to their bed when he noticed how stiff and sore he would get. Oh, how he wanted to curl up next to Asha and lay right beside her. To touch her, to smell her, too...

Suval shook his head to clear his thoughts. Lately, he noticed that it was easier for him to become more distracted. There was one point, as he was walking down an empty hall in the mansion, that he questioned if he was in someone's dream or if he was awake. It bothered him a bit that such a thing had happened to him and was the closest thing he had to a sobering thought.

Merik was demanding updates every couple of days. He hated taking time out of his schedule for something so pointless, but he had no choice. Merik would make him relive what his uncle did to him, and he definitely didn't want that to happen ever again. Even now, without Merik's unwanted assistance, he could all but feel his uncle's hands on his shoulder, his hot breath on his neck. The one good thing was that Merik reminded him to bathe. His lord had wrinkled his nose in disgust when he entered his meeting room a few days back. While he didn't do anything to work up a sweat, it didn't take long with the hot days for a body to have its own odor. Suval could care less what others thought of him, but, when Merik pointed out that it might be possible for others to detect that he was there long after he was gone because of a lingering odor, he decided that a quick wash would not be a bad thing.

He was just finishing his daily bath when there was a knock on his door. Quickly, he got dressed and answered it. A servant boy was standing outside his door, fidgeting nervously.

"Lord Merik requests your presence right away," the servant said.

Before Suval could utter a protest, the young boy turned and ran down the hall, too afraid to be in Suval's presence any longer than he had to. This was ridiculous. He wasn't scheduled to meet with Merik until tomorrow. There could be no reason for this. He gathered a few things and hurried to Merik. When he got the room Merik often used to receive important people, Suval didn't bother knocking on the door but barged right in. Normally a stickler for etiquette, Merik didn't say a thing about his unannounced entrance and, on the contrary, was quite happy to see him.

"Ah, Suval, so good of you to come so quickly," Merik said.

"Lord Merik, I need to be going soon. It is getting late and I do need to be at Liam's soon," Suval said pleadingly.

"Not tonight."

"What! You can't take him away from me."

"Calm, my good man. I am taking nothing away from you. In fact, you will still have Liam, kind of."

"What do you mean?" Suval asked.

"Earlier today, I was informed that Lucky Liam had been captured," Merik said.

"Nooo," he cried out. "It can't be!"

"Relax, I know where he is."

"Where? Tell me now," Suval cried out desperately.

The weight of firm hands pressed on his shoulders and he could feel the sensation of his pants being yanked down. His cry of outrage turned into a whimper. The feeling stayed there, as if frozen in time. Merik stared at him a good long while, then it vanished as quickly as it came.

"While I am in a good mood, I will not tolerate outbursts like that. Remember your place, Suval."

"I, I, I'm sorry, my lord. Please forgive me."

"Only because I am in such a great mood."

"Uh, why the good news?" Suval whimpered

"Ah, yes. I was just getting to that before your little outburst. As I was saying, Lucky Liam was captured today." There was a pregnant pause to see if Suval would cry out again and, once Merik was satisfied that Suval was in control of himself, he continued. "It turns out that the people who captured him work for Botun. Why Botun wants Liam, I could care less. What I do care about is, I know where Botun will be."

"How?"

A startled, puzzled look flashed across Merik's face. "How? Did you just ask me how I know something? Do I need to remind you again what I can do?" Merik berated.

"No! No, please don't! I just meant, who told you this?" Suval whimpered.

"Oh, well, as it happens, it turns out that it was the man who shot Liam."

"Shot?" Suval exclaimed as he interrupted Merik.

"Yes, yes. Liam was shot. Relax, it was a clean shot to the leg. The kid should be fine. I have seen many wounds like that before, and they heal up just fine. Anyway, the man who shot Liam and was responsible for his capture told me this. Told me everything about Liam's capture and where he was taken. Needless to say, I want you to run over there and watch the place. If you see Botun enter, then I want you to alert the guards. I will have a patrol stationed a few blocks away with a herald, and you can alert them when Botun arrives.

"Now, I do not want you going into their hideout at all. If Botun happens to be there before you get there, and you see him leave, do not follow him. I don't want you to risk losing him. Stay put and wait for him to return. I have our good captain on standby, ready to kick their doors in once I have word that Botun is there. Don't worry, I will make sure that Liam won't be harmed in the raid. From what our friend said, it seems that Botun is having a hard time traveling about the city. So, hopefully, you can get there before he does, and we can end this shortly.

"What I am trusting you with is very important. Botun is the last holdout from Djinar's rule. Once I get rid of him, then my place here in Crestburn will be secured completely. Can I count on you for this important task?"

"Yes, my lord," Suval replied.

"Good. Once you get close, I want you to go to the herald and let them establish a telepathic link, this way once you are in position you don't have to worry about leaving. Do you understand?"

"Yes, my lord."

"Good. Don't screw this up."

CHAPTER 71

BOTUN

Tonight, they met in a cafe that was closed for the evening. The owner had run up quite the bill with Zahra and was willing to let her use it for the night. She told him she had a client with a unique desire, and the man didn't bother asking any questions. He was just happy to have his debt reduced.

"I am still a bit confused as to how someone gets into debt with you through one of your girls," spoke Hargod. "I mean, don't the customers pay up front for the services?"

"Yes, but they pay for a certain amount of time and are told if they run over then they will owe for the extra time."

"I know a few of your girls. I figured they would have a man finished early and have time to kill," Hargod said with a grin.

Zahra gave a throaty laugh. "Usually, that's how it goes. Regulars, however, tend to lean towards pillow talk. Often we let them get away with a few minutes here and there. It's no big deal, because the girls have downtime between clients to freshen up. Once in a while, someone loses track of time. An extra hour or two goes by and they end up owing more than what they have on them."

"So, they owe you and eventually you collect, one way or another."

"You got that right, darling," Zahra replied.

"I think, perhaps, I should get into that line of work."

This time Zahra laughed so hard she snorted and wiped a tear away from her eye.

"Hargod, you are a sweetheart, but you don't have what it takes to be in this business. I mean, you're cute and all, but there is a subtlety that is required to finesse both coin and information out of a client that you just don't have darling."

The back door creaked open. Hargod stood up and placed a hand on his cudgel. Zahra shifted her hand to a dagger she kept hidden on the small of her back. Floorboards creaked in the steady rhythm of someone who was not worried about concealing their approach. A moment later Botun emerged from the shadowed hallway.

"Good to see you both here already."

"Yea. Zahra was just crushing my dreams about switching careers."

"Oh, and what career would that be?"

"A working girl. What else?"

Zahra shook her head and tried to suppress a grin.

"Aren't you supposed to have a guard with you?" asked Zahra

"Yes," replied Botun.

"Then why don't you?"

"We were being followed, so he stayed back to take care of it. You two seem in a good mood."

"Well, things have been better."

"I take it that the meeting at the warehouse went well?"

"It was very small, but nobody interrupted it. Of course, with the captain of the guards gone or missing, the city guards might be a bit more relaxed," commented Hargod.

"She is not gone, Hargod. My informant in the mansion says she is there. Apparently, something happened and she went on a drinking binge for several days."

Zahra gave Botun a puzzled look "Merik allowed this?"

"Yes. What's more, he has a new guest at the mansion as well."

"Who?"

"A young man by the name of Jaxus. The informant didn't have much information about him other than he is young, looks rough around the edges, and his clothes were of poorer cut."

"I will see what my girls can come up with. Maybe we will get lucky and he will stop in for a visit. Then, we can get some knowledge first hand."

"I doubt it, but there is always a chance. Recently, I have made contact with a few of the nearby towns. So far, no one has seen Djinar. At this point, I am beginning to think he tried to escape and maybe made it to a safe house where he died somehow."

"That would be a stretch, don't you think?" commented Hargod.

"It is but, at this point, I don't know what else to think. Djinar was not the type of man for patience. There would be no way he could have been held up this many days. No one outside of Crestburn has had word of him, either. So, he either has a luxurious hiding place away from things or he made it somewhere only to have something befall him. Betrayal or an accident."

"Hell, that fat bastard could have just had a heart attack," said Hargod.

Botun nodded in assent.

"Given the amount of alcohol, drugs, and foods that he consumed regularly, a heart attack would not be an unreasonable assumption," Zahra commented.

"At this point, I am going to back off on searching for him. Now, I won't stop searching for him completely, but I think our resources could be better spent strengthening our position here. Given the captain's recent episode of drinking, things may not be as stable with Merik. I am hoping our informant there can provide us with more information in the near future.

"I want another meeting held at the warehouse. Your man will agree with doing another one, Zahra?"

"Yes, that shouldn't be a problem. The first meeting was very uneventful, with only a handful of people. The nice thing about that is that it will be easier for him to host another meeting."

"Good. We are going to need another person or two to host other meetings, as well. I don't want any of these groups to know about each other, at least not yet. If Merik catches wind of one then the others should be safe. Additionally, if he discovers there are several different groups plotting against him, he won't be ready for when they all stick together."

"Are we not using the man as bait then?" asked Zahra.

"I haven't made a final decision about that yet, but don't get your hopes up."

There was a knock on the back door.

Eyes darted about from co-conspirator to co-conspirator. Again, there was a knock on the back door.

"My guy didn't know where I was heading. Are you two expecting anyone else?" Botun asked.

Hargod and Zahra both shook their heads as the knock was heard again. Botun gestured to Hargod, who got up and headed down the hallway. Slowly, he opened the door and saw a beautiful young woman standing before him. She was wearing a thin black cloak to hide.

"I need to speak to Mistress Zahra," she said.

"Who?"

"Mistress Zahra. I need to speak with her right away. It is urgent. She knows me, I am one of her special girls. My name is Emilee."

"There is no Zahra here. You have the wrong place," Hargod said and shut the door. He turned and walked back to the others who were waiting with bated breath.

"It was a young girl named Emilee. She said she was one of your special girls."

Zahra breathed a sigh of relief. "Yes, she is. She handles a lot of the information gathering that I do. I don't go anywhere without letting her know where I am, although I don't tell her what I am doing or who I'm with. Just wait here."

Without another word, she headed down the hallway and out the door. Hargod and Botun waited in silence for her return. Soon, the back door opened again and Zahra made her way back into the room.

"It seems that your crew, Hargod, managed to capture Lucky Liam."

"What," exclaimed Hargod.

"Apparently, they somehow managed to capture Lucky Liam. They have him secured at the hideout on Porter St."

"How in the hell did those sons of bitches do that?"

"I don't know. Emilee said he was caught earlier today. When they couldn't find you, Botun, someone was smart enough to think of talking with one of my girls. I suggest you head over there."

"You damn right we are going to head over there," Hargod angrily exclaimed.

"No," Botun said.

"Excuse me?"

"We are not going to head over there. I will. You will find something else to occupy your time with, Hargod."

"What do you mean I am not going?" Hargod asked.

"Exactly what I said. You are not going. I am not about to risk losing Lucky Liam by having you nearby. You are too emotionally involved."

"Damned right I am emotionally involved. That little punk made me look like a fool."

"Which you are acting like as we speak. While I don't believe Liam is lucky, I do believe he is a very talented and skilled individual. I need to be focused on him while dealing with him. That is something I can't do with you around."

"But, I..." Hargod stammered as Botun stared at him. He fell silent and clenched his fists, and his nostrils flared as he exhaled.

"Fine, whatever you want. You're the boss."

"Good. I will question Liam and figure out what is going on. I will see you two later," and with that Botun got up and left.

Hargod remained still until after Botun had been gone for a few minutes, then he slammed his fist on the table.

"That no good, lucky son of a bitch. It should have been me to have caught that little bastard. His ass should have been mine. How on earth did those fools manage to catch him?" Hargod complained.

"I don't know, hun. Emilee didn't say. It doesn't matter. Besides, you know Botun. Once he is done with Liam, he will let you deal with him. In the meantime, why don't you come with me back to my place? You can work out your frustrations with one of my girls," Zarah offered.

CHAPTER 72

ASHA

Asha's leg throbbed from the wound. Whoever her captives were, they hadn't bothered to remove the arrow that stuck out of her leg. Unless she was very careful with her movements, she would bump the arrow and pain would course through her body. They had at least done her the courtesy of wrapping a secure bandage around the wound. When it became obvious that they weren't going to remove the arrow, she tried to do it herself, but she was told to leave it alone by a rough looking guard. Whether out of fear of what she could do with an arrow or the increased mobility that she would have been granted with its removal, they weren't taking any chances with Lucky Liam.

After being shot by that young man, whose face she made damn sure never to forget, they bound and hooded her. Quickly, she was secreted off to their hiding place. They made many false turns and doubled back to prevent her from figuring out where they had taken her. Now, they just sat and waited for Botun while they drank. Her guard didn't drink, and they were very careful to rotate out her guard with another sober person so that her luck would be minimized and she couldn't perform a miraculous escape.

It was kind of flattering that they took such efforts to keep her captive, well flattering and annoying. From the looks of things, Asha didn't think the arrow would cause any permanent damage. She would have to lay low for several weeks until the wound was completely healed. That would be rough and eat into her savings, but, at this point in time, she had no other real options. The last thing she wanted was for someone to realize that Asha happened to have the same kind of injury as Lucky Liam and start asking questions.

Between chasing the crow and not being able to remember when she had a night of sleep undisturbed by bad dreams, she was exhausted. She wanted to sleep, but she was worried that one of the guards might have a thing for young boys. If one of them tried to take advantage of her, they would realize that he was, in fact, a she. So, Asha sat propped up against a wall and did her best to pay attention to her surroundings.

None of this would have happened if she hadn't been so damn tired. Asha knew better than to risk her neck chasing after something when she was not on top of her game. It was not like her, but, then again, there was nothing like her, except for Jariek. He was the only one who she knew who had a new ability. God, what it must be like to be able to control animals with your mind. Definitely a lot more exciting than being able to see what powers someone had. To be fair, her ability, while not exciting, did provide her with one hell of an advantage when dealing with people.

There was no limit to what powers a person could have, other than being limited to touching another person's mind. Even with that requirement, there were so many different possibilities of what powers a person could have. It was kind of odd, she often thought, that there had only been a dozen or so powers that people had. At one point in time, she had made a list of possible powers that might be out there. Eventually, that list grew quite long and she made another list of the ones she thought were more probable. Man, she hadn't thought of that list in ages. What was on it? She did her best to try and remember but, between the wound and the lack of sleep, her mind was fuzzy.

Mind fuzzy? Oh, that was one of the powers. The ability to make it so someone couldn't concentrate. That was one of her favorites, as well as the power to make them see things that weren't there.

A man made his way over to her and tapped the foot of her good leg with his. She looked up at him, slowly. In his hand was a bowl of something steaming with a hunk of bread and a tankard of something in the other.

"Here kid, I got you something to eat. You will need something in your system, especially when it comes time to take that arrow out. Anyway, I brought you some stew and some water. There is more if you want it, but I wouldn't recommend eating too much just yet. It's going to hurt like hell when we pull that arrow out of your leg, and you're liable to puke if you eat too much now. A little bit will be fine and it looks like you could use it."

Asha gave a small nod and he sat the food down beside her, just out of her reach, and quickly backed away. Just great. She had to move a bit to reach for the food, and that would jar her bad leg. The man might be kind, but he still wasn't about to take any chances with her. Slowly, she leaned forward and shifted her good leg a bit to get a better angle. She was just about to grasp the bowl when the arrow in her leg pushed against the floor and sent sparks of agony through her leg.

Asha slammed back against the wall panting in agony as sweat dripped off her brow. Man, that hurt like hell. Soon the pain began to subside, and she again tried for the bowl. This time, as she was about to reach it, she leaned further and was prepared for the pain. She grabbed the bowl and mug and leaned back against the wall as quickly as she could, sloshing some of the hot stew out and burning her hand a bit. It took longer for the pain to fade. The stew was good, really good. Either that or she was just extremely hungry. The water was nice and fresh, too. Yeah, it had to be her hunger that caused her to enjoy the meal.

She finished her bowl in short order and then banged her empty mug on the floor. "Yo wench," she said. "I need another tankard, and make it da good stuff. Tat last mug tasted a bit watered down."

This drew a round of chuckles from men drinking. As the guy who gave her the food and drink got up from the table and crossed the room, one of his inebriated friends reached over and pinched him on the ass and yelled, "Come serve me next wench." The other guys at the table started laughing again. Asha made sure to give him her best grin as he came over and grabbed her mug. When he came back, he handed it to her instead of putting it on the floor. Good, they were letting their guard down around her.

Asha scanned the room looking for the one who shot her. He was nowhere to be seen. That necessarily didn't mean anything, but she figured that the person who shot Lucky Liam would be celebrating hard with his companions. Given how secretive they were with her when they took her to their hideout, she didn't think that they wanted her capture to be known, or at least not yet.

"Botun!" A round of cries went up as the former seneschal entered the room. The man wasted no time. He walked straight over to her and looked her over.

"Heya, boss man. Was wondering when you showed up. You wouldn't have tat buxom lady here with you too?" she asked.

"No, Liam, she is not here."

"What a shame. I really liked her, and I know she couldn't keep her hands off of me. I guess tat's why you didn't bring her along. Might be too distracting, watching her getting all handsy with me." Botun just scowled at her. "She's not your girl, is she? I mean, I am sorry if she is, but the ladies are always like tat with me. Can't help it if I am a dashing, sexy rouge and all. Hey, while you're standing there a boss man, can you order one of your lackeys ta get me an ale. Tey have been nice and all that, but tey only give me water ta drink."

"I don't think so, Liam. We need to talk," Botun replied.

"Yeah, I kind of figured as much, what wit da arrow in me leg."

Botun turned and looked at the others. One by one they fell silent under his gaze. "Why does this man still have an arrow in his leg?" No one dared to answer. Each man found someplace else to look other than Botun. He waited. The silence stretched out and, eventually, one of the men murmured something.

"What was that? I couldn't hear you," Botun said, as if he were a parent speaking to a misbehaving child.

"We didn't want him to use his luck to get away, sir," one of the less inebriated thugs said.

"And yet you didn't think that getting drunk would give him an opportunity as well?"

"We're not drunk, sir. We were just celebrating a little bit. After all, we did catch Lucky Liam."

Botun just shook his head in disbelief. "I want that arrow removed and that leg bandaged up immediately." Turning to Liam, he said, "I am sorry for the way they treated you, Liam. It is true that I wanted you brought in to answer some of my questions. Given you well earned your reputation for luck, they did have to employ more forceful methods to get you to come in, although it does not excuse their lack of care once you were brought in.

"As a show of good faith, because I want to believe you are innocent, I will give you a few hours to recover. Then, you and I are going to have a conversation about some missing friends of mine and what happened to them. I am not sure if you are at fault, but I can't find anyone else who could be responsible for what happened."

CHAPTER 73

KERWIN

Days began to blur into one and another. With very little sleep and not being able to see the sun, Kerwin had no way of telling how much time had passed. There was a bit of a cycle, though. Occasionally, he would be allowed to sleep, and he would have overwhelming dreams. The dreams weren't nightmares but a chaotic explosion of images and sounds. It was hard to think in such a constantly exhausted state. He had been taught to endure exposure and pain, wary of mind games and even limited sleep deprivation, but this was something else.

He was not positive, but he was pretty certain that Merik or one of his lackeys had been influencing his sleep. It stood to reason that Merik was not the only person to have a new power, and that his ability to pull memories wasn't the only new power that had emerged. If his dreams hadn't changed shortly after being held prisoner, he might not have even realized his dreams were being influenced. Nothing in his training had prepared him for this. He wasn't even sure how he could resist someone while he was asleep. The only thing he could do was get through each day as best as he could.

Thankfully, not all of his dreams were a chaotic mess. At some point each day, the guards would come in, wake him up, and take him to another section of the basement where he was to exercise. Other times, whenever he dozed off, they would make a loud noise and pretend that it was not on purpose. He figured this out by pretending to be asleep, which in his exhausted state was a lot more difficult than he realized, and listened to them repeatedly make a noise until he pretended to wake up.

Since the guards were physically keeping him awake for part of the time, he figured that whoever was stirring his dreams had to either to get sleep or had other people to work on as well. To help alleviate some of his lack of sleep, he would wait until the guards came in, then he would sit with his back against the wall and his hands in his lap and meditate with his eyes open. Whenever a guard came in to check on him, he made sure to look at them and let them see that he was awake. Eventually, they got used to this and bothered him less frequently. He was able to meditate for longer periods of time, and a few times he managed to fall asleep with his eyes open for a little bit. While this didn't cure his exhaustion, it did a good deal to help alleviate it. Additionally, while he meditated, he had been able to think about his situation and the problems that Merik presented.

The first question that he had was whether or not the Cashek Society knew about the existence of new powers. For a while, he toyed with the idea that it was plausible that they knew and even had a set of protocols to deal with that. The wardens could easily handle that the same way as when the secrecy of the society was compromised. The longer he thought about it, the more he realized it was utter foolishness. New powers would be all but impossible to keep secret, even with the wardens doing the dirty work of silencing people. Besides, the wardens were the council's boogeymen and were quick to be blamed on anything bad or mysterious that happened.

If the Cashek Society didn't know about new powers, then how would that affect how they handled Merik. As a whole, the council members were a conservative lot. They wouldn't take the news of new powers very seriously. That means Merik could quickly gain the upper hand without their assistance. At that point, he would be in a stable enough position that they would have no choice but to back him. Probably, they would have Merik eliminated before he had a chance to make much use of his unique power, and any claims of him having new powers would be regarded as mere flights of fantasy from a worn and burnt out operative and an inexperienced informant.

This was the more realistic of the two scenarios. That would be bad for the society in the long run, because all their people would now be at risk from others with similar new abilities like Merik. Eventually, this situation would repeat itself and the Cashek Society could come out worse for it. There had to be a way to get the society to believe that new powers existed. The problem is that a warden would arrive and begin the cleanup work. Kerwin was hard pressed to believe that any warden would let Merik live, especially when they found out that Merik knew about them. There was no way to hide that bit of information. One of the first things a warden will do after freeing him is ask him if Cashek Society has been compromised. While he was great at lying to people, he doubted he had what it would take to deceive a warden, especially after several days without any sleep.

Plain and simple, Merik was a dead man. There was little to no chance he could survive an attack from the warden. Whoever the society sent would catch Merik unaware and it would end very quickly for Crestburn's new psylord. Unless, no he couldn't. It would go against his training. Then again, what other choice did he have? Without warning, Merik would die and the new powers would go undiscovered, putting the society at potentially greater risk in the years to come. If Merik survived the attack, then there would be time to open talks with the society.

"Guards!" he yelled.

The door opened and two dour and bored looking guards came into his cell and locked the door behind them. Neither spoke, they only looked at him.

"I need to speak to Lord Merik immediately. I have something very important to tell him. It will save his life."

One of the guards snorted while the other shook her head. "Now, why should we believe you?" a guard replied.

"You don't have to. If there is an attempt on Merik, he will go looking for answers. I am sure I will be one of the first people he questions. I will have no problem informing him that I tried to have him warned about it, but you two decided not to pass along the message. Now, you know what kind of a ruler Merik is. How do you think he will take it?"

The guards turned and looked at one another then unlocked the door and left. He could barely make out the whispers as they talked it over. It was now out of his hands. Kerwin leaned back and closed his eyes. Screw it, he was going to get some sleep whether or not they liked it.

He was awoken with a rough kick to find the guards, along with Merik, standing before him. Kerwin let out a long yawn and started to rise but, seeing the guards' hands going to their blades, he decided against it.

"Sorry about that. I seem to have nodded off while waiting for you," Kerwin said.

"The guards tell me you know about an attempt on my life," Merik replied.

"Kind of."

"Kind of? I do not have time to waste with games. You know what I can do, and I will not tolerate any kind of deception from you. I take it you are referring to the fact that a warden will be sent here to extract you?"

"Yes. The fact that you know about the Cashek Society puts you in danger. They value their secrecy above all else. That fact that you know they exist makes you a threat to them, or so they will believe."

With that, Kerwin started remembering his training classes when they went over operative protocols when something bad happened. He then jumped to times he heard that wardens had been sent to clean up various messes. There was enough there to let Merik know that he was not messing around.

"Believe me," Kerwin asked.

"Do you know who will come and when?" Merik questioned.

"No, but you now have a chance to prepare."

"I see. You want me to live in hopes that it might buy you more time. Perhaps even curry favor with gratitude for saving my life."

"Something like that."

CHAPTER 74

SUVAL

The sky was clear and the temperature was a bit cooler than it had been. Normally, it would have been a wonderful night to be out. It was great weather for stalking new prey, but he was in a foul mood. How dare someone take his prize toy away from him. How dare they harm her. He hoped that she was ok, and, more importantly, he hoped that they hadn't discovered her secret. That was his special thing to know. The shared secret made him feel closer to her.

Suval had barely said two words to the herald as he walked by the guard patrol a few blocks back. He just glared at the man and told him to link up with him. Once connected, the herald tried to engage him telepathically, but he was in no mood for conversation. Quickly, he let the herald know to keep silent and leave him alone to do his assignment.

The alley was between two fruit stands. Other than that, there was nothing special about it. Then again, a hideout probably had to be nondescript. He walked down to the end of the block, turned away from the hideout, and went down another block. Without bothering to look around, he walked over to a building and sent out a mental command to the neighboring minds not to notice his presence. Mechanically, he scaled the building and made his way back to a position opposite the alley. He found a good spot at the peak of a roof and laid down and watched the alley.

Merik had told him where the entrance was, but he had problems making it out. Oh well, eventually someone would come by and use it. Then he would know where to look. He had been there an hour when a door opened midway down the alley. He almost failed to notice it because the door was so silent he thought it was merely a shadow from a moving cloud. A tall man came out and made his way towards the street, only to pause to pull up a hood before he slipped into the crowded street. The man had been fast and stealthy, but Suval had managed to recognize him.

It was Botun. He was going to get away. Suval scrambled over the peak of the roof and started following him. The man was adept at blending into a crowd. It was amazing that someone without the psychic ability to make a mind not recognize them could disappear so well. Suval was about to jump to the next building when he remembered Merik's warning. He froze,

287

dangerously close to the edge. Botun moved further away and, if he didn't jump now, he would lose him.

Agony tore through his body as mixed emotions warred against each other. Fear of reliving those painful memories versus his desire to slip inside her dreams and sit next to her. How he longed for her. He wouldn't admit it to himself, but dreams were the only way he could connect with another person. Asha was like him, or so he believed - another lost soul with a deep secret that was hidden from the rest of the world. As the emotional torrent flooded his mind, his body stayed frozen and the choice was taken from him as Botun disappeared.

He let out an anguished howl that carried through the night. People stopped and looked around, but no one could seem to find the source of the dreadful cry. Suval collapsed on the edge and broke down in tears. The notion of ending it all danced across his mind as he considered taking a plunge to the street.

The night wore on and his tears dried up. Somehow he found the strength to stand again and make his way back to his lookout position. Gently, he laid down on the roof and watched the alley across the street. He wanted to drift off in a drug-induced haze to forget about his emptiness, and then drift off to sleep. As much as tried, he couldn't remember the last time he slept. It had been over a week ago. The strain of being conscious nonstop had started to be too much for him. When Botun got back, he would report it and then see about sleep. Suval wasn't sure if he could sleep after being in others dreams for so long, but that didn't bother him, for he made sure to always carry a little something that would cloud his mind and force him to slumber. He wouldn't even go back to his room in the mansion. Merik could worry about where he was for a day or so while sleeping right here on the rooftop.

CHAPTER 75

ASHA

She wasn't sure if her leg felt better or worse now that the arrow had finally been taken out. They had not bothered to give her anything for the pain, other than a piece of leather to bite down on. Asha was pretty thrilled with the fact that she did not pass out as they slid it out of the wound. Some high proof booze and a clean set of bandages, and she was good as new.

They gave her plenty of water and some more stew, so that her body would have plenty of fuel for the healing processes. Now that Botun was back, the revelry in the main room had died down. There were two guards who watched over her in this smaller room and, from the sounds of things, possibly one more on the other side of the door. For now, she was stuck. At least with Botun around, she was less likely to be mistreated. She tried to stay awake, but everything that had happened to her along with the lack of sleep was more than her body could handle. She drifted off to sleep.

"Liam. Wake up," a voice said.

Asha kept her eyes closed and pretended to be asleep a little longer so she could get her bearings. The firm authoritative voice was very familiar. Botun, that's right. She had recently dealt with him. Her mind was a bit fuzzy with sleep but began to clear up when she noticed how bad her leg throbbed. She had been shot on the roof. They had captured her, or Lucky Liam. Asha stretched and let out a long slow yawn.

"Morning Botun. Ta bad, it had ta be your face I see first thing. Noting personal man, I mean, you're not a bad looking man, but I prefer tat buxom friend of yours. What was her name? Sarha, Serria?"

"Zahra. Given your attempt at wit, I take it you are feeling better," Botun replied.

"I wouldn't go tat far. I mean, tanks ta your man who shot me, I won't be dancing anytime soon."

"Yes, well, you will heal just fine. Nothing serious was damaged and now you have another story for your luck."

"Not so sure I will tell this story. Kind of kills de theme of me being lucky and all, wat wit me being shot and captured."

"Yes. Now, I have some questions for you."

"Fire away. No, on second tought, don't. Tings didn't turn out ta good fer me last time some fired away at me," Asha said with a smirk.

"What happened to the people I paid you to lead out of town the night of the festival?" Botun asked.

"I lead tem out of town."

"Then what?"

"Well, tere was a party going on and wine, dancing, and beautiful women."

"So, you did not follow the group out of town?"

"No, why would I do tat? I would have missed de party. Who da you tink I am?"

"So, you were with a woman that night?"

"Well, I was wit a few, but I can't remember teir names ta well. I was drinking pretty good myself."

"That is rather unfortunate for you that you can't remember their names. If you could provide a witness to your whereabouts, it might do you a favor," Botun said.

"Oh, well, I am sure I could find tem," Asha replied.

"Even if you did, there is still the chance you might have told someone about the group leaving."

"Not a soul. I keep me mouth shut. Kiss and tell sure, you bet. But talk about a job, absolutely not."

"Then that wasn't you that the guards brought in the next morning cloaked and hooded."

Shit. Now she knew why Hargod had become so suddenly disinterested in her and left the balcony. He had thought that it was Lucky Liam hidden under the cloak. Whoever it was had been close to her size. It had to be one of the sons of someone in the group. Someone had betrayed them and, since they couldn't see who it was, they thought it had been her. Damn.

"Ah, no," but she already saw it had taken her too long to reply. Even if he believed her, Botun realized that she knew something about that day. She could tell him the truth, but then that would end Lucky Liam. There was no way she could run messages again, and, eventually, word would get out that she was Liam and someone would hunt her down. Part of the reason she survived so long as Lucky Liam was that she could make him disappear by being herself.

"I am not exactly sure I believe you, Liam. Our friends never made it to the rendezvous point. The guards butchered them before they got there. I need to be sure it wasn't you who sold them out. For the next couple of days, you will be our guest." Without another word, Botun got up and left.

Asha was stunned by the news. She had no idea that the people she led out of town had been cut down by the guards. At the time, she thought it was odd that the guards entered the town with a concealed prisoner. However, with a new psylord, there were a lot of unusual things that happened, so she didn't think much about it at the time. Thinking back to that moment, it was very easy to see why they thought that it was Lucky Liam cloaked up and hooded.

After her job was completed, she attended the celebration festivities that were going on, but she did so as herself. There was no way that she could prove Liam was doing anything. Not for the first time, Asha wished that she had never come up with that alternative persona. Even though it has put her in a serious bind right now, being Liam was as much a part of who she was as anything else she did.

She tried to think of a way to convince Botun that Liam was innocent without jeopardizing her secret. That would be very difficult. Botun was not only intelligent but he had a great memory. Any story that she would come up with would have to be airtight. Asha went over her various contacts to see if there were any who might be willing to help her, but she came up empty. She was rarely Liam outside of work. Someone would put out the word that they wanted to hire Liam, and she would show up as him for the job. Occasionally, she would be seen out and about as Liam, but those were always planned ahead of time and well between jobs. The way she had used Liam had boxed her in.

In order for Botun to believe that Liam was not involved with the massacre, he would have to find out who the mystery person was that the guards had with them that morning. Odds were against that. The person was cloaked and hooded for a reason. Merik didn't want that individual's identity known for fear of Botun's people finding out that they had been betrayed. That meant Botun had to find one of the people who had left with the group, who was now in hiding. To make matters worse, the betrayer could be dead or hiding in another town. In other words, she was screwed. By now, the bodies were probably too picked over by scavengers to identify who was missing.

Asha grew frustrated and angry. In the future, she would have to make sure she had an alibi ready for Liam. She toyed with the idea of coming clean with Botun, but she knew he would eventually use that secret as leverage over her. Telling him would be the same as joining his group. Actually, it was worse because members of his crew could slink away with next to no reprisals.

She closed her eyes and leaned against the wall. There had to be a way out of this, she thought. That was the last thing that went through her mind as sleep swept her away. Again, for the second time, her dreams were peaceful, and she was able to get rest.

CHAPTER 76

TIANNA

"Listen up everyone!" Tianna shouted at the guards in formation. "Word has just come in. Botun has been spotted. He is in a safe house in the Garish District. We are going in with overwhelming numbers. Most of you won't see action today. I want two perimeter rings set up around the building. One at one block away and another three blocks. No one goes in or gets out. Citizens of Crestburn who try to get through will be directed back to their homes, place of business, or anywhere else to hold up.

"Once the perimeter rings have been established, we will move on to the safe house and remove any loyalists to Djinar or Botun that we find. Anyone who resists is to be killed. Those who surrender will be treated as prisoners. Botun is to be harmed only if necessary. Our Lord Merik wants to make a public example of him. I have been told that a local person of some fame, a Lucky Liam, has been seen there as well." At this, there were several murmurs from the crowd, mainly from the original town guards who knew Liam's reputation.

"I have heard stories of this person. Know that there is no such thing as luck powers. Liam is just probably very skilled at using what he has and making it appear as if he is lucky. Regardless, Merik wants to question this young man as well, and he is to be taken alive. Bonuses will be given to everyone with the capture of Botun." To that announcement, a cheer went through the gathered soldiers.

"Sergeant Herlt."

"Yes, Mam," replied the old sergeant.

"Get them moving."

"Right away, Captain."

Tianna sat upon her steed and watched as they marched through the gates and out onto the street. This was almost the size of the force that she used to capture the city. Granted, that force was all mercenaries who were already seasoned in bloodshed, while half of these only had the one skirmish under their belt. Merik walked over to her, along with the young man she saw the other day.

"Wonderful speech, Captain," he said.

"Thank you, sir."

"I would like to introduce you to Jaxus. He is the reason for today's events, as well as the man who shot Lucky Liam." Tianna nodded her head in a polite greeting to Jaxus as she looked him over. There was nothing that stood out about him. He was of average height and kind of lanky with shoulder-length brown hair.

"I want him to accompany you. He will make sure to stay out of your way."

"I have more than enough guards to make sure Botun doesn't get away," Tianna replied.

"This is just an extra precaution. I have no doubt you will be successful in today's endeavors. However, I am sure you noticed how the guards got a bit nervous at the mention of Lucky Liam," Merik said.

"Not sure I would call it nervous, exactly, but yes they did react to the news."

"Think what a calming effect it would be to have the man who shot Lucky Liam in their presence. Jaxus would be good for morale. Besides, he is quite the marksman with the bow. There is a chance that you might need his skills to take him."

She frowned and nodded. "We'll get him a horse and he can ride with me."

"Excellent."

There was an awkward silence as they waited for a servant to fetch a horse for Jaxus. A servant came a few minutes later, and Jaxus mounted the beast without any problems. If nothing else, it looked like he could handle a horse, and she shouldn't worry about him letting his mount cause an issue.

Merik turned towards her. "When you are done, I wish to speak to both of you. It seems that there will more than likely be an attempt on my life in the near future."

"Sir, do you want me to double your guards?" Tianna inquired.

"Oh no, I don't think so. Not yet, anyway. I can go over with you what I have learned from our special guest. We should have several days before the would-be assassin arrives."

"If that is your wish. I will see you when we are done with the operation."

They left at a canter and quickly caught up with the formation.

"So, you shot Lucky Liam. How did you pull that off?" Tianna asked.

"I sat and waited for him to come by. I used some other thugs to flush him from his spot and drive him to me."

"Sounds like you're a hunter."

"Yeah. Gettin Liam wasn't any different than gettin a deer, really."

"Other than deers don't have royal blood."

"True, but there wasn't much Liam could do mid jump, especially since he couldn't tell I was there."

"I see," Tianna repelid.

So he had at least one ability. Tianna made sure not to be surprised if all of a sudden she didn't see him at her side.

"Once both perimeter rings are set up, I will be deploying three squads to clear out the building. One will remain outside and the other two will enter. Given what you told me, how would you feel if I put you on the roof of a nearby building? You can be a lookout, as well as be in a vantage point to shoot someone if they try slipping away."

"Sure, I can do that. I can enhance my senses so ya won't have to worry about me not seein anyone."

God, she thought, this guy is either really trusting or foolish by being so free with his powers. Perhaps he was ordered by Merik to be fully cooperative with her.

"Excellent. Now, before you get into position, I want you in link with a telepath. This way, if you see something, you can relay it immediately."

"Gotcha," Jaxus replied.

"Captain."

"Captain?"

"Yes. My rank is Captain and, even though you are not one of my guards, I still would like you to address me by my rank."

"Oh, sure. Captain."

CHAPTER 77

JARIEK

Once again Jariek was enjoying the freedom of flight when someone sent a stern telepathic message to wake up. Begrudenling, he let go of his control of the bird and sent a reply.

"Whose is this?"

"Don't play games with me."

"I am not playing any games, sir, just merely waiting for a business partner."

"That's me kid. I am your business partner, or at least that's what I am supposed to say. I am the warden the society sent to clean up this damn mess. My name's Grevin. Now, follow me up to my room."

Jariek eased open one eye and saw a stern man with an intimidating build turn and walk away. Quickly, he linked his mind to the man's sight and watched the stranger through his eyes as he headed to his room. Jariek waited a few minutes before he got up, went upstairs, and knocked on the door to the room the man had entered. The door opened a sliver as the man checked to make sure no one else was in the hall. Once he was satisfied, he opened it a little more, giving Jariek barely enough room to slip by.

"Took you long enough," Grevin said.

"I thought it might be best if I wasn't seen following you. I realize that my chances of working here in Crestburn again are slim to none, but I didn't want to jeopardize things or put you at risk."

The man laughed and shook his head "Put me at risk. You have no idea how much risk I live with a kid. How did you know which room was mine?"

"I have kept an eye on who comes and goes here and what rooms they are staying in, plus I watched where you went through your eyes."

"Not bad. So can you tell me anything about recent events?"

"A little, not too much. There was a large patrol sent out today. Looks as if they were going to raid another safe house. Most of that has died off, but occasionally they still find people who are either still loyal to Djinar or not happy with Merik. After the recent executions from the tavern fight, the second group has started to grow. The other day, a guard patrol was sent to where I used to work, inquiring about me. They left and seemed satisfied that I hadn't been back there."

"Good. How did you get all this information?"

"Same way I found your room. There are enough people who come and go from here, and my room has a balcony. It can be a bit boring seeing and hearing through random people, but, if you hang in there, you can learn a good deal and occasionally you get lucky. So, what are your plans?"

"I am going to scout out the Mansion. Coming through town, I saw a large group of guards heading out. With something going on, today might be a good chance to sneak in and see if I can find Kerwin. Do you know if he is still there?"

"No. I haven't seen him since I made my final report," Jariek replied.

"Very well. I will take a look and see what I can find. I will head out soon. Go back to the courtyard and hang out there. Feel free to link up with my sight, but I doubt you will be able to maintain a link at the distance I will be at," Grevin said.

Jariek smiled "Don't worry. I can cover several miles. I happen to be very strong with clairaudience and clairvoyance. My telepathy is not so much and will lose touch when you get a few blocks away."

CHAPTER 78

BOTUN

"Guards spotted in the alley," someone yelled. Everyone in the safe house froze. Again, the alarm came out, this time with a second squad at the other end of the alley. Everyone in the safehouse traded worried glances. Eventually, they all looked towards Botun for guidance.

"This is something we have prepared for. We knew when we started this that one-day Merik's people may find us. Now is not the time to let panic set in. You all know where the escape door is. I need volunteers to help hold them off until the rest can make it out."

A couple of the older guys stepped up and offered to hold off the guards. The rest began to head to the kitchen and pull aside a rug to reveal a trap door. Others went to the common room and grabbed a bookcase that had been specially reinforced.

"They are marching down the alley now," came the cry from the lookout.

"Quickly, people. We need to move the bookcase in front of the door." At this, several more hands grabbed the bookcase and helped carry it to the front door. They tipped the bookcase so that the bottom would be against the wall and the top wedged against the door about two-thirds of the way up. They got it into position just as a large thump came from the other side of the door, and everyone froze in their tracks. Again, another thump as the door shook in its frame. Voices could be heard from the alley outside.

"Now more than ever, we need to remain calm," came Botun's voice above the steady thumps and rattles that came from the entrance. "Get the panel into place next to the door, just below the bookcase to help block their way in. The rest of you, get going down the tunnel and into the sewers. Wait until the person in front of you is down and out of the way before you start your descent. It will do us all no good if you get jammed up. Once you are in the sewer, make your own way for several turns before coming to the surface. By then, you should be several blocks away., It should be safe enough to leave the sewers and find a place to hide."

There had been some shoving at the escape tunnel, but once the first few people made it down into the sewers the rest began to calm down a bit.

While people were waiting their turn, someone brought the trap door and wedged it into position.

The thumping stopped.

"Do you think they had enough?" asked a nervous man who had volunteered to act as a guard. Botun merely shook his head and waved at the people in the kitchen, who had frozen in place, to continue their escape.

"Get bows and spears ready," Botun whispered to those gathered by the door. The men nodded and did as they were ordered as the door jostled a bit in its place. The guards looked at each other with startled expressions as groaning sounds came from the door and matching sounds came from the guards outside.

When the noise stopped, there was a gap by the hinges that let daylight in. The daylight was short lived as a metal bar was thrust into that gap. This time, the door barely shook as the door hinge bent with the blow.

"They are trying to pop the hinges. It won't be much longer until the door is gone," Boutun warned.

Botun glanced back and saw that most of the people were gone. If the hinges could hold out for a few more minutes, then maybe they all might make it out. That hope was quickly dispelled as another loud pop sounded, followed by another, and metallic scratching as a hinge bent from the frame. More light peaked in around the edge of the door as the guards set to work on the second hinge. It was destroyed in just a few strikes and the door fell into the alley. With nothing to support it, the bookcase came crashing down, flattening the trapdoor that had been moved out of its place from the blows to the door.

Guards appeared near the door and his men drew back on their bows. Each one lingered a bit before letting their arrows fly, which gave the guards enough time to get their shields up. The guards with the shields dropped to a knee and the ones behind them fired arrows at those inside. Everyone by the entrance was hit, but they didn't move. They just stood there as a second volley of arrows took flight and struck home, this time in more vital spots.

Botun turned to run and got a dozen steps before he froze in place. Try as he might, he couldn't move. The paralysis only lasted a few seconds and he managed several more steps before it happened again. Botun could hear shouting by the door as the guards came in. When the paralysis ended, this time he didn't move. He waited for a second and then leaped forward.

That was a bad idea. While he did manage to get a lot further towards the trap door, he was off balance when the paralysis struck and he came crashing down onto the floor. He tried to get up, but each time he did his body would freeze. By the time Botun managed to get himself sitting upright, he was surrounded by several guards.

"Make way for the Captain," came a shout over by the entrance. A moment later, she was in the room with him. While the scar might mar her looks, it did nothing to her authority. Quickly, the guards searched the rooms and reported that no one else was there.

"I want a squad down that trapdoor to chase after any who got away," Tianna said.

"Yes, ma'am."

"Botun?" Tianna asked.

He nodded his head. It would do no good to lie. When they got him back to the mansion, there would be more than enough people who could identify him.

"I am sure you realize now that there is no chance for you to get away."

"I think it is quite obvious that you are in control of the situation," Botun said.

"Good. In just a little bit, we will have one of the guard wagons brought up and you will be escorted to the mansion."

"At which point, I am sure I will be questioned thoroughly and roughed up a bit. A few days shall go by, and I will be presented on that stage built in the Merchant's Courtyard and executed like those poor people in the bar fight."

Tianna flinched at that last comment. It had been fast and hardly noticeable, but Botun was well adept at noticing the smallest expressions. So it seems that she didn't enjoy that. If there was anything he could do to drive a wedge between her and Merik, he would try it. At that point, he had nothing to lose and only his life to gain.

"Captain, if I am to be executed, I have no problem with taking my own life. I can do so without your assistance," he said.

"You won't have a choice in the matter." There was a defeated look that flashed in her eyes as she said it. It was as if she wanted to add 'and neither will I'. Quickly, she turned away from him and asked one of her officers for a status update.

"The tunnel leads into the sewers, but it seems that they had barricades ready to block the pipes at the first intersection. Right now, the men are clearing them away, but it will take a few minutes since they don't have much room and the sewer water is rising," the guard said.

"How much is it rising?"

"Not much, ma'am. Just enough to make things more difficult. It might be backed up a foot deep at most."

"Get the barricades cleared out and continue the search of the sewers. I want additional patrols in this section of town. Pull them from nearby streets and have any guard that can walk out on detail in the streets. They need to be looking for dirty, wet people who smell like shit. Keep an eye out for people who are either barefoot or with soaked and soiled shoes. If they are remotely suspicious, detain them until a herald can clear them."

"Yes, ma'am!"

CHAPTER 79

KERWIN

"Wake up," a voice said.

Kerwin's eyes opened and a puzzled look came across his face.

"You're new. I haven't seen your face before," he said.

"That's because you hadn't screwed up enough to see it before now," Grevin replied.

Comprehension light behind his eyes as Kerwin slowly nodded.

"Excuse me for being a bit slow. They have a new way to deprive a person of sleep."

"What all does Merik know?"

"A lot, unfortunately. He knows the Cashek Society exists."

"How?"

"He claimed to pull it from my mind and that he has an undiscovered ability."

"There is no such thing," Grevin stated.

"I told him as such, but, nevertheless, he knew a fair amount about us."

"Then he dies."

Kerwin yawned and stretched as he got up. "Yes, I understand what the rules are."

"Then why are you still commenting?"

"There is much more to the situation than I first thought."

"Doesn't really matter. I will kill Merik and then deal with the rest of the situation. We need to get moving because all his guards are out."

"They have had raids before and never needed more than a squad or two to deal with them."

"It seems like they captured the leader."

"Djinar has been found?" Kerwin asked.

"Who cares? It's not my problem," Grevin said.

"Oh, I see. Well, Merik is a very hands-on psylord. He is probably in the city overseeing things as we speak. I think it would be best to leave the mansion. Judging by the blood on your armor, I take it that the guards down here are dead."

"Yes."

"Good, then we can make it look like I overpowered one, took his weapon, and killed them."

Grevin shook his head in disgust.

"I know you are not happy with the idea. I am not trying to steal your thunder. I just want to get out of here. Once we find out where Merik is, you can go after him. This is the best way." Kerwin let out a long yawn before continuing. "Besides, you want to catch him unprepared and that would."

"What?" Grevin asked.

"Huh?"

"You just said catch him unprepared. Why would he be prepared?"

There was a long pause before Kerwin spoke again. "I, ah, ah, told you that, ah, he knew about the Cashek Society. He knows how we operate. It wouldn't surprise me if he knew a warden was coming. If we make it look like I escaped, then there would be no reason for a warden to come, and he would let down his guard eventually."

"You took too long to answer me."

"Sorry, I am exhausted and, like I said, they have a new way to deny a person sleep."

"You are also trying really hard to not have me kill Merik."

"I just think it's the best of a bad situation," Kerwin replied calmly.

"You told him, didn't you? You sold out the Cashek Society to this petty psylord. Hell, I bet he even convinced you that he has new powers," Grevin said angrily.

"No! Not at all! It's nothing like that!"

"Nothing like that? That is perhaps the most guilty phrase I've ever heard.

"Fine, don't believe me. Take me back to the Cashek Society and have me stand trial with the council."

"Why, so you can betray me as we make our way out of here. Or, perhaps you plan to mark the trail so Merik can follow us."

"No. That's stupid. I could have just told him how to get there."

"So, you admit to telling him about us."

"That's not what I just said."

"It doesn't matter. I have heard more than enough," with that Grevin drew his sword, crossed the room in two long strides, and sunk the blade deep into Kerwin's belly.

"Please," Kerwin gasps.

"It's too late, traitor."

"You fool. Merik does have new abilities, and he is not the only one. Watch your thoughts because he can use them, too."

With a shove, Grevin pushed Kerwin off his blade. Kerwin fell to his knees. He put his hands on the wound and felt his hot blood soaking his hands. His vision grew hazy and his strength faded. Sweat beaded on his forehead, and he grew pale and clammy as his body went into shock. His eyes closed and did not open again.

CHAPTER 80

MERIK

The window in his office was open, allowing a nice breeze in. His body was warm with both liquor and the joy of victory. Tianna had performed admirably from the reports that he received. Botun had been captured and, once again, none of his guards had been killed in the fight. Soon, Merik would have the man before him, and he could hopefully put an end to the whereabouts of Djinar.

Right now, the guards were scouring the city for the ones who had escaped. Tianna was not taking any chances and had the guards detain anyone they thought were suspicious. It was taking the heralds time to sift through them all. Thankfully, they had been dumb enough to flee through the sewers. The guards could probably smell them before ever laying eyes on them.

Merik lowered his glass and heard the rattle of ice. Finished already? Well, he could have another. It was a day for celebration, was it not? He walked over to the liquor cabinet and poured himself another drink, splashing a little bit of the liquor on his hand holding the glass.

This was a good day indeed. Not only had he secured his hold here in Crestburn, but he can now take steps to expand. It had all happened so quickly. Just to think, several months ago he was unheard of. He had been nothing more than a scribe copying books and contracts. Now, here he was, a psylord. No not "a" psylord, "the" psylord. He would be the one to rebuild what no one else was capable of.

He returned to his desk and looked again at the letter that he had received this morning. Shortly after Tianna left with the guards, the courier knocked on his door. At first, he thought it was a status update from Tianna. She was to keep him informed of the progress of the raid. Merik was surprised to see the young messenger he had sent away just a few days ago. The young man had ridden long and hard in order to return so quickly.

The letter was a response to his offer. Merik knew he would need allies in the days to come. With luck, this would be the first of many. It would make things a lot easier if the other psylords would refrain from going after him. He wasn't foolish enough to believe it, but a man could always hope. As it were, he had one ally, for now. One who he would have to watch very closely. It was a dangerous path to go down, but Merik knew that he would be up to the challenge of dealing with it. Besides, greater risks meant greater reward, and soon he would be secure in his position, not just in Crestburn but the neighboring cities as well.

There was a knock on the door. "Come in," he responded. The door opened and the herald entered and bowed.

"Sorry for the intrusion, Sire, but I have a message for you from Captain Tianna."

"Proceed, herald," Merik replied with a wave of his hand.

"The guards have detained about a hundred people. So far, seven people have been found that were in the hideout with Botun. Currently, the heralds are going through the rest. Most of the guards are being dismissed or returned back to regular duty. Tianna will be on her way back here with Botun in tow in just a little while."

"Wonderful!"

"The Captain would like to know if you wish to see either the prisoner or herself right away," the herald asked.

"I want Botun tossed in a cell,m and I wish to speak with the good Captain. How long before their arrival?"

"They should be here in just a few minutes. I will head out immediately to intercept them and let the herald with her know your desires."

"Excellent. You're dismissed."

Merik leaned back in his chair and smiled. Today was a great day. He should let the chef know to make something special for dinner tonight. A large dinner with all the council members and the representatives from the neighboring town. Shit, he had forgotten all about them. Ever since Jaxus informed him about Botun's location, he had been focused on the man's capture. Well, he was sure that Botun's capture would show them that their wait was a worthwhile sacrifice.

Merik took a long sip, closed his eyes, and relaxed. The door to the room opened.e frowned and sat up ready to chastise the servant for not knocking first. Standing in the partially opened doorway was a man in a dark tunic. Silently, he stepped into the room and shut the door behind him.

"I was wondering when you would show up," Merik said.

"You knowing about me changes nothing," replied Grevin coldly.

"Oh, I disagree."

"Talk all you want, but I will kill you all just the same."

"You must do what you must do, as well as I, but do you know what I can do?"

"I don't care."

"So serious and so boring. The quintessential killer. Focused on nothing but his prey."

"If you realize this, then you should know how pointless it is to talk to me."

"Normally, I would agree with you, but, then again, I possess something you and your secret society needs. Something that will allow me to rebuild the Kysian Empire."

The man slowly made his way across the room, drawing his swords as he went. Each step was slow and measured, as if he was expecting a trap. Excellent, thought Merik, for this gave him more time to stall and, hopefully, find a memory that he could lose him in.

Merik reached out to the man's mind and had a hard time grasping onto a memory. This happened only a few times before in the past. When someone was so focused on a task at hand, they were living in the moment and had no place in their mind for memories right then. He needed a distraction and rather quickly. Something to divert the man's attention for just a bit.

"Do you know what makes me different?" he asked. The question was met with stony silence. "I have the ability to go through people's memories."

"You might have tricked Kerwin with some kind of trick, but you won't fool me. There are no new powers nor will there ever be."

"While I might have issues with Kerwin, the man is no fool. Would you like me to release him to you, as a gesture of goodwill?" Merik asked.

"Kerwin is dead," Greven flatly stated.

"No, he is quite alive. I have him in a guest room."

"No, he is dead. I killed him, along with the four guards downstairs."

As he was trying to think of something to respond to that, the man lunged. Merik screamed and flung himself backward, causing the chair to topple over. He scrambled to his feet and clutched his arm where the man's blade had sliced him high on the upper arm.

Merik kept his desk between him and his assailant. His attacker merely shook his head at this tactic and jumped up on the desk. He smiled down at Merik before he swung at his head. The blade came a lot faster than Merik thought it would, and he was just barely able to get out of the way by unceremoniously throwing himself onto the floor. Quickly, he scrambled under his desk and hoped it would shield him from the next strike. Thank god he never got around to replacing this desk. His attacker laughed. The man actually laughed at him.

"What a coward. I can't believe that a coward such as yourself actually thinks he stands a chance to rebuild the Empire."

There was a soft thud as the man leaped down from the desk. Seeing which side the man's boots landedon, Merik scurried away from him until he was well past his desk before he dared to stand up. Merik dashed towards the door but collapsed as a sharp piercing pain bit deep into his leg. He looked down and saw a dagger buried into his calf.

"Did you really think that I would come down behind the desk without a plan, just so you could scurry towards the door?"

Merik whimpered and tears rolled down his face as he tried to remove the dagger. His attacker walked slowly around the desk and threw another dagger at Merik. The second dagger nicked his thigh with a long cut. Again, Merik yelped.

"You don't realize the size of the mistake you are making," Merik pleaded.

The man merely snorted as he came steadily closer. This can not be the way it ends. He was destined to be the one to rebuild Kysia. There had to be more to his story than dying at the hands of a nameless assassin. Once again, Merik reached out and tried to find a memory that he could draw his attacker into, if just for a few minutes. There was nothing. The warden now stood at his feet, sword raised high.

CHAPTER 81

TIANNA

The raid had been very successful. Not only was Botun captured and secured in a guard wagon, but several of his helpers had been found as well. There was only one injury, and that was from one of the guards who helped remove the barricades down in the sewers.

Botun was being very compliant, but, then again, it wouldn't do him much good to cause problems. The guard detail assigned to watch him was a special unit of stunners that she hand-picked for today. The second he looked like he would try anything, one of them would stun him. Combine that with all the guards in the area, and that young archer playing lookout, and there was no hope for Botun.

Most stunners could only stop a person for a few seconds at a time, a bit longer if they concentrated, then they would need a moment or two before being able to do so again. Tianna had gathered a squad of guards who had this talent and made them practice stunning a target one after the other. They had spent the night before practicing and had gotten decent at working together. Each man learned how long the others could halt someone's body, and they quickly established a firing order with very little tinkering. The end result was that they could keep a person stunned for three minutes before they started getting exhausted and the time between each stun started lengthening.

Thankfully, there had been enough guards, along with a few conscripted heralds, that she was able to pull it off. She needed to figure out what psychic abilities the city guards had. Tianna had a fair idea of what the mercenaries who came with Merik could do. Mercenaries were pretty open about any royal blood, because it meant they could charge more. At least, they were open about their offensive abilities. Any resistance to powers was kept a secret, so as to give them an edge against someone who possessed a power they were immune to.

Now that they had Botun captured, perhaps she could set up a team that could give her an accurate account of what everyone could do. Additionally, she could talk to the training sergeants and make sure that they get this information from all incoming recruits. Today's success should help encourage others to be more forthcoming about their abilities. Perhaps she could even talk Merik into giving a bonus for those who have powers. He had been talking about rebuilding the wardens, after all.

"Excuse me, Captain," someone said.

Tianna pulled away from her thoughts and turned to see who was addressing her. It was the young man who Merik sent to tag along. What was his name again? Jacob? No, it was something else.

"Jaxus," she responded questiongly.

"Yes, ma'am. I was wonderin if there was anythin ya need me to do."

"Not at this moment. The raid went off smoothly, and we didn't' have need of you. Perhaps next time you might see some action."

"Alright. Hey, by the way, there was some strange guy passed out on the roof next to the buildin where I was."

"And?" Tianna asked.

"I don't know. Not used to seein someone passed out on a rooftop, I guess. Didn't know if it was important or not," Jaxus said a bit sheepishly.

"I can't think of any reason why it would be. Probably just some bum, nothing for us to worry about. Can you stun?"

"Ah, yea. Why?"

"What other powers do you have?"

"Why do ya want to know?"

Tianna wondered how much she wanted to tell him. Jaxus was apparently a special guest of Merik, since he shot Lucky Liam. Thinking of Liam, where was he? She held up a hand to Jaxus and yelled for a guard.

"Do any of the people we captured match the description of Lucky Liam?"

"I don't know, Captain. I can find out," a guard said.

"Jaxus, you shot Liam, so you know what he looks like. I want you to go with the guard and check the people we have rounded up. See if Liam is amongst them."

"Sure."

"I want you to report back to me only on this matter."

The guard turned to Jaxus and said, "Follow me, sir. We are putting all of the people we are rounding up into one holding area to make it easier for the heralds. It's not too far from here."

While Jaxus checked on the people being detained, she went over to guard's wagon to talk to Botun. There were ten guards surrounding the wagon. Two in front, ready to drive off at a moment's notice and pair on each corner of the wagon. Each guard was heavily armored and carried a large metal shield. They looked more like heavy infantry soldiers than town guards. Given Botun's reputation, she was not about to take any chances that he had a contingency plan ready in case he had been captured.

The back of the wagon was flat with a heavy door. There was a small step just below the door that hung on the back of the wagon. Tianna stood on the step and looked in through the small barred window in the door. Botun sat peacefully facing the door.

"Ah, Captain, what can I do for you?" he said as he noticed her.

"I was told that you had a prisoner, Lucky Liam," Tianna said.

"Yes, he was in our care."

"Was?"

"I use the past tense only because, in my current situation, I am in no position to care for anyone."

"Do you know where he is?"

"No."

"That was rather quick."

"It was an easy answer. I am sure you think that I might be lying to you, but I don't see any point in doing so. I know you will be taking me to Merik, where he will have done to me what he did to Jenal. He will have his best telepaths listening to my thoughts, ready to detect the first trace of falsehood. It is far easier for me to tell you the truth and be done with it, especially since I don't care one way or the other what happens to Liam."

"Why did you have him shot?"

"I didn't have him shot. That was," Botun paused to think for a moment, "perhaps a result of his reputation. Liam had quite the reputation for being uncatchable. I had some questions for him, and the guys were a little zealous in their methods to bring him in. I take it that the one who shot him was the one who told you where we were located?"

"What makes you think that?"

"The men told me how Liam was captured. I noticed that the young fellow who had shot Liam was nowhere to be seen and you showed up a few hours later."

Tianna stepped down from the back of the wagon. She could already see Jaxus coming back. That was rather fast, which meant that Liam was not amongst them. Merik would not be happy about that, but Liam was only a minor concern of his.

"Ah, Captain Tianna, Sir, uh, mam," Jaxus said, unsure of himself.

"Captain will do. I take it you didn't see Liam."

"No. I even made it so that anyone there wouldn't notice me."

"Good idea."

Jaxus had good instincts it seemed but needed work dealing with people.

"Jaxus, guards tend to go with sir because it's traditional, but either sir, mam, or captain will work. I am about to take the prisoner to the mansion. I want you to ride along with me to make sure he gets there safely."

"Yeah, sure." He gave a sloppy salute and went to get his mount.

Tianna turned to the guards watching over the prisoner. "Be ready to move out in just a couple of minutes." They gave her a salute and turned to face the front of the wagon. The next couple of minutes she spent with the senior most officer present, giving him orders on how she wanted things to proceed. Jaxus rode over with her mount in tow.

The ride to the mansion was uneventful. At the mansion, they pulled up to a rarely used servant's entrance. Several of the guards left the wagon to make sure the way was clear to the cells beneath the mansion. Tianna dismounted and waited for the guards to come back to tell her the path was clear of servants. The sound of rapidly approaching footsteps caught her attention. She turned and saw one of the guards returning at a sprint.

"To arms!" he yelled out as he approached. The guards drew their swords and put their backs to the wagon. Tianna drew hers as well and scanned the area for any signs of a threat.

"The guards, they are dead." huffed the man between breaths.

"Which ones?" Tianna asked.

"The ones by the cells. A bloodbath." the man painted his reply.

Tianna turned to the guard driving the wagon. "I want this wagon secured and extra guards here on the double. Stay here until I return." The man nodded.

She entered the mansion and ran down the hall. As she hit the first intersection, she almost collided with other guards who were carefully making their way back. "To the wagon now! I am getting Lord Merik," she yelled as she passed them and dashed up the nearby stairs. It seemed like it took forever for her to cross the mansion. As she ran down the halls with her blade out, servants screamed and got out of her way.

"Lord Merik is in danger, where is he?" she cried out.

One timid servant stammered a reply that she thought he was in his office. Good, that was the direction she had been heading. Quickly, she ran and took another flight of stairs three steps at a time. As she neared his office, she heard someone cry out. Without another thought, she crashed into the door shoulder first and blasted it open.

A stranger stood over a prone and bleeding Merik with his sword raised, ready to swing. Tianna lunged forward, barely deflecting the assailant's blade as he slashed down at Merik. The man recovered quickly and thrust his blade at her, hoping to catch her off balance before she could recover from her overextended lunge. Not bothering to pull back, Tianna turned her lunge into a side roll and brought her falcata in front of her at an angle to block the attack.

The man made several thrusts at her. She blocked each one, which gave her a chance to adjust her position so she could more easily rise from her crouched position. Out of the corner of her eye, she could see a bleeding Merik crawl away from the duel.

Without warning, her head began to shriek in agony worse than any morning after a night of drinks had ever done. Disorientated by the quick onset of such an intense headache, she wobbled and fell back, just barely catching herself with her free hand. Behind her, Merik let out a loud cry and she could see him as he grabbed his head. The assailant, who was unaffected by whatever it was, landed a wicked cut along her sword arm.

She tried to reach out to his mind and control his body, but she couldn't focus her thoughts with her head screeching in agony. It was all she could do to block his strikes. Her only saving grace was being able to fight by reflex. Her attacker had not expected her to defend herself so well and now he was being a little more cautious.

An arrow jutted through his arm and Tianna took the opportunity to roll away from him and come up in a crouch. The man growled as he snapped the arrow off near his flesh and started forward toward Jaxus, who leaned against the door frame. Tianna rushed the assassin. Now that she was no longer crouched backward, she was able to meet him stroke for stroke.

Behind her, she could hear Merik being dragged away. Good. Now that her lord was no longer in immediate danger, she could focus solely on the fight. Her head still screamed and the light from the windows hurt her eyes. Thankfully, Jaxus' arrow had even the playing field a bit. Hopefully, he would be back soon.

The two exchanged strikes, neither landing anything significant on the other person. Blood ran down their arms and legs from several small lacerations. Carefully she began to shift her position away from the door. By now, Merik should be far enough away that the man would not be able to find him before the guards came.

Tianna looked past his shoulder and saw Jaxus slowly making his way forward. He moved painfully slowly and his eyes were barely opened. Whatever it was that had affected her and Merik, it must have affected him as well. Jaxus' bow wobbled as he drew back the string. Tianna dropped to a knee, making herself as small as she dared and yet still be able to defend herself.

The arrow flew and struck the man in his rear. He stumbled a bit, and Tianna popped up and blocked his sword with hers while she threw a quick upper cut at the bottom of his jaw. He staggered back and her head no longer hurt. The lack of pain was almost as much of a shock as it's initial onslaught had been. Tianna recovered quickly and pressed her advantage. Now that her head no longer screamed in agony, she could focus on the fight. He was no match for her.

An overhand stroke scored a nasty cut on his free arm. She blocked a poorly aimed swing at her midsection and countered with a kick to his chest. As he staggered back, she swiped down, sinking the tip of her blade deep into the meat of his thigh, all the way to the bone. She stepped forward, coming inside his strike range, and landed another uppercut, followed by a headbutt to his nose just as his head came back from the first blow.His nose broke with a wet crunch and he staggered to the floor.

"Captain, I have him covered," said Jaxus.

Trusting the young man, she stepped, back leaving her falcata in his thigh. The carpet was soaked with blood from their duel. Sparing a quick glance, she saw that Jaxus had his bow trained on the would-be assassin, and this time his aim was steady.

From down the hall, she could hear the commotion. It must be the guards, now that more had been alerted to what was going on.

"Who are you?" she asked.

"A dead man," Grevin said matter of factly.

He was growing paler by the second. Another minute or two and he would be dead from blood loss.

"If you cooperate, we can save you," Tianna offered.

"No. I won't allow it, not that you could anyway."

"Who sent you?"

"No one."

"Don't lie to me."

"You won't get any answers from me. You are too good of a swordswoman. You butchered me up fast. You. . ."

He said no more as his body stopped moving and his bleeding became a trickle.

CHAPTER 82

MERIK

To say his arm and legs hurt was an understatement. How on earth did soldiers handle it? The assassin must have struck just the right spots to cause more pain. A cruel move intended to torture a victim before dealing a fatal blow. Merik wished he could have a drink, but the healer who had bandaged him up told him it was best not to drink tonight, for he had lost a fair amount of blood. He thought about taking some Twilight Haze but decided against it. What he wanted was for the pain to go away, not for his mind to be numbed.

Kerwin had tried to warn him but, in his arrogance, Merik thought he was safe. He thought that it would take time for the secret society to get word about what happened and send someone. Never did he expect it to be so fast. They had to have a place nearby. He would have to look at a map again and try and figure out where this menace was possibly hiding. Once he found them, he would wipe them out, provided they didn't bow down to him.

From now on, he would need bodyguards. Tianna would be great to start with, and so would Jaxus. He wondered if Lucky Liam might be convinced to work for him. Probably not, since it was Jaxus who shot him. Although, he did have other plans for Jaxus, so he may not be around much. It could possibly work out. He would have to deal with Suval if that happened. For some reason, the creep was infatuated with Lucky Liam. He would have to check the man's memories and see if he could figure out what it was about Liam that drew Suval to him. It was a shame he couldn't see the memories of the dreams that Suval entered.

To hell with what the healer said; his wounds hurt too damn much. He got up from his chair and damned near fell to the floor when he put weight on his injured leg. Damn, that hurt like hell. He managed to sit back down and yelled for a servant.

"Yes, sire," the servant said.

"Fix me a drink."

"I thought that the healer…"

"I don't give a damn what the healer said," Merik shouted at the man. "You will fix me a drink right now and without another comment or else you will find yourself on the stage in Merchant's Courtyard before sundown."

The terrified servant ran over to the liquor cabinet and damn near crashed into the thing. He splashed half of it over his shaking hands as he poured the drink. He started to rush back to Merik and stopped suddenly, sloshing half of the drink onto the ground. He walked the last several steps slowly and handed Merik a half-empty glass that was wet to the touch.

"Really?"

"Sorry, my lord. I will make you another right away." The servant dashed back to the cabinet and made a second drink with slightly less shaky hands. By the time he got back, Merik had the first one finished and was ready for a full glass. He downed this one almost as fast and was about ready to ask for another when he felt a bit light headed. Apparently, the healer wasn't kidding when he said that alcohol and other things would affect him quickly for the next few days.

"Another."

This new glass he nursed and, even then, he was very light headed for quite some time. The sun had set when the effects of the alcohol had worn off enough that he could begin to think straight.

"I want Captain Tianna, Erlin, Suval, and Jaxus to meet with me."

"Will you be meeting them here?" a nervous servant asked tentatively.

Merik looked around and realized he was in a small lounge, one he didn't recall ever being in before. "No. Have them meet me on the balcony. Also, I want some food, too. I think I am hungry. Yes, I am hungry. Let the chef know I want food. Make sure he has enough food for all of us. Oh, and get me one more glass before you go and then get me a cane."

He sat up and drank about a third of the glass while he waited for the servant to return. Things were going to change. Merik was glad that he had pulled enough people towards him to make everything possible. When he had read Palreon's manuscript, he never realized there were people who were waiting for someone like him to figure out the clues. Had Merik known that, he would have waited until his position here in Crestburn was secure. Perhaps then the society wouldn't have been in such a hurry to kill him. That part still puzzled him. Why kill him for merely knowing about them?

He took another long sip and noticed the servant had returned with a cane.

"Took you long enough," Merik mumbled into his glass, trying not to slur his words.

"My apologies, my lord. Everyone is busy trying to catch up on work lost due to today's incident."

Merik snorted. Today's incident. It was no damn incident, it was an attempt on his life. The servant handed him the cane. He looked down at the glass and thought about finishing it off but decided against it. The room wasn't quite spinning, but it definitely wasn't standing perfectly still, either. Carefully, he sat the glass down and struggled to rise. It took three attempts, but he was able to eventually stand.

Limping, he slowly made his way down the hall. At the stairs, he paused before beginning the arduous climb up. He paused twice on the staircase and once again on the landing before heading down the hallway. The mansion was eerily quiet. Didn't the servant say everyone was busy working? If so, where was everyone? Also, where was the damn balcony?

Merik stopped to give his leg a rest and noticed a window in the room across the hall from him. Something was off with the view. He hobbled towards it until he got a better view, and then realized that not only was he on the wrong floor, he was also in the wrong wing. As he looked down, he could see the balcony and a couple of people were already there waiting. Shit. He turned around and started making his way back. By the time he got down to the balcony, his head was more stable and the food was being brought out.

Doing his best not to show any weakness, he slowly made his way across the balcony. As he sat down, he smiled at everyone.

"So, how was everyone's day?" he asked playfully.

Silence.

Merik laughed. "It was a joke. If we can't laugh, especially after tragic events, then what is the point of going on?"

Erlin was the first to speak, "I take it you are feeling well my lord?"

"Well enough, all things considered. Where is Suval?"

"No one has seen him since the other day when you sent him out."

Merik shook his head. "Tianna, my good Captain, how are you? I heard that you were wounded in my defense."

Tianna was wearing a sleeveless outfit, which was unheard of for her, due to the bandages up and down her arms. She looked tired but not too worse for the wear.

"I am fine. Our friend was a decent swordsman, but, with Jaxus' help, I was able to kill him. As far as my wounds go, most are minor cuts and will heal in a few days' time."

"Good, good," he replied as he stuffed his face with buttered mash potato. Now that he had food before him, he realized how hungry he was. Jaxus was seated across from Tianna and was merely picking at his food.

"The food is not to your liking, Jaxus? I can have the cook make something else for you."

He turned his head towards Merik, but his gaze was to something well past him. There was a hauntedness to that gaze. "The food is fine, my Lord Merik, I just don't seem to have much of an appetite."

"Don't worry," commented Tianna "most people tend not to have an appetite after their first life and death fight. Give it some time and you will be hungry enough."

Jaxus gave a weak smile and nodded his head, then he returned to picking at his food. For the next several minutes, they all ate in silence. Once Merik finished his second plate, he spoke up again.

"I do believe I remember the assassin telling me that Kerwin was dead. I assumed that he had been bluffing at the time," Merik stated.

Tianna and Erlin exchanged glances and his chief herald cleared his throat. "He told you the truth. Kerwin is dead. It seems our intruder snuck in and killed the guards downstairs and then murdered Kerwin before heading towards you."

"When the guards and I returned with Botun," Tianna said, "I had a couple of them go down the cells to make sure they were ready for him, as well as to make sure no staff got in our way. One of them came running back and reported that the guards had been killed. At that point, I set off running, trying to find you."

"Let me get this straight. He came in and murdered his own man, and then he tried to kill me?"

"So it seems," replied Erlin. "It also might be a bit more complicated. After being informed about the attempt on your life, I went down to the cells to investigate matters. The guards were killed rather quickly and there was a lot of blood at the table, yet bodies weren't at the table. Kerwin's body was also in that room. I took the liberty to check his cell and found one of the guard's bodies there. I am guessing that the assassin killed the guards, then killed Kerwin in his cell, and then made it seem as if he died in an attempt to escape.

"I wish I could say to what purpose, but, to be honest, any reason to do so eludes me. Perhaps with some more time, I can come up with some."

"Cover," came the quiet reply from Jaxus.

"Cover? Do explain, please," prompted Erlin.

"He didn't want it to seem that Kerwin was killed by him. He wanted to make it look like he died tryin' to escape. The attacker wanted to cover up the fact that he killed the prisoner, this Kerwin."

"Why would he do that?" asked Merik.

Jaxus merely shrugged. "Perhaps because a prisoner died attackin the guards raises a lot fewer questions than one who was killed in his cell."

"It is as good an explanation as any we will get. The big question is: why was he killed?" asked Erlin.

"I believe he was killed because of what he told me. Kerwin was a part of some secret society that is waiting to help bring back the Kysian Empire. I didn't learn much from him, other than this organization does exist. He even warned me that they would send someone who might try to kill me. A warden, if you can believe it."

"When did he tell you this?" asked Tianna.

"Well, that was yesterday. I was planning on setting up personal bodyguards after you handled Botun. There was no way I could have predicted that the assassin would come so quickly."

"His accomplice must have sent word shortly after he was captured," surmised Erlin.

"Have you narrowed down who this Jariek could be?" Merik asked.

"Yes. I was planning on bringing this up tomorrow, actually, what with you being busy with getting Botun." Erlin paused to turn to Tianna before continuing, "By the way, congratulations on the successful operation, Captain."

"Thank you," she replied.

"One of the young men with that name, who we checked on, was an apprentice falconer to a Master Gerwald. Recently, he has disappeared and this happens to be right around the time Kerwin became your guest."

"Then it must be this boy," Merik stated matter of factly.

"It would seem so, my lord. I took the liberty to have the guards and heralds be on the lookout for him. Additionally, I would recommend a sweep of the inns in town. There is a good chance that, if he has not left, he might be hiding out in one of them."

"Or, he could have already left the city, which was how an assassin was sent to me."

"Yes, it is also another possibility," Erlin agreed.

Merik took a drink and then asked, "You said he is a falconer right?"

"That is correct, sire."

"Then he could have easily used one of the falcons to get word to this secret society of theirs. Kerwin mentioned that they had some kind of special communication network in place. They called it the second caravan, but that name might be just to throw people off, have people looking for merchant wagons instead of birds. If they sent a message shortly after we detained Kerwin, then that could very well explain how one of their wardens arrived here so quickly."

"That is a possibility," Erlin mused.

"I want this Master Gerwald and his staff arrested for treason."

"All of them?" Erlin inquired.

"Yes, everyone. If everyone is arrested, then someone who knows something, but is not directly involved, will be more likely to report it to prevent being executed along with the others."

"As you wish."

"With this attack on me, it is now more important than ever that I am protected. Tianna, for the time being you will be my personal bodyguard. The city guard will be able to operate fine without you for a while, as we recently learned with your break. I want you to pick people you trust, who are excellent fighters, and have strong imperial blood to serve as my bodyguard. I want you to have a list of candidates ready by tomorrow afternoon."

"I can do that my lord. I don't think it is necessary to remove me."

"What is more important, my life or your wants?" Merik interrupted with a shout.

"Your life, of course," Tianna said apologetically.

"I can not rebuild the Kysian Empire if I am dead. Don't think of this as a demotion. Quite the opposite. I am trusting you with the most precious of all things, my life. There is no one who is better suited to keeping me alive than you. Today, you proved that beyond a doubt. A lesser person would have been butchered by him at the onset of that headache. Did you even feel it?"

She nodded. "Yes, I felt it and it was all that I could do to keep his blade at bay."

"Yeah, what was that?" chimed in Jaxus.

"I think it was a new power," Merik said with a smirk.

"Yeah, right", Jaxus laughed until he realized no one else was laughing and was, in fact, very serious.

"Jaxus, I am about to let you in on a very big secret. The only reason I am even telling you this is out of pure gratitude for your part in saving my life. There are a few people out there with new powers. The man who beat our good captain in a duel could give people false memories. I can go through a person's memories and even make them experience them again."

Jaxus looked to the other two seated at the table, and they both nodded to confirm what he had been told.

"No way. No one has new powers," the young man said with disbelief.

"I know it's hard to believe, so how about a quick demonstration?"

"Ok," Jaxus said nervously.

"Think about your village and growing up. I will find something that will suit my purposes and you will relive it."

Jaxus shrugged and closed his eyes. Merik gave him a moment then looked into his memories. Before him was a small fishing and hunting village. A nice sunny day and his parents were there. Merik shifted it to another memory of Jaxus' parents. Then another of him hunting with his father. There were several hunting memories, too many to count or shift through. It turned out that Jaxus had a lot of memories of being in the woods. Here was one of him alone and crying with his bow in his head. Promising, but he needed something more emotional than this. Why was he crying? Ah, yes, bullies.

There were several memories of bullies. Quickly, Merik shifted through them until he found one where Jaxus had taken a solid beating from them. He couldn't be much more than ten at the time. Merik started the memory at the first punch and made it intense. In his chair, Jaxus' head reeled back as if he had gotten hit in real life. Merik let the memory continue to the end of the fight then started it all over again. He let it repeat a few times before stopping.

Tears rolled down Jaxus' face.

"I am sorry to have to do that to you, my friend, but people learn better if there is a price attached to the lesson. Don't worry, you are not alone. All of my inner circle has experienced something similar," Merik said without remorse.

"Like what?" he said as he dried his eyes on his sleeves.

"It's not my place to tell, only to show you what I can do. Now, do you believe me?" Merik asked.

"Yes. What about you two, what can you do?"

Merik laughed. "They don't possess unique powers. In fact, there are only two or three others that I know of who do, and one of them is dead. Tianna and Erlin do have something in common, though. They are both unusually strong in several talents. There is yet a person whose body Tianna has failed to control. Not only can she control a person's body, but she can go from person to person quickly. Erlin has a range of telepathy that can cover the entire Merchant's Courtyard.

"You see, Jaxus, times are changing. People are changing. There are those with unbelievable strength in their talents while others have appeared with new abilities. I believe now more than ever that Kysia will be rebuilt, and I am the man to do it. One of the nice things with my special gift is that I can use it to help find others like me. I can go through their memories and find when they used a never before seen power. I will also be able to detect the fakers who will come posing as someone with a new power.

It is not quite time to reveal to the world what I can do. Once word gets out, there will be no end to the threats on my life. So, I need you to keep this a secret. I am trusting you with my life. Soon, I will let the world know, but not before we are ready. We need to be prepared because the other psylords will come at me hard and fast once they realize how powerful I am and what I represent. Can I trust you, my dear friend?" Merik asked as he sowed a feeling of hope and joy in Jaxus.

"Oh yeah, absolutely, Merik. I mean, Lord Merik."

"It's quite alright, just don't do it again. So, what were we talking about?"

"The headaches you three experienced," Erlin answered.

"Ah yes. That was awful. I couldn't concentrate to use any of my abilities," Merik said.

"Neither could I," replied Tianna.

"Same here. Hell, I could barely hold my bow steady to shoot."

"How was it you were able to fight when the rest of us were almost crippled by the headache?" Merik asked.

"I've trained a lot. It's to the point where it is instinctual. I barely even think in a fight."

"So, you fought on reflex then?"

"Yes. I tried to control him, but I couldn't focus at all to do so."

"I also had a problem using my abilities. Part of the reason that I am as good of a shot as I am is that I can enhance my senses. When I gots near the room, my head hurt and my senses went back to normal," Jaxus said.

"You said your head hurt when you got near the room?" inquired Erlin.

"Yes. I was fine, then all of a sudden there was sudden pain."

"How far away from the room where you when the pain started?" Erlin asked.

"About fifteen feet or so. Actually, ya can find the spot because," Jaxus paused as his cheeks reddened "I kind of had a misfire."

"Misfire? Do explain," Erlin asked puzzled.

"Yeah. As I was tryin to follow the captain, all of a sudden my head exploded with pain. I wasn't ready for it and let gos of my bowstring and accidently shot an arrow into the floor."

"Well, I am sure our Lord Merik won't mind a small hole in the carpet, especially since it gives me a better way to estimate the range of the dead man's power. I can check to see if the servants were affected. I am curious to learn if those without royal blood suffered from it as well. It might be worth putting a few people without powers in your guard, my Lord. At least for now, until we can better learn about this ability."

"I can do that. Do we have any idea what kind of threat this secret society is? Any ideas on their numbers or what other unique powers they may possess?" Tianna asked.

Merik leaned back into his chair, "Unfortunately, no. But, I might have a way to learn more about them. You know that I have a small collection of rare manuscripts from Emperor Palreon. There is a hidden truth within them. I always thought it was an inner truth, something metaphysical, that the emperors knew about and didn't share with the rest of the world. With this special knowledge, I thought that I would be better suited to establish Kysia than other psylords. It seems that perhaps the truth in the books isn't metaphysical but a code or something to attract this secret society's attention. I am going to have to spend some time rereading them, as well as my notes, and see if there was something else hidden in them."

"What more could there be?" asked Erlin.

"Honestly, I have no idea. It could be as simple as a hidden message within a hidden message," Merik said with a shrug.

"That doesn't sound very simple, my Lord," Jaxus commented.

"Perhaps not to you, Jaxus, but I am well read. You know I used to be a scribe. I have read quite extensively and have learned a lot from books. That is partially why I am doing a better job of rebuilding Kysia than others."

"Do you want me to increase the guards at the gate and have an order that no messengers, including birds, are to leave?" asked Tianna.

"I don't think so. Right now, they don't know what has happened. I want Master Gerwald rounded up first. Besides, we will be having a guest arrive soon and that will drastically change things."

"A guest?" asked Tianna.

"Several in fact. I have made an alliance with another psylord, and he will be bringing his forces to bolster our numbers."

"Are you sure this is wise my lord?" asked Erlin.

"Everything will be fine. We are going to need allies, and I happen to know his secret, so he won't be a threat."

"Who is this psylord and what size is his force?" questioned Tianna.

"You all have enough to worry about over the next several days. Our barracks for the guards need to be increased, extra tabards are to be sewn, and bodyguards need to be selected and trained. With the addition of this new force, we can finally see about setting up the wardens earlier than planned. Also, we need to find Suval. I definitely want him here. Of course, there is Botun to question and this Jariek to find, if he is still in the city. It is going to be a very busy week or two for us.

"I know I told you, Jaxus, that you could have plenty of time to decide about what we talked about. Unfortunately, I am going to need your decision sooner rather than later, due to recent events. After your actions today, I can honestly say that I want you to be a part of what I am building here." Merik sent the feeling of pride to the young man's mind. "You have been included in my secret and together the chances of rebuilding Kysia will be much greater. Now, I realize that there will be things that I ask of you that will be hard, and that you may not wish to do. Know this. Both Erlin and Tianna have done the same. Like you, they do the hard and necessary tasks that a lesser person would balk at. There will be times that what I require of you will seem cruel and unnecessary, but I promise you that it will be what is needed for the greater good."

While he talked, servants had removed their plates and produced dessert. Not bothering to wait for a response, Merik started on the dessert. It was a rich creamy chocolate mousse with diced fruits and a topping of powdered nuts. Taking his lead, the others ate their desserts in silence. After the day's excitement and a full meal, exhaustion came over him. He would turn in early tonight, but not before he concluded a bit of business after the others had left.

"My lord." came the timid voice from Jaxus.

"Yes."

"I don't need to wait to make up my mind. Ya have been extremely kind to me. Not only did ya trust me with yar secret, but ya also included me in today's operations. Neither of these things ya had to do. With what ya told me, I agree that now more than any other time is the best chance we will have to rebuild Kysia. I want to be a part of that. Ya reminded me why I left home. I have nothing there. All I did was hunt and hide out in the woods to avoid bullies. With ya, I can be somethin. Ya are going to be a threat to the way things are. That's ok, because we must change things in order to bring back the Kysian Empire. They will see ya as a threat and try to get rid of ya, like they attempted today. I don't want that to happen. So, I am yars, and use me however ya see fit," Jaxus said solemnly.

"Thank you. I am humbled by your words and gladly accept your service. Tianna, I want you to include him in the training you give the bodyguards. While I do have other plans for you, Jaxus, I think learning about bodyguards will benefit you greatly, even if it is only for a short while. It has been a long day, and I need to recover from the wounds that I received. Erlin, if you don't mind, I would like to speak to you for a few minutes longer in private."

"Of course."

Merik waited till Jaxus, Tianna, and the servants cleared the balcony. "With Tianna being in charge of my bodyguards, I want you to take over running the city guards. You have been doing an excellent job with the heralds, and I would like to see the two combined, eventually. I think a herald should be included with each guard patrol."

"If this is what you wish."

"It is. Also, you will be having a smaller guard force to work with, as I will be using a lot of the guards to form my army. Now that an attempt has been made on my life, I need to strengthen my position. At some point, I may have to show the world what I can do."

"That seems reasonable. I take it that once the transition from city guard to the army is complete, you will have Captain Tianna in charge of the latter. That is, after the bodyguards are fully trained."

"We will see what the future holds. While she is a decent commander, she may be better suited to keeping me alive, especially if I should happen to come across someone else who is a talented military commander," Merik said with a smirk.

"I see."

CHAPTER 83

ASHA

Maybe she really did have luck, Asha pondered when she heard shouting from the other room and realized that the place was about to be raided. Hopefully, she could disappear in the chaos, and, if not, there might be a chance to in the aftermath. Thankfully she was a light sleeper or else she could have woken up to guards standing over her. Carefully, so as not to risk reopening her wound, she managed to get herself into a sitting. Hobling slowly, she crept towards the door and put her ear to it.

It seemed that the city guards were approaching. Botun ordered a bookcase to be moved in front of the door to block it, as well as something about a trap door. Excellent. A way out of here that didn't mean leaving by the front door. Even if she waited till everyone was gone, it would be preferable to leave by an exit no one was watching. It might be possible that the guards would have lookouts watching the place for a short time after the raid. You never know who might try to sneak in or was missed in the initial raid. Besides, lookouts tended to be people with enhanced senses, and that could be a problem.

Asha turned and surveyed the room to see what her best options were. The room was little more than a glorified closet. There was a bed and a trunk, that was it. She hobbled over to the trunk and opened it. Nothing but a few blankets, excellent. Asha examined the latch to see if there was a way to make sure it wouldn't close completely and leave her trapped inside.

Reaching into her hair she found a pin that she kept hidden there. Since Liam was the person they captured, they didn't bother to go through her hair and search for things that might help her escape, such as the pin. After all, it was women who usually hid things in their hair. More than once, she would have to change where she hid things on her body based on the gender she was portraying. Her life would be so much easier if men and women were treated the same but, then again, it would be even easier if she didn't adopt Liam as part of her life. Honestly, she wouldn't know what to do with herself if she wasn't both Asha and Liam, or what would happen if one day she never needed to become Liam again.

Those thoughts were for a later day. For now, she needed to make sure the latch won't trap her inside the trunk. Asha sent out an unfocused thought that would keep people from noticing her as she worked on the trunk. It didn't take long for her to pry out the pin that held the latch to the trunk. With that removed, the latch fell off and she used it to add a few extra scuff marks to the trunk to make it look worse. Then she opened the lid and crawled inside.

Now, all she had to do was wait. Asha was bored inside the trunk. She could hear less than she did before. Although, when the guards started beating down the door, she could make out the crashing thumps as they bashed the door. She could hear a few voices after that, and then it was relatively quiet. The guards must have made their way into the hideout. Now, all she had to do was sit and wait.

Only a few minutes had passed when she heard the door to the room open and she could hear the muffled sounds of footsteps coming closer. Asha gazed a few seconds into the future and, sure enough, a guard was opening the trunk to see if anyone was hiding in it. No problem. When the moment arrived, she was ready and, the second the trunk started opening, she reached out with her mind and sent a focused thought for the guard not to notice her. A couple of seconds later, he shut the trunk lid and she could hear him walking away.

Occasionally, she could hear voices from the other room, but, otherwise, things had seemed to settle down. It was stuffy in the trunk and she had to focus in order not to drift off to sleep. She wasn't sure how much time passed, but, once again, she heard footsteps come into the room. Too much time had passed from the first check for the guards to come and get her because she had been spotted. This was probably the guards performing a final check before they cleared out. Now, it seemed that things were wrapping up and, eventually, she could get out of the trunk. Again, she reached out and touched the guard's mind, this time it was a woman, as the trunk lid started to open. After the guard left, she counted to a thousand, for there was nothing better to do. At the end of the count, she planned on getting out of the trunk and walking out of the hideout. Asha opened up her mind's eye to the future and saw herself perform the intended actions. Due to her bad leg, however, she moved a lot slower than she normally would and the vision ended before she reached the front door, although she did see a trap door in the floor of the kitchen that was open.

Cautiously, she opened the trunk and stood up. Giving herself a minute to make sure her wounded leg could support her weight, she carefully made her way to the door, which was left open. At the door, she repeated the process of intending to walk out the front entrance and then opened herself up to what the future held. This time, she made it outside and was able to turn to walk down the alley when she saw a guard wagon and several guards, along with Captain Tianna, standing close by. She opened her eyes and cleared her mind. This time she thought about using the escape tunnel that she noticed in her first walk through. Asha got to the trap door, which was open, and dropped down into the sewers that had dangerously high waters. Several guards seemed to be struggling to remove something. Nope.

Damn. So much for getting away from here early.

It may be a while, she realized. Asha looked over at the bed and longed to lie down on it and sleep. She couldn't remember the last time she got a good night's rest, and the wound drained her more than she realized. As much as she wanted to sleep on the bed, she knew it was too risky. At best, she could only see about a minute or so into the future. To do enough to guarantee a safe sleep would require a strength in precognition that hadn't been seen since the last Emperor went mad.

Sighing, Asha limped her way back to the trunk. She took a moment to stretch her stiff muscles, because she wasn't sure how long she would have to hide. If she didn't, there would probably be hell to pay when she finally got out of the trunk. Carefully, she crawled back inside and shut the lid again. Asha yawned and did her best to fight off sleep but, with all that she had been through, it was too much of an uphill battle for her to last more than a few minutes.

Sometime later, she awoke, stiff and sore and slightly confused. Once the fog of sleep slipped from her mind, she was able to recall recent events. A quick scan of the future showed her successfully getting out of the trunk and sitting on the bed. So, that was what she did. Once on the bed, she stretched a bit and worked her muscles till they had loosened up enough to walk safely.

Asha listened and could hear nothing. She walked to the door and thought about her actions. She checked to make sure the future didn't hold any immediate surprises. With the coast clear, she checked out the hideout. The trap door was in place, and she thought about exiting that way, but the idea of running around in the sewers with a wounded leg did not appeal to her.

The bookcase was near the entrance and there was some debris by the ruin of the door. It looked like they tried to make a barricade. No one bothered to replace the shattered front door, and she could see a faint light coming from the alley. It wasn't much light, but it did give her a few minutes to search the hideout. Everything was pretty much left intact. With a quick search of the place, she found a few coins and, under a floorboard but in a back room, she found a pouch with several coins and a few small gemstones. This had to have belonged to Botun. It was probably how he was funding the operation. Thankfully, the guards were more worried about capturing him than looking for loot.

Asha made her way back to the entrance and noticed how much lighter it was getting outside. So, it was sunrise and not sunset, which meant she had spent the entire night in the trunk. When she saw that the immediate future looked clear, she carefully made her way out of the hideout and onto the street, all the while maintaining a thought not to be recognized.

As she made her way down the street, her stomach growled. She hadn't eaten since the night before the raid and was starving. Seeing no guards in the area, she dropped her unrecognizability as she turned a corner and started to look for a food vendor. A few streets over, Asha found a vendor selling an egg and vegetable wrap. She ordered one and noticed him eyeing her bandaged leg.

"Did you get hurt yesterday?" the vendor asked.

"Naw. It was two nights ago, man. We were playing cards and the guy called me a cheat. Insulted him back and he took a swing at me. My cousin is a guard and he taught me a trick or two. So, I managed to toss his ass on the ground and gave him a few swift kicks to the ribs. When I turned to walk away, he stuck me with a knife."

"Sure, kid."

"I'm telling you the truth, man," she said exasperatedly as she sent a feeling of disbelief to the merchant.

"Yeah, a little runt like you tossed a man to the ground and beat him up only to get stabbed? Sure you did, and I am the Emperor."

"I said I had a cousin who was a guard," this time she sent humor along with the disbelief.

"Yea, and he taught you tricks. What he should have taught you, kid, was not to run your mouth. Now, here is your wrap."

Asha paid the man and left, wolfing down the wrap as she went. The purpose had not been to get him to believe her but to distract him from the wound and not take her seriously. If she wasn't someone to be taken seriously, then she probably wasn't involved in the raid yesterday.

With her hunger backed off, she went to another store and bought a new outfit. She waited until the lady was busy with several customers before she came up to pay for it, counting on the fact that she would be too busy to notice the wound. It worked. Asha headed into the street and sent out a thought not to be recognized as she looked for an alley to change in. While she could change in the street, there was still the chance that someone would accidentally bump into her.

Once changed, she set out to find something else to eat, as well as learn what happened yesterday. Surely, there would be rumors about the raid, especially if Djinar's former seneschal was captured. She made her way to a busy part of town and selected an inn that was fairly busy that morning. After ordering a large meal, another advantage of being male was that no one looked at you twice when you ordered a lot of food, she listened to what people were talking about.

Inns and coffee houses were two of the best sources of information that a person could go to any time of the day. The constant flow of customers provided a wide variety of topics you could listen in on. Most people didn't bother keeping their conversations discreet, for there was telepathy for that, not to mention that there could be someone with enhanced senses nearby. It was by far the best way to get caught up on current news. In theory, you could always go to a herald and ask for what happened in the last day or two, but she got the feeling that with Lord Merik any kind of requests for information would be noted in a report. The heralds felt more like the eyes of the psylord instead of his mouthpiece.

There were only two things of major importance that she learned while devouring breakfast. The first was that Botun had been captured. She knew that already, but the details helped frame her experience of the events. Several squads of guards were brought in and the raid was performed swiftly. An unknown number of people escaped through the sewers, of which several were captured. Afterward, there was a general round-up of people in the area. Heralds were used to determine if a suspected person had been in the hideout or just an innocent bystander. Several hundred people had been detained and about a dozen or so of Botun's people were captured. Even though her back and neck would disagree, it was a good thing that she stayed hidden in the trunk overnight.

The second big news was that there had been some kind of attack at the mansion. No one knew what happened, but there were plenty of competing rumors. What the rumors did agree on was that the attack happened shortly after Botun was brought to the mansion. Most of the staff was not released until late that night and wouldn't say what had happened, several of which were still frightened of the day's events. Merik was alive, but his health varied from rumor to rumor.

As to what happened, there were several competing theories. First, there was the idea that Botun had managed to break free at the mansion and tried to kill Merik, a sub rumor to that was that his capture was a trick to get him close to Merik. A more believable version was that several of Botun's people tried to rescue him at the mansion. The rest of the rumors didn't involve Botun or his people in any way. In them, it was just happenstance that an assassination attempt happened on Merik at roughly the same time as Botun's roundup. If not happenstance, then someone took advantage of the fact that the guards were busy and used that opportunity to make their attempt.

Heralds had yet to make an announcement of any kind. At the gates, the guards had not been increased and it seemed like business as usual for Crestburn. Naturally, people debated what that meant. Did nothing happen at the mansion, or was Merik just playing it cool? No one really knew.

Upon finishing her meal, she went to the innkeeper and ordered a room for a couple of days. With her stomach full of food and head full of rumors, Asha left the inn and began her real search to find out what really happened. The rumors gave her a starting point and, from there, she could check with more reliable resources. As she made her way through Crestburn, she noticed that the guard patrols stayed about the same. So it seemed that it was in fact business as usual. Her first stop was to get some better and more feminine clothes. Liam had too much of a reputation for her to just wander the streets as him.

She toyed with going back to her place to change but wasn't sure if that was safe. There was a chance, a slim one, that her place could be watched. Asha knew that she was being paranoid, but, given the fact that for the first time since she started being Lucky Liam she had been caught, she didn't think a bit of paranoia was out of place. So, heading to the merchant's courtyard and shopping for new outfits was her first order of business.

The first was a simple dress that would allow her to blend into the crowd well. Again, she switched outfits on a side street before she began to shop for something a lot fancier. Asha relaxed a bit, now that she was no longer dressing boyishly and risked being spotted as Liam. Taking her time, she posed as a servant buying things for her lady, all in the outer ring of the Merchant's Courtyard. Nice makeup at one vendor, jewelry at another, and an outfit at a final merchant. Unlike with the previous outfit, she did not change right away. For now, the plain dress was more useful and allowed her to move through Crestburn unnoticed. Her first stop was to drop off the new dress at her room at the inn. From there, she could go to her various contacts and see what she could learn.

CHAPTER 84

MERIK

Merik did his best to look like he wasn't uncomfortable. His wounds pained him a fair amount, and the bandages hindered his movements just a bit. He wanted everything to appear as if things were perfectly normal. There was no way they could hide everything that had happened yesterday from Botun. After all, the man did have to go through the room where the guards had been slaughtered. He would know some things had happened, but he didn't need to know that Merik had been wounded. From what Merik had learned about him, the man had a dazzling intellect and was probably one of the few people smarter than himself.

"How do I look?" he asked the servant who was with him on the balcony.

"You look fine, my Lord."

Merik sighed. "I don't need a flattering compliment right now. If you didn't know that I was wounded in a fight yesterday, could you tell that just by looking at me?"

The servant gazed at him carefully. "I can't see any bandages, however you are a bit pale. though, my lord."

"Since he hasn't seen me before, then he wouldn't know that. Go ahead and have the guards bring him in."

He sat waiting and sipping juice with a bit of flavored liquor in it to help take the edge off of his pain. It seemed to take forever but, eventually, Botun was brought in and placed across from him at the table.

"Good morning, Botun. I hope you had a pleasant night," Merik smiled.

"It was fine," replied Botun

"Excellent. Well, there will be plenty to eat. I kept Djinar's chef. You remember him, don't you? Hell of a cook."

Botun merely nodded his head.

"So, what am I going to do with you, my friend?"

"Torture me for information and execute me publicly."

"A blunt one," replied Merik.

"I don't see any sense in dancing around the subject. You overthrew Djinar and killed those who didn't swear loyalty to you fast enough. I was his seneschal and hid from you. I even tried to smuggle people out of the city, but you took care of that."

Merik smiled and took another drink.

"You don't deny you butchered those people?" Botun questioned.

"I didn't kill anyone," Merik said with a smirk.

"I am not playing word games with you, Merik, so please treat me with the same respect and stop playing them with me."

"Yes, I ordered my guards to kill them. Like I said at the beginning of this endeavor, people had by morning to declare their loyalty to me. They chose not to. I couldn't risk having them run off and possibly come back in the future to retake the city, especially if they had Djinar with them."

"They didn't."

"I know that now. My informant told me everyone who was a part of that group, and he wasn't one. Besides, if he had been, Captain Tianna would have captured him."

"Your informant. You mean Lucky Liam?"

"So that is why you had him shot and brought into you," Merik laughed. He shook his head "No, Lucky Liam doesn't work for me, but, given the lad's reputation, I would be willing to forget that he led those people out of town and allow him the chance to work for me."

"Who was it then?" Botun asked.

"Antove."

"Gerson's boy? I have to admit that I did not see that coming. Where is he?"

"Dead. I had him killed after we talked. I couldn't risk him being spotted by your people and, like I said, he didn't swear loyalty to me in the beginning."

"Is Djnar dead?"

"Since you are asking that question, I would assume so. I haven't seen him at all."

"I last saw him the night you took over. I bade him leave as I tried to rally the guards," Botun said.

"Commendable effort, but too little too late. Then he must have managed to escape the mansion and died in some back alley or some other dirty place that he was trying to get too. God knows this place had enough dark allies and abandoned buildings when I first took over."

"No more than most other cities."

"Either way, it doesn't matter. What does matter is whether or not you are willing to cooperate with me."

"If not, I will be tortured."

"Yes. I have with me a man who will turn your dreams into nightmares, depriving you of sleep. In your exhausted state, I won't have any problems going through your memories."

"I thought we were going to be honest with one another."

"I am, and I will prove it to you. Pick a memory and I will describe it to you."

Merik gave the man a moment and then linked with his mind. Botun thought about standing on this balcony on a chilly autumn day when it was pouring rain. A rather banal memory, Merik thought.

"Wow, I am underwhelmed at your choice. This balcony on a cold rainy day. Why that?" Merik satated.

"I figured you had some kind of trick you were pulling, so I thought of the most boring and mundane thing that I could," Botun replied.

"Do I need to do it again? I can even make a memory so real that you are experiencing it all over again." Merik reached out again to Botun's mind, this time making the memory seem as if it was happening right then.

"Amazing."

"Yes, I am. There is even a man who can make people have false memories, and another who can cause anyone with royal blood to have a migraine."

"Why now?"

"I don't know. Of course, the history books will tell that they came about because the person who reforged the Kysian Empire was born and created a new era for man."

"Let me guess; you are that man."

"Humility is not one of my traits. So, I have an offer for you. I am willing to forgive all that you have done if you tell me everything you know. People, hideouts, caches, you name it. Tell me everything and swear loyalty to me, and I will let you live. You practically ran this city for Djinar. I know. I did my research. Djinar had nothing to offer the future, which is why I took him out. You, on the other hand, could be a part of this. No one knows Crestburn as you do." As Merik finished, he sent a feeling of trust to Botun.

"You want me to betray those who loyally follow me to help you, even though I didn't swear loyalty to you when you first took over," Botun said.

"Yes. Look, Botun, you have something to offer that the others don't. You know this city and can help me run it, make it better than the drug slums that Djinar turned it into."

"I need to think about it."

"What is there to think about? Are you worried about someone? Now, if you had a couple of people who were very skilled and worth keeping around, I might be willing to consider giving them a chance," Meriks said.

"Who is to say that I won't betray you later on?"

Merik laughed. "I can read your memories. How are you going to plot my betrayal when I can look inside your head? It's not just the memories that you chose to think about that I can see. When we are connected, I can pick through all your memories and sift through them to find what I want. Needless to say, I can easily find anything that even hints at treachery."

"It seems that I have no choice. I can say no, but then I would be tortured and you would then go through my memories. If you promise to let me live, then I can tell you everything I know about Crestburn."

"Excellent. You can begin after breakfast. Now, you will be watched by a guard during the day and kept in the cell at night. While I am trusting, I am not foolish. When you finish telling my scribes what you know, then we can talk more about your situation. The more forthcoming you are with your information, the more favorably I will look upon you." Once again he sent out a feeling of trust, as well as hope.

CHAPTER 85

ASHA

Asha walked back to her room, doing her best not to limp too much. At the inn, several wagons escorted by city guards came rolling down the street. Everyone made room for them as they went by. It looked like another roundup. With Botun captured, his followers wouldn't stand much of a chance. The way things were going in Crestburn, it might not be a bad idea to leave the city. Between the gemstones she recovered from the hideout and her own savings, she would be able to live decently for some time. Perhaps she could buy a business and become a merchant in another town. As she toyed with that notion, Asha couldn't help but notice a crow that seemed to follow the wagons. She opened up her psychic senses and saw a familiar aura around the crow. Jariek. Whoever the guards transported, it was someone of interest to the young man. Could it possibly be Kerwin? That would explain why she had not seen the man for quite some time. If he and Jariek were up to something, then that would give good reason for Kerwin to be detained by the guards.

Asha would have to pay Jariek a visit. It had only been two days since she first saw the crow. Hopefully, he should still be at the same inn. She yawned. Tomorrow. There was still some more sleep that she needed to catch up on.

CHAPTER 86

MERIK

Merik skimmed the report the scribe had brought in. This one contained the locations of the various hidden caches and hideouts that Djinar had scattered throughout Crestburn. Yesterday, Botun had spent all day with a pair of scribes. Already the man had provided a wealth of information. Two secret rooms and a hidden staircase were revealed in the mansion. To think that they had been there all this time.

He leaned back in his chair and stretched carefully, so as not to reopen his wounds. It frustrated him how every little motion could aggravate them. How on earth did warriors put up with them? In the stories, warriors would shrug off sword blows as if they had been scratched from a house cat. It was ridiculous. While the pain was manageable, it was definitely something that impeded his ability to think and plan. Perhaps that is why people thought of warriors as being dumb. Dealing with their wounds kept them from doing any serious thinking.

Drinking helped. Thankfully, it didn't take much for the alcohol to affect him in his current condition. More than once, he contemplated using twilight haze to dull the pain. The only problem was that it dulled the mind just as much as it did the body. Perhaps he could use a little bit of it tonight when he went to bed. Last night, he woke up several times, because when he tossed and turned in his sleep he would bump one of his wounds. Some twilight haze just before bed would allow him to sleep through the night and get well rested. He was, after all, going to have to look his best when he gave his next speech.

Merik put aside the report from Botun and grabbed the one from Tianna. Master Gerwald and his staff had been rounded up with no problems and were currently in a holding cell. The process for bodyguards was already underway. She was giving priority to people who could enhance their senses, make themselves not be noticed, or could dominate another's mind. He would definitely have to meet with the group and give them a sense of loyalty to him. A nice thing about emotions was that the more often a person felt them, the more they became a part of who they were. Daily doses of thoughts of loyalty would eventually give way to true loyalty. It was merely a matter of conditioning. As it were, Tianna found twenty-four candidates, and she was planning on training them starting tomorrow. She recommended that the guards worked in groups of four, for four-hour shifts. Additionally, she requested a different uniform for them, so that they would stand out from the normal guards.

Not a bad idea, he thought. He already had seamstresses working overtime to provide enough tabards for his new ally's force, but this would only be twenty-four more outfits. Merik stopped for a moment to write a note reminding himself to order a new uniform for his guards. Ahh, someone would have to design them and that would take time. Shit. He shook his head in frustration and tried to recall what he remembered about the royal guards of Kysia. Were they different from the wardens? He wasn't sure, but he didn't think so. What he could do was make their uniforms similar to the guards. Might as well get them looking the part now instead of having to switch things when he eventually does become emperor.

What was he thinking? His bodyguards would be wearing armor. Shaking his head at such an obvious mistake, he cursed the wounds, for he knew such a lapse was their fault. They would definitely need uniform armor and weapons. The helms and shields could be the key to distinguish them from the rest of the guards. Yes, that was it. For the next two hours, he began drawing up his plans for his bodyguards' armor. When he was done, he stood up and slowly made his way to the liquor cabinet with the use of a cane. He hated the damn thing and only used it when he was alone, since he didn't want to appear weak.

Merik poured himself a glass and drank half of it before heading back to his desk. The healer said he needed some light exercise to aid in the healing process. Thankfully, walking across the mansion would suit his purposes. That was another thing. How come the history books never told of the hero's going for a walk to get some exercise while they recover? History made it seem like a few days of bed rest and then they were perfectly good as new. Such a thing was not even remotely possible, besides who could handle several days of bed rest? After the attack, Merik went from his room to the balcony and his new office, which happened to be on the same floor as the balcony. It was driving him crazy to be limited to such a small area to work in. Ever since he escaped from the banality of coping books, he couldn't stand being in one room for too long. Hopefully, his body would heal soon, and he could start moving about the mansion more.

Plopping himself down into his chair, Merik grabbed another report and started reading. This one came from his new ally. Shortly after he started his march towards Crestburn, he drafted a letter detailing his troop strength. It seems that they were moving at night and should be here any day now. He had twelve hundred warriors with him. That was a lot more than Merik had planned on, which was both good and bad. Thankfully, he had Tianna, who could dominate him should the man step out of line. As it were, he wouldn't be around too long. Merik already planned on making quick use of him by having him attack one of his neighbors. Merik hadn't decided who would be the first to fall in his conquest. Right now, he had the more pressing matter of deciding where to house that many soldiers. The new barracks he ordered for the city guard wouldn't come close to holding them.

"Servant," he yelled and the door creaked open.

"Yes, my lord."

"Fetch me an accurate map of the city. Do so right away. I am in a hurry. Also, send Jaxus to me."

"Yes, my lord. Right away, my lord."

Merik turned back to the report and finished reading it. He was half way done with the next report when there was a knock on the door.

"Enter," Merik said.

"Ya wish to see me, Lord Merik," Jaxus said.

"Ah yes, Jaxus. Come in my good man."

"How are ya recoverin, my lord."

"Quite all right. Thanks to you and Tianna, I only sustained minor wounds. They are healing nicely, and, in a short time, I will be back to things as usual. In the meantime, I have plenty to keep me busy. Now, as you know from the other night, I have an army that is coming here to serve me."

"Yes."

"Can I trust you with something extremely important?" Merik asked as he seeded Jaxus' mind with emotions of pride and gratification.

Jaxus swelled with pride. "Absolutely, Lord Merik. I am yar man. Whatever ya need, I will do it."

"Excellent. These days you can't be too careful in who you trust. Now what I am about to tell you, no one else knows. Not even Captain Tianna, and for very good reason."

"Ok, sir, ya can count on me."

"Good. The leader of the army, and my new ally, is a psylord named Argent."

"Never heard of him," Jaxus said.

"He served in Kour's mercenary band at the same time as Tianna. In fact, he was the one who beat our good captain in the duel and caused her to get kicked out and be given the mark."

"Oh."

"As you can imagine, she will not be taking this very well. She has a lot of bad feelings towards him and rightfully so. Unfortunately, I need his army more than I need her to be happy. There is also the complication in the fact that he can alter memories."

"He can do what?"

"Alter memories. Apparently, his power is similar to mine. Thankfully, fate is on our side, for I can detect the false memories that he puts into people. I need you to be my backup plan, my secret weapon if you will."

"How will I do that?" Jaxus asked.

"By not existing. I want you to become a shadowy rumor. Something that others will fear because they can not see you nor predict you, let alone find you."

"How on earth can I do that? I don't have anythin special about me. I am not like ya or Erlin or Tianna."

Merik raised his hand to silence Jaxus. This time he sent faith and certainty.

"You have two powers that, when combined with your own skills, make you a natural assassin. Deadly with the bow and knowledgeable in hunting, correct?"

"Yeah, but."

"With hunting, you learned to be stealthy, as well as how to survive on your own."

"Yes."

"I bet you know which berries to eat and which will make you sick."

"Any decent woodsman knows that."

"Yes, but most woodsmen can't combine that with your two psychic powers and my money. I had a new bow, traveling cloak, and armor commissioned for you. You will have the best horse in Crestburn and more than enough coin to pay for what you may need. When you leave here, you can live off the land and disappear from everyone. No one will know where you are, until it is too late. With your skill with the bow, you can strike from afar with poisoned arrows then disappear again. I can set you up with a home in a nearby town where you can live comfortably, until your next assignment."

"How is this goins to help against Argent, my lord?" Jaxus asked.

Merik laughed "Because, my good man, you are going to kill him should anything ever happen to me. You will become an invisible knife to threaten him with. Someone he will never see and never be able to sway with false memories. You will be handsomely paid for your work. If anyone asks you, tell them your father was a nobleman who didn't swear his loyalty to me as fast as you did. He was killed, but you were allowed to live a meager existence in a nearby village. Well, meager for a nobleman anyway."

"How will I know where to go and who to kill?"

"I have it all planned out. You will take up the hobby of falconry. As it turns out, I just acquired an avery. We can use the birds to send messages to one another. If you go more than a fortnight without hearing from me, then know that I have been compromised and Argent is to be killed."

"What if someone else compromises ya?"

"Let's not worry about that. As it is, we have enough to deal with, and Argent will have a difficult time trying to influence me. Now, I need you to have a reputation fairly quickly so I have a list of names. They are not powerful people but well known enough in other cities to cause a stir when they all die by the same method."

"Poisoned arrows."

"Exactly. I even had special arrows made so they stand out. They will be unique and, when each victim has one in their heart, then all will know that they were not random attacks but a part of something greater. You do want to be a part of something greater don't you, Jaxus?"

"Yes, sir."

"Good, because there is little time to waste. Now, as I stated, I need you to be a threat to Argent. He is heading to us with his army. He intends to pledge loyalty to me, but I want to make sure he knows that I can get to him anytime. I need you to deliver that message before he gets here. Do you think you could shoot his horse out from under him in one shot?"

"Yea, that shouldn't be any trouble."

"Good to hear."

"His army may find me, though."

"Oh, I am sure you're more than capable of avoiding them. After all, don't animals sometimes escape hunters; even one as good as you?"

Jaxus blushed and nodded, "Yeah, the smarts hunker down and don't move. I've had to beat a patch a brush or tall grass more than a few times to kick game that I knew was hidden."

"And that game doesn't have your psychic powers. You will be fine. Take your shot and stay hidden until you are positive the army has moved south, then stay hidden a while longer."

"Yeah, that could work."

"Excellent. Tonight will be your last night here. Say nothing of this to anyone. I want you to go to Harken's Street and see the armorer there. He will finish fitting your armor as well as give you your new bow."

Merik pulled open a drawer and pulled out a hefty bag of coins. He tossed it Jaxus. "This should be more than enough for you to live off of for a month. The armor is already paid, and you will find a sheet in your room later tonight with a list of names. At sunrise, you will disappear and make history."

"Yes, sir," Jaxus said smiling. The young man was nervous, but Merik could tell he was excited about the assignment and the trust that Merik placed in him. As Jaxus left, a servant entered carrying a large rolled up sheet of parchment.

"I have a map of the city you requested, my lord."

"Excellent," Merik replied, taking the map. After a minute or two of reshuffling paperwork on his desk, he was soon able to roll out the map. It wasn't nearly as detailed as he had hoped for, but it would be better than nothing. At least he would have a better idea of where he could put his army. After a few minutes studying the map, he found a section of town near the eastern gate that would probably work.

Things were coming along rather nicely. He had originally planned on beginning his conquest of the other psylords in the spring, but, now that he had found a willing ally, he may be able to grab a city before winter hits. A lot could happen between now and then, but if things went well with Argent's force, then he could move his time table up a bit. The last thing he wanted to do was spend the winter in the same city as a man who could make false memories. No matter how vigilant he would be, there would still be many opportunities for that man to undermine him. It would be better for him to be somewhere else.

It was a risk, for Argent could establish whichever city he was sent to conquer as his own stronghold, but, hopefully, fear of the mysterious assassin would keep the general in line. He wondered if he should invent a new power for Jaxus to have, something that would explain why he was as good as Merik hoped he would be. A little misdirection would be nice and help keep people from finding out that the kid was merely some backwoods hunter.

Perhaps there were more people like Jaxus in the small hunting towns who could help. One assassin was nice, but a small team of them would be even better. Especially since he could then send them to different locations that were somewhat close to each other, but just far enough apart to make it seem like one person had managed to travel all those miles in such a short time to make those kills.

CHAPTER 87

ASHA

Asha had debated dressing as herself to go see Jariek. Things were liable to be tense with him, and she knew that she would have to do something drastic to earn his trust. The more she thought about it, the more Asha realized that it would be better to tell him about the fact that she could see when people used their psychic powers. If things went bad with him, she might need the advantage of changing her appearance to escape.

The thought of telling him about her unique power made her sick to her stomach. Normally not one to be afraid of anything, the idea of confiding in someone bothered her greatly. Originally, she had planned to set out first thing after she had gotten up. It was during breakfast that she realized what she would probably have to do to win his trust. Now it was early afternoon, and she was still outside the inn where he was staying, thinking about the best way to do that.

Asha closed her eyes and counted to ten and then took her first step, putting herself in motion towards the front door before opening her eyes again. Had she ever been this afraid, other than when she was first cast out into the streets?

The inn was not a cheap place and was frequented by well-to-do merchants. Slowly, she made her way through the inn and hoped to lay eyes on him first. It would complicate matters greatly if he were to see her first and then run away. For all he knew, she could be here to kill him. After all, how was she supposed to know where he was?

What would she do if he tried to run or, worse yet, try to attack her? It was possible he had more than one unique power and that would give him a good advantage over her. Slowly and purposefully, she made her way from the foyer to an indoor courtyard. It was empty. Asha decided that it would be best if she sat down where she could see the foyer and waited to see if Jariek came down from his room. Although, she fearfully admitted to herself, it was possible that he had moved from this inn to another.

She had waited for almost two hours when he finally came downstairs. Unlike a lot of inns, this one had a large room for dining that was not a part of the common area. Yawning, Jariek, dressed in an unconventional outfit with his head shaved, went into the dinning area and took a seat as a serving girl with long brown hair and a friendly smile came by and gave him a glass of wine. Now or never, Asha thought to herself. Quickly, she got up and walked into the dining area and to a chair opposite him at his table.

"Hey, my friend, it's been a while," she said to Jariek.

Jariek gave a startled jerk and it was obvious that he was surprised to see her. He recovered fairly quickly and said, "Yes it has been." To his credit, he remained calm and didn't bother checking to see if she was alone.

"I have heard things have been tough for you lately. I remember when we met, you were a bit horse. It's been a while, and I thought to myself I ought to go see you. After all, it's only a short distance as a crow flies. Nice hair cut, by the way. Bald looks good on you," Asha said without Liam's typical uneducated street accent.

The color drained from his face, and he had to stop to compose himself a few times before giving an articulate response.

"You always had a way to turn a phrase," Jariekd replied in a cautious, measured pace.

"Thanks. I figured with your line of work you would excel at noticing subtle things," she said.

Before he could say anything further, the serving girl brought over a steaming meat pie with a large wedge of cheese. "Here you go, sweety. I see you have a friend with you tonight. Will he be joining you?"

"Yes, Nicka, give him the same as what I am having."

"Right away," the serving girl replied.

Asha turned back to Jariek and smiled. "I must say that I almost didn't recognize you."

Jariek turned towards his meat pie and began to eat as he mumbled something under his breath. A short while later, Asha was enjoying her food as well. They ate in tense silence. She tried to start a conversation, but, after the third failed attempt, she stopped trying. Jariek ate swiftly and mechanically, not bothering to savor the meal. The meat pie was delightfully seasoned and the wine complimented it splendidly. She would definitely have to come back here sometime. He waited patiently for her to finish, not bothering to say anything until she was done and then it was only, "Come."

She nodded and fell in behind him as he made his way out of the dining room and up the stairs. A short walk down the hall and he unlocked a door and entered his room. Asha looked over her shoulder and, seeing no one down the hall, she stepped into the room. Jariek shut the door and locked it before he crossed the room to sit on the edge of the bed.

"How did you find me," he asked.

Asha swallowed nervously and closed her eyes for a second before responding, "I am like you in the fact that I have a psychic ability that is different." His only response was a cold and stony gaze, so she continued, "While you can use your abilities on animals, I can see when people are using their abilities. It forms a cloud around their heads. Different colors and intensities signify different abilities and strengths.

"When we first met, you dominated the horse and made it charge into the alley and attack Hargod and his crew. Later, I saw a crow with the same psychic cloud around its head. I followed it here, but, unfortunately, I got delayed coming here. Then, yesterday, I saw the crow again and noticed you were watching the prisoner wagon that the guards were using. So I decided that I wanted to talk to you, because ,up until now, I have never known anyone else with a unique power. You're the first person who is like me."

"We are not alike," he stated flatly.

"Look, man, we may not be a lot alike, but we do have at least one thing in common. What about Kerwin? Does he have a unique power, too?"

At the mention of Kerwin Jariek's tough facade crumbled, and he shook his head while his body trembled. When he looked back up at Asha, she could see that he had the look of utter defeat in his eyes.

"What's wrong?" she asked.

"Nothing you can fix."

She let out a hearty laugh. "Dude, I'm Lucky Liam. You have no clue what I can or can't do. I am beyond the bounds of normal people."

"Is luck one of your unique powers?"

She paused, why hadn't she thought about that question. Time crept forward and she slowly shook her head. "No. It is not. Luck is merely a story I weave. I am really good at misdirection and using people's imagination against them. Plus being able to see what powers a person is using gives me a great advantage against them."

"I bet it does, but, unfortunately, it won't help me," Jaxus said with a heavy sigh.

"Tell me what the problem is. I do have lots of contacts and more than a fair share of people who owe me a favor or two."

"That may be so, Liam, but you don't have anywhere near the resources Kerwin and Grevin had at their disposal. And, look how much good it did them."

"Grevin, who is that?"

"Look, I have already said too much."

"You're a part of something aren't you? Some kind of group or something."

"I already said too much," Jariek said as he looked down at the floor.

"Yeah, I was thinking that myself, what with all the juicy secrets you've been telling me. You forget who you are talking to. Besides, Kerwin has yet to pay me, so I have to help, if for no other reason than to get paid."

"Didn't Kerwin buy you a couple of outfits and give you a few meals at a tavern?"

"That was all a part of the job. Look, man, let me help. Just because Kerwin and this Grevin guy had a lot of resources doesn't mean they had the right resources. I am going to guess that they got captured by Lord Merik," Asha asked.

"Kerwin got caught. It was the night you helped him," he said as he shifted his gaze from the floor to her. "They must have got him when he went back to the inn."

"That would explain why I haven't heard from him," she mused.

"Yes. Grevin was sent by the," he paused "Grevin was sent to get him out, and I haven't seen anything of him since he went in. I do know there was a fight at the mansion and several bodies were brought out in a wagon that night, but they were covered so I couldn't tell if Grevin was amongst them."

"So who was Grevin?"

Jariek sighed heavily and got off the bed. He paced back and forth across the room. She could tell he was trying to decide how much to tell, or even if to tell her anything at all. Asha decided to give him some space. She sat at the table and waited patiently.

"I can't tell you much. Just even acknowledging what I am a part of could get me into serious trouble."

"Don't worry. I won't tell anyone, man. Look, I trusted you with my secret so you can trust me with yours. Who knows, maybe the fact that, like you guys, I have a new power may get you off the hook or at least lessen the punishment."

Jariekd laughed at that, "The thing is my people don't know I have a new power, either. I have kept it secret from them. It was hard, and I think that I would be in more trouble for that than telling you about them."

"Why didn't you tell them?"

"I really don't want to get into that right now. As it is, we have enough problems to deal with. Perhaps another time, Liam."

"Sure, man, whatever you want," she said, holding her hands up in a passive gesture.

"I belong to a group of people that want to see the Kysian Empire rebuilt."

"So, that's no big deal. Who wouldn't want that?"

"We have been around for a long - and I mean a long - time. I serve as the group's eyes and ears in Crestburn. When Merik looked like someone we could possibly support, I notified those above me, and they sent Kerwin to investigate matters."

"Oh, shit. Kerwin got caught while checking out Merik. So where does Grevin come into play?"

"He was sent by the soc... the group to see what happened to Kerwin."

This last sentence was a lot slower and more measured, as if he was trying to be more careful about what he was saying. What about Grevin did he not want her to know? Maybe he wasn't sent to rescue Kerwin but to silence him.

"How do you know Merik has Kerwin?" she asked.

"I saw him. Before I went into hiding, I used one of Master Gerwald's falcons to spy on Merik. I saw Kerwin and him eating together on a balcony."

"That doesn't sound bad."

"At first it wasn't, then at one point Kerwin discovered that," he stopped and stared off into space.

"What did Kerwin discover?"

Jariek took a deep breath. "That Merik is like us."

"What?!"

"Merik has the ability to go through people's memories. Kerwin figured it out somehow. Merik was pissed about it. There was an argument, and Kerwin was dragged away. I haven't seen him since."

"Damn. So did Merik learn about your group?"

"Yeah."

"That's why Grevin was sent in, to kill Merik? And, if Merik has been seen since Grevin went after…"

"Grevin is either dead or in prison and, given that I saw wrapped bodies being loaded into a wagon at night, I think it is safe to assume the first," Jariek interrupted. "Wait. If you can see when people use their psych powers, then how come you didn't know Merik was like us? Weren't you with Kerwin when he met with Merik?"

"Yea, but I didn't use my ability," she said.

"Why not?"

"It's not like I run around using it all the time, man. Besides, I was doing my best to keep a low profile. Merik is a psylord and I," she faltered, not sure of what to say next.

"You what?"

She looked away before responding. "I was afraid he would notice me."

"How would he notice you?"

"If he had the exact same power as me, then he would see me using it when I checked him out. Why would I be the only one with the ability to see other peoples psychic powers? I mean, there are countless telepaths right?"

"Yeah, but don't you go around pretending to have luck powers?"

"That's different. Like I said, it's all about misdirection. Even if someone else could see what powers I was using, they would just see the powers that other people have. Using powers one on one with a psylord that took over the city in a single night was way too risky."

"I can understand that," Jariek said.

"So, who was in the wagon yesterday?" she asked, changing the subject.

Jariek's body shuddered, and he did his best to control the turmoil inside him, but tears ran down his face. Asha wanted to comfort the young man but knew as Liam she dared not go up and hug him. At last, she said, "Look, man, if you don't want to talk about it, that's fine."

He stood up as he waged war with his emotions before he finally spoke. "The people in the wagon were Master Gerwald and his workers. The apprentices and journeymen, as well as his family. Merik took them because of me. They are going to die because of me."

"You don't know that for positive."

"Yeah, I do. I have been using birds to keep an eye on things while I remain in hiding. A few days ago, I was watching Master Gerwald's place and saw guards come in and question them. They didn't know anything, but they did confirm that I had recently disappeared. That must have been more than enough for Merik, who probably pulled my name from Kerwin's memory. Now they are all going to be executed because of me."

"You don't know that for sure, Jariek."

He shook his head. "Merik had those people killed just for getting into a bar fight with his guards. What do you think he will do to someone harboring a spy?"

"Did they know what you did?"

"No."

"Then, they should be fine. Look, you said Merik can pull people's memories right?"

"Yea."

"Then Merik can go through their memories and see that they have nothing to do with you," Asha said.

"Maybe. I could use a drink," Jariek replied.

Asha smiled. "That sounds like a good idea, but change your outfit. What the hell kind of clothing are you wearing anyway."

"It's supposed to be fashionable in another city."

"How would you know that?"

"Well, the group I am with set me up with this room as well as the clothes. It must be true,else I would stick out."

She laughed "Man, you do stick out. Personally, I think it's a prank on you, but whatever. Let's go get a drink and see how you feel. I know a place not too far from here. Don't worry, it's discreet."

"I still don't know if I should go out."

"Have you been holed up here this entire time? If that's the case, then you definitely need to get out."

"Actually, I get out daily through the crows. I have a couple of them that have been coming back daily now for food. You see, when I am in one, I can have it steal better food than when they scavenge on their own. Crows are pretty smart, and they know that if they come here, at the end of their time with me they will have a nice meal."

"I am not sure what to say to that."

Jariek shrugged. "Look, I appreciate your offer, but, honestly, I would rather not risk leaving here. I'll tell you what. Come back tomorrow and we can have supper again. I could use some company that doesn't squawk."

CHAPTER 88

TIANNA

Again, they ate on the balcony, just the four of them. Suval was nowhere to be seen. No one had laid eyes on him since the day they had captured Botun. At dinner, Merik told them that Jaxus would be going away on a special mission, and that they were not to mention anything about him. He talked about the army that was coming but danced around who was leading it. This set her on edge. She would like to know who was going to be taking her place. Botun was under watch but free to move around the mansion. He had agreed to help Merik out and swore to be his ally. Merik met with him each night to scan his memories to learn more about the city and to make sure the man was not plotting anything else. During the day, Botun spent time in a room with a pair of scribes detailing everything he knew about Crestburn and Djinar's operations. It felt odd.

She had been so busy the last couple of days, she barely followed the conversation at dinner. Merik was looking a bit better and seemed to back off on his drinking. Erlin, as usual, was saying just enough to be polite and a part of the conversation without really contributing to it. Jaxus was smiling and in a great mood. Whatever it was that he was about to do for Merik, he was definitely happy about it. Good for him.

"Tianna," Merik said.

"Uh, sorry, I was lost in thought," she replied.

"It's ok. I would like to speak to you after dinner in private."

"Of course, my lord."

The servants brought out a rich cake smothered in a sweet caramel icing. It was too rich for her taste, and she ate only a little bit. Jaxus wolfed his down and then got up and asked for them to forgive him, for he had an early morning. They all wished him well and shortly after that Erlin left.

"What is it you wanted to talk about, Lord Merik?" she asked.

"I have been putting off telling you something because I know you are not going to like what I have to say. In fact, you will probably be downright furious with me, and rightfully so, but I need you to trust me. After all, I have gotten us this far, haven't I?"

She thought about everything they had accomplished, and even though she may have disagreed with him, he had done what he said. Tianna had no choice but to trust him.

"What is it?" she asked.

"I want you to promise me that you will listen to me and wait till I am done before reacting."

"I promise." What on earth could it be, she wondered? She took a breath and felt a little calmer.

"There is a reason I don't want you in charge of the army, for now. The person who is willing to ally with me is someone who can't be trusted, and I need you to keep me safe. It will be hard for you, and I know it will be difficult to let him take over what you have been doing, but I need an army and he has one. We may get lucky and he will die in the first couple of battles. Then you, my dear, can resume control. Until then, I need you to keep me safe from him. You are the only one I can trust to do this."

She nodded, not yet daring to speak.

"I was planning on forming the army over the winter, as originally planned. and hopefully by spring be able to send you out. As it so happens, I have a chance to get an army now and send them before winter hits. It will be much easier for us in the long run if we can gain several territories right away. To the rest of the world, it will look like it was my right to reforge Kysia, and I can finally let the world know about my unique talent."

He was stalling. Merik had the tendency to be a bit grandiose when talking, but this was a bit different. He was delaying telling her who was coming.

"It really is for the best. I know it will be hard on you, unimaginably hard, but I have to do what is best for the future empire. Once others have joined our cause, and he is not the only warrior out there fighting for me, then I can remove him and put you where you belong. Until then, I need you to keep me safe. From him, as well as other threats, and, believe me, there will be plenty of people who will try to see me dead."

Who on earth could it be? She had no issues with anyone. No it couldn't be. He wouldn't dare.

"Like I said, I need you to trust me. Please say you trust me."

She wanted to keep silent but found herself saying, "I trust you my lord," and somewhere inside of her she did.

"Good. It is Argent who is coming here with his mercenary band."

No! What on earth was he thinking? How could he do this to her? It took all her will power and control to resist leaving the table. Merik was saying something, but she had no clue what it was. Something was placed before her and she looked down to see a glass with a rusty color liquid inside.

"Drink," Merik ordered.

She drank, and her throat burned. Tianna slammed the glass down on the table and a servant filled it again. This time, she drank it a bit more slowly.

She could feel the alcohol hit her system, even after that fine meal she had just had. Whatever this stuff was, it was strong as hell. Merik sat there, waiting patiently for her. Eventually, she felt calm enough to speak.

"Why?" she said angerly.

"Because he has an army at his disposal."

"An army? He only has a few hundred men. When I was with them, Kour had at most four hundred warriors."

"Argent is now in command, and he has a little over a thousand."

She was speechless. Kour was done and Argent was in command. More than that, he had more than double their numbers. How was that possible? Kour was a brilliant leader who existed as long as he did because he knew better than to get too big.

"How can you even think about trusting him?" she asked.

"I can't. Trust is not an option with him, unlike you, who I trust with my life. I know this will be hard, but think about this. With him close, you now have a chance for vengeance against him. Eventually, I will have enough soldiers fighting for me that his force won't be as important. Then ,you can be free to take him out."

"You won't even be able to trust your own memories once you have been around him."

"I have ways to deal with him, thanks to Jaxus and Erlin. I know this is hard, but trust me when I say this is the best path for us to take."

"I don't know what to say." Emotions warred within her, betrayal and anger against trust and devotion. The longer she sat there, the more the later seemed important.

"Then don't say anything, but let me give you something to think about. All that he did to you, all that he took from you, and yet here you stand. You lead my forces in the takeover of Crestburn, you run the city guard, and now rise to be the head of my bodyguards, who you get to hand pick. You survived bearing Kour's mark and knew that there was something wrong with that duel. His power couldn't latch onto you. Show him how little power he has over you. Show him that despite everything, you have become what you are now. That, my dear, will be the second best kind of revenge. The first of course you can have once I am through with him, providing he doesn't die on the battlefield."

"Ok" she found herself saying as a feeling of vengeance and justice enveloped her.

CHAPTER 89

SUVAL

Suval sat alone in the dark. She was gone, but she would be back soon, he hoped. Last night, he slipped into the mansion and did not find her in the cells. To his surprise, a good deal of blood had been spilled, and Kerwin was gone, too. Well, at least now Merik won't have a need for him right away.

He wasn't sure what to do at first. For the first hour or so, he aimlessly wandered the streets, hoping to come across her. It was foolishness. She was like him, a predator. Predators had lairs, and so he went back to hers and waited.

There was no telling how long it would be before she came back to her hovel, so, on his way back there, he made a side trip. The man was surprised to see him so soon after his last purchase, but Suval turned down the offer for more sleeping drugs. He needed something different, something to keep him awake, for days if need be. Naturally, the dealer was more than happy to supply him with something. The man was glad to expand his business with a regular customer.

Now, he sat alone in the dark waiting for her to come home, waiting for her to embrace sleep, so that he could embrace her dreams, and they could be together.

CHAPTER 90

ASHA

Asha puzzled over a way to get Jariek to talk more about the society he was a part of. Originally, she had hoped that they were the key to his ability to affect animals and that maybe, just maybe, she could join them. It would have been nice to finally be around people like herself. But, who was she kidding? There was no one like her. Jariek was close, but he had a sheltered life. He had no idea what it was like to be cast out and forced to make your way in a world ready to tear you apart at the first moment of weakness, to be burdened with having to carry secrets.

The last part was unfair. Jariek definitely knew what it was like to carry secrets; he was a spy, after all. Then, there was the fact that he kept his ability to affect animals hidden from the group he belongs to.

She toyed with the idea of seducing him. It would be easy. Asha didn't think he had much experience with women. The fact that he knew her as Liam and not Asha wouldn't matter. She could reveal her other secret to him and perhaps that act might be enough to get him to talk. However, for some reason, it didn't feel right to do so. That was odd, for in the past she had no problems seducing people when the need fit. Granted, it was always more enjoyable to seduce a woman, but seduction was never about pleasure, at least for her anyway. If she couldn't get him to open up more about this secret group he belonged to, then perhaps she would reconsider seducing him.

Right now, she had other things to worry about, namely checking on her home. She hadn't been back to it since she had been wounded. Now that she was rested and her wound had begun to heal, it was time to make sure it was safe to return home. Casually, she walked up and down the street to see if there was anyone watching the place. Everything seemed normal. The street wasn't a busy one. In fact, this neighborhood didn't have a lot of people in it.

She saw a guard patrol coming down the street. They stopped and said something, but she couldn't hear what it was. Again, the guards started down the street, only to stop at the next intersection to have one of them say something. Great, this could not be good. Whatever it was, it had to be big, because the guards were making sure everyone knew about it. Off in the distance, she could hear other guards shouting as well and, judging by the cadence, it sounded like the same thing.

Now the guards were at the end of the block. Asha could finally learn what they were announcing. The guards stopped and a herald, whom she hadn't noticed before, stepped out and began to speak.

"People of Crestburn, our Lord Merik wishes to address you. He shall grace us with his presence and wisdom at the stage in the Merchant's Courtyard. After his speech, there will be the public execution of the traitor Botun, as well as Master Gerwald and other nefarious people," the herald proclaimed.

Oh, shit. Asha slowly made her way up the street as the patrol made its way to the next intersection. Once she was a safe distance away, she picked up the pace and hurried back to the inn to make a quick change of outfits. Checking out her home would have to wait for another day. She was just thankful that the inn she was staying in was along the way to the one where Jariek was staying.

It only took a moment for her to swap her clothes, then she sat on the bed and gave herself a moment to think. Even though she was in a hurry, it wouldn't do her any good to rush to Jariek without a plan. More than likely, he would be wanting to do something rash and stupid to rescue his former master. Asha would need a plan to counter that. Time was of the essence, and she had an idea of what to do. Hopefully, she could come up with something on her way there.

As she neared the inn, she came across another patrol. Just great. Odds were definitely against Jariek not knowing. Hopefully, he was still in his room and hadn't done anything rash. Quickly, she checked the lounge to make sure he wasn't there and then went up to his room and gave two swift knocks.

"Come in," came the muffled reply.

She opened the door and saw him pacing back and forth. His hands were clenched at his sides and tears were running down his face.

"I came as quick as I could when I heard the news," she said.

"There is nothing I can do, Liam. It's my fault," Jariek cried.

"Surely, you can't believe that, man."

Jariek whirled at her and shouted, "They were captured because of me, because of what I do and now they are going to die."

"Quiet down, man. Do you want someone to hear you shouting? I know you are upset, but now is not the time to attract attention to yourself. Maybe someone from your group will come in time to stop it."

He laughed and shook his head. "The society won't get involved. They care about rebuilding Kysia, not people. How many people have they let die over the years just so that they wouldn't be discovered? No, they won't do a damn thing, and neither can I."

"I don't know what to say," Asha said.

"There is nothing to say. My friends are going to die because of me, and I have to let it happen. I can't risk going to Merik and surrendering because there is no guarantee he would let them go. If anything, he would execute me along with them and that wouldn't solve anything. I have to let them die. I know it sounds horrible, and I won't be surprised if you hate me for it, but it is what's necessary, for the greater good."

"Jariek, I don't hate you, man. I can't believe you have to make a choice like this, but I don't hate you. Shit, I don't think I would be strong enough, or loyal enough, to do as you are."

He gave a weak half laugh and wiped the tears coming from his eyes. "Thanks. I appreciate it, Liam. This sucks. You know, when they were training me, they said he would have to watch the people that we live amongst and care about die. That inevitably someone would upset a psylord and get murdered. We would have to do nothing because to do something would compromise all that we have worked for. That it wouldn't be fair to all those who have died in the past if, in a moment of weakness, we betrayed the presence of the society and undermined the years of sacrifice."

"Knowing and experiencing are two different things, buddy. Learned that myself when I started living on the streets. Won't say it compares with what you're dealing with, man, but I can empathize a bit."

"Thanks, Liam, you're a good man," Jariekd said.

"So, what are you going to do?" Asha asked.

"Not sure. A lot depends on this execution."

"Are you going?"

"No. I will stay here and probably watch from a bird."

"Why?" she said, stunned.

"I owe it to them to at least watch it. To be there, since it should be me up on the stage. Then, depending on what Merik says, I will probably leave town."

"Where will you go?"

"Back to the society."

"Oh."

"I'll stay with them for a while and eventually get reassigned to a new city."

"I see. Uhh, I hate to ask."

"Don't worry, I won't mention you. There will be no need for you to worry about a warden coming to make sure you can't tell anyone."

Asha sighed with relief, not that she was worried but because that was expected of her. As it was, she had already considered leaving Crestburn. Things were changing way too fast here, and she wasn't sure how safe she would be here. With the money that Botun had, along with what she had saved up, she could travel to another city and start over."

"Do you think you can make it out of the city?"

"Why wouldn't I?" Jariekd replied, confused by the question.

"Well, if Merik has Master Gerwald, then he definitely knows what you look like. By now, every guard will be looking for you. They announced only two names of the people being executed tomorrow. Botun and your master. Botun is no surprise. Merik has been searching for him since he took over, but why Master Gerwald? The only reason is to get your attention and try to flush you out. Even if you don't go to the execution, then the guards at the gates will have an eye out for you."

"Then what should I do? I really can't risk staying here any longer."

"I know a way out of town. Can you be ready tonight?"

"Tonight?"

"Yes. I can get you over the wall tonight, and you can be safely out of town before the execution happens. You said you plan on watching them as a bird, as it was, so what difference does it make which side of the wall you are on?"

She could see that he was thinking things over. After a moment or two of silence, he looked at her and said, "I guess it makes no difference."

"Good, then we leave tonight," she said with a smile that she did not feel.

"Thank you, Liam, you are a good friend," Jariek said.

"Don't mention it, man. It's nice to have someone like me around. I mean someone who has another ability that others don't."

Jariek smiled. "Yeah, it is kind of nice to be able to finally talk about it with someone."

"Definitely going to miss that."

"Me too."

"Uh."

"What?" Jariek asked.

"Well, we don't have to miss it," Asha said tentatively.

"What do you mean?"

"I was thinking that maybe I could come along, at least part way. Crestburn is getting dangerous, and I don't want to stick around here. I know I can't go with you to your secret society group, but I thought maybe we could share the road together for a little way at least."

Jariek smiled. "Yeah, I would like that."

Asha couldn't help but smile back. "Great. Look, I am going to get some things that I need. I will be back here with some dark clothes for you and probably a normal looking outfit for the road. Don't do anything stupid, ok?"

"You got it, Liam. Oh, here is some money for the clothes. I have plenty."

Jariek handed over a small pouch of coins, which would be more than enough for a couple of outfits. This was going better than she had planned, much better.

CHAPTER 91

BOTUN

Botun had never talked so much in his life as he did since his capture. Merik had been a genial host, even if there was always an armed guard standing by and his nights were spent in the cells underneath the mansion. He had been told it was just for a short while, until Merik was sure he could trust him. Botun knew this was all a lie. Now that he was done giving Merik everything he knew about Crestburn and other psylords, Merik would probably execute him.

While he had many secrets, the one that no one knew was that he was immune to emotional influence. He could feel when someone was trying to influence his emotions, as Merik had when he made his offer to Botun. It only took context for Botun to figure out what Merik was hoping to get from him, hope and trust. Whenever Merik came to check in on him, there was always a feeling or two of emotional manipulation. Merik would not know that his power had no effect on him. Despite Merik's failed attempt to influence how he felt, he still fulfilled his part of the agreement.

It had been a huge shock to learn that Merik had possessed a new power. His unique gift would be a game changer and would greatly disrupt the status quo. That, combined with powerful psychics like Tianna and Erlin, and he should have little problem carving himself out a nice kingdom to rule. The odds of Merik actually rebuilding Kysia was slim, but they were probably better than anyone in a long time, possibly even since the fall of Kysia. His odds for escaping were about the same, maybe even less, since Tianna could control his body with barely a glance.

As much as he regretted that his life was ending, he regretted the fact that he would not be around to see what could become the next era of history. It was little consolation that his role in the events would at best be a footnote in the history books that would one day be written. That was perhaps the biggest reason he was fulfilling his side of the bargain. That and the dire hope that he had misread Merik. If nothing else, Merik might allow his contribution to be noted and his name to go on for quite some time.

Botun got up and stretched. "That is all there is. I am afraid," he told the scribe. The small woman nodded and made a few more notes, then she got up and left with her papers. In the corner, the guard looked bored.

"If you don't mind," he addressed the guard, "I would like to sit on the balcony for a while before going down to my cell." The guard shrugged and went over to open the door. It was a short walk to the balcony. He gazed up at the stars; what a beautiful night it was.

"Do you need anything, sir?" a timid voice asked from behind him.

Botun turned and saw Vera standing behind him. How brave of her to come up to him. He had seen her in the halls of the mansion but, being under watch, he didn't dare risk speaking to her.

"I would love a nice wine, my dear. Nothing makes you feel as if everything will be just fine and that you are safe and secure than a good glass of wine."

She paused for a moment and then nodded her head. Hopefully, she was smart enough to catch his double meaning and would not fret about him turning her in. Such a thought hadn't even crossed his mind. He might be a lot of things, but a betrayer wasn't one of them. Sure, he gave Merik a whole list of names, but those people were dead or out of the city. All he did was confirm what was already known. People like Zahra and Hargod would be safe, or at least until Merik started plucking his memories.

"Here you go, sir," as she handed him the glass she sent *"thank you."*

Good, she got it. He hadn't wanted to risk sending her a telepathic message, just in case Merik could see those somehow as he went through a person's memories. He stood at the balcony alone with his thoughts, gazing at the night sky. It was beautiful.

His glass had been empty for some time when he heard Merik approach. "Good evening, Botun. I have been informed that you are done."

"Yes. Now, all we have left is my execution."

Merik's face quickly tensed and, just as quickly, relaxed. Most people wouldn't have noticed the slip of control, but Botun was adept at dealing with liars and con artists. "Now, what makes you think that?"

"Let's be honest. You made a big deal out of capturing me. To let me go, even if I was now working for you, would appear as a weakness. Additionally, why would you need to have what I know written down if I was to be around?"

"You're a smart man, Botun."

"So, I am correct."

"Yes. You will be executed publicly. I am sure you heard how Tianna executed the men who got into a fight with my guards."

"All of Crestburn is aware of how that was handled."

"Excellent," Merik said with a smile.

"You have upset many people by doing that," Botun said.

"I am a ruler, and rulers will inevitably upset people. Besides, Tianna will be stepping down as captain of the guards. That should go a long way in pacifying the rabble."

"Don't be too sure about it."

Merik rolled his eyes. "Well, if I want any advice from you, I can just read it."

"I am curious. If you planned on executing me all along, then why bother to have me write down what I know?" Botun asked.

"For the sake of knowledge. I know the value of a good book, and you do have a lot of knowledge to share. Since you won't be around, I can have your knowledge at my disposal. Now, I don't plan to read much of it myself but will more than likely give copies to people who will be running Crestburn as I focus my attention on larger things."

"The rebuilding of Kysia."

"Exactly. Now, I am curious. If you knew that you were going to be executed, why bother helping at all?"

"Several reasons. It gave me more time, time that wasn't spent being tortured."

"A very good reason."

"Also, I do care for the city. Djinar has ruled Crestburn for quite some time, but, for most of that, I did most of the decision making. It was my policies and suggestions that kept this city from falling apart. Once Djinar was in power, all he really cared about was food, girls, drugs, and maintaining his power. Ruling what he controlled was an annoyance to him. So, I ran things in his name.

"I will fully admit a large part of the reason that I wrote down what I know was for my own ego. I want this city to continue not just because I care for it, but because I put in years of hard work making it what it is. When was the last time someone built anything that lasted long after their death? We have not been attacked during Djinar's reign, and the stability of Crestburn is something that I accomplished and am very proud of.

"With the revelation that you have a new power, and that there are others like you, there is a chance that you could actually succeed. I would like to be a part of that, even if it is a tiny part, after I die. I realize my contributions won't be much more than a footnote in the history books, but that is still more than most men get. Finally, there is also the hope, or there was the hope, that you might change your mind and not execute me."

"I am almost sorry that you are going to die tomorrow. You would have made a good ally, I think. But, as I have already made too big of a deal about capturing you, I dare not change things. The announcement about you and the others has gone out. By now, all of Crestburn will know your fate."

Botun merely nodded his head. It was as he feared.

"Go ahead and have another glass or two; enjoy your last night. I can make you this promise, though. When things are all said and done, I can make sure that you will get mentioned in the history books. Now that I know it was you who was really running things here in Crestburn, I can honestly downplay Djinar's part, and he can become the footnote. You can be elevated to the position of my cunning opponent who took a good deal of effort to capture.

Your success with running Crestburn will be the reason why I chose this city and not because I knew Djinar to be an easy target. This way, your accomplishments will not only live on but be known for years to come. Will that suffice?"

At that Botun smiled. "Yes. Thank you. That would be nice"

Without another word, Merik sauntered off. Botun sighed heavily and looked at his empty glass. Perhaps he will have another. Normally, he rarely indulged but, at this point, it no longer mattered, and it was a beautiful night.

CHAPTER 92

SUVAL

It was early evening when he heard the sound of someone slipping under the door. Quickly, he sent out the thought not to be recognized just as she walked into the room. Asha was back, his sweet secret. How he missed her. Suval watched her as she made her way around the room and gathered things to put them on the bed. Boy's clothes, her dagger, and a pouch full of coins that she had hidden under a floorboard.

She was going somewhere, and as Lucky Liam. As she walked around the room, he noticed that she was favoring one leg. Was that where she had been shot? Was that why she hadn't been back, because she was wounded?

He waited off to the side, longing to reach out and touch her. Oh, how he missed her. Missed her dreams and the fun that they had together when she slept. Soon, she will be his again. If she was leaving, then he would have to follow her. It would be important to Merik to know where Lucky Liam went, or so he told himself. Carefully, he slid back into a corner as she went about her business of packing up. Finally, she was satisfied with what she had and turned and gave the room a final look. A smile crept across her lips. She bent over, gathered up her things, and made her way out. He followed.

CHAPTER 93

MERIK

A messenger had arrived first thing that morning with a request for a meeting. Merik smiled at the request and told the messenger that his master can come along with a choice of four of his personal bodyguards. He had been expecting this and, in fact, had a room ready for the meeting. It was going to be a busy day. Breakfast, then the meeting, and, of course, the speech and public execution, and hopefully the introduction of his new army. Tianna had done good work in getting a group of guards ready to serve as his personal bodyguards. They had five suites of matching armor that seven of them could wear. This would be fine for a couple of days. Already, the armorers were hammering out the rest of the breastplates and other apparel. They should be done in a few more days.

The big question on his mind was whether or not Jaxus had been caught. He hoped that the young boy had managed to get away after his first target had been taken care of. It wasn't as much that Merik cared for the boy as it would have been such a waste of a potential resource. Either way, it was out of his hands, and Merik would adapt to whatever situation developed. That was the key to being a great leader, the ability to adapt. Too many were rigid in their ways and couldn't change to unpredicted circumstances.

Merik strolled out onto the balcony, flanked by two of his new bodyguards. The table was already loaded with food and Erlin and Tianna had started without him. "Such a good morning."

"Yes, it is my lord," came the measured reply from Erlin.

"Tianna, excellent job with getting my personal guards ready. Thank you."

"You're welcome, my lord," she replied.

Merik sat down and helped himself to the food as Erlin began going over the schedule. He listened with half an ear, as he was already well versed with the itinerary of the day. Eventually, he grew tired of it and waved Erlin to silence.

"My good man, I know quite well what is going on. Now, I received word just a little bit ago that we will be having a meeting with a representative from Argent's army. The messenger didn't say who, so it may not be their leader. Either way, I do want you there, Tianna."

"Yes, sir," she all but growled.

"Remember, your success in life is a slap in the face to everything he has done. Now, let's enjoy this meal." Her back straightened as she felt the sense of pride he sent her.

"I do have a question that may sour the mood a bit, but I find it a necessary one," Erlin said.

Merik sighed and then nodded his ascent.

"How did Botun take the news?"

"Quite well. In fact, he had it figured out. The man is really intelligent. Honestly, it's a shame we have to kill him, or rather you have to kill him, Tianna." The former captain grimaced at the mention of her role later that day. "I wish he had sworn allegiance to us right away, but oh well. We will destroy many things as we rebuild Kysia."

They ate in silence for a few minutes, until a servant arrived at the table. "Excuse me, my lord, but the party has arrived and is waiting."

"Excellent. Have them shown to a lounge, and we will meet with them in a little bit."

The servant nodded and left to inform the guests. "Well, this is good news. I am glad they wasted no time," Merik said.

"We can go wherever you are ready, sir," commented Tianna.

"There is no hurry, my good captain." Merik laughed, "Actually, I should say captains, since you are now Captain of the Guards, Erlin. Anyway, we have a busy day ahead of us, so please, eat up and enjoy yourselves. They can wait. In fact, it would be good for them to wait a bit."

They sat and ate for a half hour, then each retired to their room to freshen up just a bit before joining him in the conference room. It was the room he used to meet with the council that oversaw things in Crestburn. This time, there were only four chairs, three of which were on his side of the room. He sat in the middle while Tianna and Erlin flanked him. Two guards stood in the corner and two more outside the door. When their guest arrived, the guards came in with them and stood next to the other two. Unbeknownst to his guest, there were several telepaths in the other room. Each one telepathically linked with Merik, Erlin and Tianna to watch over their minds. These telepaths had telepaths of their own linked to them as an extra precaution. Additionally, there was a scribe who, through a peephole, spied on the meeting and transcribed the conversation.

Argent looked exhausted and frustrated. In his hand, he carried one of the special arrows that Jaxus was to use on his missions. Excellent, so he succeeded.

"Please, sit my good man," Merik said.

Argent sat and stared at Merik. "I see your telepath wasted no time connecting with me. Afraid that I will start playing with your memories? You remember what that is like, don't you dear?"

Tianna, for her part, smiled and remained calm.

"Now, my good friend, you can't blame me for taking safety measures. I mean, you did manage to trick my good captain, albeit only for a short while. As to your power, I am not afraid of it, but I am a busy man and would rather not have to take the time to go through everyone's memories to make sure you didn't leave something behind. It's more of a matter of efficiency than out of fear of you."

"Efficiency." Argent laughed and tossed the arrow on the table. "Is that why you tried to have me shot?"

"You are mistaken, my friend. If I had wanted you dead, then that arrow would have been in your neck and not your horses." Argent paused and a look of shock crossed his face. "We are not the only ones with unique abilities. Since I can see people's memories, I can see their past and it makes it so much easier in finding those like us. I have several and one of them... Well, I don't want to give away that secret just yet, but, as you can imagine, it makes him the most ideal assassin.

"Now, you won't have to worry about him as long as my people are left alone. The moment I find one false memory in a servant, guard, or an ally, you will die. Word will be sent and my friend will aim for your neck instead of your steeds. Do I make myself clear?"

Anger came across Argent's face, and Merik could tell he was biting back a retort. Good, this was working out very well.

"By the way, I would be careful with handling the arrow. There might still be some poison left on it."

Argent froze and then carefully put the arrow on the table and did his best not to appear that he had wiped his hands on his pants after putting them on his lap.

Merik smiled.

"Over the next couple of weeks, my friend will be delivering more of those gifts that you received, only this time it won't be their mounts that will be shot. Now, you look like a man who knows how to get along with others."

Argent merely nodded.

"Good. Now, as to what I need from you General Argent. Currently, we are in the process of refurbishing several buildings to serve as a garrison for your troops. I have had seamstresses busy making tabards for your soldiers, as well as a couple of new banners. There are a couple of wagons loaded with these by the Eastern Gate. Take these to your men. I want them marching here and ready to show off at the executions."

"How do you know I won't betray you the second I get inside the walls with my soldiers?" Argent sneered.

Merik laughed and turned to Tianna "God, you were so right about him. Who said my friend has started his other assignment yet? Besides, you really don't have a clue how strong Tianna is. Anyone drawing a blade would find themselves using it on the man next to them. Fear will run through your ranks as each person becomes afraid that their neighbors' blade might find them."

"I see," replied Argent cautiously.

"For your troop's sake, I hope so. Now, I am not completely foolish. You could be stupid enough to try something. So, before we leave, I will go through you and your guards' memories just to make sure."

CHAPTER 94

ASHA

She rose from the bush where she had been sleeping. Jariek had been true to his word and let her come with him after they left Crestburn. Last night, they had gone only a few miles out of town when they found a nice place to hole up. He wanted to remain close to the city so that he could control an animal and fly it into Crestburn to watch the execution. Jariek wasn't too sure how many miles away he could control an animal and hadn't wanted to risk being too far from Crestburn, lest he miss the execution. He owed it to Master Gerwald and the others to at least witness their end.

She looked over and saw that Jariek was still asleep. Judging from where the sun was, it was still morning. It looked like it was still fairly early. It would be a long and emotional day for him, so she decided to let him sleep a bit longer. After all, he would have nothing to do but worry about his friends' inevitable demise when he was awake.

Quietly, she dug through her pack, careful not to disturb the small cage that she had strapped to it. The cage was covered in a heavy cloth and inside was a dove. On a whim, she bought it last night before meeting with Jariek. She knew that the next day was going to be emotional for him, and she thought that perhaps if he watched the execution with a beautiful bird it might help him. It was a dumb idea, but she wanted to curry favor with him because he was the only other psychic with a new power that she was aware of. If she could get him to like her, then perhaps Jariek might delay going back to his secret society right away and they could… She didn't know what they could do, but she did know that she wanted to spend more time around him to learn. About what, she wasn't exactly sure.

Slowly, she ate some of the bread that she had packed for their journey and listened to the birds singing. Jariek moaned in his sleep. He must have been having bad dreams, which would be no surprise, given what he was dealing with. Turning her attention back to the birds' song, Asha frowned in confusion. What had happened to the birds? They were singing just a few minutes ago. Asha sat still and heard a noise off in the distance that began to get louder.

After a few minutes, she could see a column of soldiers marching towards Crestburn. It was a good thing that they had gotten out of the city when they did. She had no desire to be in the middle of a war zone. Her debate on whether or not to wake Jariek was cut short when the young man began to stir.

"Shhhh. We have company," she whispered.

"Uh, what?" Jariekd asked sleepy

"There is an army marching towards Crestburn."

"An army?" he exclaimed and bolted up.

"Get down, you fool," she hissed "or else they might see you."

Thankfully, he listened and dropped down, making only a moderate level of noise. Carefully, she made her way next to him. "It won't do us any good if you get us caught by whoever they are."

"Sorry."

"I get it, buddy. You see an army and think that perhaps your former master has a chance if they attack the city in time."

"Yeah, I." he didn't finish his thought as he looked away.

"Dude, that is perfectly understandable and maybe it will happen that way. But, it won't happen if they see us out here."

"I guess you're right," a sullen Jariek replied. He was quiet for a moment as they watched the troops march down the road off in the distance. After a few minutes, Jariek started looking up into the trees and sky. Frustration splayed across his face and she gave him a puzzled look.

"I want to get a closer look, but there are no animals near."

Asha nodded, smiled, and held up a finger for him to wait. Quietly, she grabbed her pack and untied the small box she had on top. Jariek had asked her what it was when they met, but she told him it was a surprise. Asha went back over and whispered to Jariek "I got you something to make your final goodbye a bit more special," and, with that, she took off the cover to show that the box was really a small cage and inside was a dove. The bird barely fit into the cage and blinked a few times to get used to the light.

"I know you are taking it hard, with your master being executed. I thought perhaps you could use the dove to watch the execution and, I don't know, maybe fly by him or something."

Jariek was at a loss for words.

"I'm sorry, it was a stupid idea," Asha said.

"No, man, it is a great idea. Thank you."

"Good, now you do your thing, and I will sit here and be the lookout. I take it that when you control an animal it's no different than when you control a person."

"There's a bit of a difference but it's more about the way their minds work and their instinct, which is stronger than ours, can be tapped into. When I am with a predator, I can make use of some of their natural instincts. It's as if I can feel what they want to do. Anyway, sorry, I was rambling."

"It's ok, man."

"Thanks, Liam.

CHAPTER 95

MERIK

The Merchant's Courtyard had all but closed down an hour or so before the speech and execution. Only a few of the outer ring merchants were still doing business and even that was sparse. The middle was cleared of all blanket traders, and a large crowd had gathered around the stage. There was a nervous excitement in the air.

A squad of guards stood around the stage, making sure no one approached too close. More guards were scattered throughout the crowd, many not in uniform as an extra safety precaution. Finally, at the main gate, there was a group of guards over a hundred strong.

At his signal, the processional made their way from the mansion towards the Merchant's Courtyard. In the very front, clearing the way for the rest, was a pair of heralds who set a slow but steady pace. Behind them, a squad of guards, followed by two of his new bodyguards. Next came Merik, Erlin, and Tianna, followed by two more bodyguards and another squad of guards. After this group of guards were three wagons filled with the condemned, then another group of guards, and the final heralds.

A large guard patrol had left the mansion a half hour before, taking the exact same route. They were to make sure the way was clear, and at each major intersection, a squad of city guards was stationed. Nothing was going to interfere with today's event. When the sun set in the west, what happened would be remembered by all and recorded for the history books. Needless to say, Merik had agonized over many of the details, since it would be remembered for all time.

As they made their way down the streets, people stopped whatever they were doing and watched the procession go by. More than a few bowed their heads as their new lord rode by. The crowd that had gathered at the end of their route could be seen several blocks away from the Merchant's Courtyard. While he had dreamed of being met with cheers and applause, reality was a much more somber affair. As he drew near, the crowd drew quiet and, by the time he stepped onto the stage, the Merchant's Courtyard was silent.

He waited a moment then nodded towards Erlin to announce him, both out loud and in everyone's mind. "Good people of Crestburn. Lord Merik has great news to share with you. Today, you are witnessing history in the making. Today, you see that Lord Merik is not like other psylords but our one true hope to rebuild the dream that is Kysia." There was applause at the introduction. It was not nearly loud enough as befitting this special occasion, but it would do. They will learn in time.

Merik stepped forward and sent out feelings of awe and hope as he began his speech.

"My friends, not long ago I freed you from the rule of the dictator Djinar. For years, he held this fair city hostage as he exploited its youth and robbed you of your hopes and dreams. In return, he gave you a drug that helped you forget how much you were suffering. That time is over. The last vestige of Djinar's rule has been captured and now awaits justice." At that time, guards brought Botun out on stage for everyone to see. "Look, with your own eyes, and see that I tell the truth. Not long ago, I told you I would bring him to justice. That Botun would not be able to hide forever, and that one day you will be safe from his tyranny. Djinar may have been the Lord of Crestburn, but I can assure you, my friends, he was merely a puppet, a figured head drowning in vice while Botun was the mastermind of this fair city. It was Botun who drafted the laws, influenced the city guards, and turned this fair city into the den of crime and vice that it became. He made it so that only the clever and unscrupulous could rise through the ranks. While you thought the peace that this fair city had from other psylords was for your benefit, the truth was the opposite. Botun made deals that, should he fall, this fair city would be threatened and thus keeping you safe but also his prisoner. He used the years of peace to enrich himself." Now, Merik sewed anger and resentment into the crowd. He paused and waited as a few people near the stage started to boo and shout. While he kept a straight face, inwardly he smiled. This was going well, and he was so glad that Botun was willing to be cast as the villainous mastermind so he could at least be remembered by history.

Merik gave the crowd a few minutes to let out their anger and frustrations at Botun, who, for his part, took the abuse well. Most just shouted, but a few dared to throw rotten food at him. When the crowd had a taste of catharsis, Merik raised his hands over the crowd until they calmed down.

This time it was calm, and hope, he seeped in the people's mind. "Since I have taken over Crestburn, crime has been reduced, streets are safer than they have been in ages, and corruption has been lanced from the system. Yes, it is not perfect, but each day is better than the one before. People can safely walk late at night. The innocent do not have to fear accidentally getting punished, for the heralds will see that they are telling the truth and let them go. Opportunities never before seen will now allow for a much better life than previously thought possible. It doesn't matter if you're a street orphan or a wealthy merchant's son, for all will have a chance to prove themselves within the new government.

"Already, many have taken my invitation and joined the city guard. As of my last speech, just over three hundred new members have begun their training for your safety. Guards are great for our city, my friends, but guards do not forge an empire. To do that, you need an army and soldiers. I wish I could tell you that we won't go to war, but I can not lie to you. I will not lie to you. Eventually, battle will be necessary. There will be those who see what we are building and come to tear it down and take it from us." He paused to stare at Botun for a moment before beginning again. "We must not let that happen. Kysia is a dream that we all share and a dream that will soon become a reality as the old empire is reborn."

At that, the crowd cheered and he dropped his emotional influence. He nodded towards Tianna, who stepped forward. "Now, my good friends," Merik continued, "we come to a part of today's event that I regret is a necessity. When I took over this city, I gave the powers that be a chance to swear their allegiance to me. Most took me up on this offer, while a few," he paused to look at Botun again, "chose to fight me, to sow seeds of insurrection. If we are to become as great as the Kysian Empire, we must be a society of law and order. Those who disrupt the law must pay the price. So, now, I turn things over to Captain Tianna."

CHAPTER 96

JARIEK

Jariek could hardly believe the gift that Liam had gotten him. It had taken him several breaths to calm down and all his will power not to cry. God, that would have been embarrassing. There was definitely a lot more to Lucky Liam than the brash and cocky youth let on. It was a shame that he couldn't find a way to take him to the society. The council had a strict rule about outsiders, and Liam was probably not willing to let them know about his ability to see psychic powers. Hell, he was a member of the society and never let them know about his ability with animals. Well, maybe he could delay going back just a few days so that he and Liam can learn more about each other's unique powers.

Off in the distance, the soldiers marched on towards Crestburn. He hoped that they would attack the city in time to stop the executions. It was a small hope. If they were an attacking force, then there was also the chance that Merik could be disposed of and that would be a great benefit to the society. Their existence would still remain secret, and he could start over in another city.

He took control of the dove while it was still in the cage. Liam opened the door and pulled it out. Stretching its wings, he took flight towards the nearest tree. Going from branch to branch, he made his way closer to the soldiers. As he drew near, his heart fell. The soldiers were wearing Merik's colors. There was no mistaking it, these were Merik's soldiers. Where did he get so many? Any chance of Master Gerwald being rescued was over.

Taking off from the tree he was in, Jariek had the dove race through the sky. He allowed himself a few minutes to be lost in the joys of flight before doing what must be done. While there was nothing that could be done for Master Gerwald, there was something he could do for the society.

Jariek spoke with his body telling Liam to pay attention to what he was about to say. Jariek flew the dove over the army several times. Each time he noted troop size, equipment, and other things of importance. His body said what he observed with the dove and hoped that Liam was paying attention. He would remember most of it himself, but he also knew that things were going to get emotional and it was possible he could forget.

With his reconnaissance of the army done, Jariek flew the dove towards Crestburn. Already, the stalls and trade blankets of Merchant's Courtyard had been packed up to make room for the crowd that was beginning to form. Back and forth he flew across the city, taking it all in one last time. He noticed a detachment of guards leaving the mansion. A short while later, a large group formed up. Near the back of the group were three wagons. He settled down in a nearby tree and watched.

Guards milled about in loose formation. A grizzled old man, well compared to the other guards, came out and started giving orders. Their formation tightened up and all came to attention. He barked out another order and a pair of guards brought Botun out and placed him in the lead wagon. Once Botun was secure, guards brought Master Gerwald and his staff out and placed them in the other wagons.

Jariek's heart fell. Gerwald looked disheveled and staggered as if he was in a daze. Several of the apprentices were crying, and some of the journeymen were nursing fresh wounds. All of this was because of him, because he worked there. Back in the woods, tears streamed down his face. He had been trained to expect things like this to happen. At the time, he didn't pay much heed to the idea. After all, the instructors were just trying to scare the kids a bit so that they wouldn't take unnecessary risks. Now, he knew that they had been all too right.

The doors to the wagons slammed shut with a haunting finality. Out of the mansion came Lord Merik, Tianna, and Erlin, along with a small group of guards. These guards were a bit different, better armored and carried swords. Bodyguards. It seems that Grevin's attack did scare Merik enough to get his own bodyguards. Another useful bit of information for the society.

Once Merik and his group were mounted, the guards headed away from the mansion. Taking flight, Jariek flew above the procession as they slowly made their way to the Merchant's Courtyard. When they came to a stop, he found a rooftop to perch on. While the dove was nice, it didn't have near as good eyesight as the falcons he was used to.

Merik walked out onto the stage and started speaking to the crowd. After a bit, Botun was brought before them and Merik continued to speak. It was a rousing speech and the crowd cheered at the end. Tianna stepped forward and addressed the crowd. She was very straight forward. She named Botun and then began listing his long list of crimes. At the end of it, she turned and asked him if he had any final words, to which he nodded.

"People of Crestburn, I would ask for your forgiveness, but I realize there is little chance of that. Only too late have I realized my mistake of not siding with Lord Merik. He is a wise man, and his plans for the future will lead to the rebuilding of the Kysian Empire. How I wish I could see that."

Stunned silence enveloped the crowd. This was not even close to what they were expecting. Botun turned to Tianna, nodded, and closed his eyes. She walked behind him, drew a dagger, and thrust it into the small of his back. He went rigid and she grabbed him and lowered him to the stage. Retrieving her dagger, she addressed the crowd.

"Lord Merik has decided that since, in the end, Botun saw the error of his ways, he was to receive a merciful death. The next group still refuse to deny their involvement in seditious acts, as well as being spies. Next to Botun, they represented the single biggest threat to Lord Merik's rule."

The guards opened the two wagons that held Master Gerwald and his staff. Slowly, they walked out of the wagon and were led onto the stage. Jariek scanned the crowds and saw several dozen guards. Even if he had been heavily armed with a squad of wardens, they wouldn't stand a chance of making it to the stage.

It was agonizing to watch, and he hated the feeling of helplessness. Taking wing, he flew down to the stage and circled the condemned. The crowd's jeering faltered by his second lap and went completely silent when he landed in Master Gerwald's hand. He looked up at his former master and cooed softly. Tears were streaming down the old man's face.

"During the reign of Empress Kyleanna," Merik spoke up "she would sometimes present the condemned with a dove. As long as they kept it alive, she would stay their execution. Upon the bird's death, she would see if the person had reformed their ways and, if so, she would pardon them. As we rebuild the Kysian Empire, we need to live as they did, so I will graciously allow Master Gerwald to pick one of his apprentices to receive the dove, so that they may learn to live a faithful life full of service to our dream."

Empress Kyleanna had done no such thing, nor had any other emperor or empress. The Cashek Society had a record of everyone who led the empire since its founding. Merik had to be making it up in order to take advantage of the situation. Judging by the cheers from the crowd, they were eating it up, and why not? A bird had just circled the condemned three times and landed in one of their hands. Such a thing did not happen. Inadvertently, he just helped cement Merik's hold over the city. Well, at least one of them will now be spared.

Master Gerwald had to be told a second time before he even realized what Merik was saying. The man nodded, then walked down the line of the condemned and handed the dove to Lucius. If only one was to survive, Lucius was an excellent choice. The kid was mild mannered and quick to laugh. He was an orphan who Master Gerwald had taken in when his family had died in a fire several years back. Master Gerwald had been friends with the boy's parents. Lucius started sobbing when he received the dove.

Master Gerwald started to walk back to his spot in the line when he froze and turned towards the crowd. Tianna held out the dagger and Master Gewald reached out and took it, then held it up for everyone to see. As he held it aloft, the crowd cheered. It is obvious that now Tianna was in control of his body. When the last of the crowd fell silent, he plunged the dagger into his own heart. His wife screamed in anguish and several journeymen surged forward, only to be halted by the guards.

Tianna took control of his wife next and had her retrieve the dagger from her husband's corpse. Once again, it was held aloft for a time before sinking into the breast, to still the beating heart that lay beneath. One by one, each of the condemned repeated the process until only Lucius remained. Tianna bent down and retrieved her dagger as Merik walked across the stage and addressed the crowd.

"Now that justice has been served, and our biggest internal threat eliminated," he began, "we can move forward and make this city safe from those that would dare try to harm us." At that point, the city gates opened and the army that Jariek had seen earlier marched in. The column split in two and went on either side of the Merchant's Courtyard. A stunned silence descended upon the crowd. From the gate, a small group of people rode towards the stage. When they drew near, one man got down and came over and stood by Merik.

"Good people of Crestburn, I present to you General Argent. He will be in charge of the army. Should another psylord dare threaten us, he will be our shield. General Argent is merely the first of many who shall come to our side and join us as we rebuild the Kysian Empire. For Kysia!"

The crowd erupted in thunderous applause and cheering. Some started up the chant of "For Kysia," which was quickly picked up.

Jariek let go of his connection with the dove and saw Liam watching him intently. "You ok, man?" he asked.

"Yeah. Thanks to you and your dove we got to save one life." He wiped his face, which was wet with tears.

"How did that happen?"

Jariek got up and grabbed his pack. Off in the distance, he thought he could just barely make out the chanting in Crestburn. "Grab your stuff, man, and let's go. I can tell you along the way."

CHAPTER 97

SUVAL

It was never really a debate: go back to Merik or follow Asha and her friend. They had been very quiet as they crossed Crestburn in the dead of the night. He didn't even hesitate as they headed north of the city. Merik would be upset that he was gone, but Merik was always upset. Merik was a cruel man and often made Suval relive the nightmare that was his uncle. Now, he was free and able to do as he pleased. Right now, that was following her. The young man she was traveling with didn't even realize that she was not a he. She was so good at keeping her secret.

Suval found out that his name was Jariek, and he would stop and look back at Crestburn with painful longing. Whatever it was, he was not happy to leave it behind. Perhaps this was the boy who Merik was trying to find. If so, then him following them would be a good thing. He just hoped that they did not split apart.

They had stopped only a few miles north of the city. Bedding down in bushes, they were fast asleep in no time. Suval crept forward and entered the young boy's dreams first. He wanted hers, but, now that she was his again, he could hold off a little bit. It would be better for him to play with the young man's dreams for a bit before jumping into hers.

He dreamed of death, of friends lost. It took Suval very little effort to stir up his dreams. At one point, he had to calm them down or else risk waking the boy up. Asha, on the other hand, was dreaming peacefully and it took a little bit to stir them up. Achingly, he stopped after a short while. There was a chance that Merik might send people to look for them. It wouldn't do to have them captured, and lack of sleep would definitely aid in that.

Backing off to hide in a nearby tree, Suval watched them from a distance. Liam was up only a few hours later. It wasn't until a large army came marching near that Jariek awoke. After a bit of discussion, Liam showed Jariek a bird. Jareik was thrilled and soon was sitting still and not saying a word. Liam released the bird, a dove, and it took flight. Jareik wasn't doing anything for a while, but then he started talking. Suval couldn't hear what he was saying, but Liam was paying apt attention. After that, he was quiet again for a long time.

Eventually, he got up and grabbed his pack. They talked just a bit before Liam grabbed hers and followed him north. What was with Jariek setting like that, he wondered. It was as if he was in some kind of trance. Could it be that he had been controlling the bird? If so, then Jariek was like Merik and him. That could explain why Merik was looking for him. Suval had to follow him, now. There was no choice in the matter, for Merik would be very upset to lose a psychic with a new ability.

EPILOGUE

It was a warm day in the plaza and several well to do merchants were seated amongst the benches, catching up on the latest gossip. A chuckle escaped. It was the irony of their situation, for as they gossiped they were about to become the gossip that others would soon talk about. The chuckle grew into a laugh that became louder the longer it went on. Several of the merchants in the plaza scowled and shook their heads. Little did they know they were soon to be a part of history.

For hundreds of years, since the fall of Kysia, people warred and fought amongst themselves with little hope of salvation or change. Many had pondered over the years as to why Kysia fell, but he knew the truth. Somehow, mankind fell from grace and the peace and prosperity that they knew had been stripped from them. Before Kysia could be reestablished, humanity must first redeem itself.

Today, the first step along that long and arduous road towards redemption would begin. It would begin with their pledge to serve something greater than themselves. In service to others, they would pave the way to redemption and let Kysia be a dream no more. For, somehow, a new power had been gifted, one that had never been seen before. It didn't matter how. What mattered was this new power was one that others could not deny. This power shall serve as a beacon, and they shall flock to him, seeking sanctuary and servitude

It was time.

Almost at once, the cry came from those nearby as their sight was stripped away, followed by their sense of touch, taste, and smell. Their hearing was left, for a message had to be delivered. Several minutes went by.

"You all have erred in your ways. You sought out profit and power for yourselves. The ways of Kysia have been lost to you. Beg for forgiveness, and I shall restore your sense of touch. Swear to me that you will change your ways, and you shall have your sense of smell. Give to me, and I will give you your sense of taste back. Promise to spread the word of what happened, and I will give you your sight back."

Slowly, they came, crawling to the sound of the voice. Their wails had turned to desperate pleading and promises to do all that he asked. Their senses returned, one sense at a time. They gathered around, on their hands and knees, waiting, for never before had there ever been a psylord who could strip the senses from a person. This was something new, never seen before.

"Go, my children and spread word of what has happened here. Let the world know that I am the chosen one. That with me, Kysia will be rebuilt. Any who oppose me shall be stripped of their senses."

The End

Dear Reader,

Writing a novel has been a lifelong dream of mine. And, I'm sure there are many of you out there with a story or two to tell of your own. Eventually, I stopped being afraid and started writing. I realized that I was a storyteller. Hell, I had been telling stories for over 20 years as a dungeon master. If I could do that, then I could write a book. I put my self-esteem issues aside and began writing. It wasn't easy. There were a lot of growing pains, but I did it and I hope you enjoyed it. There is nothing like getting caught up in a good story.

I read a lot through junior high and high school. Once my school work was finished, I popped out whatever paperback I was reading and left the classroom behind. Back then it was a lot of Piers Anthony, Robert Jordan, Fred Saberhagen, and Stephen King. And, don't forget the Dragon Lance and Forgotten Realms novels.

We played a lot of Dungeons and Dragons back in High School. Occasionally, we tried other games, like Shadowrun, but it was mainly good old D&D. While we all took turns being the Dungeon Master, I got the roll a lot more often than the others. At times, it's annoying being a forever DM. But, once and a while, life throws you a break. My buddy Rob started running a Shadowrun 5th Edition game and almost all of the old crew are able to make it. What's even cooler is that he let my son join in.

Now, I still play Dungeons and Dragons. I have a small game that I run for my three kids that takes place in Kalgun, in Aram Vartian's world of Godsfall. Additionally, I run a game with my kids plus my brother, his wife, and three kids. A party of 8 is a royal pain but it is worth it. We even managed a live session when we visited them last summer. My darling wife just shook her head at me when I had twice as many suitcases for my D&D books, minis, terrain, dice etc… as I did clothes. But, I will tell you what, dear reader, it was worth it. We took over my parent's dining room and there were pizza boxes and Vess Root Beer everywhere, just like when I was a teenager; except it was 2 in the afternoon and not 2 in morning. It's more than just a game, more than just dice, or heroic deeds; it's a story that we will all share together, and the events that transpired will be retold for years.

I still tell stories about the old games we used to play. For me, my main character was an elven wizard named Jargulous. There were others, such Dregard Bloodaxe, who I bring back from time to time when I need a mercenary protagonist; and boy does my step-daughter hate him. Somehow, I still have Dregard's original character sheet. It was kind of funny because Dregard was there at the beginning.

Our gaming group was small. Often it would be two players and a DM. Sometimes, we would run two characters so that there was a party of four. I had just picked up The Complete Psionics Handbook for 2ed AD&D. Needless to say, every character we had who wasn't a psionicist, rolled for a wild talent. While Dregard had nothing, the other character, Grax, hit the motherload. I had so many wild talents that when the character switched classes from fighter to psionicist, he was overpowered and no fun to play.

Since Grax wasn't any fun, I decided to make him a villain in a campaign I ran a few months later. Annoyed that psionicists didn't get enough love in the Forgotten Realms, I decided that during the Time of Troubles a psionicist was one of the heroes who returned the Tablets of Fate. In this reality, not only was there a god of psionicists but a metal that was almost as strong as steel but didn't interfere with psionic powers. Grax was in charge of a vast empire and a lot of his soldiers had psychic powers. The players had a great time and eventually took down Grax and made it back home to their reality.

It wasn't until many years later that the idea of a psychic empire came back to me. I love psionics because it is much more limiting in what it can do than magic. A few times, I tried to write something but it never ended well. You know, I shouldn't say that. I should be truthful to you, dear reader, at least. Those attempts never even took off. It wasn't until after reading an article about how Brandon Sanderson was changing things with the new Mistborn books, the Wax and Wayne Series, that I started thinking. While I had an idea for the book about when the Kysian Empire fell, I never looked beyond that. So, I stole from Brandon and advanced my world a few hundred years and figured out what would happen to it. Now, I had something I could write. From there, to be cliché, the rest is history.

I wish I could end this with a cliché, but I promised myself something. If I ever published a novel, I would do what Piers Anthony did in his author notes. As a young man with depression, it meant something to me to see 1-800-SUICIDE (1-800-784-2433) at the back of each book. While I no longer struggle with being suicidal, I know that many of you do. Please don't. I know that I am just a stranger, and I don't know your story or your pain. I won't pretend it was like mine. I know it hurts and is heavy in ways that others cannot conceive, but hang in there. Mental health help is a hell of a lot more available and less stigmatized than when I was growing up. So, this is my promise to you, dear reader. I will include that lifesaving number in each of my author's notes and a link at the bottom of my website. Please use it if you need it.

Jason R Sank
12/4/21

NATIONAL

SUICIDE
PREVENTION
LIFELINE™

1-800-273-TALK
www.suicidepreventionlifeline.org

www.ingramcontent.com/pod-product-compliance
Lightning Source LLC
Chambersburg PA
CBHW030240030726
47493CB00023B/276